R.W.W. Greene

TWENTY-FIVE TO LIFE

ANGRY ROBOT

ANGRY ROBOT
An imprint of Watkins Media Ltd

Unit 11, Shepperton House
89-93 Shepperton Road
London N1 3DF
UK

angryrobotbooks.com
twitter.com/angryrobotbooks
Roadtrip 'till the end of the world

An Angry Robot paperback original, 2021

Cover by Glen Wilkins
Edited by Eleanor Teasdale and Andrew Hook
Map by Kieryn Tyler
Set in Meridien

ISBN 978 0 85766 920 9
Ebook ISBN 978 0 85766 921 6

Printed and bound in the United Kingdom by TJ Books Ltd.

9 8 7 6 5 4 3 2 1

To everyone who voluntarily and without complaint wore a mask during the COVID 19 pandemic. You probably saved some lives.

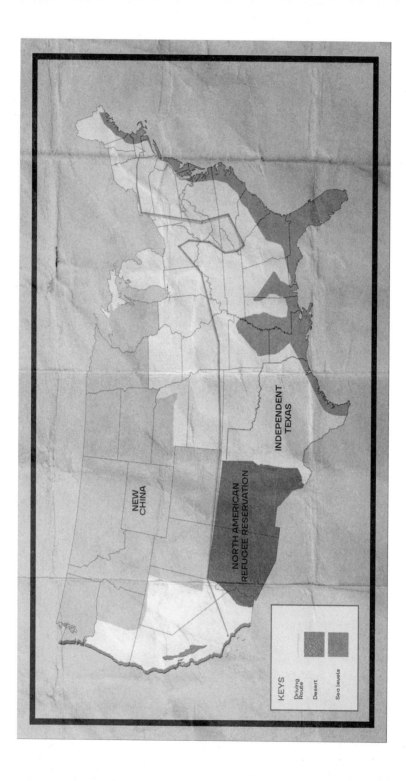

It doesn't matter how smart teens are or how well they scored on the SAT or ACT. Good judgment isn't something they can excel in, at least not yet.

The rational part of a teen's brain isn't fully developed and won't be until age 25 or so.

In fact, recent research has found that adult and teen brains work differently. Adults think with the prefrontal cortex, the brain's rational part. This is the part of the brain that responds to situations with good judgment and an awareness of long-term consequences. Teens process information with the amygdala. This is the emotional part.

In teens' brains, the connections between the emotional part of the brain and the decision-making center are still developing – and not always at the same rate. That's why when teens have overwhelming emotional input, they can't explain later what they were thinking. They weren't thinking as much as they were feeling.[1]

---

1 Research used to support passage of the Thirtieth Amendment. University of Rochester Medical Center, "Health Encyclopedia" reviewed by Joseph Campelone, MD and Raymond Kent Turley, BSN MSN RN

ONE

Julie's eyes rolled. It was the end of the world, and the deejay had no better response to it than industrial techno.

The invitation Ben had slipped her the week before described the fete as "The Party to End Everything" and promised twelve hours of music and madness. After all, the font screamed, "It's all downhill from here!!!"

All week, Ben had been referring to it as "The PEE."

Whatever direction the hill was headed, the music was too fucking loud. A migraine bass line, a rattle of synth-snare, choral loops, robot-assembler clashes, dark notes, and washtub thumps. Instinct demanded Julie crouch and cover her head, and she might have done had she been alone and had Ben given her room. "Quit stepping on my heels!" she said again.

Ben shuffled back an inch or two. It had been years since either of them had seen so many people – real, sweating, laughing, body-heat people – crowded into one place, and his sense of security seemed to hinge on how close to her he could stand, his cinnamon-scented breath puffing against the side of her face.

"Great party," he said. "Really glad we came."

"This was your idea."

His idea, sure, but Julie had agreed to go and gotten her mother to sign the release. Two more years lay ahead of her twenty-fifth birthday, which meant asking Mommy for permission to have fun. "I don't care if you drink and have sex and raise hell, but, for god's sake, don't let anyone get it on camera!" Julie's mother had warned and authorized the autocab that carried them to the event.

"We'll get some drinks and relax," Julie said. "If we don't like it we can leave early." *And then what? Spend the end of the world in ThirdEye or in front of the vid? Break into Mom's medicine cabinet again for some happy patches?*

When they reached the head of the line, Ben showed his invitation to a woman sitting at a table beneath a banner advertising Mela-Tonic, the party's corporate sponsor. She smiled. Some of her sliver-glitter lipstick had come off on her teeth. "Come get mellow, guys!" She reached below the table and came out with a Mela-Tonic swag bag for each of them. Julie waved hers off.

His own bag in hand, Ben joined Julie at the doorway of the ballroom. She grimaced. The PEE was an under-25 event hosted by a soft-drink company, so it was about as grassroots hip as the McDonald's Birthday Bash Julie's parents had organized for her ninth. Still, the organizers could have made an effort, rented out an old warehouse or mall space rather than the ballroom at the highway Marriott. The three-sided video unit overhead hardly bothered to cover the garish chandelier it surrounded. Instead, it alternated showing particolored rhythmscapes, Mela-Tonic commercials, and a mover of PorQ Pig saying, "That's it, folks!" in Hindi.

A girl in tribal bodypaint slunk up beside Julie. "What do you have?" she said.

"What?" Julie said.

The woman patted her left clavicle. "Apple, Tronic?"

"Oh!" Julie flushed. "It's a Tronic. Is there a mod?"

The girl handed Julie a plastic card.

"Can I get one?" Ben said.

"It only works if you have a pharma emplant," Bodypaint said. "Won't do shit if you don't." She drifted back into the shadows near the door. Her partner was there, pointing a scanner at people as they entered.

Julie ran her right index finger over the raised design on the card and made a fist to send the scan to the miniature computer under her clavicle. The emplant flashed a warning and grudgingly surrendered. The mod took an inventory of Julie's pharma and forced it to spit something more interesting than usual into her bloodstream.

Ben gazed at the girl in the bodypaint, who was now handing out cards to a group of three. "Do you think she's really naked?"

"Probably."

He pulled his eyes back to Julie. "Are you feeling the mod yet?"

"Yep." The hack was doing something lovely to Julie's endorphin and serotonin levels. She felt good, warm, loose. She took Ben's hand. "Let's get a drink."

The refreshment tables were loaded with Mela-Tonics, six flavors of carbonated water chock full of melatonin, valerian root, and seventeen other mood-altering herbs and spices! Ben opened a Lemon Lowdown. Julie picked a Strawberry Siesta. "Sip and chill," it said on the aluminum bottle.

"How do they expect people to dance after drinking these?" Ben said.

"They're mostly swaying," Julie said. A couple of dozen brave souls had taken to the dance floor. The rest of the party-goers were at the tables, barely looking at each other and playing holo games on their emplants.

"This is lame. I'm sorry," Ben said.

Julie ran her hand up and down the back of his shirt sleeve. It was incredibly smooth, but at the same time it seemed like she could feel every fiber. "I love you, Ben."

He shook his head sorrowfully. "That's just the drugs talking."

"Yeah, it is." She drained her drink. "Do you want to dance?"

"You go ahead. I'll just hang out over there." He gestured at one of the empty tables.

"Benjamin Esposito, you are such a slug." She grabbed his arm and dragged him back toward the entrance. Bodypaint's partner had left her standing alone looking bored. "Hey. My friend's brain is too normal to need a pharma. Do you have anything else?"

"Like real drugs?"

"Yeah."

The girl spread her arms and turned in a slow circle. She'd done the do-you-have-an-emplant? pantomime so many times she had a bare spot above her left breast. She also had a denuded place on her ass from where she'd been leaning against the wall. Otherwise, it was just her and the paint against the end of the world. "Do I look like I'm holding anything?"

Julie blinked owlishly. "Nope. You are definitely naked. What about the guy you were with?"

"My brother. Do you know how much trouble we could get into selling drugs at an under-age party?"

"So don't sell it." Julie held out her hand. "Give. It's the end of fucking everything."

The girl started to scratch her neck but caught herself. "He's in the bathroom. Send Mr Normal in there and tell him Cassandra says it's OK."

Julie waited outside the bathroom while Ben went in to negotiate. He came out slowly, holding his fist at waist level.

"What did you get?"

Ben opened his hand to reveal a single green pill. "No idea. Could be twelvemolly, could be a laxative."

"Either one will help you get rid of some of that shit you're packing." Julie handed him a fresh Lemon Lowdown. "Take."

Sixty minutes later, Ben and his drug dealer's little sister were in the corner messing up her paint job. Julie was on the dance floor. The techno tracks and her dance partners blended into each other in a wave of colored lights, rhythm, and touch. She was a hot, sticky mess and liked that just fine. When her high started to fade, she did the thing with the card again and let her mind go. She might pay for it later, but how much later was there, really?

The music stopped at 1:09am. The overhead screens played a short film designed to sell Mela-Tonic, then the view flipped to the news channels. The president gave a speech about hope and the future. A rabbi said a prayer. A newshead did an interview with three of "America's best and brightest," a scientist, a kindergarten teacher, and a famous cello player. There was a montage of faces and goodbyes.

Two-hundred and fifty-four miles up, rockets fired, moving the six colony ships out of low-Earth orbit and beginning an eighty-six year voyage to Proxima Centauri, humanity's new home, leaving ten billion people to die on the old one.

In spite of the mods and the gallons of Mela-Tonic consumed, some of the partygoers were crying. Ben slung a sweaty arm around Julie's shoulders. His hand smelled like bodypaint and foreplay. "Are you OK?"

Julie bit her lip. "Am I supposed to feel good knowing Anji's up there? That she has a chance? I don't think I do."

Ben snorted. "She'll be an old woman before they even get close to the place."

The screens showed the big ships moving away from the second International Space Station. The point-of-view switched, and the cameras on the ships looked back at Earth. More newsheads. Suicide rates were expected to spike again. Tech stocks – especially aerospace and VR – were surging.

The American Dream, Julie thought. *Escape or die.*

"What's the opposite of survivor guilt?" one newshead said.

His partner chuckled. "Resentment of the doomed?"

The deejay cut the feeds and started in with the industrial techno again. More ads for Mela-Tonic flickered on the screens.

Julie couldn't move. No one else could either.

The three-way screen cut back to PorQ Pig. *That's it, folks!*

* * *

Julie's head was starting to clear when the autocab dropped her home around 2:30am. She changed into sweats and slippers and went to the kitchen for a snack. The smart screen embedded in the fridge door recognized her and began playing her mother's theme music. Julie squeezed her left eye shut and tried to focus on the fridge, which was showing a recut of a piece her mother had done the month prior.

Julie's mom, "Carson S Riley", the top-rated newshead in the third-largest American market, smiled for the camera. She looked at least thirty years younger than she should. "They're off! Everyone's favorite family, the O'Briens – Mom, Dad, sister Anjali, and little brother Deshi – have left Earth. Next stop: Proxima Centauri!"

Julie couldn't tell if her mother had recorded the alternate introduction or if the news crew had just faked it with the AI. It hardly mattered. She'd been at the O'Briens' going-away party, too, but had studiously avoided her mother's camera. The video cut to Anji's father, Chuck. A drone hung behind him, flashing a game company's logo. Brian Case, one of Ben's friends, had a sponsorship and had to get the logo out in front of people whenever he could. "We were as surprised as anyone to be picked," Anji's father said, oblivious to the marketing going on behind him, "but we've spent the last fifteen years getting ready."

The next cut was to Deshi, Anji's adopted little brother. "It's so cool!" he said. "I'm going to live on a spaceship!" He began listing all the generation ship's technical specifications.

"Will it be hard to leave all your friends?" Carson asked Anji when her turn came.

Anji rubbed at a pimple on her forehead. Another journalist might have edited the blemish out, but Carson S Riley was hoping for a few more hard-news laurels before she retired.

"I wish I could take them all with me," Anji said. "It feels like there's nothing here for them anymore."

The story editor let Anji's mom Upasana have the last word. "It's difficult, of course, to be leaving so much and so many behind." She smiled. "We'll just have to work hard to make the mission a success."

The segment cut to the studio. Carson S and her co-anchor Dr Owen Wang faced each other over a low coffee table.

"What do you think of that, Owen?"

Owen Wang was the prototypical cuddly conservative. He spread his hands. "It's a long shot, Carson. I've always said it. Nearly a century of travel and then what? Who knows what they'll find there? Who knows if they'll find anything? It's a crying shame that it's come to this."

Julie had a T-shirt with Wang's tagline, "It's a crying shame", printed on it. He said it at least once every broadcast. The sterilization of Mexico City. The water wars in southern Europe. The HIV-Too epidemic. The North Korean missile launch on Seoul. COVID-90. The failure of the latest generation of antibiotics. Crying shames, all of them. People like Wang and his pals were the reason the ecosystem was dying, and that was a crying shame, too.

Julie waved the screen off. There'd be nothing else on the news she wanted to see. Short of deistic intervention or the invention of time travel, there wasn't much that could catch her eye anymore. Her chest felt hollow. Before she was tempted to put a name to the feeling growing there, she pulled the plastic card out of her pocket and traced the mod again. She swayed, momentarily dizzy from the sudden change in brain chemistry. Everything was fine. She took the feeling to bed before it faded.

"Twenty-Five Saves Lives!" *A slogan used by proponents of the Thirtieth Amendment, a law that repealed the Twenty-Sixth amendment, which had set the voting age at eighteen. The Thirtieth Amendment went on to limit things like adulthood and full citizenship to persons "who are twenty-five years of age or older." The amendment had been designed to protect the job market, eliminate housing shortages, and take the pressure off aging infrastructure.*

—Wikipedia

TWO

Julie propped her elbows on the breakfast bar and used her hands to keep her head in place. Her fourth tumbler of citrus-flavored electrolyte water and a nearly empty plate of scrambled eggs sat beside her. She felt hollow, tired, achy, depressed... just about all of the symptoms on the comedown list her pharma had downloaded with the party mod. Her emplant would reassert itself and make her feel better when it checked into the Cloud in a couple of hours, but for now it was useless. Julie was all alone with her brain chemistry and hangover.

Things might get even worse after the emplant synced because it would rat her out – report it had been modded without proper authorization – and Julie's mother and doctor would both get a call. Julie lowered her head to the bar. The cool granite was no help, but it took the weight off her hands.

Julie's mother swept into the kitchen wearing slippers and a silk robe. "Was it worth it?" she said.

"Maybe," Julie mumbled into the bar top. "Am I dead?"

"Not according to your emplant. And since none of my alerts went off, it looks like you kept your clothes on and your name off the public 'net. Even Dallas couldn't find anything. Congratulations."

Julie twirled her finger in the air. "The perfect daughter."

"You're not so bad." She massaged the back of Julie's neck and dug into her shoulders. "You should make an appointment

17

with Tabitha. You're like a rock." She stepped back. "Public nudity, over-sharing... what youthful indiscretion did I miss?"

Julie pushed herself upright. "I modded my emplant."

Julie felt her mother's patented hard-interview stare bore into her eyes. *The worst thing about journalists is that they know shit.*

"Hard mod or soft?" Carson S Riley said.

"Soft." Julie slid Bodypaint's card across the bar. "Only good for three uses. It's registered."

Carson inspected the card before sliding it into the pocket of her robe. "At least I'll know who to sue if you die. Did you make coffee?" Without waiting for an answer, she pulled her favorite mug off the rack and placed it inside the coffee machine. Julie had topped the thing off with water and beans as soon as she stumbled into the kitchen, so it was ready to go. It erupted into life, filling the kitchen with the smell of dark roast.

"So, we're good?" Julie said. "You'll cover me with Dr Spenser? I have an appointment Thursday."

"I suppose." Her mother frowned. "Can't expect you to go to a party and not get a little altered. I'll send her office a message and tell her I forgot to approve it in advance."

Julie's shoulders loosened. The worst that could happen was an extra therapy session or two, but she'd already had enough of those for a lifetime. "Thank you."

"Hey, I voted against the Thirtieth, you know. We're not all bad, kiddo."

Julie smiled wanly. She had heard it before. In the past, it had often been followed by a reminder that her father had voted for it, but he hadn't factored into their arguments for a while. "How's Mark?"

"Lovely." She pinkened. "He's a lovely, lovely man. I don't know why you refuse to meet him."

"You guys never go out around here. You're always in the city."

The coffee machine pinged. Carson removed her mug. "Do you want one?"

Julie came around the breakfast bar and put her now empty mug into the machine. It hesitated, updating its recipe with Julie's user preferences, and went to work.

"You should meet him," Julie's mother said. "Let's all go out to dinner tomorrow."

"Maybe."

"No, it's time. We have things to talk about."

Things to talk about. Julie's stomach, the only thing the mod hangover had not depressed, dropped. "Like what?"

"It can wait until we have dinner."

"No. You want to do that thing where you bring me out somewhere so I won't be able to cause a scene while you fuck with my life."

"When have I ever done that?"

Julie's coffee signaled that it was ready, but she ignored it. "When you and Dad got divorced," she counted on her fingers, "when you sent me to Ohio to live with him for a year. When you sent me to live with him the seco–"

"Fine." Carson held up her hands. "I have something important to share that you're going to be selfish about and shit all over, so I want to do it in public when you're on your best behavior."

Julie crossed her arms. "You're marrying Mark."

Carson laughed. "Hardly. I make way more money than he does, and I'm not stupid enough to open myself up to divorce court again."

"What then?"

"I'm selling the house."

"You said you wouldn't do that until I left."

"I said that when you were a kid." Carson glanced at her reflection in the refrigerator screen and made an effort to relax her forehead. "I'm not getting any younger, Jules, and there's no point in keeping this house any longer than I have to. Do you have any idea how much I'll save in police and fire protection alone?"

Julie stabbed her finger at her mother. "You said you'd wait!"

"I did wait. Now, you'll live with me in the city until you're twenty-five then get your own place."

"A cube."

"It doesn't have to be. Get a job, save some money, petition for an upgrade. A little studio in the upper levels, maybe." She smiled. "We can be neighbors."

Julie slapped the bar top. "You say 'get a job' like it's so fucking easy. Like I'm even allowed to work full-time for another two years."

"Nothing comes easily, Jules. When I was your age–"

"When you were my age you had options! You could leave home, move across the country, drive a fucking car!"

"I didn't screw up the climate." It was Carson's turn to use her fingers as bullet points. "I didn't vote for President Carlson, and I didn't invent autodrive."

"But you got to live your life before it all kicked in, Mom!" Julie's face was flushed. Tears threatened, but she willed them away. "When you were my age, you had your whole life ahead of you. Now–"

Carson laughed again. There was anger in her face, but her emplant was keeping the worst of it away. Pre-pharma, the coffee mug Carson was holding would have been dashed to the floor, followed by whatever else was nearby and grabbable. "Your whole life *is* ahead of you. It's not like everyone's going to drop dead tomorrow, Jules!"

"What about my kids?" Julie jabbed her index finger into her own chest. "Your grandkids? You're just fine with them living out their lives as slugs."

Carson rolled her eyes. "Not everyone who lives in a cube becomes a VR addict. I've seen the studies. By the time you have grandkids – if you have grandkids – things could be different."

"Do you know what the odds of me ever being able to afford my own house are? I've seen the studies, too, Mother. Unless everyone your age dies off in the next ten to fifteen years, I'm not even going to have a career!"

Carson's knuckles were whitening on her mug. "If you want a career, work for it. If you waste your life waiting for a spot to open up, that's your damned fault!"

"This is my home! This is where I grew up. I should have a say in what happens to it."

"My name is the only one on the deed. The decision is made, Julie. I signed the papers two weeks ago."

"Fuck you!"

"OK, now that we've talked about it, I guess we don't need to have dinner after all." Carson set her mug back on the counter. "And you're on your own with Dr Spenser."

THREE

"Have you tried to see this from your mother's perspective?" Dr Spenser said.

Julie had fessed up to the mod at the top of the session and accepted her sentence of a hundred and eighty minutes of substance-abuse counseling sessions without complaint. It had been a good buzz, after all, and the confession put the payback on the installment plan.

Dr Spenser's ThirdEye avatar was deliberately nonthreatening: average height and weight, early thirties, blandly multiracial. At least that was the face she showed Julie. It was entirely possible she had a custom skin for each patient. "Dr Spenser" might have been a face shared by a half dozen counselors and therabots. There was no way of knowing.

"Has she tried to see it from mine?" Julie said. She was using a formal skin on her avatar. It was a little taller than she was in real life and way better put together.

Dr Spenser leaned forward. "We've talked about this before. The only person you can legitimately control is yourself. Your mother will see what she sees. I'm asking you what you see. Can you understand where your mother is coming from?"

Easily. Carson S Riley had, on the outside, twenty or twenty-five good years remaining and wanted to make the best of them. The best did not include hours spent commuting from the city, where she worked and played, and the suburbs, which she was only bound to by a house and her legally dependent daughter. Julie reported her understanding to the doctor. "But it's still not fair."

"None of it is." The doctor's avatar rubbed the bridge of its nose. "It wasn't fair when they told your mother's generation…" she laughed, "…*my* generation, that there were only twelve years until the point of no return. Scientists had been warning us for fifty years, and just like that, we only had twelve years left. I had nightmares almost every night."

"Mom was part of the second-gen school strikers. She even had Greta Thunberg braids."

"We all did. There was so much passion in those days. We really thought we might change things. When those twelve years came and went," the avatar flickered through several expressions, "life kept going. We took our braids out and tried to make the best of things."

"That was easier to do when you had choices," Julie said. "Now, it's a straight road to a cube and virtual-reality addiction."

"Addiction is common enough to be alarming, but it's not ubiquitous. I live in the city. Upper mid-level suite. Probably a few floors below what your mother is buying. There are parks and gyms. Playgrounds for the children. Coffee shops. It takes some willpower. You have to challenge yourself. But you can still have a fairly normal life."

"In a hundred square feet."

"That's only if you stay inside." She sighed. "Look, I don't envy the young as much as I used to. But none of us choose the world we're born into, Julie. We have to take what we're given and build something with it." She cleared her throat. "Our time is up for the day. Did you need a pharma refill?"

"Probably."

"I'll send over a script." The avatar's eyes narrowed. "I don't have to tell you again to avoid mods, do I? Some of them, I'm sure, are safe or safeish, but your luck can change quickly. I don't want to read your obituary, Julie."

After the appointment, Julie hit the treadmill, running in place while ThirdEye tried to convince her she was on an anonymous country road somewhere. Gravel crunched under her feet. The trees overhead were nicely rendered. Birds sang. Julie had taken up running as part of the virtual police academy all her vocational tests had pointed her to. It was either that or be a forest ranger in a world where forests didn't much matter anymore or train as a receptionist.

She surfed the news feeds as she ran. The religious fundamentalists were still grousing about the colony mission, saying it flew in the face of their various gods' plans to put an end to things and bring the faithful home. A spokeswoman for the mission called the Fundies' threats "negligible," especially since the six ships were already getting clear of Earth as fast as they could.

Green letters flashed above the road ahead, saying it was time for a cool down. The treadmill slowed, and Julie dropped to a jog, then a walk. She pulled off the VR headset and stepped off the machine. The scrunchie holding her ponytail together took some hair with it as it came off and fell to the desk. Julie brushed out her hair with her fingers and did some stretches.

She hadn't begun to pack, although moving day was less than three weeks away. Her mother had sent her a virtual tour of the new condo, high up in the Menino Tower. Julie's new room was half the size of the one she had now.

Running was easier than thinking, so she did a lot of it. It took care of her body, and the pharma emplant kept her emotions in check. No highs, no lows... just a human drone jogging into the future. It was a good thing; otherwise what she was planning might send her into a panic.

Julie showered and lay down on her bed to go back into ThirdEye. Her room – the one with molecules – disappeared, and the one she actually had some measure of control over rezzed up. Her lack of spending money in the real world was no barrier to good taste here. The room was red brick with black leather couches and chairs and lots of pillows. The ceiling was a night sky with more stars than she'd ever seen in the real. Out the south window was Times Square, circa 1976. To the north were sliding doors and a balcony that looked out over the Latin Quarter in Paris. The lights of the Eiffel Tower shone in the distance. The large picture window to the east appeared to be set in the rocky walls of the Grand Canyon. The sun was shining there, painting long, strange shadows on the red rocks.

On the west wall was the door to Julie's walk-in closet, where she kept the skins for her avatar. She went through the door and dropped into the leather armchair in front of the runway.

Twelve years worth of saved skins paraded past her, from cartoon characters to those she used in the ThirdEye sex clubs. She deleted them all, experiencing the barest of second thoughts when the first one she'd made, a cat-eared anime princess, looked at her like she'd broken its heart.

"I said, 'Delete.'"

The skin bowed, faded to gray, and vanished.

Somewhere else, her legs ached from the exercise. In high school, she'd been on the steeplechase team, competing on a virtual two-thousand-meter loop with hurdles and water jumps. She had trophies and a varsity letter to prove it, awards for working hard and never actually going anywhere.

"Give me a blank. My height and build."

The new skin appeared, waiting for her to dress it up and tell it do something. It reminded Julie of many of the people she knew. Her high school and university classmates. Everyone moving into the city where it was safe and comfortable. The skin seemed almost grateful when Julie gave it identity and purpose, tweaking it to resemble herself.

It would have been gauche beyond belief to make the skin an exact twin, but she got the idea across. It was Julie with cherry-red hair and dark eye makeup. She dressed it from a collection slugged "bohemian" and pulled it out of the closet to wear.

She ported the avatar to a makerspace, a place where programmers and artists met to share ideas and work. Such places were full of wonders and abominations. One day, a group might be working on an emulation of the Mexico City fire bombing. Another, they'd be building a rainbow of semi-independent, self-replicating polygons. The creations usually faded an hour or so after their creators left the area, but sometimes pieces lingered. There'd be a building in the distance, but on closer inspection all that remained would be a single, towering wall. A steampunk airship someone had parked and left behind would be nothing but an empty shell, de-rezzing from the inside out.

All the really weird, creative people loved the makerspaces. It was where they tried out all their new ideas. And since artists and hackers tended to know the kind of people Julie wanted to talk to, hanging around the makerspaces was a good place to start.

This one, though, seemed pretty empty. Julie dialed up the magnification and tried to find a likely target. Her peripheral vision shrank to a cone.

"Jump!" someone yelled.

The surprise shout was followed a surge of motion sickness as Julie's avatar made an emergency port to avoid being run down by two hovercycles. It was completely unnecessary. The vehicles could have zipped right through her without harm, but that would have spoiled the illusion. As a result, Julie found herself twenty meters to the right of where she started, watching the hovercycles scream toward the horizon.

"They've been doing that all day."

Julie's avatar turned toward the source of the voice.

"They buzzed me twice." A thin woman in a loose robe pointed at a jumble of white cubes beside her. "The first time the automatics reacted so fast I had to start this over."

"What is it?" Julie said.

"It's – it will be an arch. Like the one in St Louis. Right now it's just pieces."

"Did they knock it down?"

The woman lifted a cube twice her size and levitated it into place. "Some assembly required. Those kids won't come near me a third time. I have a hack. Turns their little penis substitutes into pretty pink ponies." She smiled. "I almost wish they would come back so I could show you."

"Me, too." Julie's avatar floated back a few meters to get a better look at the project. She didn't see any arching going on, but there were a lot of blocks left to stack.

The arch maker rubbed her hands together to clean off imaginary dust. "Do you want to help?"

What would I do?"

The woman's avatar grinned. "Talk to me. Move some blocks. Check my math. Keep me from looking stupid."

"I can do that." She extended her avatar's hand. "Julie."

"Ariel. What are you doing here besides helping me and dodging assholes?"

"Actually," Julie said, "I'm looking for a ride."

FOUR

Carson S paid for top-shelf ad-free stream access, but Julie's vid binge started with a commercial.

The androgyne in the ad smiled like a goblin. "It's hip to be cubed!"

A parody of an ancient pop song picked the howl up as a refrain, weaving it through the action on the screen. In cut scenes, the happy humanoid cavorted around the living space, rictus sardonicus firmly in place, to demonstrate the cube's amenities. Fold-out kitchen. Pull-down bed. Self-cleaning shower and toilet unit that revolved into the wall. All of it packed into a space smaller than Julie's bedroom. Pony up the future to the national government, sign on the dotted link, and the cube was free forever. No worries, no problems. Plus, it came with a super-fast ThirdEye connection and the latest in full-body VR gear. In return, the government got a population that was safely housed, fed, entertained, and not rioting in the streets, breaking into warehouses, or sabotaging robofactories.

"I never need to leave it!" The goblin cackled and slid into the ThirdEye capsule, presumably to log on forever. The commercial ended with a 'net address and a promise. "Get a branded T-shirt for your ThirdEye avatar by clicking through for additional information!"

Its public-service penance paid, the entertainment center returned to Julie's control, and the nostalgia she'd cued up started playing. A girl in a cheerleader outfit walked through a cemetery. A boy in a varsity-sports jacket was hiding behind a headstone. He pounced. The blond girl flipped the boy, really a vampire, onto his back and drove a wooden stake into his chest. He exploded into dust.

Julie smiled. *Take that, asshole.*

The vid froze as Carson S Riley swept into the living room.

"Enough!" she said. "You've been sulking about this for days, and you still haven't started packing. You and Ben are going to a YA party in Menino Towers tonight. It's all been arranged."

"I have no interest in that whatsoever." Julie pulled the couch throw up around her shoulders. She'd been avoiding people, virtual and otherwise, as the move approached and binging *Buffy the Vampire Slayer*. It was the show's one-hundredth anniversary, and season four was showing a lot of promise.

Carson set her face to Brook No Arguments "You are putting roots into that couch."

Julie put her hands behind her head and leaned into the pillows she'd piled against the arm of the couch. "I ran five miles today."

"Healthy but not social."

"I'm just not in the mood, Mom." Julie folded her legs to make room for her mother to sit.

"I know you're sad about Anji leaving. And angry at me." Carson offered a practiced Mom smile. "But she's not coming back, and I'm not changing my mind."

Julie considered the frozen screen. Something evil had stolen all the voices in Sunnydale, and Buffy and her crew had to save the day. She could identify. She was voiceless, too, but it was also possible she lacked anything interesting or original to say. Whatever. The world wasn't doing such a great job of changing for her, either.

"I'm fine," she said.

"I hope so. The cab will be here in two hours with Ben inside. I have Dr Spenser on special retainer if you need someone to talk you through it."

Dr Spenser had turned the avatar over to a therabot for their appointment that morning. The honesty about fairness and perspective in the session before had sent the shrink running for the hills. The bot was an insufferable asshole, barely worthy of working in tech support much less passing the Turing Test. Twice it had threatened to sic the cops on Julie for using unregistered pharma mods. "Fine. I'll go to the dance."

"Huzzah! My daughter is normal." Carson called to the entertainment center, and Buffy's on-screen troubles were replaced by a shopping window. "Let's see what we can find for you to wear."

Two and half hours later Julie and Ben were at the party, an in-person mixer for all the eighteen- to twenty-four year-olds living in Menino Towers. Julie's admittedly stunted fashion sense was besieged by an array of neon stockings and tutus, baby-doll dresses and bloomers, cat ears and tube tops, lace slips and black boots. The youngsters presenting as male were even worse. Overall, they favored athleisure and ratty T-shirts, but two guys were wearing tuxedos, one had on fake plate-mail armor, and three, standing awkwardly together, were wearing pirate outfits. Most of the costumes didn't fit well, none of them looked comfortable. There was not a drug or mod dealer in sight.

"This is a nightmare," Julie said.

Ben's hand floated to his mouth. "They're dressing as their ThirdEye avatars."

Julie had done it in her early teens, too, but gave it up when she realized most of the outfits wouldn't let her do much more than stand and creak to the music. Only the pointy ears lingered until her eighteenth birthday party. For this mixer, Carson had ordered a blue dress with spaghetti straps and flats to match. It was corn silk, maybe a little better printed than standard, but still cheap and good only for a wear or two. It looked expensive and stylish, and that was the important part. Carson's maternal skills might have been limited to doctor's visits and veiled threats, but she knew her fashion.

The Menino YA Social Committee had set up arcade-style dance games along the walls, and a few boys were showing off moves to each other. Most of the partiers were sitting off to the sides playing games on their emplants. The legally-mandated chaperones were talking to each other in small groups.

"You think the chaperones are armed?" Ben was wearing a black suit over a cheap-print gray T-shirt on which he'd glitter-painted the word "Clone." "I wonder if they can use force to make us have fun."

According to the permission slip Carson had signed, the parents of the party-goers were fiscally and legally responsible for any pregnancies, assaults, or hurt feeling that occurred at the party.

"I don't think there's much chance of fun breaking out otherwise," Julie said.

Ben looked around the room. "It's kind of pathetic. Our jailors are the only ones interacting."

"And this is supposed to cheer me up," Julie mumbled.

"What?"

A din broke out in the far corner. Two of the dance-game groups were celebrating simultaneously but completely apart.

"Never mind. Let's see if we can get some people together to dance." Julie pointed. "You try the geeks at those machines. I'll talk to the ones over there."

Ben grinned. "Meet you back here in two minutes, even if it's a crappy song."

It was a very crappy song. Some kind of new-new-wave shitstorm popular on the college feeds. Ben gave Julie an "Oh, well" look when he got back with a couple of princesses in tow. They hit the dance floor anyway, trying to find the joy in a song that sounded like teeth grinding. "Sleep, little children, don't you weep," the singer growled. "Your world's been eaten by the electric sheep."

"The Ice Miners." Ben did a dance move that made him look as if he had shit himself and was trying to climb a ladder. "It's new. From the Mars colony."

Hardly anyone on the floor was looking at anyone else. They ran through steps they'd learned from vids and dance games and actively tried not to catch each other's eyes.

Julie stopped moving. No one noticed. She folded her arms and waited.

Ben caught on just as the next song started. "What's wrong?"

"This is stupid."

He looked around. One girl's cat ears were falling off her head as she gyrated by herself. "Yeah, well, pop up."

"I can't do this."

Ben caught her arm. "Are you all right?"

She shrugged him off. "I'm fine. I'm just going to the bathroom."

"You're a cliché. Nobody cries in the bathroom anymore."

"Fuck off."

He smiled. "Let's go out on the balcony, instead."

"We're not allowed."

"Who's watching?" He pointed back over his shoulder at the chaperones. One was wearing a portable ThirdEye rig; the others were engrossed in their emplants. "C'mon, I downloaded the floor plan."

Ben led the way out a side exit, down a hallway, to a set of double doors. "Do you remember what the weather was like out there?"

Julie shook her head. "I wasn't paying attention."

"Me, either. Only one way to find out." He pushed the left-hand door, and it scraped open. They followed it outside and emerged onto an enclosed balcony. "Guess it doesn't matter."

The balcony ran the width of the building, jutting twenty or so feet from its face. Safety glass curved up from a rail the height of Julie's chest and met the building about ten feet above the door. Below and beyond, what remained of Boston's skyline twinkled and loomed.

"It looks like ThirdEye," Julie said. "I wonder why they didn't have the party out here. It's not like anyone could fall off."

"Or jump," Ben said. "Probably agoraphobia. C'est common among the cubed."

Menino Towers was one of a dozen new ultra high-rises built in a part of Boston once known as Bellevue Hill. The hill was three hundred feet above sea level, and city planners figured it had a good chance of staying dry in the decades ahead. Already, thirty percent of the old city was underwater and sea levels were only getting higher.

Julie put her palms on the safety glass. "I wonder what it used to look like."

"I've seen pictures," Ben said. "I could show you them."

She pointed. "They used to play baseball over there. I know that much."

The area around Fenway Park had been a Stage-Two casualty, bulldozed and converted back to wetlands in an effort to absorb the higher tides. Boston's seafront had been lost to Stage One.

"Nine World Championships this century," Ben said. "I always thought calling it that was stupid. Nobody but the US played in them."

"Well, Canada. And Japan for awhile. And Cuba at the end. Before... you know." Desertification, desperate emigration, hostilities at the US border, war. Poof, no more Cuba.

"Still stupid," Ben said. "The World ThirdEye Games really are worldwide. No false advertising there."

Julie put her forehead against the glass. "I don't want to live this way, Ben."

"It's really not that much different from how you live now. Grit your teeth and get through the next two years. See what your options are then."

Options.

The moon hung heavy and full in the eastern sky. One-hundred and twenty-three people still lived at its south pole, on Chandrayaan Base, but they'd be the last. There weren't enough resources on the moon to allow the base to operate independently, and now that the Proxima Centauri mission was underway, there was no point in maintaining it. The base staff, many of them unable to return and live safely on Earth, remained up there to close up shop and live out the remainder of their lives. *The options suck.* "If the glass wasn't here, I might think about jumping," she said.

"You wouldn't go through with it."

"I might."

"Never jump unless you see a nice soft place to land. It's just basic escape tactics. Pop up, Jules. No soft place to land, no escape. Pick another option."

"Good advice."

"You ready to go back in?"

"Not just yet." Julie scrubbed at the mark her skin had left on the window. "It's weird hanging out without her."

It was Ben's turn to study the moon. "I wonder how it looks from the colony ships." He cleared his throat. "I always felt like we were competing for her."

"For Anji?"

"Stupid idea, maybe." He rubbed his face. "I told her I loved her more than once, but I don't even know if I meant it."

"What does that make us?"

"I don't know."

"I'm leaving soon," Julie said. "I don't need you to come with me, but I can't stay."

Ben's face twisted. He'd been an eager participant in the first escape attempt three months before, but that had been when they thought Anjali would come with them. When she hadn't shown up for the ride he had arranged for them all, his interest vanished. "That bad, huh?"

"If I stay here I'm going to dissolve. Just log into ThirdEye one day and never come out." Julie leaned into him, feeling his warmth through the thin fabric of his T-shirt. "I'm ready to go."

"Tonight?"

She smiled. "Just home for now. But soon."

Ben led the way back to the double door.

"Wait." Julie had to stand on tiptoes to kiss him on the cheek.

"What was that for?" he said.

"For dancing with me, maybe. Maybe just for being good competition."

They took the autocab back to the suburbs. It dropped Ben off first, and after the door closed behind him Julie used her emplant to compose a new message. She entered an address she'd gotten from the woman she had met in the makerspace and hit "send."

After two episodes of *Buffy*, Julie felt recovered enough for a walk. She checked the charge on her filtermask and went outside.

It had been months since she'd been outdoors longer than the trip from the front door to a cab required. The sky's black depth, yellowed as it was by a blanket of light-reflective smog, gave her vertigo. She fought the urge to fling herself on the sidewalk and hold on for her life. She overrode her pharma emplant and focused on sucking air through the filtermask and counting like they had taught her in the hospital. Her heart slowed. Her shoulders relaxed.

"I did it."

The sound of her voice dissipated like it had never existed. Like she would, eventually. Like they all would. Julie pulled the hood of her sweatshirt up and walked to the end of the driveway. A decade ago, she would have been greeted by the lights of her neighbors' houses, cheery beacons of civilization and life. Now most of the neighbors were gone, moved to suites and condominiums in the city. Humanity was circling its wagons, and anything left outside would be on its own.

She picked a direction at random and walked. Her head was clearing. The night air, though muggy, helped.

It would be Halloween soon. She'd been ten the last time she went out trick-or-treating. Her father had walked her around the neighborhood with Anji, Ben, and a few other kids. They'd knocked on doors for hours then gone back to Anji's house to divide the spoils. Ben had eaten too much and thrown up. His father had carried him home on his back, superhero costume and all. Julie had spent the night at Anji's house, and they had stayed up late talking about, well, everything.

The next year bombs fell on the other side of the world, and parents were advised to keep their kids inside safe from the fallout. Halloween was canceled. Julie logged on to ThirdEye to play games. Anji and Ben met her there. Nobody threw up, but they hadn't talked as much. Cracking the shells of the "Crab Army Invasion" hadn't left much time for conversation.

Only every ninth or tenth house on the block had lights burning now. Julie tried to put names and faces to the empties she passed. Megan Something had lived in the single-story ranch on the corner. She'd had a pool and invited the kids she liked to swim in it. One time Brian had pantsed Ben there, and Ben had dived into the water – nachos and all – to cover his embarrassment. Brian called him "Needle Dink" for the next two years.

Megan's family had traded their house for a suite in the towers, mid-level but nice. Julie remembered seeing pictures somewhere. Megan's father had been an artist, but her mother earned real money somehow. The house and pool, now federal property and boarded up, had been empty for the last eight years.

Megan's next door neighbors had been older. Two men. Dave and... Not Dave. Dave had lived there alone after Not

Dave died. He had sort of faded out of Julie's awareness at some point, but she remembered his cat, Oliver. Black with a single white foot. His tongue had felt scratchy on Julie's fingers.

Julie took another left. The route would take her back home in a few minutes. The indicator light on her filtermask was yellow, there was about an hour left on the charge, but her steps were slowing and her feet starting to drag. Sleep sounded like a good idea.

A police drone whined low overhead and directed its spotlight on her. Julie held her left hand out, palm up, so the drone could scan her. The drone operator was probably hoping she was a squatter, so he could deploy his taser net or, better yet, shoot her and claim a bonus. No such luck tonight. The drone dipped and flew away to find someone else to harass.

Julie watched it go. If she waited long enough, and kept her eyes open and record clean, the operator might retire, and Julie could apply for his job. Most cops worked from home, running drones via ThirdEye. An ever smaller number waited at the police depots for deployment. Maybe Julie would get lucky, and the cop behind the drone would choke on his dinner and leave his spot open for a young up-and-comer. The last job she'd applied for had more than four thousand applicants. She had the classes, the certificate, and more than enough simulation time, but she hadn't even made it past the first round of cuts. If she had, she might already be worried about being made redundant by one of the new AIs the corporations were rolling out right and left.

She turned again and ended up back at her driveway, her sneaker toes on the line dividing the recycled asphalt of the street and the vulcanized rubber of the drive. Julie's filtermask hissed, catching two hundred years of pollution on one side and releasing mint-scented sterility on the other. The lights were still on in her house. The empty homes, dark-eyed and staring, looked envious.

There was nowhere to go but back. She wiggled her toes a little further onto the driveway. The surface gave slightly under the balls of her feet, rocking her forward. The tiny weight shift tipped the balance, and she walked the rest of the way to the door.

FIVE

Julie logged out and stretched, testing her arms and legs against the stiffness that had set in. It was her fourth time through the award-winning virt-doc, *Just Plain Volks*, and she'd squeezed as much information out of it as she could. The volksgeist, the so-called "spirit of the people," was a name made up by an academic who did the first study on the movement. It started in the 2050s when a mass of senior citizens fled Florida's rising tides in their RVs and campers. Later, artists, writers, mediocre guitar players, and other creatives joined. Nowadays, the volksgeist was a rolling freak show, a home for runaways, criminals, and anyone else who didn't fit in or want to live in a cube. *Perfect.*

"Lights."

The ceiling mounted LEDs stuttered on, revealing nothing of interest. She had woken up in the room nearly every day for the past twenty-three years. Only the paint color had changed and that only twice.

"Time."

"Eight pm" said her bedside clock in the voice of a famous actor she no longer cared about and barely remembered.

Julie's stomach growled. She had been in ThirdEye through lunch and dinner, so she went downstairs to the kitchen. The hallway and stairwell lights flickered on ahead of her and dimmed in her wake like lobotomized will-o-the-wisps leading her somewhere totally devoid of magic and charm.

A message flashed on the refrigerator. Julie ignored it while she made herself two sesame-butter sandwiches and poured herself a glass of whatever milk substitute her mother had been duped into ordering that week. Sandwich in hand, she leaned against the kitchen island and poked the message icon. It expanded to fill the screen.

"Julie. It's Mom." Carson brushed the hair off her forehead and smiled at someone out of the camera's range. "We're heading into the city after the eleven o'clock news to see a show and are planning to spend the rest of the week there." A low voice mumbled something Julie could not hear, but it made her mother smile at someone off camera. "We'll be back late Sunday night. If you stay up, you can finally meet Mark. He can talk to you about that program I told you about." Julie's mother reached toward the camera, its lens automatically focusing on her fingers instead of her face. "Love you," the blurred mouth said. "Stay safe. Don't spend all your time online."

The message ended. Julie swiped it closed and dragged it to the trash icon at the edge of the fridge screen. None of the men her mother had brought home for inspection since the divorce had been bad, but neither had they been memorable. Broad shoulders, white teeth, artfully applied gray accents at the temples... they might as well have come out of a clone vat labeled "Roger", after Julie's father. Love had not lasted with him, and her mother's latest affair would fall apart, too. In a couple of months she'd get her pharma emplant adjusted and start the dating cycle all over again.

Julie went to her bedroom to pack.

There wasn't much she wanted to bring. She stuffed some clothes and extra power clips for her best filtermask into a small backpack. Her ThirdEye gear stayed put. Her life was finally going to be real. There'd be no time, hopefully no reason, for anything else.

Julie walked into her bathroom and slid open the medicine cabinet. She grabbed two boxes of the antidepressant patches she'd used before she got her emplant installed, added a toothbrush and her face lotion, and closed the cabinet. She considered using the mirror's built-in camera to record a message for her mother but left the room without saying a word. If her mother didn't already understand why she was leaving, an explanation wouldn't help.

Julie's wrist tingled. The message scrolled from the inside of her elbow to her palm.

–I'm here–

The interior of the car smelled like foodbars and dirty underwear. The driver smelled worse. "All the way to Pennsylvania, right?"

That was the plan, and it had taken awhile to come together. The contact Ariel provided passed Julie along to someone else. That someone shared a link to an app that refused to work in ThirdEye or on Julie's emplant, and in spite of her plans for a clean break, she had to get Ben involved. They'd tried five of his antique phones before finding one that would accept the app and begin the three hour search for the volksnet, a primitive-looking bulletin board the travelers used to plan routes, swap rides, and apparently share cooking tips. Julie had waded through hundreds of entries and threads before finding those she needed.

"Long drive. About eleven hours plus the ferry." The driver squinted. "You sure you're twenty-five?"

"I'm old enough," Julie said. "Let's go." She climbed into the car. The seatbelt whined into place, and she tried to minimize the amount of skin that came into contact with the car's ratty upholstery.

The driver put his hands on the steering wheel. The car signaled and pulled away from the curb. "Drives itself, but I have to keep my hands on the steering wheel. Safety feature."

"Great."

"Your post said you had your license."

"Sure."

"We're headed south for most of the trip." He cleared his throat. "I've never had much luck in New York."

Julie hummed noncommittally.

"Like I said, this thing will pilot itself. If you drive for some of it, we can shoot straight through. If you need to sleep you can crawl into the back."

Julie looked over her shoulder. The rear seat of the little hatchback had been folded flat, and the space was nearly filled with blankets. "Do you live in here?"

"Mostly." He drummed his fingers on the wheel. "I'm visiting an Army buddy in Tennessee, though. Just a couple of days. All I can stand. Nowadays it's roam or become a slug. I'd rather be mobile."

Julie turned her head to see if she could still glimpse her house. *My mother's house.* The driver took his hand off the wheel to pluck at his crotch, and the car slowed. Julie looked out the side window again. The streets were growing strange.

I'm running, Anj. Not as far as you, but as far as I can go.

"Do you have a real name?" Julie said after awhile.

"What?"

"I'm guessing you weren't born StudMan." His bulletin-board handle had put her off initially, but he had a good rating from former passengers.

"No one uses their real names out here. It's like a tradition or something. Started calling myself StudMan when I got out of the service. It was a joke then. Now it's just kind of stupid." He stuck his hand out. "Martin Walsh. Call me Marty."

"Julie. You were in the Army?"

"Ten years. Only way I could get out of the house. Spent most of my time patrolling the refugee camps west of Texas." He yawned. "Why don't you crawl back and get a couple hours sleep? You can take over for me when you wake up."

"Can't I just sleep up here?"

"It's your neck."

Julie leaned her head against the window and, to her surprise, dropped off almost immediately. By the time she woke, they'd been on the road long enough to feel the sun coming up behind them. The driver tapped a dashboard telltale. "We're getting close to empty. You got any money?"

Julie neck was stiff. They were on the highway. Marty kept to the slow lane, staying well clear of the long-haul robotrucks and mass-passenports that left the little hatchback rocking in their wakes. "What?"

"Money. You told me you'd have some."

"I can hold up my end," she said.

There was little need for Marty to pay attention to the road, but he kept his eyes straight ahead, chasing the headlights. He chewed his lips. A sign announced a rest stop ahead. "We'll get off there. You can stretch your legs while I charge up, then you can watch the car while I take a piss."

"Where are we?" Julie said.

"About twenty miles outside Hartford."

Julie peered at a road sign as they shot by it. Ten miles to the exit. "You grow up around here?"

Marty chewed his lips some more. He looked older than his volksnet profile claimed. He was balding, and his clothes were worn. His body was a mix of scrawny and fat, like he didn't eat enough and didn't get much exercise. "Not far. Rhode Island. Lost most of my family to Trevor."

Julie blanched. Hurricane Trevor had been the third of the half dozen superstorms that had crawled up the Old Coast in the '60s. The first one had resulted in the drowning of Miami and the evacuation of eastern Florida.

"I'm sorry." The words seemed empty as soon as she said them. None of her work-skills classes had included roleplays about comforting strangers.

"Old data." Marty sat up straighter. "I was just a kid when it happened. Went into a group home after that. When I got out of the Army, I claimed my half of the family pool and bought the car. Been driving around ever since."

It was not much of a life story, but Julie didn't have better. "How long ago was that?"

"About three years."

Julie tried to make a sound that read as noncommittal and unconcerned. "Do you like it out here?"

"Beats being a snotty 'Burban." His smile took some of the sting out of it. "My little sister took the trade. Gave up her half of the pool and got a ten-by-ten cube in Cleveland. She never logs out of VR." His mouth tightened. "Beats the hell out of that."

"Is that why you joined volksgeist?"

Marty snorted. "Those idiots? Nah. I just can't sit still. Docs say it's PTSD. I do this because I have to. None of that looking-for-humanity's-final-purpose bullshit. If it's really going to be over in a generation or two, I got better ways to waste my time."

The car took the exit to the rest stop and pulled up to the bio-diesel pumps. Marty and Julie got out. She pulled her filtermask back over her face. Marty didn't seem to have one. Julie used the restroom and stretched her legs in the parking lot until Marty waved her back to the car. He pointed to the fuel pump. "Fuel's on you, 'Burb. I'm hitting the head."

Julie activated her emplant and used it to pay for the fuel. She hoped they wouldn't need another fill-up before Marty dropped her off. He probably lived on Basic, but she couldn't sign up for it until her twenty-fifth birthday. The money she had in her account needed to last.

Marty grunted when he saw Julie waiting at the car. "Get in." He pointed at the driver's door.

She got behind the wheel and tried to get comfortable as he rubbed the dirt off the windshield with a sloppy squeegee. It confused her. She didn't need to see in order to drive. She wondered if, maybe, he was trying to impress her.

"What do I do?" she said when Marty had gotten back in the car.

"Put your hands on the wheel." He showed her. "When the car asks you say 'yes' or 'OK.' Or poke the screen there."

The car pulled away from the pumps smoothly with Julie behind the wheel. It merged with traffic, and in minutes they were back on the highway. The wheel moved gently in Julie's grip, guiding her and keeping her hands in position in case she had to suddenly take over.

"How old is this thing?" she said.

Operating Marty's car didn't really require any more concentration or knowledge than did riding in an autocab, but she could feel the road in a way she never had before. It felt...

I'm driving!

"Doing OK?" Marty said. "You have a weird look on your face."

"I've never driven a car this old before."

"You want a recording or a still for your networks?"

"No." She rolled tension out of her shoulders. Anji was halfway to Venus by now, her mother was a big part of what she was running from, and Ben, with his last-generation slang and collections of antiques, would probably give her shit for it. Not to mention what she was doing was completely illegal. "There's no one I want to tell."

"You like music?" Marty fiddled with buttons until he found the feed he wanted. "How 'bout oldies? Beyonce before she went country, that kind of thing. My mother liked it."

"I like it OK. I like most music."

"What do you like the best?"

"Best...?" Julie rubbed her chin. "I don't know. I guess I just listen to whatever my bot comes up with."

"You can do better than that."

"No. Really. I like mostly everything."

"Make a choice, kid. How 'bout the Ice Miners?" The feed switched from old-time pop to the clanks and groans of the latest hit from the Martian industrial band. He hit the button again. "How about opera?" The music swelled like a scream from the car's tinny speakers. "Volksgeist folk?" The whiny singer on the feed plucked a guitar and mewled about the trials of life on the move.

"Stop it," Julie said.

"What about AI?" The music switched to the weird tootling and rhythmic clicks produced by the latest generation of near-smart computers.

"Why is it so important to you anyway?"

"Gotta get used to making choices. It's your will or someone else's. Get mad and stay that way. It's a lot safer. You got a gun? It's not always whimsy and bullshit out here."

"I don't have a gun."

"A stunner? A knife? Anything?"

"I'll get something." Julie got the message. There wasn't much room for nice or wishy-washy on the road. "Put it back on the oldies."

"You're sure?"

"I'm sure."

"That's your favorite?"

Julie's jaw clenched. "I fucking love it."

While Marty snored through three hours of early twenty-first century pop, she watched the world go by through the car's windows. There wasn't much to see. Some big, old buildings built up against the highway, many of them unoccupied. She found the most entertainment in watching the other drivers whip by, seemingly oblivious of the fact they were traveling at eighty to ninety miles an hour. They fooled around with their emplants, watched vids, napped, picked their noses... One group of three, Julie was sure, was fucking.

The car's navigation system chimed, and Marty snorted awake. "Should be coming up on Yonkers." The car slowed and took an exit. Marty swore.

"What?" Julie said.

"Sign back there said the ferry's been delayed." He cleared his throat. "Car, check and see if the 11:40 ferry from Yonkers to Newark is on time."

The car spoke with an English accent. "The 11:40 ferry from Yonkers to Newark has been delayed four hours. Passengers are being diverted to," it listed a parking lot number.

"Not much we can do about it," Julie said.

"Not a thing." Marty poked a button on the navigation system. The car took the very next exit and pulled into the parking lot of an abandoned shopping plaza.

"Why are we stopping here?" Julie's safety belt unhooked itself and whined back into the seat.

"I'm not interested in paying for parking. You?"

"I guess not." The lot was empty except for a few wrecked cars. Every store in the plaza was closed and boarded up.

"I'm sorry about before," Marty said. "With the music. I can get a little intense sometimes."

"It's OK."

"But it's not safe out here." His eyes narrowed. "Don't ever forget that."

"I won't."

Marty reclined his seat. "Do you want to have sex or something? Pass a little time?"

"I think I'm good."

"Figured I'd check. You never know what people want to do." He closed his eyes. "Car, set an alarm for four o'clock."

The car announced the alarm was set. Julie reclined her own seat and closed her eyes.

Marty cleared his throat. "I get, like, night terrors sometimes when I'm parked. I'm on meds for them, but they don't always work. I might start yelling and thrashing around."

"OK."

"The car will turn the overhead light on and unlock the doors. If you feel unsafe, just get out and wait until it's over."

"Sure."

"Alright, see you in a few."

Julie closed her eyes again. The volksgeist caravan she planned to meet up with in Pennsylvania would be parked for another two days. The delayed ferry wouldn't have much effect on the rendezvous, and anyway, the volk supposedly had a pretty slippery grasp on time and schedules. *'Course, that also means they could leave early.* Julie pushed the thought away. *Everything will be fine.* She tried to sleep, but Marty's snores sounded like an angry pig.

The car's interior light flashed on, and the horn sounded. The doors shot open. Marty sat up and looked around wildly. Two police drones had come down right behind the car, silent as sharks, and hacked the car's control system.

Marty made it four running steps away from the car before the drones brought him down with a taser net. He screamed repeatedly before dropping into harsh sobs. The drones' radios squawked as they hovered nearby. A speaker crackled, and one of the flying robots called Julie by name.

"Julie Riley, please remain in the car. A human officer will arrive in thirty minutes to take you both into custody." The machine paused. "Do you require medical assistance?"

Julie shook her head before remembering the drone's operator probably couldn't see her. "He wasn't going to hurt me. He was–"

"Please remain in the car." The doors of Marty's car clunked closed and locked. The drone continued, now speaking through the car's entertainment system. "A human officer will be here in twenty-nine minutes to take you both into custody."

SIX

Sometime in the distant past, a committee of shrinks and sociologists had decided teal and white would be a good color scheme for a jail barracks, and now Julie was stuck with it. The white was gray with grime now, and the muting of the sterile, forced cheerfulness of the tones was one of two things keeping Julie from screaming. The other was the smell. The barracks offered every strain of body stink, and taking a scream-worthy inhale would have required getting some of it in her mouth.

Instead, she huddled on her bunk and tried to be invisible.

It wasn't working well. Every few minutes someone poked her and asked if she had any drugs or snacks. After lunch, a wild-haired woman had threatened to kill her, insisting that Julie had fucked her over the last time they were in Malibu together. After that confrontation, Julie had pulled the thin blanket over her head, passing the remainder of the day in a mix of boredom and terror.

Marty had been charged with resisting arrest and transporting a minor across state lines. If convicted, he'd lose his freedom and his car. He had been crying as police led him away. Julie told the police everything – how she'd lied to Marty about her age and having a license – hoping to spare him further trouble. When she'd run out of things to confess, the cops booked her as a runaway and called her mother. Carson S Riley, firm of mouth and narrow of eye, suggested a few days in stir might be just what Julie needed to get with the program. She refused bail and left Julie to the mercies of a public-defense bot less personable than a multiple-choice quiz. The only hint of personality it offered was a buzzing "hmmm" when Julie told it she had trained to be a cop. Rule one of cop school had been "don't break the law", so the hard-won certificate was likely no longer worth the electrons it was made from anyway. The lawyerbot scheduled an appointment with Dr Spenser on day three, the only communication with the outside Julie was allowed until her court appearance on day five.

On day two, Julie traced a mod she found carved into the bottom of her bunk and spent the next six hours in a near panic convinced the barracks was a cave and the floor below her bunk alive with rats. When the hallucinations faded, she did it again.

On the evening of day three, after a barely-better-than-the-rats visit with one of the Drs Spenser, a heavy foot thudded into the side of Julie's bunk. "Looks like you might be here for a while, 'Burb. What do you have that I want?" the owner of the foot said. Her voice was insistent but bored.

Julie stayed under the thin blanket. The next kick struck her in the leg.

"Don't ignore me." The foot wielder whistled, and two sets of hands pulled Julie's blanket away and dragged her to her feet.

Julie's eyes stung, assaulted by the unshielded LEDs embedded in the ceiling. It was as good an excuse as any for the welled tears that blurred her view of the gray-haired kicker and the two grave-looking women who flanked her. "You're new here. Maybe you don't know the rules. Pop up, when Brickhouse," the largest woman pointed at the foot-wielder with her thumb, "asks you a question, you answer it."

The smaller henchwoman had a bone-crushing grip on Julie's arm. There were a couple of ways to break free –

moves Julie had learned in police hand-to-hand training –
but fighting three larger opponents without backup seemed
like a bad idea.

"Let's try this again." Brickhouse was shorter by a third than
her henchwomen. "What do you have that I want?"

"I don't have anything," Julie said. The rats were looking
better and better.

"You sure about that? How about those shoes?"

"You can have them."

"I don't want your shoes. They're stupid. What about that
jacket?"

"Sure." Julie started to unzip her fleece.

"I don't want that, either." Brickhouse squinted. "You're a
juve, betcha. You get tired of all that good food and shelter
your parents are required to give you? Did your daddy feel you
up too many times?"

"That wasn't it."

"I don't care." Brickhouse looked Julie up and down. "What
if I want your body?"

"What?"

"Ess. Eee. Ex. You ever been with a woman before?"

"Not really." *Anji, but we were just kids. Just fooling around. Five
or twelve times.*

The woman laughed. "Not for real, you mean. ThirdEye
virgin. Probably never been with anything that doesn't need
to be charged up."

"I really don't have anything for you."

"What about that fancy filtermask?"

The air inside the jailhouse was none too clean, as the mask
helpfully reminded her every thirty minutes or so, and Julie was
one of the few people in the barracks wearing a modern mask. The
rest, including Brickhouse and her goons, covered their mouths
and noses with a range of cloth masks, scarves, or bandanas.

"It's a Sony, right? Good for viruses and particulates
down to thirty nanometers? Better than my kids ever had."

Brickhouse held out her hand. Her knuckles were scarred. "I want it."

"I need it," Julie said. "The air–"

"When you get home, stay inside until Mommy buys you a new one." She made a fist. "Give or my ladies will take. We'll give you something to keep the jailhouse cooties away."

Julie's hands were shaking. *My will or someone else's.* "What do I get out of it?"

Brickhouse barked a laugh. "A pain-free night. Good deal, right?"

"I want more." Julie's throat was dry. She held back a cough. "I don't want to go home."

"Kill yourself. It's all the rage since the colony ships left orbit." She glanced at the larger henchwoman. "We lost how many?"

"Seven," the woman rumbled.

"Seven women here last week. Bunch on the men's side, too."

Julie crossed her arms.

"Takes a lot more than a filtermask to get you what you want," Brickhouse said.

"If you can get it, I have some pharmaceutical patches in my backpack."

"What kind?"

"Antidepressants."

"Everyone has antidepressants." Brickhouse gestured, and her henchwomen grabbed Julie's arms. The gray-haired woman stuck her hand up Julie's shirt, sliding it up over her bra to her collarbone. "How long since your pharma was refreshed?"

"Couple of weeks."

"The cops can track you with it, you know. Give me the mask and the pharma without throwing a fit, I get you out."

"The pharma's inside me. How can I give it to you?"

The smaller henchwoman produced a crude, little knife.

"You scream, deal's off," Brickhouse said.

The knife moved closer. "Wait!" Julie said.

The knife paused.

"I also need a ride."

SEVEN

The dumpster was full of soiled uniforms, dirty underwear and socks, packing material, empty food cartons, and other recyclables bound for the printers where they would be unmade and turned back into something useful. Somewhere in the middle of it all was Julie, wholly uncomfortable and trying to keep her sutures from getting wet. Three hours, Brickhouse had said. Three hours before the bin slid out onto the street, and she could make a run for it.

The removal of Julie's pharma had disabled her standard emplant, and without it she had only a vague idea how much time had passed. *Either it could happen any minute, or I still have hours to go.*

Primitive man could have measured time's passage in the sun or stars, but Julie had nothing to go on but the smell of the garbage around her, and the growing ache in her abused left arm. The pain was approaching the intensity of an Ice Miners' solo. Brickhouse's surgeon had sprayed Julie's skin with an anesthetic-antiseptic combo before digging in with her shank, but the numbness had faded fast. Now, Julie almost welcomed the pain. The worse it got, the more time had passed, and the quicker she could get out of the damned dumpster.

Julie ran six seasons of *Buffy the Vampire Slayer* through her head, episode by episode, cursing herself for leaving home before she could watch the seventh and final season. She nearly yelled in surprise when the dumpster finally shuddered into motion, sliding through a door in the wall to the parking lot to await pick up by the recycling truck. She counted to ninety twice, as she'd been told, and fought clear of the garbage. The top of the dumpster wouldn't open, but she gritted her teeth and tried it from a different angle. It was just heavier than she'd expected. She cracked it open and slithered out onto the pavement, thanking the gods of budget cuts and poor security. There wasn't much point on putting good locks on the jail when the outside was usually worse than being in.

Julie was wearing a cheap-print mask Brickhouse had provided in lieu of the high-tech she'd had given up for the deal. It reeked of a former owner's sour-cream-and-onion exhalations. There are kids in developing countries who don't have masks as nice as yours, Julie's father had recited whenever her younger self complained about having to wear a mask outside. *Now I'm the one with inadequate protection. Good thing I've had all my shots.*

It was dark out, maybe midnight or a little better. Julie crouched beside the dumpster and reviewed her instructions. A left turn then four straight blocks then another left, a right, and eight more blocks to a safe house where she could hole up while she waited for her ride out of town. Brickhouse had traded a half pack of cigarettes for another long-term inmate's weekly call home and set everything up in five minutes. Julie didn't have a lot of confidence in the results but options were limited. She pulled off her fleece and tied it around her waist. Hartford was deep in an autumn heatwave, twenty-plus-days of ninety-degree temperatures. She made the left and started counting city blocks.

The area surrounding the jail was a ghost town. Most of the communities south of the city had been bulldozed and left to re-marsh as a buffer against the rising waters of the Long Island Sound. There'd been some flooding in the city, too, and most of the population had headed to higher ground courtesy of their own tower projects. Julie passed a boarded-up car rental place, a vacant doughnut shop, and any number of bail bondsman offices before taking another left onto an equally deserted street. In months or years or decades, depending on the budget, the city would raze the entire area to prevent squatters.

The directions Brickhouse provided led to an abandoned hotel off the highway, a two-story derelict with flood damage and a mostly caved-in roof. Julie went in through the front door. The guy sitting behind the front desk was lean and skinny like a coyote.

Julie cleared her throat. "Brickhouse sent me."

"Who?" the guy said.

"Brickhouse. At the jail. She said I could get a place to sleep."

His mouth twisted. "Does this look like the kind of place that takes reservations?"

Julie took a step back. "I thought–"

"That you'd drop some bitch's name, and I'd roll out the red carpet for you?" He laughed. "If you're lucky enough to find a place to sleep tonight, you better guard it with your life. Someone bigger and meaner than you's liable to snap it up. Snap you up, too, if you aren't careful."

I really need to get a knife or something. "What are you doing here then?"

The man waved his hand over the check-in desk. "Pharma mods and patches. You want anything?"

Tempting, but without a working emplant, money had become a real problem. "No."

"Then get the fuck out of my face."

Julie climbed to the second floor in search of an empty room and finally found one at the end of a long hallway. The bare mattress was badly stained, and black mold was creeping up the walls. There were three locks on the warped door, all of them busted. Julie shoved a bureau against it and pushed a sagging chair against that. Her backpack was still in police lockup, but Brickhouse had given her a shoulder bag someone had sewn together from pillow cases and let her fill it from a stash of supplies pilfered from the jail kitchen and clinic. Julie lifted her shirt and smoothed a pain-killer patch onto her skin. It wouldn't be nearly as effective as her pharma had been, but it might take the edge off and let her sleep a couple of hours. Her ride, assuming it showed up at all, would be there in the morning.

Two men were arguing loudly in the room next door. A body or something thudded heavily into the adjoining wall, sending a framed print on Julie's side to the floor. Julie sat in the sagging chair and sipped from one of the water packets she'd taken from Brickhouse's stash.

Someone downstairs screamed.

Julie unwrapped a foodbar and planted her feet on the floor. *Gonna be a long night.*

EIGHT

Her ride showed up at noon. The vehicle was nearly shapeless, all rust and primer, and covered with aftermarket and bespoke add-ons. The driver leaned across the front seat to open the passenger door. "It doesn't always work from the outside." She craned her neck to look at Julie. "Can you drive a manual?"

"I've done some simulations. Mostly racing games."

The woman sighed. "I guess I won't be letting you behind the wheel until you dump that data. Get in."

The driver was in her late thirties, maybe, with lines on her face Carson S Riley wouldn't have dreamed of allowing. Her hair was divided into several thick braids. Draped over the back of her seat was a long coat that might have been leather once but now was mostly patches. She pointed into the van with her thumb. "You can toss your bag back there for now. I'm Ranger."

Julie looked where Ranger had pointed and saw a narrow bed and a work surface. Boxes and bags were stacked around the sides and tied to the walls. She added her pack to the closest pile.

"You ready?" Ranger said.

Julie climbed in. The rust-pocked van was at least twenty-five years old. She had to adjust the seat by hand. Ranger thumped the dashboard with the side of her fist, and the dim holomap projected there brightened and stuttered into sharper focus. The van's location was marked with an icon shaped like a rude gesture. Ranger stuck her finger in the map to indicate her destination and waited while the navigator figured out the best route. She showed Julie how to fasten the seatbelt, and they were off in a cloud of smoke that smelled like french fries. The sun was creeping up the sky behind them.

"You can take the mask off," Ranger said. "My vax are up to date."

Julie slid the grubby cheap-print off her face and held it in her lap. "Mine, too."

"Figured. Hope you aren't in a hurry to get anywhere. I mostly take back roads. Juniper doesn't like the highways much."

"Juniper?" The van was certainly big enough for two people, but there was no sign of a partner.

Ranger patted the dashboard. "Juniper. Juniper Two, really. My second ride. Used to belong to an arborist."

"It's nice."

"She's perfect." Ranger emphasized the pronoun. "How do you know Brickhouse?"

"I just met her."

"I 'just' met her outside Chicago a couple of years ago. She helped me out of a jam. Well, it was a mutual jam. We helped each other out of it."

Julie's arm was throbbing from the jailhouse surgery. "How much did it cost you?"

"A big lithium battery and a favor to be used later. That's where you come in." Ranger took a corner wide. The van rocked and shook on its springs.

Julie used her left arm to brace herself and sucked air in through her teeth. "Why aren't you using autodrive?"

"I pulled all that shit out years ago. No strings on me. Even the navigator is self-contained. No satellites looking over our shoulder. Juniper, love, say hello to the new girl."

The van's navigation system spoke with a Southern accent. "Hey there! Where you headed?"

"I've no idea," Julie said.

"Where were you headed when the pigs got you?" Ranger said.

Julie frowned. "Pigs?"

"The police."

"Pennsylvania. I was trying to meet up with a caravan parked there."

"Probably gone now. What's your backup plan?" Ranger took another wide turn.

Julie clutched her seatbelt. "I don't really have one."

"We'll get on the volksnet later and find you one. What did Brickhouse charge for springing you?"

"My pharma emplant. They stitched me up with dental floss."

"Not unheard of but surely not comfortable." She slowed the van to merge with a line of cars and cabs waiting at an intersection. "She might have done you a favor. Are you a runaway?"

"How is that your business?"

"Giving a runaway a ride would be a felony, and I don't want to rot in prison because you fucked around with me when I asked you a question. Are you a runaway?"

"I'm twenty-three."

"How much of your emplant did she leave in there?"

"She cut me here," Julie raised her forearm, "and under my collarbone. I don't know what she took out. I tried not to look."

Ranger sucked her teeth. "Might be OK. Might not. Do you have a Faraday sleeve?"

Julie looked at her in confusion.

"We have to cut off the signal to and from whatever might be left in there. Look in the glove compartment."

Julie popped it open and half the contents fell out on her feet. She sorted through the mess on the floor for a minute or two before realizing the item she needed was still inside. The sleeve looked and felt like a long black mesh glove with silver threading. "Why are you helping me?"

"You came highly recommended. Put it on. There's probably a strip of painkillers in there, too."

Julie slid the glove on her left hand. Nothing happened.

"Now they can't use the network to find you." Ranger rolled her shoulders a few times.

"You're not turning me in?" Julie said.

"I ran, too. Younger than you, but that was way before the Thirtieth kicked in. I split from a foster home." She took a breath that stalled in the middle. "Dead parents. I tried to live with my grandmother, but she didn't want me. Then she died, and I got her money." She patted the dashboard. "Guess Gran gave me a home after all."

Julie cleaned up the mess on the floor and stuffed it back into the glove compartment. She pulled a pain-relief patch off a ragged strip she found there and smoothed it onto her forearm.

Hartford gave way to the suburban wastelands outside the city. Here and there a well-tended house testified to privileged contrariness, but mostly it was filled-in foundations and pointless driveways.

Ranger cleared her throat. "Longish term, I'm headed to California. It's been awhile since I've seen the Pacific."

"How long?"

"After the Chinese but before Texas. Maybe ten years ago."

The US had signed over most of its middle to the People's Republic in the '70s, paying off years of accumulated debt and raising the funds needed for the tower projects. Many of the sixty-seven million native Chinese displaced by rising seas had ended up in America's former heartland, along with most of the population of the Marshall Islands, Indonesia, and the Philippines. After the secession of Texas in 2088, the only remaining land link to the West Coast was the Oklahoma panhandle. "I hear the crossing is dangerous."

"Getting through can be a little tricky." Ranger rubbed the steering wheel with her thumbs. "I'm not going to Pennsylvania this trip, but I can get you up to Albany. We can spend the night near there and look for something in the morning. Got a gig coming up escorting some grays down to their summer hunting grounds in a week or so. Maybe you can hook up with them."

"Sounds good."

Ranger's mouth twisted. "Hold off on that until you meet them. If you're looking for peace and quiet, this group ain't it. But they're nice enough. Good people." She rode out a sudden coughing fit. "Settle in and get some sleep. Bet you didn't get much rest in that shit hole."

Julie didn't know if Ranger was talking about the jail or the squat, but either would have worked. She was tired, nearing exhaustion, and her arm hurt. Ranger started humming to herself, following the red line the navigation system had drawn on the holo map.

Julie closed her eyes and let the potholes rock her to sleep.

NINE

When Julie blinked awake, the van was coming to a stop among a loose circle of mismatched vehicles. "We're in Massachusetts," Ranger said. "The weather is about to do something weird, and it's better to get off the road."

The sky was overcast and the light had a gray tone that was unsettling. "Where are we?"

"Near Springfield. It's a little after five."

"Oh, jeez." Julie fumbled for her seatbelt. "I'm sorry. I didn't mean to sleep–"

"You were pretty out." Ranger took the van out of gear and turned off the holo map floating above the dash. "Help me put the storm shutters down and I'll forgive you."

The van had five windows – windshield, passenger and driver's side, and two small squares in the rear doors. Julie put on her mask, and Ranger showed her how to pull the metal shutters off the storage rack on top of the van and mount them on the tracks bordering each window.

"What's it supposed to do?" Julie said.

"Hail, maybe. Sleet." Ranger rested her hands on her hips and watched as Julie bolted the last shutter in place. "Could be nothing. Could be a calamity. Better to be safe."

The heavy leather coat Julie had spotted on the back of Ranger's seat was now draped over the woman's shoulders, almost like armor. She was wearing boots, thick work pants, and a denim shirt. Around her waist was a utility belt. Carson

S Riley might not have approved of Ranger's fashion sense, but the ensemble made her look extremely competent.

"You hungry?" Ranger said.

"A little."

Ranger held up a box of protein crackers. "Let's go meet the neighbors."

A campfire burned at the center of the circled vehicles, and people were clustered around it. Strings of fairy lights twinkled on and around the parked trucks and vans.

"Don't tell anyone your real name and don't ask for theirs," Ranger said before they came within earshot of the group. "If anyone here is wired, their emplant might be listening and dime you out to the pigs."

Julie stopped walking. "Who should I be?"

"Bad luck to pick your own road name," Ranger considered. "It's supposed to come up naturally."

"I don't believe in luck. How about Pilgrim or Wanderer? Or Scout?"

"Gods, no." Ranger resumed her walk to the campfire. "Maybe just don't talk."

A woman with a zipper tattooed on the side of her head raised her hand as they approached. "Howzit?"

Ranger put her hands on her hips. "Fair. Figured we'd park early to avoid the storm."

Zipper woman's head dipped. "Got anything to share?"

"Box of crackers."

"Welcome to the park. There's soup."

"Real soup?" Ranger said.

Zipper woman smiled. "It's wet and there are edible things in it. I'm Zip."

Ranger tossed the crackers on top of a pile of assorted food items. "Ranger." She indicated Julie with her thumb. "This is Runner. We're just out of Hartford. Everyone's shots up to date?"

A chorus of nods and "yeahs" answered. The two people beside Zip scooted over to make room by the fire. Julie followed Ranger to the ground. She focused on the mug of soup someone handed her while Zip quizzed Ranger about the road to Hartford. The thin soup was mostly re-hydrated vegetables and soba. It benefited greatly from the handful of seasoned crackers she crumbled into it.

"Where you from, Runner?"

The man who asked the question was thin, maybe fifty years old, his rainbow-colored hair drawn up into a ponytail.

Julie cleared her throat. "Boston." *Close enough to true.* "You?"

"Texas, originally." He introduced the man beside him, a little younger with several facial piercings. "This is my husband, Crunch. I'm Alamo. We left when Texas went independent."

Texas had gotten pretty crazy toward the end, nationalistic, macho, very bootstraps and traditional values. It could easily have made someone like Alamo uncomfortable.

Alamo introduced the rest of the folk around the fire. He was probably the oldest. Zip fell somewhere in the middle. The youngest were a set of three men, almost boys really, called Huey, Dewey, and Louie.

"They came on together." Alamo leaned over as if to confide in Julie. "Seemed like we should recognize them as a set. I call 'em the 'ducklings.'"

The three spoke English with a thick accent.

Easel and Squeak were a middle-aged married couple from Virginia. They traveled in a brutalist-looking pickup truck. Squeak had drawn kitchen duty, and the soup was his responsibility. Crunch contributed dessert: two boxes of slightly stale toaster pastries, warmed over the fire. After the dinner things were recycled or burned in the fire, Magnolia, an older woman on her own, shared a jug of wine.

Alamo was the easiest to talk to, but there was hardly a need to be choosy. They all had stories to share. Even the trio of boys talked guardedly about life on the other side of The Wall.

It was nearly nine when the rain started, sluggish and considerate of bodies and minds slowed by cheap merlot.

Ranger pulled out her phone to check the weather. "Looks like the hail is canceled," she said. "Just rain."

Zip and her caravan were headed south in the morning, so Ranger and Julie offered goodnights and goodlucks and walked back to the van.

"Runner, huh?" Julie said as soon as she felt it was safe. The wine made her feel loose and comfortable. "A little obvious."

Ranger yawned. "I've met a dozen Runners out here. You'll have to pick a modifier if more than two of you are in a group, otherwise it'll be fine. No one will question it."

"Midnight Runner," Julie offered. "Road Runner."

"More like Carpet Runner or Table Runner."

"I actually do like running," Julie said. "For exercise."

"Kismet." Ranger unlocked the van. "You take the front seat. I'll wake you up in about four hours, and we'll switch." She pulled a battered sleeping bag out of the back and tossed it on the front seat. "I think this still has some juice left. There's a reader full of books in the glove box if you can't sleep."

"What if I have to go to the bathroom?"

"Paper is in there." Ranger pointed to driver's side door. "Bottom pocket. Don't go crazy with it. The bushes over there to the left are probably safe. That's where I'd go."

Julie smiled.

"What?"

"I had fun tonight. With people. That's not normal for me."

"That's just the wine talking."

"It was great. It's just like the documentary."

Ranger's forehead creased. "Yeah, well… It can be that way. Sometimes."

TEN

The van rocked, and Julie took it as a signal to stretch and yawn herself awake. "Time to go?"

Ranger peered over the seat at her. "Was. Then it wasn't. Zip's guys have a mechanical problem we're trying to suss out."

"Can I help?"

"Know anything about antique cars?"

"Nothing."

"You're on the clean-up crew then. Coffee is on the fire. Breakfast is whatever you can find. Check in with Squeak for a to-do list."

Julie lingered inside the sleeping bag for a couple of extra minutes. It smelled like it hadn't been washed in a while, but it was warm and difficult to leave. The need to pee finally forced her outside, and, that taken care of, she walked to the fire and poured herself a mug of the murky coffee heating in a saucepan there. The first sip made her grimace.

"Filter the grounds through your teeth." Squeak dropped the recycling bag he was carrying.

She tried it again. The second sip made her grimace, too.

"It takes some practice," he said.

The coffee was hot and bitter and bold. Completely lacking in subtlety. Probably just what she needed to get her heart started and her brain running right. "Ranger said there was some kind of trouble."

"Huey, Dewey, and Louie... the Spanish kids? Their car

won't start." Squeak brushed his thinning hair back and wound it into a bun with one of the hair ties he wore on his wrist. "I don't know how it's stayed running this long. The thing's almost as old as I am."

"Can Zip fix it?"

"Zip? Nah. We're just a pick-up group. Closest thing we have to a mechanic is Easel, and she doesn't know anything about hydros."

"Can we call someone?"

Squeak laughed, and Julie finally understood where he got his name. "Like who? It would cost more than the car's worth to get someone out here, and there's no telling how long that would take." He poked the trash bag with the toe of his boot. "Nah. If we can't get it started they'll have to ditch it. We can't park here for another night."

"So–?" Julie started.

"Ranger and Zip say I can put you to work." He pointed out the piled-up remainders of the prior evening's potluck. "Salvage anything edible and/or appetizing and toss the rest in the bag. If you see anything you want to eat, grab it and call it breakfast."

"What do I do with the rest?"

"Bring it over to Magnolia. She's in charge of stores until we break up." He rubbed the back of his neck. "We were supposed to be on the road by now. Might want to ask her what she wants to do about lunch."

Julie finished her coffee and turned her attention to the pile of boxes and containers. Most were empty and went straight in the bag. She grabbed a peanut butter-and-jelly bar out of a mostly empty box and washed it down with another cup of coffee. A few of the containers were sealed but past their expiration date. Julie decided to tote them over to Magnolia and let her provide the answers. She carried Squeak's recycle bag back to his truck and lugged the salvage to the station wagon Magnolia traveled in. The older woman was repacking the small trailer she towed behind it. "Hey, Runner," she said.

"Got some things for you," Julie said. "Some of it's expired."

"That's usually more of a suggestion than a hard stop," Magnolia said, "but I'll take a look at them." She straightened and pressed the small of her back with both hands. "Any news about the ducklings' ride?"

"I haven't heard anything." Julie piled the containers on the trailer's surviving fender. "What happens if it won't start?"

"Nothing good. We're only together for another two hundred miles or so, and none of us are set up to take three extra riders." She frowned through the transparency of her filtermask. "Everything those boys have is wrapped up in that car. Losing it would be a disaster."

There were seven climate-refugee camps in the Arizona-New Mexico Buffer Zone, jointly funded by the governments of the Unites States, Mexico, and Independent Texas. Ref life was simple: no one got enough, everyone was mistreated equally, and the only sure way out was death.

"They're brothers," Magnolia said. "Their grandmother had a little money set by. She arranged for a smuggler to take them to Las Vegas, and they bought the car there. Got royally screwed on it you ask me."

"Squeak said I should ask you about lunch."

She shifted the box of leftovers Julie had carried over. "There ought to be enough here. We'll have to clear out before six, though. I hope Zip realizes that."

"What will happen if you don't?"

"If no one is paying attention, nothing. More likely the drones will come chase us out. It's private property. The malls are sort of grandfathered in with old laws, but we still can't park at most of them for more than a day or two."

"Can we put a message up on the volksnet? There has to be someone who can help."

Magnolia frowned. "The boys were extremely lucky they found us. Not everyone is as enthusiastic about helping the wretched refuse as we are."

"But… I…" Julie stopped, confused. Altruism was practically a volksgeist commandment.

Magnolia's eyes widened. "You've seen that movie." She smiled to herself. "I've watched it a couple of times just for the laughs."

"I don't get the joke," Julie said.

"I mean, it's better spin than the government-propo vids about us. Drug- and disease-ridden parades of the damned, freaks too stupid to get out of the rain. That documentary…" her lips curled, "the only people they talked to were the crazies, the zealots. No one elected them to tell our story."

Julie frowned.

"Pop up, babe, I didn't always live in a station wagon. I did my doctoral anthropology study on lumberjacks in the northeastern US and Canada. Wish like hell I could do it over knowing everything I know now. That film barely went ankle-deep into life out here." She scrubbed at her forehead with her sleeve. "Living on the road isn't for the weak. It's exhausting, and kindness is rarely rewarded. The only reason I do it is because it's a lesser hell than taking a cube."

Magnolia returned to her packing and inventory, and Julie wandered back to sit in the van. She ran the *Just Volks* documentary back through her mind. The participants hadn't seemed crazy, or at least no crazier than anyone else. *What the fuck is the point of this if–?*

Ranger broke into Julie's downward spiral by rapping on the window. "I need your help."

"With what?"

"We may have gotten real lucky on this whole breakdown thing."

Julie helped Ranger unpack equipment from the back of the van. The volksnet, Ranger explained, was not a single network. Instead, each caravan, organized or ad hoc, carried its own copy. Anytime caravans met, or a new vehicle joined an existing group, all the phones and computers hosting a copy of the volksnet compared notes and updated themselves based on who was carrying the most recent version.

"It's a security measure." Ranger grunted, lifting a multi-limbed contraption out of the van. "It keeps the pigs from knowing too much about what we're talking about. Juniper," she slapped the side of the van, "just happens to have the freshest bread, and that bread just happens to have manuals and printer files from a hydro-car hobbyist up in Maine."

Ranger and Julie carried the pile of gear to the middle of the circle of vehicles and watched as Alamo hooked it up to his generator.

"Two parts," Ranger said. "It will take a few hours to powder enough feedstock, and a couple more to print, but I think we can get on the road by two or three o'clock."

Alamo loaded the broken bits he'd removed from the boys' car into the scanner and set to work. "I'll do them in plastic first to check the fit."

Julie looked dubiously at the battered 3-D printer she'd unknowingly been sleeping beside. "Does that thing even work?"

"Probably," Ranger said. "What's for lunch?"

ELEVEN

Julie waited until Ranger had thunked the navigation system into life and pulled back onto the road.

"Why aren't we traveling with a caravan?" she said.

"We were literally with a caravan ten minutes ago." Ranger pointed to the monitor linked to the backup camera. "Zoom in real quick and you might see their sweeper."

"You know what I mean."

"I'm a professional." Ranger slowed the van through a moonscape of potholes. "When I was first out here I always ran with a caravan. Recently, though," she smothered a cough, "recently I'd rather be alone. It just works out better. Don't have to worry about finding someone headed my way."

"What happens if you have mechanical trouble?"

"I fix it." She patted the steering wheel. "I know every inch of her. There's not a thing she could do that would surprise me."

"Plus, there's the volksnet."

Ranger jabbed a thumb at her jacket. "That reminds me. Reach into the big pocket closest to you. Be careful, there might be a couple of sharps."

Julie reached gingerly into the pocket Ranger indicated. "What am I looking for?"

"'Bout four inches wide, flat, smooth–"

"Got it." Julie slid the object out of Ranger's pocket. "It's a phone."

"Yours. Alamo gave it to me to give to you. His specialty. It's all wiped and rigged. New battery. The pigs can't find it, but the volksnet can."

Julie woke the phone and read the message that appeared on the screen. "Says it's updating." She looked closer. "It's today's date. How–?"

"Juniper always has the most recent version of the volksnet."

"I thought the only updates came from caravan-to-caravan sharing."

"Juney and I are a little special."

The van's navigation system broke in with a soft chime. "Hey, sugar, the bridge we're headed for was declared unsafe about thirty minutes ago."

Ranger swore under her breath. "Find us a way around, baby girl."

"Will do, darlin'," the nav said.

Ranger worked her shoulders. "This drive is going to take a little longer than I thought."

Thirty miles an hour was ten times the average human walking speed. More than twice the speed of a marathon runner.

But Julie felt like she was crawling. Ranger's van had probably never been speedy, but it had long ago sacrificed whatever quickness it had to add-ons and age. The roadways didn't help. Pitted, cracked, washed out completely in places... the locals gave up on maintenance as soon as it was politically expedient. What need for road repair if no one important traveled them?

It was nearly dark, and well into the third play-through of *Malala: The Musical,* when Ranger pointed at a glow on the horizon. "That's Albany."

They went north of the city. Ranger consulted her ancient phone and grunted. "Looks like Thacher will be safe tonight."

"Who's Thacher?" Julie said.

"State park. Cops flew over it last night, and they usually don't do that twice in a row."

There was no one else on the road. Ranger took a left turn without signaling or slowing down for the stop sign. Years of neglect had nearly reduced the roadway to gravel, and the van wallowed comfortably. A faded sign on the gate revealed the park's full name: John Boyd Thacher State Park. Ranger showed Julie how to pop the gate and close it so it looked secure. A man in a poncho waved them down as they drove onto the site. Ranger slid down her window.

"No fires," the man said, "and no fighting."

"Trading OK?"

The man stepped closer to peer inside the van. "What do you have?"

"Knit goods, mostly. Sundries. I have a pair of purple-and-gray mittens that would probably fit you."

"I got mittens. 'Sides, it's a million degrees out here." The man pointed. "Go up that way. You'll see where everyone else is."

"Who's here?"

"Small caravan. Long-term group." He waved them on. "Welcome to the park."

Ranger put the van in gear and took it along a weaving, uphill road that looked like it might crumble under the tires at any minute.

"Who was that guy?" Julie said.

"Caretaker. Self-appointed. Keeps things up and probably lives in the visitors' center when he's not ducking the pigs. If it's a good stay, we're supposed to tip him on the way out."

The hill flattened out into a plateau. Ranger pointed Juniper toward a motley collection of vehicles scattered at one end of the small parking lot. The largest was an old school bus, repainted in rainbow colors. If the park seemed less communal than the last site, it might have been the effect of the dead and charred trees that surrounded it.

"Is it safe?" Julie said.

"Safe enough. Honor among tramps and all that. No one wants the cops out here." Ranger pulled into an empty space and killed the engine. "Let's go meet the neighbors. Maybe don't talk much unless I give you the go-ahead." She took a deep breath of the moist air and spat. "Bad today."

Julie fumbled the cheap print out of her pocket and tied it around her face. "I never see you wearing a mask."

"Once upon a time, you'd never catch me without one. Now I'll only wear one if I'm sick or there's a new bug going 'round."

"What about all the shit in the air?"

"When it's only my life I'm risking," she cleared her throat, "doesn't seem as important."

Julie followed Ranger to the center of the camping area. About a dozen people, most of them women, were sitting around a fire built inside a low iron ring.

"Caretaker said something about no fires," Ranger said.

"This is the only one he authorized. Had to show him we had enough water on hand to put it out." A tall man with curly hair gestured to an empty spot. "Sit down and take a load off. Welcome to the park."

"Hope everyone's had their shots." Ranger hunkered down. Julie studied the ground carefully before joining her.

The tall man laughed at her. "Nothing big enough here to eat you. Call me Kinks."

"Ranger. This is Runner. How long have you been traveling together?"

Ranger directed the question to the women in the group, but Kinks appeared to be the only one in a talking mood. The travelers were clean, well-fed, but none of the women met Ranger or Julie's eyes.

"Few months," Kinks said. "Found each other west of here and joined up for safety. We're looking for somewhere to spend the winter. Spent the last one with my brother in LA, and I don't want to do that again."

"I know a couple of places you could hole up near West Virginia. I can send them to your nav unit."

"Appreciate that. Which way you two headed?"

Ranger poked at the fire with a stick. "This way and that. We like to keep our options open."

"Got anything to trade?"

"Good chance."

"We have showers," one of the other men in the circle said. "Hot as you like."

Ranger pulled a foodbar out of her pocket. She unwrapped it and handed half to Julie. "I'm plenty clean, but I have some trade-ables that could make your bath time a little happier."

Julie chewed on her half of the foodbar. It tasted vaguely like chocolate. "I'd love a shower." She hadn't had one since the day she'd left home and subsequent itchiness had her worried the bunk in the jail barracks or the squat had been infested.

"Bet you would." Kinks shifted a burning log. "Just how dirty are you?"

Ranger put her hand on Julie's ankle to get her attention and offered her a minute head shake. "She's fresh enough for me. How was the Panhandle?"

"Not bad." Kinks scratched his patchy beard. "We traveled at night, kept quiet. Missed a lot of the checkpoints that way. Stopped once to wait out a storm."

"Big?"

"Lot of wind and rain. Could have been worse. Between the fence the Chinese built and the Texans' shoot-on-sight policy we didn't have many options."

"Who's running the checkpoints now?"

Kinks snorted. "Anyone with the means to put up a road block. Cops. Squatters. Raiders. Neighborhood watch. Kids with lemonade stands. They all have their hands out, and some of them ain't too polite about asking."

"But you got through."

"Like I said, we avoided lot of them." Kinks grinned at the

man who'd talked about the showers. "Paid the tolls when we couldn't."

"Good for you." Ranger smothered a yawn. "It's been a long day. Think we'll turn in early."

"We're leaving about nine. If you catch us, maybe we can make some deals."

"Might do that." Ranger stood and patted Julie's cheek affectionately. "Let's go, baby."

Julie's eyes widened, but she got up and followed Ranger back to the van "What's going on?"

"Cock Blocking 101. I don't think Kinks and I would stay chummy if we talked much more."

"What's wrong with him?"

"I know his type. He's running a shower show out of that bus of his. You'd get your hot water, and he'd take stills and vid, and you'd be all over the x-feeds by morning." She pulled the van door open.

"Do people still do that?"

"A lot of people get off on voyeurism. It's a predation thing."

"But in ThirdEye–"

"In ThirdEye you can do anything. Nothing is forbidden or taboo, and it's all fake. Takes some of the fun out of it." Ranger climbed into the front seat. "You can start in the back tonight. If a shower is worth it to you, talk to him in the morning."

"Have you ever... you know?"

"There are always other options." She considered. "Almost always."

TWELVE

Ranger snored hard for four hours in the front seat and didn't let up after they switched places. Julie resolved to get earplugs before too many more nights passed, but she slept, too, albeit fitfully. Ranger was already out of the car doing stretching exercises when Julie woke for the final time and clambered, blinking, out of the van.

"I made tea." Ranger pointed to a table she'd unfolded from the side of the van. "I also rustled up a breakfast out of some of the stuff from your bag."

"What time is it?"

"About seven. I figured you could eat and pee, walk back over to see if Kinks and his people have anything we want."

Breakfast was another foodbar, fruit-flavored, and a small tub of bland protein pudding. Julie ate the spoon, too, which tasted like cinnamon, and folded the container flat.

"We'll hit a recycler down the road and get rid of the trash." Ranger pulled a patched backpack out of the van. "Don't forget your mask."

"You said it wasn't important."

"I said it wasn't important to me," she said. "You make the call, but no one is going to harass you for wanting to keep your lungs intact."

Julie retrieved the malodorous mask and pulled it over her face. "What are you trading?"

"Stuff I've picked up. And I knit when I have time. And make soap."

"Soap?"

She smiled. "You'd be surprised what you can get for soap out here."

Julie closed the van door. "Why are we trading with Kinks if he's a bad guy?"

"The realities of the situation. Everyone is someone's bad guy, and if Kinks has something I need or want..." She shouldered the pack. "Plus, I doubt he's awake, yet. This might be the only chance to talk to his ladies without him."

Julie followed Ranger back to the fire pit. One of the women from the night before was heating a pot of water. Ranger waved. "We saw you last night, but we didn't get your name."

"Boo."

She opened the backpack under the woman's nose. "Know anyone who'd be interested?"

Boo reached inside the bag and pulled out a hand-cut bar of soap. "Lemon!"

"Lemongrass. But close enough," Ranger said. "And mint. A few other things. All natural."

The woman smiled. "Let me get some of the others."

Boo steered clear of Kinks' bus but soon had seven or eight women looking over Ranger's wares. Ranger traded a half dozen bars of soap for two jugs of waste cooking oil, a couple of clean cheap-print masks, and a pair of gently used boots. She put the oil in her backpack and gave the masks and shoes to Julie to carry.

"You really from out west?" Ranger said.

Boo nodded. "Utah. Three of us left the towers in Salt Lake about six months ago. We picked up the others along the way."

"When did you meet Kinks?"

She grimaced. "Right after Salt Lake. He convinced us we needed an escort through the Panhandle and then stuck around. Started supplying a few of us with drugs."

"And showers," Julie said.

Boo's smile was thin. "Give it a couple weeks, kid. You'd be surprised at what you're willing to do to get rid of the stink."

"You need to ditch him," Ranger said. "You're already letting him speak for you, and it's going to get worse. How much of the convoy does he own?"

"One car and the bus," Boo said. "But–"

"Is he armed?"

"Nothing lethal."

"Can you access the volksnet?"

"One of the girls has it on her phone."

"Leave a message for me there once you're clear." Ranger reached into one of the many pockets of her coat. "Take this in case he has a problem with you leaving."

Boo weighed the stunner Ranger had put in her hand. "I've never–"

"Safety off." Ranger pointed at the switch. "Aim and shoot. Repeat until he stops trying to get up. Zap the other guys, too. You have fifteen shots. Then disable his vehicles. Grab the drugs, get your friends, and drive away. Stick together."

Boo put the stunner in her jacket pocket.

"The next time I see you, I don't want to see him." Ranger closed her backpack. "It's bad enough out here without feeding ourselves to the snakes."

Julie hauled the boots and cooking oil back to the van, and let Ranger show her where to stow them. "You really don't like him."

Ranger put her keys in the ignition. "Freedom from people like Kinks is important."

"You do that kind of thing a lot?"

"Not as much as I used to." She opened a hatch in the console between the front seats and pulled out another stunner. She plugged it into a charging port. "There are three more in the back. I'll charge one up for you. You know how to use it?"

Julie did. Most of her experience was simulated, but she'd put a lot of time in.

Ranger let several miles pass between them and Kinks' caravan before waking her phone to access the volksnet. She kept one eye on the road as she scrolled through the posts. "Got it. Small caravan. Heading west. If we hustle we can catch up with them in an hour."

"Why's it so important to be in a group now?"

"Rough country ahead. I need to get to Buffalo to meet my clients, and I don't want any more delays."

Ranger found the group before it broke camp. She and Julie took the middle position, with a rickety RV running about a half mile back, a converted ambulance behind that, and two young guys in a modern compact taking the lead. Every so often Ranger used her phone to check in with the other drivers.

"The guys in front and back are keeping a lookout for pigs," she said, glancing from the road to Julie. Without autodrive, she couldn't afford to take her eyes away for long. "If they see any, we'll get off the road for a couple of hours and keep you out of sight."

Tramping wasn't illegal, but the police assigned to the back roads got bored sometimes. Ranger shaded the dashboard clock with her hand so she could see the green numbers there. "We'll probably drive for another three hours. Then we'll park until nightfall. That will give me a chance to give you a driving lesson." She rolled her head from side to side to stretch her neck.

Ranger's smartphone squealed. She peered at the screen and dropped it in her lap. She gripped the steering wheel harder. "A couple of pigs coming up behind us."

Julie had no idea why Ranger kept calling them pigs. Police drones looked like, well, like drones. She craned her neck to look out the back window. "What do we do?"

"We need to get off the road."

The battered van shook and rattled when Ranger asked it for more speed, but with a lurch and a whine it agreed. The view outside the windows didn't exactly become a blur, but it started going by at a better clip.

The phone squealed again.

"Can you get that?" Ranger said.

Julie snatched up the handheld and looked at the message flashing on the screen. "The RV driver says they got pulled over."

"As long as they're not carrying anything they'll be alright. You're the only contraband I'm worried about." The road ahead ended in a rotary. "Pick an exit."

Julie picked the second right, which took them onto what, ten or fifteen years ago, had been a major retail strip. Now the stores and chain restaurants along the roadway were shuttered.

"We couldn't have planned this any better." Ranger sped through a dead traffic light and took the next right into a parking lot. She steered toward the small cluster of vehicles already parked there and pulled into a spot. "Stay put for a couple of minutes. I'll be right back."

She exited, locking the doors behind her, and approached the people setting up camp. Julie watched for a few seconds then decided to be helpful by picking up the mess inside the van. Packages of wetnaps. Sample bottles of shampoo. A superhero figurine. A toothbrush still in the wrapper. Random condiments. A battered sheriff's star. Another phone, this one missing its battery.

She stuffed most of it into the glove compartment, but hesitated on a picture, printed out old-style on stiff paper. It was Ranger, smiling and holding hands with another woman. Ranger's hair had not changed, but she looked less worn, even happy. The other woman was pretty, almost tiny, with mechanized braces on her arms and legs. She was wearing a Faraday sleeve that looked just like the one Julie had on.

Ranger reappeared and flung open the passenger-side door. "We're all set. These guys don't care if we stay here tonight."

Julie handed her the picture. Ranger spent a few silent seconds looking at the faces.

"Her name was Euchre. It's a card game. I'll show you sometime. She loved taking pictures. Had a whole book of them printed out like this." Her voice sounded like someone had a fist around it.

"Did you break up?"

Ranger chewed on her bottom lip. "Died about two years ago. Suicide."

"I'm sorry."

"Me, too." Ranger lay the picture atop the junk in the glove compartment. "Let's go introduce you to the neighbors."

The members of the caravan were all senior citizens, refugees from Florida. They shared their dinner and kept Ranger and Julie up late with tales of the days before the Slide and the Emergency Powers Act. "I used to drive an hour and a half to get to work every day," an old woman with pink hair – the others called her Cotton Candy – said. "Each way! Can you believe it?"

"I drove two hours." A skinny man named Trainwreck shook his head in disgust. "Big house in the suburbs, and I commuted into the city every day. Everyone I know did!"

Ranger and Julie gave up the fight just after midnight and left the elders to tend their fire and swap stories. It was Ranger's turn to start the night in the back, and Julie waited to hear her snore. A long silence rang in her ears.

Ranger rolled over and sighed. "Euch was a runaway, too. Late onset. She was in a bad marriage, but she was fleeing society as much as anything. That's her sleeve you're wearing."

The skin under the sleeve started itching. Julie reached to scratch it and cracked her elbow against the dashboard. Ranger laughed dryly. "Relax. She wasn't wearing it when she died."

"Why did she kill herself?"

The resulting silence was louder and longer, and Julie took a deep breath to fuel an apology. Ranger cut her off before she could push any of it out. "A lot of reasons."

Julie pulled herself up so she could see Ranger's face.

"She would have been a great mother, but she couldn't have kids. Mercury poisoning. It messed with her motor control, too. Her husband got to be a real dick about it. Then, she got low when the results of the colony lottery were announced." She sighed. "I met her after she'd been on the road for about a year. She'd had some bad times." Julie couldn't tell whether the noise Ranger made was a cough or a laugh. "She said she wanted a reboot. A do-over. Really knocked the guts out of me for awhile."

"What was her real name?"

"Don't know. No one comes out here to live in the past, pal."

"I had a… friend back home. She's part of the mission to Proxima Centauri."

Ranger grunted. "Must be quite a gal. Not a lot of people made the cut."

"You called me 'baby' before, with Kinks," Julie said.

"That was just cover. You're not a replacement. You're too young for me, and I'm way too tired to start training you up."

Julie hadn't realized she'd been holding her breath until she let it out. Ranger cackled, loud in the darkness of the car. "Euchre was looking for something out here and didn't find it. It happens a lot. Some people give up and go home. Some…" Ranger rolled over. "Some don't."

Julie tugged the sleeping bag up to her neck. Life was very different outside the cities.

Ranger folded and pounded her pillow. "I'm going to sleep."

The snores kicked in a few minutes later. The glow of the park, where the oldsters were finally banking the fire and heading for bed, was alive in the side window. Julie worked to get comfortable. The inside of the van didn't smell good. Her own funk was adding to the miasma baked into the cracked seats and faded dashboard. Her room in Menino Towers probably didn't smell like anything. The bathroom wasn't a bush. The bed was flat and wide enough to sprawl on. She was supposed to be out here with Anji, but...

Julie rubbed her eyes and yawned. She needed to find a way to let Carson S know she was alive. Her father might want to know, too. She squirmed deeper into the sleeping bag and made a mental note to plug it into charge in the morning. The day would start early.

Euchre had gotten off the road and taken a big part of Ranger with her. Hopefully, staying on the move would work out better for everyone.

THIRTEEN

The campfire crowd reconvened at breakfast, the lady with the pink hair beckoning Julie and Ranger to join them and share their food. While they ate, a man in a grubby lab coat sat to the side muttering about "doing the math on Mars."

Julie leaned closer to Cotton Candy. "Who's that?" she whispered.

She glanced at the mumbling man. "That's the Professor. He says he worked for NASA back in the day but," she lowered her voice, "he's not what he used to be."

"I heard that!" the man growled. "I'll be three times what you are on my worst day!"

"Here we go." Trainwreck tossed a piece of scrap on the fire. "Rule Number One: Do Not Engage the Mad Scientist Before the Coffee Kicks In."

"Mad!" The Professor's face reddened. "You're not crazy if you're right."

"Mad is not the right word." Candy bumped Julie with her shoulder. "He's just excitable."

The Professor ran his hands through what was left of his hair, making it stand up in white licks. "A fool could see it." His eyes fixed on Julie. "They fired me to hide the results. The colony on Mars won't be self-sustaining for a century or better. What are the odds Earth will be in good enough shape to keep it supplied until then? Zero!" His face crumpled. "They're all going to die up there, and I helped them do it!"

Julie wrapped her arms around her chest. The old man might be right. The mission to Proxima Centauri had been launched, according to the newsheads, to ensure the human diaspora could spread beyond the solar system while the resources were available. "Mars for the present, PC for the future!" went the slogan. But there had been other voices, many of them rhyming with the old scientist's lament. Ten thousand people on Mars doomed to starvation. "Did he really work for NASA?"

"I looked it up when he joined us a few years ago," Trainwreck said. "A Dr Gabriel Kittridge was on the Mars planning team back in the '40s. Whether it's the same guy or not..." He see-sawed his hand.

"It's him," Candy said. "He looks like hell, but it's him. None of us are as pretty as we used to be."

Like most American kids, Julie had sent friendship videos to agemates in the Mars colony. A slightly cross-eyed Martian named Ash had responded, and they'd messaged back and forth for a few years.

"They wouldn't do that," Julie said. "They wouldn't just send people up to another planet and forget about them."

The Professor's eyes sharpened, and he suddenly looked like someone with authority and expertise instead of a sad, old man who lived in his car. "Do you think the PC mission is going to fare any better, young lady? Bread and circuses. Give us something to root for, heroes to cheer, and let us die with hope in our hearts." He spat into the fire.

"We should get going," Ranger said. "We're on a schedule."

Julie lurched to her feet where she swayed, abruptly dizzy. Her stomach clenched, and she thought she might throw up.

"Are you alright?" Ranger said. "You got pale all of a sudden."

Julie's lips were tight above the urge to regurgitate her breakfast into Cotton Candy's lap. The dull headache she'd been nursing since she crawled out of the van surged. She let Ranger make the goodbyes and followed her back to Juniper.

"I think he's wrong," Ranger said. "About Mars and the PC mission. I think we went into both with the best of intentions."

"What do intentions matter?"

"Everything," Ranger said. "There's no shame in failing, but fuck you if you don't at least make the effort. Your friend's going to be OK. At least as OK as we are."

Julie's stomach was rolling again. An hour down the road, she felt even worse. She shouted for Ranger to stop the van and threw up in the scrub beside the road. Ranger wrapped the sleeping bag around Julie's shoulders and guided her back to the van.

"What the hell is wrong with me?" Julie's throat burned, and her mouth tasted like bile. "I keep getting these–!" She grunted in surprise. It felt like someone had applied a live wire to her brain. "These shocks."

"I suppose you could be dying from something terrible, but I'm betting it's withdrawal."

"Withdrawal from what?" Julie's shoulder muscles spasmed painfully.

"Your pharma emplant. You've been on depression and anti-anxiety meds for years, and your brain has no idea what to do without them."

"How long will it last?"

"Weeks, probably. And whatever problems the meds were treating will start kicking in again."

"Maybe I'm not depressed anymore."

Ranger's mouth quirked. "Maybe. It might be just a habit with you. More likely it's the way your brain's made." She ducked into the van, and Julie heard her rummaging around inside. "Do you have any idea what your little buddy was pumping into you?" she called.

"Not really. Serotonin something-something. I wasn't really paying attention. I just wanted to feel better."

Ranger emerged from the van and tossed Julie a small box.

"Try these. Put one on your arm." She pointed at her own tricep. "If it helps with the symptoms, we'll keep it up. If not, we'll try something else."

Julie pulled one of the dermapatches out of the box and reached into her shirt to apply it. "Where did you get it?"

"I got a little bit of everything." She offered Julie a hand up. "Let's get going. It's not smart to park along the road this long. You going to puke again?"

Julie tried to evaluate her condition. "Maybe."

Ranger pulled a small tin of candy out of her pocket. "Peppermints. All-natural nausea remedy. Suck, don't chew. If nothing else it will take the taste out of your mouth."

Julie had assumed her head ached too badly to leave room for embarrassment, but she'd been wrong. "I'm so sorry about this," she said. "I know this isn't what–"

"It's not a problem. I'll let you know if it ever becomes one, OK?" She waited until Julie answered with a reluctant nod. "Just help out the next person who needs it. Anyone. Might be someone you haven't met, yet. Could even be me."

Ranger got the van back on the road and headed toward her rendezvous in Buffalo. Julie gave the aching weight of her head to the worn upholstery behind it. "Why are you keeping me around?"

The van rocked and pitched over a frost heave. "Pardon?" Ranger said.

"You could have left me with Cotton Candy and Trainwreck. Or with Zip. Hell, you could have turned me over to Kinks. Why am I still here?"

"I wouldn't leave a sexbot with Kinks," Ranger said. "Man like that deserves a long, involuntarily celibate life."

"You didn't answer my question."

Ranger turned down the music playing on the entertainment center. "I can get on the phone and find you somewhere safe between here and Buffalo if you want."

"I think you want me to stay."

"I think I have a client waiting for me, and I don't want to waste a lot of time playing autocab."

"I don't know much about being out here," Julie said.

"You're certainly not very good with job interviews."

Julie fell silent. In spite of the sway of the van, the mints were helping with her stomach. "I'd like to stay with you."

Ranger smiled. "You'd have to do what I say. Back my plays *and* my bullshit."

"I can use a stunner. I know a little hand-to-hand. At least in ThirdEye sims. My tests said I should be a police officer, so I took all the courses. I got the certificate and everything."

"I'll try not to hold that against you." Ranger reached for the volume slide. "As long as you can forget most of that shit, you're hired. I'll start teaching you how to drive when we get to Buffalo."

FOURTEEN

"Stay to the right. The right!"

Julie twisted the wheel, swerving away from the faded lane marker.

"Brake!" Ranger practically stood in her seat as she applied maximum pressure to the brake pedal, which, in reality, was under Julie's feet. The van bumped over a low curb and came to a stop half-on and half-off a sidewalk. Ranger reached over and turned off the ignition. She took a long, slow breath. "That could've gone better."

If Julie had spoken, she might have started crying, and she'd vowed that wasn't going to happen. The dermapatch had gotten rid of the worst of the withdrawal symptoms, but her lows felt more intense than they should, and she was tearing up at even stupid things. Ranger had taught her some breathing exercises that helped some.

"We'll try it again when we've both calmed down a little." Ranger climbed out of the passenger-side door and walked, a little unsteadily, across the traffic island and into the neighboring parking lot. She didn't bother to shut the door.

Julie leaned back in the seat and closed her eyes. Driving required a ridiculous amount of attention and control. It was little like the simulation games she'd played. She got out of the van and walked opposite the direction Ranger took. The air felt heavy and tasted like metal. Julie scuffed her shoe in a half circle, kicking up a low cloud of dusty soil. There was a headache growing behind her right eye. She wasn't wearing a mask, and the air was full of shit she shouldn't be breathing. Carson S would be appalled.

The parking lot they'd been practicing in was vast but abandoned except for the van and a family caravan that had parked for the night. The mall was huge, colors faded like a child's toy left in the sun too long. Gaps in the plywood nailed up over the entrances revealed the milky cataract of glass windows and doors. ThirdEye was full of models and games created by urban spelunkers who claimed they had broken into such places, but Julie didn't personally know anyone who'd dared. A low whine coming from the police drones passing by overhead reminded her why. The law said the caravans could use the parking lots short-term, but looters could be shot on sight.

A horn honked. Julie shaded her eyes and peered at the van. Ranger was in the passenger seat and waving at her through the windshield.

Back to school.

Later that day, while they waited for their client caravan to show, Ranger showed her how to bum fuel. Federal law required homeowners and restaurants to recycle all of their cooking oils but getting a few free gallons was mostly a matter of showing up before the recycling trucks. They drove out to a pizza plant and a Chinese-food franchise and came back to the mall with seven gallons of grossness. Juniper Two was a hybrid. She could run on electric or biodiesel and, when the converter worked, could use the biodiesel motor to charge her batteries.

Ranger opened the van's back doors and pulled out four boards, two foldable sawhorses, a fish tank, and a cardboard box. She used the boards and sawhorses to make a table. Julie helped her wrestle the fish tank on top of it

"Time to feed the baby," Ranger said. "Pay attention. You might be doing this next time."

They filtered the cooking gook until it ran clean and thinned the liquid out in the fish tank with a mixture of lye and alcohol. Over the next couple of hours the mixture separated: gold-colored liquid on top, clear on the bottom. Ranger used a pump to take off the top layer and funneled it into Juniper. "Biodiesel," she said.

She poured the clear liquid into a plastic jug. "Glycerin."

Ranger sent Julie to a dumpster with the filter and showed her how to pack everything back in the van. "That will get us a few miles further down the road." She stretched and winced as something in her back cracked. "Too much sitting, not enough moving. You ever do any yoga?"

"Just running."

"Hard to do that without a treadmill."

Ranger grabbed two mats out of the van and herded Julie to a spot about a hundred yards away. It was starting to get dark and a chill was setting in. Ranger rolled the mats out and proceeded to wear Julie out with a one-on-one yoga class. After twenty minutes Julie wasn't feeling the cold anymore. After an hour she was feeling warm and relaxed and ready for a nap.

"Shower time," Ranger said. "I traded with the neighbors for two five-minute showers. It's my trade, so I get firsts."

The low-pressure, lukewarm shower, even in the cramped quarters of an RV, was the best of Julie's life. Distance-wise, time-wise, she hadn't come all that far: maybe five hundred miles and a couple of weeks. In her head, though, she was a world away. Ranger, Magnolia, even Marty were more real to her than nearly everyone in her old life.

"Are we part of the volksgeist?" she asked Ranger back at the van.

The older woman rolled her eyes. "We're never going to escape that damned film."

Julie had watched the documentary twice in the year before Anji's goodbye party and four times after. Narrated by some has-been actor, the filmmakers interviewed dozens of people who had opted for life on the road rather than in a cube.

"If I was part of it I'd have to say that we're all part of it, right? One big happy family." Ranger's eyes rolled. "That movie was hipster-rainbow bullshit. Some Harvard anthropologist came up the whole 'volksgeist' thing. We're tramps. Travelers. Malcontents. Lots of people choose to be out here, sure, but some don't have a good option." She pointed at the cluster of vehicles around the RV. "They're not out here for a ThirdEye show. They lost almost everything to desertification, and the government's answer was to offer 'em cubes. There's no guarantee they'd even be close to each other. How can they be expected to give up whatever they've got left for something they know isn't real?"

They had a potluck dinner with the family. Ranger showed Julie how to turn chicken-flavored protein pudding into patties and fry them up with some of the filtered cooking oil they'd kept aside. Mom, a tattooed woman named Lydia, made some kind of noodle casserole, and her husband made fry bread over the campfire.

They sat for awhile and swapped stories. The kids, two teenagers, were poring over the volksnet update from Ranger's "special" computer. Julie didn't want to let on she was a runaway, so she mostly listened. The family was looking for a new temporary home, and Ranger had something to share about every possible destination they mentioned.

"I'm thinking the park outside Memphis might be your best bet," she said. "You'll be close enough to the city to buy supplies, and there's a good view of the highway from there. You'll have at least fifteen minutes' warning before trouble pulls up."

The caravans weren't well liked. The government had made it clear it would rather have everyone in the cities, under control and safely logged into ThirdEye. Spending more than a couple of weeks in one place was a good way to attract attention, so the caravans usually stayed moving.

"It's not the po-po we're worried about these days. They're mostly closing up shop and focusing on the cities," Lydia's father, Flash, said. He was the group's scout, zipping ahead of everyone on a motorcycle with his boyfriend bundled in the sidecar. "They leave us alone mostly. It's the gangs we want to avoid. They're starting to get bad."

"I haven't been out this far in awhile," Ranger said. "How bad are we talking about?"

"More aggressive and more of them," Lydia said. "Better armed. Rumor has it a few caravans have disappeared entirely. Everyone killed."

Later, back in the car for the night, Ranger started shifting around and pillow-punching again.

"What?" Julie said.

Ranger growled. "This is getting too much like work. Ten years ago, we'd never heard of gangs. Now we're actively dodging them."

The documentary hadn't said anything about gangs. "Where do they come from?"

"They start out as caravans. Then they get desperate. Or lazy. Or listen to the wrong person. It doesn't take much to turn a beggar into a thief."

"Like Kinks." Julie tried get comfortable in the front seat.

"Kinks has probably always been a predator. He'd be an asshole in any context."

A couple of days before, Julie had spotted a volksnet post from Boo, the woman Ranger gave a stunner to. She'd followed Ranger's instructions, formed her own group, and headed south.

"Aren't they worried Kinks is going to see that and go after them?" Julie had asked.

Ranger smiled. "He's been cut off. No access for him unless he changes out all his tech and gets a new ID."

Ranger's special relationship with the volksnet remained a mystery, although Julie had scoured the site to find out more about it. There were posts about Ranger, mostly thank yous, all over the place, but their frequency had decreased over the past couple of years. What did that make her? A guard dog? A hero? One of the good guys, at least. What did that make Julie? A tagalong? A runaway?

Julie stretched her toes in the sleeping bag. *For now, a partner.*

FIFTEEN

Ranger ducked into the van in a hurry.

"Something wrong?" Julie said.

"Clients are here. I need to get into costume." She reached under the driver's seat, pulled out a utility belt, and tightened it around her waist. Her stunner went into the belt's holster, and she slid a collapsible baton and a flashlight into loops on the other side to balance it out. She loaded her fingers with chunky metal rings, some of them featuring skulls, and donned her battered leather coat. She replaced her camp sneakers with her heavy boots. "Tah-dah!" She spread her arms and turned so Julie could see both sides. "Instant bad ass."

"I'm surprised you don't have a bandoleer and a sawed-off shotgun."

"Overkill. I need to impress these guys, not scare them."

"Should I wear an eye patch or something? Be a bad ass, too?"

Ranger reached under the seat again and pulled out a second utility belt, which she tossed to Julie. "You're my apprentice. You don't have to be a bad ass, yet."

Julie's belt also had a stunner holster and baton loops. She had practiced some with the stunner but needed a quick lesson in baton extension. It opened with a satisfying click and felt good in her hand.

"Really effective on knees and elbows," Ranger said.

"Anywhere you can hit bone. Avoid the head unless you desperately need to fuck someone up."

Julie brandished the baton aggressively. "How do I close it?"

Ranger showed her. "Keep it on your belt until I give you a few lessons. Right now it's just for show."

"Do I look OK?"

"Like a kid playing Batman. You ready?"

They walked toward the waiting caravan. Lydia and her family had headed south at daybreak. The new group was much larger.

"What exactly are they hiring us to do?" Julie said.

"In the old-old pioneer days they would have called us wagon masters. They want to go south for the winter, and it's our job to make sure they get there."

"So, we're security guards."

"Logistics, mostly." Ranger chewed her lower lip, considering. "I make sure they have the supplies they need, decide the rolling order, and see no one gets left behind. Breakdowns are usually the biggest problem. Then the pigs, but these folks say they have their papers in order. They're headed to a piece of land one of them owns in Georgia."

"Flash said there were gangs moving in down there."

"There might be some guarding, too. We'll see." She squinted at the vehicles ahead. "They're parked all over the place. They should be circled up for security." Ranger thumped herself in the chest. "That's why they need the experts."

Julie laughed. "How'd you get to be so expert?"

Ranger's face lost any trace of mirth. "I survived, chica. I survived."

"Welcome to the park," Ranger said.

"Welcome yourself." The skinny old man stuck his hand out. "Coop."

"You get the name before or after you got the car?" Ranger

nodded toward the red hatchback the old fellow had climbed out of.

"Before. Two cars before," he said. "It's short for Chicken Coop. Don't ask."

"You know who I am." Ranger took his hand in a firm shake. "This is Runner."

"I didn't expect two of you." Coop had a nice smile.

Ranger had adopted a sort of swagger, either an affectation or a result of the heavy boots she'd put on. Either way, she was doing a good job of looking like someone used to being in charge. "The ad said you've been doing this run for about twenty years."

"North to south in the fall and back up in the spring. Sometimes a few more vehicles, sometimes a few less. We're only as fast as our slowest car, and like I said in our post, our route is already mapped out. No diversions, and we have to be parked before dark." He smiled. "Old eyes, you know."

Ranger tucked her thumbs into her utility belt, framing the ornate buckle with her fingers. "I'm a little surprised you advertised. You look like you know how to take care of yourself."

"At eighty, taking care of yourself is one thing. Taking care of a pack of people is another. We took a vote and decided we wanted an expert. That's you, right?"

Ranger slid her thumbs around to her hips, making her coat flare, a gesture that might or might not have been designed to show the stunner on her belt. "I've been east to west and back twice, up and down the New Coast more times than I can count. I've got four security drones, I'm certified in emergency medicine, and I'm fun to talk to."

Julie surprised herself by opening her mouth. "I have a certificate in law enforcement," she said, and almost immediately regretted it. She caught Ranger's side eye and zipped her lip.

"Well, there you go," Ranger said. "We'll get you where you want to go."

Coop stuck his thumbs into the front pockets of his jeans. "We were about to start lunch. You two hungry?"

Ranger and Julie followed him to a fire a tall man was building in a trashcan.

"Sorry about that," Julie whispered en route. "I just wanted to help."

"Let you know if I need you to Mirandize anyone," Ranger said out of the side of her mouth. "Wait. You guys don't do that anymore, do you?"

"Not for a while."

"Remember, the cops aren't always popular out here. Even baby ones."

"I just took the classes." Julie's toe caught a rock, sending it spinning ahead. "I never actually–"

"You said you can fly drones."

"Sort of."

"Good. Only two of my drones can go full-auto. The third one needs a pilot."

"What about the fourth one?"

"It's in pieces." Ranger cleared her throat. They were in earshot of the fire. "Talk to you about it later." She squared her shoulders and let Coop make introductions.

"I'm looking forward to working with you all," she said afterward. "Which one of you is keeping track of food and water?"

A woman with short gray hair raised her hand. "I'm Rumpelstiltskin."

"I'm going to want an inventory list. Everything in stores," Ranger said. "Printed preferably, so I won't have to dick around with tech. Who's in charge of vehicle maintenance?"

The people around the fire looked at each other awkwardly. The gray-haired lady coughed.

"Died a couple of months ago," Coop said. "Nobody's really taken his place."

Ranger's mouth tightened. "I can't keep you safe unless I

know what problems are going to crop up. Do we even have enough fuel for the trip? Does everyone have spare tires?"

No one answered.

Ranger pointed at a young woman in a bright skirt. "What do you do here?"

"Poet. They call me Verses."

"Now you're my assistant vehicle manager. What do you know about cars and trucks?"

The woman paled. "Not mu–"

"You have twenty-four hours to get me the specs of all the vehicles in the caravan. Maintenance problems, fuel requirements, spare-part inventory. Got it?"

The poet turned manager nodded uncertainly.

"Which one of you is the doctor?"

A woman raised her hand. "Nurse. Retired. I already sent you my inventory."

Ranger turned to Coop. "Let's you and me talk about how you got people parked."

The caravan was majority gray, but a group of twenty- and thirty-somethings had recently joined and were trying their hardest to fit in. They gamely sipped from the jug of ethanol Coop handed around at meeting's end.

"Made it myself," he said, wiping off the neck of the jar with his shirt cuff.

Julie and Ranger escaped the experience, claiming their work required strict sobriety. Based on the faces the youngsters made after their turn with the jug, Julie was relieved.

"Some folks like it better with a mixer," Coop allowed.

Even without the booze, Julie's brain was on overload by the time lunch was over. She'd heard the origin stories of half the people around the fire, and names and faces swirled in her head.

While Julie prepped the working security drones, Ranger made the rounds, shaking hands and stomping around in her heavy boots. It was dark by the time she had the caravan circled up the way she liked it.

When she got back, she shucked off her long leather coat and hung it on one of the van's side mirrors. "People are exhausting!"

Julie ran the third drone's diagnostic again. "I have no idea why Bartleby here won't go into guard mode. The mechanics check out. The batteries are OK..." She ran a grimy hand through her hair. "No idea."

Ranger sat down to pull off her boots. "Probably a software glitch. Although Gretchen will be happy to point out that it's my fault. There's probably a super-secret preference menu I accidentally unchecked."

"Gretchen?"

"The most dangerous woman alive. She does all my tech."

Julie pointed with her screwdriver. "Well, that one's not going anywhere, those two are fine, and this one," she tapped the source of her frustration, "is brain dead."

"Launch the two that work. You can fly Bartleby around while you sit in the crow's nest for first shift."

Just the thought made Julie tired. "All the way to Georgia like that?"

Ranger put her hands on her hips. "We're professionals. Professionals don't need sleep." She handed Julie a flask of coffee. "You scared of heights?"

"I don't think so."

"You need to pee first?"

Julie shook her head.

Ranger handed her an earbud. "It's already synced to mine. If you get up there and feel the need, buzz me and we can throw a piss bucket up."

Julie inserted the bud and climbed the ladder to the van's roof. She reached down to get the lawn chair Ranger handed up.

"Catch." Ranger tossed something underhand. Night-vision goggles.

"What do I do?"

"Fly around. Keep an eye out and stay awake. If something attacks, holler loud and shoot straight."

Looking down, Julie realized she maybe *was* a little afraid of heights. Ranger waved up at her. "Do a quick loop with Bartleby and see if there's anything I should inspect when I do my foot patrol!"

"Do the other ones have names?"

"I got out of the habit. I'll leave it up to you."

Julie used her ancient phone to wake the functional drones and set them to circle the campsite. The little machines were small and quick, armed with stunner flechettes and mostly autonomous when it came to doing their jobs. Once airborne, they'd communicate with each other and work out a patrol route that gave them the best coverage. She booted up Bartleby the Defective Drone. It lifted off the table, far less steadily than its machine-controlled cousins, and whined into the air.

Flying had never been Julie's best thing. She'd barely passed the course in the ThirdEye police academy she'd enrolled in, but somehow the less-than-immersive interface of the phone made drone control easier. Piloting drones in ThirdEye had often made her queasy. After a few moments though, hovering and getting a feel for the touch-screen controls, Julie put the drone into a loose figure-eight over the shopping plaza.

She zoomed in on Ranger, who was back to swapping stories at the fire, and sent a message to the functional drones reminding them that she was friendly. The front of the shopping mall was set up at a ninety-degree angle, with the main entrance as the vertex. Taking Bartleby up and over the roof, Julie discovered the geometry had not held up in the back. Parts of the building bulged out further than others, and the irregularities had created dark crevices and alleys. Julie switched the drone's cameras to night vision and dipped down for a closer look.

"Looks like there's a campsite in back of the plaza," she radioed.

"Is it active?" Ranger said.

Julie tapped the camera interface again and switched to infrared. "I don't see any heat."

"Anything else?"

"Not yet."

Julie spun Bartleby around and juked left to dodge the approach of one of his smarter cousins. She directed more power to the fans, and the drone climbed higher. She could see the entire plaza. The central campfire was a bright dot on the infrared, the cooling vehicles and warm bodies around it a jumble of colors.

"I don't see anything alive out here but us."

"Be nice if it stays that way," Ranger said. "Geo tag that campsite, and I'll walk back there in a bit and check it out."

"Want me to go with you?"

"Nah. But you can follow me with Bartleby and make sure I get home alright."

Julie brought the drone down to patrol height and did four more circuits of the plaza before Ranger made her move.

"I'm going," she said. "You on me?"

Julie abandoned her loop and zoomed to hover over the fire. Ranger was standing, hands pressed to the small of her back in a slow stretch. She saluted Coop and headed away from the fire along the front of the plaza. Julie put Bartleby about four feet above Ranger's head and six feet behind and followed.

"I bet this is the long way around," Ranger said.

Julie activated the drone's external speakers. "Yeah. And it's really dark over here. You want me to play some creepy music?"

Ranger laughed. "I'd settle for a light."

Julie searched among the drone's menu of commands and found the spotlight. The interface was close to police specs, but there were differences, and Julie was out of practice.

"What do you think so far?" Ranger said.

"Of the job?"

"Of the caravan." Ranger had reached the end of the east wing of the plaza. She stopped to check the door of a shop that used to sell electronic cigarettes. The door pulled open about three inches and then stopped. Ranger shone a flashlight into the gap. "Chained," she said. "We'll keep an eye on it."

"The people seem nice," Julie said.

"Probably don't need us. Still," Ranger grinned at the camera, "who am I to turn down a payday?" She turned the corner and followed the wall to the back of the plaza. "There's a lot of junk back here. Might be worth a pass in daylight to see if there's anything worth taking."

"You're getting close to the campsite."

"See anything?"

Julie cycled through the cameras again. "No."

Ranger pointed her flashlight at the spot in question, which was protected on two sides by the walls of the plaza and guarded on a third by a metal dumpster. "Hello?"

Her flashlight swept the space, illuminating a small cook stove, a backpack, and a sleeping bag. She nudged the sleeping bag with her foot and crouched to pull back the top. "Corpse," she said. "A very dead one."

Julie swallowed hard. The drone's camera picked out the dome of a skull and wisps of hair. "What do we do?"

Ranger stood and resumed her walk. "Coop can call it in before we leave tomorrow. Our camper's not going to get any more dead before then, and there's no sense bringing the pigs around while we're still here."

"What do you think killed him?"

"Life." Ranger rubbed her palms on the legs of her pants. "Go ahead and land Bartleby. Do a patrol with him every couple of hours. I have a few more skulls to crack and then I'll come home to roost."

SIXTEEN

"My mother never let me have these," Julie said, going back for dinner seconds. "She said they were junk food."

"There's nothing wrong with them, health-wise," Coop said. "But not everyone is as thrilled to be eating textured insect protein as you seem to be."

"Buggets." Ranger pushed food around the plate with her spork. "Buggets and Tasty Paste. My entire childhood in a dinner buffet."

The woman named Rumpelstiltskin was in charge of provisions for the trip, and even Ranger allowed she'd done well. It was simple fare, but there was plenty of it. It would do fine until the caravan reached Georgia even if, a couple days into the trip, it was already getting repetitive.

"Were you in the foster system?" Coop said.

"Until I got out," Ranger said. "Spent two years on the lam, and that's back when they bothered looking for runaways."

Julie speared a buffalo-flavored bugget and brought it to her mouth.

"The post-scarcity world. Everyone has access to the same crap." Coop grimaced. "Either of you ever been to a barbecue? Real meat?"

"Just how old do you think I am?" Ranger said.

"I had a hot dog once," said Waldo, one of the younger tramps. He'd gotten his road name in honor of his poor sense of direction. "The kid who gave it to me said it was real meat."

"He was probably lying," Ranger said.

Julie snagged one of Ranger's buggets. "If you're not going to eat it, I will."

Rumpelstiltskin grinned. "Remember cheeseburgers?"

The Remember Game was popular at mealtimes. The younger tramps did their best to keep up, but they were often stunned to silence by their elders' tales of the world gone by. Such abundance! Such waste! Such hubris!

"I met a group once that had a rolling catfish farm," Rumpel said. Her aspirations for Georgia weren't that high, but she hoped to grow crickets and mealworms enough to keep the caravan self-sufficient through the winter and spring, with enough left over for the trip back north in June.

On the map, the route from Buffalo, New York, to the caravan's communal parking spot outside Atlanta, Georgia, was eight-hundred and ninety-one miles end to end. In a straight line, even at caravan speed, it should have taken about thirty hours of drive time to get there. Julie had done the math, once at the beginning of the trip and twice after hour thirty had come and gone.

Math and the map didn't account for the immeasurable and unpredictable delays that came from traveling in a convoy of antiques over decrepit roads. Ranger had delayed their scheduled start time by twenty-four hours when Verses' vehicle-status report had turned up a host of problems. She had insisted that four new tires be printed up and installed on a creaky old camper van that played home and transportation to a couple named Bert and Ernie, who, among other things, taught tai chi and operated a his-and-theirs puppetry troupe. Ranger also had ordered that every third day of travel be dedicated to vehicle maintenance.

There also was the mystery of the route itself. It looped and juked seemingly at random, occasionally backtracking for miles at a time. Ranger complained about it regularly, but, as wagonmaster, it was her job to make sure the clients got to their destination safely no matter what route they opted for.

"I really don't get it," she told Julie one evening after getting the parking set up the way she liked. "According to the nav, some of the places we've stopped at used to be tourist attractions, but they haven't been for years."

"What does Coop say?" Julie asked.

"That old habits die hard."

There were a dozen vehicles in the group, twenty-nine people including a four-year-old boy named Kid and a teenage girl who didn't talk much and insisted on being called Creep. The oldest member of the group was one hundred and one, born three years before the turn of the century. Like the NASA scientist Julie had met before, Family Man or Fam was well past his best days, and she half expected to wake up one morning and hear that he'd died in the night. But every morning he was up and out of his car, a first-gen autodrive, for breakfast. He showed around pictures of his grandchildren, complained that he never saw them anymore, and forgot that he'd done the exact same thing the morning before.

Waldo and his friends were artists, and they took advantage of every stop by spray-painting elaborate murals on any vertical surface available.

"We're off the road tomorrow. What's on the art agenda?" she asked him at the fire that night.

He pointed to the façade of a shuttered box store. "Big beautiful installation, twenty feet up."

Julie's eyes tracked his gesture. Once the space had been dedicated to the name of the business. Now it was a big, blank canvas. "That's going to take you all day, even if you can get up there without the drones shooting you."

"Be real helpful if someone could convince Ranger to let us borrow the ladders again." He dropped a smile on her. "Know anyone who could do that?"

Julie sighed. "Get me a copy of the plans, and I'll ask."

Approval without prior review at their Beckley, West Virginia park had resulted in a celebration of anime erotica on a billboard overlooking I-77. Ranger hadn't had a problem with it, but several seniors had complained.

"This one's going to be great. Trust me," Waldo said. "Even Coop will love it."

After dinner and the evening fire, Julie went back to the van and set the drones in motion. Flying Bartleby around was becoming second nature, and she sent the broken drone in a wide loop around the park, which had circled up in front of the façade of an abandoned DIY superstore. She glanced down at Ranger from the van roof. "I still don't see why I have to climb up here. Most of the time I'm seeing through the drone."

"And if the drone breaks down?" Ranger said. "Plus, it looks good. Do you know any other security outfit that can boast a crow's nest?"

Julie had not met any other security outfit, but she didn't bother pointing that out. Ranger had her own way of doing things, a routine as arcane in its own way as the caravan's long and winding route to Georgia.

Waldo and his crew spent the night printing stencils and mixing colors and by the end of the next day the convoy's vehicles were all judged roadworthy, and the storefront was adorned with a mural featuring the members of the caravan laughing and dining around the fire.

Waldo was gray with fatigue but couldn't seem to stop grinning. "Like to see them forget about us now," he wheezed. "That's immortality, right there. For all of us."

Julie waited until the artists led Waldo away to their truck and put him to bed before taking to the crow's nest. Ranger was leaning against the van, looking up at the mural.

"Not too bad," she said. "Reminds me a little of Banksy."

"Who?" Julie said.

"Just some dead guy. How long do you think it will last?"

"Waldo said the paint will hold up for twenty years or so." She squinted to get a better view. "Someone might take the building down before that, though."

"It's pretty isolated. Bet it's low on the priority list."

"Maybe."

Ranger folded her arms. "Won't see anything like that in a cube."

Exactly like that? No. But there were plenty of people doing and sharing art in ThirdEye without the risk of falling off an overpass or sucking in lungfuls of polluted air. None of Waldo's gang wore filtermasks regularly, and he was already exhibiting symptoms of a disease the tramps called lung rot. Julie had caught herself forgetting her own mask more than a few times. "Pretty special."

"They'll know we were here, sure enough." Ranger smothered a cough.

Julie didn't ask who "they" was. She suspected that Ranger didn't have a good answer to the question anyway. "I'm going to get the drones warmed up. You should turn in early. Busy day tomorrow."

Ranger lifted an eyebrow. "Getting kind of big for your britches, ain't you?"

"Just keeping the boss healthy."

Julie climbed onto the van roof and sent the drones whining off into the dark. She took control of Bartleby and flew it up to take a picture of the mural. The faces were easy to pick out: Ranger, Rumpel, Coop, Waldo and the other artists, Julie herself... Everyone she'd come to know and care about over the past several days.

That's immortality, right there.

SEVENTEEN

Juniper's tires gnawed at the road. On a good day a caravan could cover a hundred miles. On a bad day, what with washouts and road closures, they'd be lucky to make ten.

It had been a bad couple of days, and the battered sign for Gastonia, North Carolina, was a relief in the late-afternoon sunlight.

Coop signaled an exit, and Julie followed the caravan off the road. One right and two lefts later they were at another abandoned mall. Ahead Julie could see Verses waving her arms, directing the drivers to their places.

Julie pulled the van up. "Nice job, Juniper." They'd worked the van hard, using her to tow several other vehicles through an especially bad washout. Ranger had been everywhere at once, shouting encouragement, hooking up tow ropes, and twice making emergency repairs. Her face was tight with fatigue.

"You're getting the hang of this," she said.

Julie smiled.

"Now go, driver. Check in with the scout and bring back news. I must rest." Ranger leaned back dramatically and shut her eyes. Julie climbed out and walked up to Coop's little two-seater. He had the hood open and was doing something to his engine.

"The wagonmaster wants to know if there's anything she should know."

111

"It's going to be a cold one tonight," Coop cleaned grime off his hands with a rag, "and there's another big group parked to the side. Might be some opportunity for trade."

"I'll pass it on." Julie rubbed the small of her back where a sickly ache had been crouching all day.

The mall was huge, bigger than any building she had ever seen. A shopping mecca. But now it was just canned space, shut up, shut down, and sealed off. The ground level was wrapped in plywood and razor wire, and the upper windows, kept intact by the threat of police drones, stared darkly down. It didn't want the travelers there. Once upon a time people had given the big building purpose, now it wanted to be left to rot in peace.

Julie walked back to the van. Ranger was leaning against the hood.

"Do you mind if we skip yoga?" she said. "I'm a little tired."

"Coop says there's another group here. Could be good for trade."

Ranger's forehead creased. "I have some soap in stock, but it's never a good idea to have an empty inventory. You ready to learn something useful?"

Julie mostly wanted to eat something hot and take a nap, but she learned how to make soap instead. Any time Ranger made biodiesel, she put the leftover glycerin in a wide-mouthed plastic jar. She had Julie scoop the jar empty and melt the glycerin down in a deep pan.

Ranger had the uncanny ability to pull whatever the moment required out of the back of her van. She kept a small box of fragrant oils in a little compartment built into the passenger seat. "I make these," she said when she showed them to Julie. "I grow the herbs when I can and use Juniper as a drying shed."

Julie added scent and color to the pot and poured the result into trays.

"If we'd had some rubbing alcohol we could have gotten rid of the bubbles." Ranger held the empty mixing pot to her nose. "Smells good, though."

Julie pushed the trays under the van to cool overnight while Ranger loaded her existing stock into a backpack. They paused for a snack. The food made Julie nauseous and did nothing for the chill that was creeping into her bones.

"Can we run the heat tonight?" she said.

"We're running low on juice because of the towing today. I don't want to risk getting stuck."

Julie tried to let the wave of irritation go, but pain in her back made it difficult. She hugged herself to ward off the chill.

"Do you have a warm hat and scarf?" Ranger said.

Julie shook her head.

"We'll print up some yarn tomorrow, and I'll show you how to knit."

Julie rolled her eyes. "Why can't we just trade for them?"

"It would take twice what we just made to get one that someone else knitted."

"It's just a fucking hat."

"Just a hat, but it takes at least six hours to make a decent one. Look, you can take an advance on the soap you just made, plus the shower you were going to take tonight, and try to get something. Maybe someone can cheap-print you one, although it won't be real warm." Ranger closed the van's back doors. "Or you can learn something useful. It's up to you."

Julie stared at the ground, blinking away angry tears.

"I'm not your mom, bud. You can do what you want. Nothing out here is free. You make it yourself, or you trade for it."

"I don't need a shower."

"I just spent all day with you; I'd say different. But suit yourself." Ranger slung the pack on her back. "We got a little daylight left. Let's go meet the neighbors."

The caravan on the other side of the mall was parked in a loose semicircle. There were seven vehicles, the usual mix of vans, buses, and smaller cars. Unlike the senior caravan, all the vehicles were painted the same dirty rust-orange.

"Long-term group," Ranger said. A sickly sweet smell got stronger as they approached. She frowned. "They're just dumping their shit somewhere."

Coop's caravan was careful to recycle or reuse everything. They left nothing behind at their parking spots. Discarded food and humanure was shoveled into a pickup truck they used as a traveling compost bin. When they got to their winter park, they'd use it in the greenhouses.

Ranger's shoulders rose as they got closer to the other convoy. A smell like burning plastic and ammonia was warring with the odor of shit.

Julie had gotten used to how scruffy most tramps looked. Everything they wore was patched to within an inch of its life but usually clean. The people in the rust-orange convoy set a new mark for unkempt. It was almost easier to smell them than see them. Long greasy hair, layers of dirty clothes, yellowed teeth fighting a losing battle for a quorum.

Julie leaned close to Ranger and whispered. "You're going to be popular."

Ranger grimaced. "We won't get anything here but trouble."

They were already attracting attention, including some outright stares. As they turned to leave, two ragged men blocked their retreat.

"You got something in that bag for us?" the taller one said.

"Maybe they just looking for the good time," the other one said, elbowing the other guy in the arm. "We like the good time, don't we?"

Ranger took a half step ahead of Julie. "Like we'd have a good time with you rashers. Move your ass to the slow lane and let us by."

Julie stared at her. She expected the dirty strangers to spring on them in a rage. Instead, the tall one laughed. "How 'bout your sidecar, there? She don't look too choosy."

He touched Julie's hair and leered. She shrank back. Her hair had gone a couple of weeks without a good wash, but it must have looked good compared to the ratty-looking hairdos in the convoy.

Ranger grabbed Julie roughly around the waist with one arm. "She's with me, roadkill. Get your own."

Both men laughed this time, and one made an obscene gesture to the other.

"Muffle it, rasher," Ranger said. "We came here for the biz. What's in the trunk?"

Ranger kept talking, mostly trading insults, as the guys she called rashers brought out their few pitiful wares: a little pile of random prescription patches, a glass jar half full of something that smelled like biology class, a plastic bag of rags, five or six outdated phones, and a worn tire pump.

Julie moved to examine the rags, but Ranger squeezed her shoulder and whispered something about lice. They left the compound lighter by ten bars of soap. Ranger made Julie walk slowly, almost at a stroll. Julie clutched the tire pump and tried to hide her white knuckles.

When they got back to the van, Ranger sagged, catching herself with the palms of both hands on the hood. "We just got lucky," she said.

Julie put the tire pump on ground. "Who were those guys?"

Ranger sighed and turned around to prop her butt against the van. "A gang. A well-established one. We caught them on a good day."

"You called them 'rashers'."

"Short for 'road rash.' It's kind of a swear word among the older anarchist groups. They use it on each other but can get pretty pissed if someone they think is an outsider does."

"How did you know what to do?"

"I haven't always traveled with good people." She hefted her backpack and swore. "That's a third of our trade goods gone. That pump even work?"

Julie tried it. "Sort of."

"We need to let the others know."

* * *

"They may not stop at a few bars of soap," Ranger said.

Grimy or not, the raiders were dangerous.

"The drones and a handful of stunners won't be enough if they decide to come through." Ranger took in the people around the fire, a gathering of the caravan's leadership team. "Tomorrow's supposed to be a recovery day, but I think we should leave tonight."

"We can't." Coop glanced at Rumpel. "We can go in the morning."

"We'll just have to hope for the best," Rumpel said.

"That's not a good idea." Ranger leaned into the circle. "Even getting five or ten miles away would help."

Cooper rubbed his mouth. "You two do what you need to do. No hard feelings. We can leave right after dawn but not before."

The meeting drew to an awkward close. Julie went back to the van alone to launch the drones, and was on her way up to the crow's nest when Ranger showed.

"I just had it out with Coop," she said. "You know how I've been wondering why they keep ignoring my advice about shortcuts and alternate routes?"

Julie stepped back off the ladder.

"It's Fam," Ranger said. "His car is stuck in a travel loop. He programmed it years ago for a scenic trip up to Canada with his wife. He can't remember the password to change the program, and the car won't travel after dark."

"Can't he get it reset?"

"Company went out of business during the Slide. I told Coop I could sic Gretchen on it, but Coop doesn't think he wants it fixed. Said it reminds him of better times."

"So they'll just go with him, round and round, until–"

"Fam dies. Or everyone else does. Coop swore me to secrecy. Said it's never been a problem before, and he's worried the younger tramps won't be as sympathetic."

"I don't blame them," Julie said. "He's adding weeks to the trip."

"Time isn't the real issue, though. With all the increased gang activity, he's putting people in danger."

Julie stretched. Hunching over the drones had put a crick in her back. "Let's stuff his ass in the van and go then."

"I suggested that. Coop countered that the car is the only thing Fam has."

"Ah."

"Yeah." Ranger donned her utility belt and checked the charge on her stunner.

"Do you think there'll be trouble?" Julie said.

"We make a tempting target. They might have let you and me go just to get our guard down."

"And you're sure about staying with them."

"It's what they're paying us for."

"I'll put another pot of coffee on before I climb up."

EIGHTEEN

Ranger's eyes were red with fatigue. The night had passed without conflict but not without tension. Both she had Julie stayed up, on guard for any movement from the raiders on the other side of the park. The sun rose, fulfilling the if/then requirements of Fam's creaky autodrive.

Ranger jogged back from Coop's car. "Let's get everyone moving and put as much distance between us and them as possible," Ranger said. "You look like shit."

"I feel like shit."

"There's a to-go breakfast at the fire and a roll of stimulants in the med box if you need them. I know you want to sleep, but I need you to keep one of the drones up while I drive, Bartleby preferably, and follow us at maximum range."

Julie nodded. "Make sure they aren't coming after us. Got it."

"I hope I'm just being paranoid, but that's part of the job."

Julie filled a flask with reheated coffee and put Bartleby on an emergency recharge cycle. It wouldn't be great for his longtime battery life, but the stimulant patch she slapped on her arm probably wasn't good for hers, either.

Ranger stomped back to the van with her hands full. "Cold breakfast all around. We're ready to go. You?"

Julie used her phone to check Bartleby's vitals. His battery was about three-quarters charged. His transmission range, even with Ranger's special equipment, was about seven miles. "Good enough."

"Keep his eyes open but wait until we're at the edge of his receiving range to launch and follow. I want to watch them as long as we can. Waldo said he'll send a couple of his little painter drones out about a half mile ahead of Coop."

Waldo's drones were nearly toys, low range and low speed, basically flying cans of spray paint, but eyes were eyes. "If they see anything, maybe they can squirt it."

Julie carried Bartleby to a concrete picnic table and left him on the chipped and weathered surface. She jogged back to the van in time to see Coop, at the head of the caravan, starting to move.

"We're more vulnerable when we're on the road," Ranger said. "If they get ahead of us, they can attack from both sides."

Julie kept her eyes on her phone. It was strange watching the caravan leave from Bartleby's perspective. "I feel like we're leaving him behind."

"Better him than us," Ranger said.

The van rocked and swayed. Juniper was the last vehicle in the procession, playing sweeper in case any of the other vehicles had trouble. It was easier to stop and help than turn around and come back.

In fifteen minutes, Julie hadn't seen anything alarming through Bartleby's cameras and they were nearing the edge of his transmission range. "I need to launch," she said.

"Do it," said Ranger. "Take him as close as you can to their park, circle it, and then get him back here."

Julie set the drone's fans in motion, taking the machine up to about fifty feet, and pointed it at the gang's park. On the phone screen, it looked peaceful. A few people around campfires eating breakfast. Late bloomers crawling out of their beds to meet the day.

"Looks like they're just waking up," she said. "Wait..." One of the figures on screen was pointing at the drone. Then another.

The view from Bartleby's cameras twisted sickeningly, and his vitals went red. He flipped over and fell.

"I think they hit him with something. He's on the ground," Julie said. "I'm trying to get him back up."

The drone's remaining fans whirred helplessly. Through its cameras, Julie watched as a heavy boot lifted over it. The screen went dark.

NINETEEN

They made it to the caravan's winter park four days later.

"Victory screen, baby." Ranger pounded out a drum roll on the steering wheel. "We got everyone here in one piece." She looked like a corpse, gray-skinned and sharp-boned. She'd taken on the majority of the extra shifts their revised schedule required, arguing that all her weak spots had worn away years before.

Long hours of paranoia, fueled with caffeine and not a few stimulant patches, had left Julie's mouth dry and her mind whirling. Her head pounded and a muscle in her left arm had been twitching for the last twelve hours. "Is that really it?"

Ranger pointed. "Right through that gate."

The van was playing sweeper, bringing up the rear of the convoy to make sure no one got left behind. Coop and his little red car were already through the gate, and the other vehicles filed in and pulled into the spots indicated by the park's caretaker.

"Lot of people here," Julie said.

"Coop said, what, four groups? Looks like we might be the last to arrive."

Rumpel was already out of her car and hugging a woman who was wearing a patchwork robe.

"Looks like they've been missed," Julie said. "Are we really safe?"

"Nothing sure in life but death and the rising seas, buddy." Ranger scratched the back of her head. "But I think so. The more people at a park the less likelihood of anyone from the outside doing something stupid."

They were down to one fully functional security drone. Julie had kept them flying the whole time the caravan was on the road, stripping the batteries out of the parts drone and putting them into the charging rotation. After a wind storm sent one of the working drones into a tree, Ranger had fully cannibalized the parts donor to get its healthier sibling limping along. The van's navigation system refused to respond no matter how many times Ranger thunked. Everything they owned needed a break and an overhaul.

Julie felt twitchy and anxious. She was exhausted, but sleep was the last thing on her mind. "What now?"

Ranger chewed her lip. "I'm going to check in with the caretaker while you unpack a little and make some room. Figure we'll stay here for a bit. Put ourselves back together again."

Julie moved like a zombie, each step in the unpacking process competent and totally mechanical. The folding tables and chairs went just so. The solar-cell array unwound, pointed south, and plugged into the inverter. Recycling carried to the one of the common bins. She left the doors of the van open to air out some of the funk and ran a clothes line from the van to a stake in the ground. She was just draping the bedding on the line when Ranger came back.

"Nice work. We'll both sleep better with the crumbs shook out." She handed Julie a fresh cup of coffee. "I can see why Coop and them come back here every year."

"I'm surprised they don't stay."

Ranger sipped from her own mug. "Hurricane season and residency laws. Government isn't giving out permits for permanent structures anymore, and anything less than permanent would be gone with the wind."

"That blows."

"You must be tired if you thought that was funny." She smiled. "You ready to go meet the neighbors?"

Julie frowned. "I think I just want to sleep."

"I won't stop you, but it's a bad idea. The come down from those stims is going to make you want to kill people. You'd be better off going to sleep at a normal hour and riding it out in REM."

Julie hesitated. Ranger reached for her hand.

"Come on," she said. "They have real vegetables."

Julie let herself be led to the park kitchen, which indeed featured a shallow pan of roast vegetables, about twenty pounds of well-seasoned couscous, and three kinds of freshly baked bread.

"You ever had beer?" Ranger said.

"A few times. I didn't really like it."

Ranger filled a glass and put it beside Julie's plate. "You might like this one. I just met the woman who makes it."

The beer was dark and a little sweet, with a sort of coffee taste.

"It will help with your jitters." Ranger poured herself a beer and sat across the table. "Nice people but not high-tech. We might be able to get the drone you're calling Flutter fixed, but I doubt we're going to be able to replace Bartleby and the Sacrificial Lamb."

"Can't we print parts?"

"My printer isn't great for chips. It's more of an anvil than a scalpel." She drank some beer and smacked her lips. "We'll see what happens. I put the word out. We might be surprised."

A thin person with a shaved head approached the table. "What do you think of the stout?"

"Love it," Ranger said. "Not sure Runner is convinced, though."

Julie struggled to pull her attention together. She wanted nothing more than to lie down under the table and take a nap. "It's good. Better than other beer I've tasted."

"I'm the brewer." They extended their hand. "Beer Wench. Wench for short."

"I'm not really a beer person," Julie said, reaching for Wench's hand.

"It's mostly a matter of finding the right one." Wench squinted. "You folks just got in, right? Come back for lunch tomorrow, and we'll do a tasting. I've got seven more on tap."

"Count us in," Ranger said.

"Do you make the bread, too?" Julie said.

"One of my husbands does. The other one can't cook to save his life."

Ranger pulled out her phone and sent Julie a message. "For a good time, follow those directions." She stretched. "I have a couple of tricks to pull before it gets dark. See you in a bit."

She left Julie to eat. The vegetables demanded seconds be taken, and between that, the beer, and cup of tea, Julie was almost feeling human again. Ranger's directions led her to the park's shower and laundry facilities. Outside the shower area, a sign advertised haircuts with an arrow pointing to an orange-and-blue tent, and Julie made a detour.

"Looking for something special for the ball?" the woman inside the tent said.

"The what?"

"The party tomorrow night." The woman heaved herself out of the barber's chair and motioned Julie to sit. "To celebrate all the groups arriving."

"I hadn't heard about it."

The woman washed and combed out Julie's hair. "You've been out here, what, a month or so?"

"About that."

"You're going to ask me to cut it all off."

I'm a cliché. "Is that a thing everyone does?"

"Pretty much. It will stay that way for a couple of years, then you'll get bored with it and try growing it out again. By that time you might be traveling with an established group and have more regular access to bathing."

"By all means then, cut."

"Skin or fuzz?"

"Fuzz."

After the haircut, Julie hit the showers, which, she was surprised to see, included several large soaking tubs. She soaked while the laundry machines worked over her clothes. When she emerged from the bath, the transformation was complete: twitchy ball of nerves to human being. She got dressed and made a loop around the park. It was a mix of vehicles and temporary structures like yurts and tents. Most were residential, but many had signs advertising various services. Several people were at work in the greenhouses.

Coop waved her over when she returned to the caravan's parking spots. He looked tired but clean and well-fed. "I like your hair. What's next on your agenda?"

"Food and fourteen hours sleep," Julie said.

"I hear you. That was not the easiest run I've ever made." He cleared his throat. "You did good out there."

"I just did what Ranger told me to do."

"She knows her business." He sighed. "Pop up, kiddo, I'm not getting any younger. Don't know how many trips like that I've got in me."

Julie made a noise she hoped read as noncommittal. Coop was not a young man but pointing that out or agreeing with it didn't seem polite.

"There could be a place for you in the caravan. Permanent-like," he said. "Ride with me for a year and maybe take over as scout when I retire. I'll sign my car over to you free and clear."

"Jeez, Coop." Julie blinked. "I'm honored."

The old man smiled. "We're not a big outfit, but we're solid. Car's in good shape. Should hold up for a while. I'd like to know it's in good hands."

Julie's mind was whirling again. In less than two months, she'd gone from bitter and jobless to employed and overwhelmed. It was probably an improvement overall, but her stomach twisted. Life was easier without options. "Let me think about it."

Coop smiled. "You know where I am."

TWENTY

The park kitchen was convenient and comfortable and the food was vastly superior to that on the road, but Julie missed the campfire. Around it, there was an understanding of the need for silence and reflection. To signal such a need, all that was required was to gaze into the flames and—

A middle-aged man with slicked-back hair patted her shoulder again. "I asked if you were saved, girl." The man's smile was beautiful and terrible.

Julie sighed. There were all kinds of valid reactions to the end of the world: loss of sanity had to be in there somewhere. "I'm all set, thanks."

The man shook his head. "We must all appear before Christ to receive what is due for the things done while in the body, whether good or bad."

Do things done "in body" include ThirdEye? Julie had broken any number of the man's commandments in virtual reality, probably could have curled his hair with some of her stories. Once, she might have asked him, even enjoyed the debate, but the smiling man was the fourth to try to save her soul since she'd hauled her stimulant hangover out of bed the morning before. Julie kept her mouth shut, and he wandered off toward the dessert table. It was Pie Day.

"It's just 'cause you're new," said the woman sitting on Julie's other side. "In a couple of days, Hap will be just as content to be ignored, and he'll go back to reading his Bible."

"Hap" was short for Happy Daze. He was one of about a dozen people at the park who believed the mission to Proxima Centauri was the Rapture in disguise and that in less than seven years Christ would return to lead the rest of his people home. They were a small, undauntedly cheerful group, and why not? It was all going just like they expected. Cue the Apocalypse.

Julie got up to draw another glass of porter. At lunch the day before, Wench had plied Julie with samples until she admitted that she just might be a beer person after all. The porter was milder than the stout and went well with the vegetarian chili on offer for dinner. Rumpel caught up with Julie on route to the tap.

"Ranger's looking for you," she said. "Fam's disappeared."

Adrenaline pushed Julie's heart rate higher than coffee ever could. She followed Rumpel to the yurt that housed the park's security service. Fam's car was stuck in a travel loop. The only place it could go was back to the caravan's summer park in Canada. A carjacking then. A kidnapping. Somehow the gang had followed them and picked off their weakest link. "Do we know which way they went?"

Rumpel shook her head. "That's what we're trying to figure out."

Ranger and Coop were bent over a display table with Law Dog, the park's head of security. Julie had met him at the party and told him about her own curtailed ambitions. "Cops were getting bad twenty years ago when I got out," he had told her. "You probably got lucky."

Coop beckoned Julie over when she entered the yurt.

"What happened?" she said.

"Last anyone saw him was last night. They said he seemed confused. We only noticed he was gone about an hour ago."

Rumpel's face was pale. "He was supposed to meet us for lunch."

"Did someone take him?" Julie said.

"Doesn't look like it." Ranger tapped the viewscreen embedded in the table. "One of Dog's drones spotted him climbing into his car to sleep. In the morning, the parking spot was empty."

"Why would he leave?"

"He wouldn't." Rumpel wrung her hands. "We're all he has."

"Maybe it wasn't enough," Law Dog said. "People're doing all kinds of fucked up things since the colony mission left."

"Did the drone pick up any sound?" Julie said.

"That's what I'm trying to find out," Ranger said. "Dog's equipment is seriously out of date. I was hoping you could use the software on our drones to dig something out."

"Let me try."

Ranger's drones were nonstandard, but they had a thoroughly modern suite of analysis ware, and Julie had learned a few tricks in school. She fetched Flutter from the van and worked in silence for a few minutes. Then she played Fam's last sighting again using lip-reading software. "I just want to go home," he'd mumbled as he entered the car. "Take me home."

"Shit," Coop said.

"Is that all it would take?" Ranger said.

Coop's hand went to his mouth. "Might be. Yeah."

"I don't understand," Law Dog said.

"Fam's car was looping." Ranger closed the video clip. "Montreal to here and then back."

"So, he's–"

"On his way to Canada," Julie said.

"I'm headed out in ten minutes." Ranger looked at Julie. "You coming?"

"Let me get the drone stowed and grab a couple of sandwiches from the kitchen."

"I can't get a search party together in ten minutes," Coop protested.

"We don't need everyone," Ranger said. "Runner and I can handle it."

Julie didn't linger to listen to the debate. She deposited the drone on the folding table next to the van and dashed to the kitchen to see what provisions were easiest to grab. Three or four partial loaves of bread were on the side table, along with a block of cheese, and a bowl of cherry tomatoes. Julie grabbed it all, filled a couple of flasks with coffee, and jogged back to the van.

"I put Flutter in the back," Ranger said. "Coop and Waldo are leading. Our nav system still isn't working, and Coop's is."

"I didn't get enough food for four people," Julie said.

"Fortunately, I took part of our payment in Buggets and Tasty Paste. It's already loaded."

Julie winced. Her romance with trash food had died along the road. "Lovely." She looked at the clock. The road between the penultimate park and the caravan's summer place had required nearly ten hours of hard driving. "Where are we stopping tonight?"

"We're not." She glanced at Julie. "It's risky, but I've done dumber things for less reason. You OK with it?"

"You're the boss." Julie tugged at her bottom lip. "Do you think he's OK?"

"Probably not. But even if he is, he doesn't have any way of turning that car around and coming back. Cheap piece of automated shit." She slapped the steering wheel hard. "I had a date tonight."

"Seriously?"

"Nothing serious about it. Purely recreational. Good for body and soul. You should try it."

"You should stick to the rescue business," Julie said.

Ranger's laugh had little real humor in it. The sun was getting low, and the battered roads were even more treacherous after dark. "I hope you brought coffee."

"Coop offered me a job," Julie said.

"He told me. Would have been bad form not to." Ranger drummed her fingers on the wheel. "Are you going to take it?"

"Should I?"

"It's a good offer." Ranger woke the van's entertainment center and asked it for some Miles Davis. "You should think pretty hard on it. You'd have your own vehicle in a couple of years without spending a dime."

"I'll think about it." Julie made herself more comfortable in the seat. "Let me know when you want me to drive."

TWENTY-ONE

It was nearly 2am when they neared the darkened park.

"This is not a great idea." Coop's voice was slightly tinny through the van's speakers, but it probably had more to do with the setup on his end. Ranger hadn't scrimped on sound. "We're going to get shot."

"Only if they're paying attention," Ranger said.

Waldo laughed. His voice was tinny, too. "Parked in the middle of nowhere with gangs crawling around? What are the odds of that?"

"Just drive slow and avoid looking sneaky. Let me get out first."

There was a loose circle of vehicles parked around a dying fire. Ranger and Julie headed for the center of it. They each wore a stunner, but Ranger had left her leather coat in the van. "Keep your shoulders loose and your hands away from your belt," Ranger said out of the side of her mouth. "If they start shooting, get low and find a shadow." She cleared her throat. "Hello, the fire! We've lost a member of our caravan, and we'd like him back!"

The campfire was momentarily eclipsed as someone near it reached for something leaning against a chair. "Come on over," a voice said. "Just keep your hands where I can see them."

Julie followed Ranger into the firelight.

"It's the two of us and two more in the little red car," Ranger said. "We just want our man."

The fireside voice belonged to a tall woman with a dandelion puff of graying hair. "Think I know who you're talking about." She looked into the darkness on the other side of the circle. "He was here when we got here. We looked but didn't touch."

"Is he OK?" Julie said.

"If he's not, it weren't our doing," the woman said. "Like I said, we just looked. I don't want any trouble."

"Neither do we." Ranger took a step closer. "I'm Ranger. This is my partner, Runner."

"Silent Night, but mostly they just call me Silent."

"You security for this outfit?"

Silent's hair bounced. "Gave her the night off. I'm the chief. Figured I'd sit up and see if anyone showed up to claim him."

"Can I bring the others forward? Old guy named Coop. Young one named Waldo."

Silent's hair bounced again.

Ranger turned to Julie. "Get the boys. I'm going to sit down here with Silent."

The atmosphere around the fire was a lot more relaxed when Julie returned with the others.

Silent lifted her hand. "Welcome to the park."

"Thanks," Coop said. "Appreciate you not shooting us."

"Your friend's back there about two hundred yards. Probably right where you camped the last time you were here," Silent said, pointing again. "You want some help?"

Ranger stood. "I think we got it. Mind if we drive over?"

Coop led the way again, driving slow until Fam's car was clear in his headlights. Ranger peered through the driver's side window with a flashlight. "Glass isn't fogged, and it doesn't look like he's breathing." She rapped on the window with the flashlight. Fam didn't stir.

Coop sighed. "Well, that's that. We can probably wait until morning to get him out and figure out what to do with the car."

They left the vehicles parked and walked back to the fire. Silent was sitting with a younger woman. "This is my security."

"You probably don't remember me," the security woman said.

Ranger squinted at her. "Nope."

"I was with Kinks. You helped Boo get us out."

"And now you're security with this outfit."

The woman nodded. "Did a couple years in the ref camps with the Army. Silent figured that qualified me." She pointed. "Boo's sleeping in the truck over there."

"You girls all stay together?" Ranger said.

"Most of us. Two went back to the city. Rest of us drove around until we met up with Silent."

Silent cleared her throat. "My outfit was in decline, shall we say. We were happy to get the new blood."

"Glad it all worked out." Ranger smothered a cough. "We're going to get some sleep and take care of things in the morning. That all right with you?"

"Plenty," Silent said. "I was just about to turn things over and get some sleep of my own. I'll get up when you do in case you need some help."

"You got any breaking-and-entering tricks in that van of yours?" Coop tried the door of Fam's car for the umpteenth time.

"I suppose we could wait a few weeks for the batteries to die," Ranger said. "Foiling computerized locks is not my best thing."

Julie ended the quandary by tossing a fist-sized rock through the rear passenger window and crawling through to unlock the doors. She avoided looking at Fam, who already seemed to be shrinking into the upholstery.

"His real name was Stanley," Coop said. "Can't remember the last. His wife died in the '60s, and he lost his kids and grandkids to Sophia in '83. Soon as he got the news he hopped in the car and came out here to die. We ran into him near Allenstown. Gave him a reason to live, and he gave us a place to stay. That's his land we're all spending the winter on."

"What happens to it now?" Julie said.

"We tell the proper authorities and it reverts to the state." He smiled sadly. "Best we not tell them."

Fam's car refused to respond to their voice commands.

"Good security for such a stupid piece of shit." Ranger kicked a tire. "Any ideas?"

"We leave it here it'll get picked clean by scavengers anyway," Coop said. "I say we offer it to Silent and her crew for parts."

The tall woman nodded slowly when she heard the offer. "Be good practice for the girls to pull it apart. We'll treat it nice."

"Come by and see us on your way through," Coop said. "Plenty of room, food, and a good doctor. Lots of opportunities for trade."

"We might just do that," Silent said. "Send the numbers to my map."

The leaders of the two outfits shook hands.

They loaded Stanley into the back of Ranger's van. The old man weighed next to nothing, and Julie couldn't help but glance over her shoulder at him as they drove away.

"He's not getting up," Ranger said.

Julie flushed. "It's just strange having that... him... back there. That's our bed."

"Old age isn't contagious, but we'll wash everything good when we get back to the park."

Julie leaned into the seat and put her eyes on the road. "What's going to happen to him?"

"Service of some kind. We'll pay our respects. Then we'll cut him up and eat him. It's the way of the road."

"What!?" Julie's pulse shot up. She'd asked the question mostly to make conversation. She couldn't have heard the answer right, but it made a certain kind of sense. Tramps didn't let much go to waste.

"Just kidding." Ranger smiled. "We're not that desperate. Yet."

TWENTY-TWO

The memorial was quiet but well-attended. It seemed everyone at the park had known Fam, and from the stories they told, Julie wished she'd met him before he started to slip away. His friends described him as loyal, dependable, funny, warm, and eternally sad. Julie tried to make the description mesh with the shrouded bundle of bones and meat they'd hauled back in the van and came up empty. They buried him in the shadow of a tree that supposedly meant something to him. Julie skipped the reception and went back to the van to rest. Ranger was already there.

"You look like crap." Ranger handed over a flask of hot coffee.

"I must've slept funny." Julie peeled back the lid and sipped. "My back hurts. I guess my stomach does, too." The pain had greeted her as soon as she woke. She put her hands on her lower abdomen and probed gently. "Here. Like inside. And my head is killing me."

Ranger put her hand to Julie's forehead. "You don't have a fever. When's the last time you had your period?"

"It's been years. I'm on… Oh, shit." The last time had been the first and only time. Julie had been twelve. After it was over her mother had taken her to the doctor's office for a birth-control implant. She'd gotten a new one every few years until her pharma emplant took over the job.

"You've been off the medication for a while. Your cycle is starting to re-assert itself."

"What do I do?"

"Bleed and hurt for a couple of days. I have an emplant, but I think I have some emergency pads. Maybe the park doc has more." Ranger rummaged in the back of the van and tossed Julie a small package. "Do you need me to show you how to use them?"

"I can figure it out."

Julie pulled down her pants to inspect her underwear. Blood had started to pool in the crotch. She put the pad inside them and pulled everything back up. Pressure seemed to help the pain a little, so she reclined the seat and folded her hands over her stomach.

Ranger tapped on the window. "How are you doing?"

"Nature sucks."

"Slide the window down." She held up a bottle of water and a strip of med patches. "I got you some help. Doc says no go on a new emplant. Most folks take care of this before they come out here."

Julie took the water and let Ranger stick the patch on her forearm. "It's like knives scraping away my insides. I think I'm dying."

"Thousands of years of biology and evolution says you're wrong. Come on." She gestured. "We'll get a little exercise and see if anyone has any lady gear for you."

"I need more underwear. I've gone through all the disposables I took from jail."

"Already?" Ranger tugged the car door open. "You need to be a little less fastidious. Get a couple days out of each of them at least."

"That's disgusting."

"Park has a cheap-print facility off the laundry room, no worries. Let's walk."

"I don't want to."

"It will make the drugs work faster and help with the cramping." She took Julie's arm and helped her out of the car.

"I can't even stand straight."

"We won't go fast."

Julie shuffled a few meters. "Oh, god. I can feel it coming out." She turned to go back to the car.

Ranger pulled her around again. "You can rest at that camper." She pointed about twenty meters ahead. "Geek Girl and Super Nerd. From one of the other groups. He's bald and round; she's not. Maybe they can help you out."

Nerd excused himself at the start of the conversation, but Geek Girl had Julie seated on the camper's small couch with a hot pack within minutes.

"I'm not really set up for this," Ranger said. "We were hoping you could help."

"Doubtful. Thank biology for menopause." She tapped her chin. "But we might have some of our daughter's things in deep storage. Give me a minute."

She left Ranger and Julie alone in the trailer.

"What's she going to charge?" Julie said.

Ranger inspected the camper's small kitchenette. "Whatever the market will bear, I'm sure."

"I don't have anything."

"I'll cover you this time." She held up her hand. "She's coming back."

Geek Girl stomped back up the camper stairs. "I don't have any pads, but I found these." She thrust a half-dozen T-shirts in Julie's direction. "She was about your size."

The shirts were clean but musty from wherever they'd been stored. "What do I owe you?"

Geek Girl tsked. "Nothing. It's not like she's coming back for them."

Julie was afraid to ask.

Ranger wasn't. "Where is she?"

"Philadelphia. She moved into a cube…" She looked at the wall as if the date were written there. "Six years ago? We visited with each other a couple of times, but..." She sighed. "Never mind."

"Let us give you something," Ranger said. "What do you need?"

"Not very much," Geek Girl said. "We have food, water, plenty of fuel. We just keep moving."

Julie adjusted the heat pack. Either it or the medpatch was taking the edge off her cramps. "How long have you been with your caravan?"

"Fifteen, sixteen years? Nerd could tell you. It formed around us, really. We met Sneakerhead in Nebraska. He was a solo. I guess the Jennifers came next. They were on a tour of all the remaining national parks." She ticked the names off on her fingers. "Tracker and Dandy were broken down at a rest stop in Nevada."

"You've been to the Pacific?" Julie said.

"Oh, yes. It was easier back then. The roads were in better shape, and there were fewer checkpoints." Geek Girl poured herself a cup of coffee from an antique that was gurgling on the counter. "Do you want one?"

Julie shook her head.

"We should go." Ranger swatted Julie in the leg. "We need to find you some supplies."

Julie stood up slowly and offered the heat pack back to Geek Girl. "Thank you."

She waved the pack away. "You keep that. We have plenty more. We always keep some around for Nerd's knees. You know, the Jennifers might be able to help you out. They're sort of throwbacks. Anti-tech types."

Ranger led the way down the stairs and closed the camper door behind them. "The younger Jennifer is in her forties, I think. How are you feeling?"

"Better. How many... pads do I need?"

"No idea. It's been a while for me, too, and I was never all that regular."

The Jennifers lived and traveled in a van they'd painted in rainbow colors. Jennifer the Older was outside tending a small cooking fire. She waved at their approach. "Tea?" she said.

"No, thank you," Ranger said. "We're hoping to trade for some pads. Runner's emplant ran out of juice."

"Younger has a few boxes stashed away." Jennifer the Older rose to her feet in a way that belied her nickname and crossed to the van's side door. She knocked. "Are you decent?"

"Come in and find out," a muffled voice replied. The van door slid open, and Jennifer the Younger stepped out. "Whoops, company."

"Ranger's little friend needs some period pads," the older woman said. "I told her I thought you had some."

"I can give you one box." She looked at Julie and Ranger. "You can have them if you replace them."

"First chance we get," Ranger said.

They walked back to the van, prize in hand. "Will this be enough?" Julie said.

"Should be. We'll try to get you a new emplant before it becomes a problem again."

Julie couldn't imagine a repeat performance. She felt better, but the patch didn't seem to be knocking down any more of the discomfort. Ranger made her a cup of tea. "Rest for a bit. Eat something. Take a shower. You'll feel better in a few days."

Days!? Julie groaned.

TWENTY-THREE

Two weeks after Fam's memorial, Ranger dropped into the chair next to Julie, upsetting her beer.

"Sorry 'bout that." Ranger grabbed the glass before it tipped and held it up. The afternoon sun was barely up to piercing the dark beer and settled for making it glow. "The porter again, right?" She took a sip and smacked her lips. "Wanted you to know that I'm taking the parking brake off in a day or two. Getting back on the road."

"What's the hurry?" Julie said. It was the first she had heard of the plan. Ranger had been scarce lately, even spending her nights elsewhere.

"The nav system's repaired, and I'm bored." Ranger wiped her mouth. "And Clem's getting that 'what does the future hold for us' look." She faked a shudder. "Makes me feel like ants are crawling under my clothes."

Darling Clementine was the head of a community theater troupe run out of one of the other caravans. She was small, cute, and melodramatic. She and Ranger had started hanging out almost immediately.

Julie could identify with Ranger's feeling of infestation. Waldo had been finding excuses to drop by the van and bump into her in the kitchen under the guise of talking about Fam or sharing drone-repair tips. He was a nice guy, pretty, with gorgeous hands and long, graceful fingers, but Julie found his earnestness off-putting. Art and self expression weren't the solution to every ill society suffered. Plus, the park's flock of Rapture enthusiasts still hadn't caught on that Julie didn't need saving. "Am I invited?" she said.

"What about Coop's job offer?"

Julie had done a lot of thinking about that, but the truth was she wasn't really interested. "Too much of a commitment," she said. "Besides, I'm still a minor and can't get my driver's license for another year and a half. If I get pulled over, I'm headed back to jail, and the caravan is out a scout."

"That is a problem," Ranger chewed her bottom lip, "but I know someone who could fix it."

"A time traveler?"

"Better." She rubbed her knuckles. "Gives us some place to go at least."

"Just give me a departure time and tell me what to pack."

Ranger smiled. "How about this afternoon?"

Julie headed back to the van and began dismantling the shooting range she'd set up outside. She'd had plenty of simulated experience with stunners, but the weight of the real thing threw off her accuracy. A few days of drills had brought her back to decent and took her mind off... things.

She was folding up the table and chairs when Darling Clementine herself showed up, stiff-legged and intent.

"You're going then." Clem's eyes were red and her mouth set in a thin line.

"We never planned to stay long," Julie said.

"People like Ranger never do."

Julie wiped her hands on her pants. "I don't want to get in the middle–"

"She's dying. Did you know that? She doesn't give a shit. Do you?"

That was news to Julie. Ranger had a bad cough, sure, and sometimes stopped breathing in the middle of the night, but she always started back up again.

"She didn't tell you, did she?" Clem said. "They call it lung rot out here. Mesothelioma or close enough. Her chest is full of road shit."

"Curable?"

"If she made an effort in time," Clem's shoulders were tight, her hands in fists at her sides, "but she won't. She'd just going to lie down and die."

Ranger had a lot of bad habits, but quitting wasn't one of them. "I guess that's her business," Julie said.

"That's not how a life works, Runner! She doesn't just get to decide when to go. Tell that selfish bitch she's not the only one affected by this!"

Julie finished with the table and chairs and cleaned up around the parking spot while Clem shouted and cried herself empty. At some point, the smaller woman left without saying goodbye.

There was still more than an hour to go before Ranger's scheduled departure, so Julie walked the park and said some goodbyes of her own. Coop looked disappointed but not overly surprised when she told him she wouldn't be taking his job.

"You know where we'll be this time next year. And the next, probably," he said. "If you change your mind or just need a place to crash for awhile–" Julie cut him off with a hug.

Waldo was surly and a little weepy. Julie would likely show up in a mural eventually, maybe not flatteringly.

Jennifer the Younger reminded Julie about the replacement pads she owed.

Beer Wench loaded her down with growlers and told her to come back for some pumpkin ale in the fall.

Rumpel just gave her a hug and said she'd see Julie somewhere down the road.

Ranger was checking over the van when she got back. "Ready?" she said.

Julie climbed into the passenger seat. "Where are we going?"

"Jackson, Ohio, with a couple of stops between here and there. We'll park at Chattahoochee tonight."

"Clementine stopped by."

"Did she?" Ranger started the engine and put the van in gear. "What did she say?"

"She said you were dying."

The van backed back out of its parking spot and pointed its battered nose at the park gate. "She plays a great Helena, but I don't remember her being a doctor," Ranger said.

They waved to the caretaker and pulled back onto the road.

"'Sides, we're all dying, rook," Ranger said. "It's the end of the goddamned world."

TWENTY-FOUR

They spotted it less than twenty miles from the park. The battered cargo vehicle was barely visible at the edge of Juniper's headlights, half on and half off the road. Ranger brought the van to a halt.

"What do you think it is?" Julie said.

"Mechanical failure or fiendish trap," Ranger said. "Or maybe mechanical failure turned opportunistic trap."

"So, a one out of three chance it's just someone who needs help."

Ranger took the van out of gear. "Something like that." She triggered the horn in two short blasts. "Let's set it off."

The cargo truck's interior light flashed as the driver's side door opened and someone in a long coat stepped out. He or she waved their hands over their head.

"Are the odds worse or better now?" Julie said.

"About the same." Ranger flashed the headlights, signaling the driver that it was OK to approach. "Got your stunner?"

"It's in the back," Julie said.

"Get it." She slid the window down and smiled as the driver approached. "Having trouble?"

The driver kept his hands raised, but his long coat could have been concealing a myriad of dangerous things. "Truck just died." He pointed with his thumb. "My wife and kids are sleeping inside."

"You call for help?" Ranger said.

"Phone was tied into the nav system when it happened," the man said. "Everything shorted out."

"I can make a call for you," Ranger said.

"I'd appreciate that." The man smiled. "Appreciate it more if you took my family on to the park you're headed to. Chattahoochee?"

"That's the one." Ranger undid her seatbelt. "Step back a little there and let me get out."

Ranger opened her door and stepped out onto the cracked asphalt. Cold air from outside licked into the interior of the van. Julie checked the charge level on her stunner. Fresh out of the factory, each flechette in the magazine was fitted with a nanochip police could trace back to the stunner that fired the shot. Ranger had shown Julie how to disable the chips, which was illegal but practical. She tugged on the door handle, disengaging the lock and latch, but kept the door closed.

Ranger had left her leather coat behind, and the van's headlights clearly revealed she was unarmed. "It just died on you?" Julie heard her say.

The man pointed at his vehicle. He said something that Julie couldn't hear. Ranger turned to look in the direction he was pointing.

Julie looked the other way, to the opposite side of the road. Someone was coming out of the scrub there.

Adrenaline flooded Julie's system, and she struggled against the fear trying overwhelm her. She remembered her training. *Breathe! Look at your options!*

Option one, do nothing. Ranger was the pro. Let her handle it. True, she was unarmed and facing at least two people. True, she didn't know one of them was behind her... *No.*

Option two, go for the horn. Alert Ranger, and everyone else, that the ambush had been discovered. Then Ranger could... And the guy across the road could... *what? No.*

Option three. Julie disabled the overhead light and crept the door open. She stepped into the pool of darkness outside and steadied her stunner on the hood of the van. Ranger and the tall man were still talking, facing the cargo truck. The person who'd been hiding in the scrub was crouched low. It was a man. He crossed the roadway... he had something in his hand.

It was just like the stims and target practice, except Julie's hands were shaking like she was leaning against a washing machine in mid spin cycle. She pulled the trigger and recocked the stunner. She fired again.

The man fell. Julie shifted her aim to the guy in the long coat and tagged him with a couple of flechettes, too. As he fell, Ranger dropped into a crouch, looking around wildly. Julie pointed at the man who had come up behind her. "I think he had a weapon." Her heart was still hammering, and she felt dizzy.

"Sit down for a second. I'll check." Ranger crossed the road. "A knife." Julie heard it skitter across the asphalt into the scrub. "Ambush. We called it."

"Surprised you came out here unarmed."

"I have a holdout." She turned to look at the man in the long coat. He was groaning and showing signs of returning to his senses. "Didn't count on him having a buddy. Maybe I'm getting old." She took the stunner from Julie and shot both men again. "I'll get the binders."

They dragged the weakly protesting men to the roadside, and Julie recovered the flechettes. The legal ones were about ninety percent effective at keeping a full-grown man under wraps for about five minutes, but Ranger had doctored her loads with a mild neurotoxin. Weak protests were about all the men were capable of, and they'd feel like shit for a couple of days and be incapable of erections for a least a week.

"What do we do with them?" she said.

Ranger toed the long-coated man a little harder than necessary in the back. "If we kill them there'd be less chance of recidivism."

Ranger's words were mostly theater, but a roadside execution made a certain amount of sense. Neither of them wanted to involve themselves with the police, and the ambush had been set up awfully close to Coop and his people. Google only knew what the men would have done to them had the situation been reversed.

"Roll 'em over so I can get a good picture for the volksnet," Ranger said. "We'll put an alert out on them and their truck. Revoke their access to the 'net."

"Will that be enough?" Julie said.

"I'm open to ideas, chica," Ranger said.

Ranger studied the blaze via the backup camera. "Effective," she said.

"Too harsh?" Julie was driving. She kept her eyes on the road and off the burning cargo truck. They'd stripped the men of all their personal gear, dragged them a safe distance away, and set fire to everything they owned.

"Beats killing them," Ranger said, "but it doesn't leave them with a lot of options."

"They didn't leave us with many," Julie said. "If they're smart, they'll get off the road. Safer for everyone if they were cubed up. They can play robber to their hearts' content in ThirdEye."

In another hour, they were pulling into the park at Chattahoochee National Forest. The caretaker waved them down.

"This is not a good place to be tonight," she said. "Couple of guys robbed the caravan parked here. Took just about everything they had. Roughed some people up."

Ranger pulled out her phone. "These the guys?"

The caretaker nodded. "Looks like it."

"They won't be robbing again for awhile. Didn't notice they had abundance of supplies with them." She looked at Julie. "You?"

Julie shook her head. "Could they have dumped it?"

"More likely they cached it somewhere." The caretaker handed the phone back to Ranger. "They're local."

"We met up with them about fifteen miles that way." She pointed with her thumb. "They were running a help-me scam. We tied 'em up and torched their ride."

"Busy boys," the caretaker said.

"Anyplace around here they might have a permanent base?" Julie asked. "Complicates things, but it would make sense."

"Lots of places. If they had a phone–"

"Burned it," Ranger said.

"Well, a fifteen- or twenty-mile hike isn't beyond the pale. They could be back on base by morning."

"They know where we were planning to stay tonight," Julie said.

Ranger swore and turned to the caretaker. "We have food to share. We should probably talk to the caravan boss."

"I'll make some coffee," the caretaker said. "We won't get much sleep tonight." She smiled wryly. "Welcome to the park."

TWENTY-FIVE

The caravan was a younger group. Their vehicles were relatively modern, their clothes were in good repair, and they hadn't a clue what to do about being robbed.

"Let me get this straight," Ranger said. "There are twenty of you, and you let two guys with knives take all your shit?"

The caravan leader scowled. He was in his late twenties, sported a black eye and a swollen mouth, and introduced himself as Angel. *Not even close*, Julie thought, *more like Parker. Blah!*

"We didn't come out here to fight," he said.

"Oh, I can see that." Ranger put her hands on her hips. "Who's in charge of security for this outfit?"

Julie left Ranger to whip the youngsters into some semblance of fighting shape and refilled the caravan's food stores from the surplus in the van. She heard raised voices and looked over in time to see Ranger tag Angel in the elbow with her baton. Angel backed away clutching and swearing but soon returned to the half circle of people Ranger was lecturing. Julie was closing and locking the van doors when Ranger caught up with her.

"Angel making trouble?" Julie said.

"He's just embarrassed and showing his ass." Ranger tugged her utility belt into a more comfortable position. "They all met on ThirdEye and came out here as soon as the youngest turned twenty-five. Totally legal, completely unprepared."

"I restocked them like you said, but it took most of what we got from Coop."

Ranger shrugged. "Not a big deal. Money's not really an issue for me."

"How's that?"

"Got a silver mine."

Julie blinked.

"Never mind, old joke. Sold my grandmother's house when I was a kid and a friend invested the money. I'm not rich, but I have more to spend than anyone on Basic. Call it independently lower middle class. We can restock anytime. These twerps can't."

And she's not likely to need retirement.

The young tramps were splitting or pairing up for a couple of hours sleep, many of them munching Buggets straight from the box. They'd taken Ranger's advice and posted guards.

"Are you expecting more trouble?" Julie said.

"In retrospect, we might not have wanted to torch that truck," Ranger said. "They probably could have coped with being foiled by a couple of girls, but we might have pushed them into red zone by wrecking their ride."

"Sorry about that."

"Seemed like a good idea at the time. The law of unintended consequences." She sighed. "It will be another six or seven hours before those dudes can walk straight, and they'll have to talk each other up into doing something stupid."

"Unless they have friends."

She shoved her hands in her pockets. "Let's wake up Flutter and Nameless and send them out as backup. Tight circles around the park. We'll each take a watch shift. How's that?"

A silent alarm from Flutter alerted Julie just before dawn. There were five of them, hidden in the dead trees just outside of camp. She climbed down from the van roof to wake her partner.

"Armed?" Ranger rubbed her eyes.

"Looks like," Julie said. "Can't tell with what."

"See if you can take a couple of them out with the drones. I'll make sure the kids are awake."

Julie felt the van shift as Ranger left, but most of her attention was on the screen of her antique phone. Flying a drone on patrol was one thing; flying it into combat was quite another. She left Flutter on autopilot and brought Nameless around behind the attackers. The drones were armed with the same flechettes, double-dosed with the neurotoxin that Ranger loaded into the stunners, and the computer assist made tagging a stationary target a cinch. The leftmost attacker slipped bonelessly to the ground.

Shoot and scoot. The voice of Julie's combat instructor rang in her head. It had been little more than a video game back then, but now a fuck-up could have deadly consequences. The new leftmost attacker turned and fired blindly into the warming darkness. Nameless was already moving to the right, dropping another attacker on the way.

"Two down," Julie sent.

"Roger that," Ranger replied. "Keep it up as long as you can."

Julie ordered Flutter to shoot at anyone who fired at Nameless and piloted the drone up and back to the left. It would have been easy to get behind the remaining three and take them down with crossfire from the two drones, but that would have risked flechettes flying into the park.

"Three down."

"I've got Angel and a couple of the others beating the bushes on the other side to make sure we didn't miss anyone," Ranger sent.

Nameless rocked, clipped by a shot from one of the two remaining attackers. Flutter tagged him in the back of the neck.

"Four." The last attacker made a run for it. Julie took him down with a flechette to the ass. "Got 'em all."

"Show off." Ranger's voice crackled in Julie's ear. "Put the hounds on auto and come out and help us wrap them up."

The five attackers were bound and laid out in various states of consciousness in the center of the park. "What should we do with them?" Angel's face was a mix of satisfaction and fear.

"We're just passing through," Ranger said. "Take it up with Queen Bess." She pointed at the caretaker who was standing guard with a hunting rifle, swearing and kicking at any groaned or gurgled complaint.

"All I know is you're not leaving them here." Bess squinted at Angel. "Got enough work without turning warden."

"I don't even know what our options are," Angel said.

"We let those two go," Ranger pointed at the familiar faces, "but they didn't get any smarter."

"We're not far from Atlanta," Bess said. "Police will come out here eventually if you call them."

"'Course they'll also search your vehicles, check your pockets, run your IDs... Make your life hell for a day or two." Ranger yawned. "Whatever you do, you're doing without us."

"Onward?" Julie said.

"Miles to make and hearts to break, buddy. I'll drive."

Back in the van, Ranger slumped. "I'm getting too old for this."

Julie pulled out her phone. "I'll get on the 'net and find us a park."

Ranger rubbed her face. "I'm tempted just to go back to Coop, but I don't want to risk any of this shit coming back on them."

"Plus Clementine."

"Yeah. Clementine." She started the engine and put the van in gear. "Look for something in southwest Tennessee. Maybe Oak Ridge. If we push, we can make that by dark."

TWENTY-SIX

They bushwhacked into a highway rest stop to raid the vending machines and scrape seven gallons of old cooking oil out of the robo chef. Ranger was breathing hard by the time they got back to the van, so Julie drove the rest of the way into Tennessee.

Night had fallen by the time they checked in with the park caretaker and pulled into the plot he indicated. Ranger grunted. "I always expect this place to glow in the dark."

"What do you mean?"

"Bad science joke. Irradiated tissue just dies." She cleared her throat and sat straighter. "Los Alamos gets all the attention, but Oak Ridge was one of three towns created for atomic-bomb research."

"You've been here before," Julie said.

"Few times. Makes a good meeting point. Never had a lot of people living here and it cleared out early. Guess the residents were used to doing what the government said." She undid her seatbelt. "Let's go meet the neighbors."

It was a cold November night, and the usual campfire was built high. Ranger kept her heavy jacket on. "Hello, the fire!" she said.

"God bless you." A woman with robin tattoo on her face and a high, tight haircut tossed another branch onto the blaze. "And welcome to the park. There's some more wood that way." She pointed.

"I'll get some," Julie said. "You make friends."

Ranger sat down at the fire. Julie followed the woman's gesture to a pile of scrub and loaded her arms. By the time she got back, Ranger had everyone laughing at some joke or other.

"I told him to get his butt down the road or else!" She smothered a cough.

Julie dropped her armload of wood. The fire was doing a nice job of beating back the chill. "What's the news?" she said.

"Pie," Ranger gestured to the woman, "and her crew are headed west."

"How far?" Julie took a seat near the fire.

"All the way." Pie smiled. "We've been called to serve in the ref camps for a couple of months."

Julie let her eyes wander across the faces around the fire. She guessed many of them were in their forties and fifties, but several were about her age. "All of you?"

Pie closed her eyes and raised her palms to chest level. "Everyone in this chapter of the Rolling Church Ministries of Jesus Christ Tramp. Praise Jesus and Amen."

Murmurs of "amen" circled the fire. Ranger caught Julie's eye and winked.

"Are you ladies saved?" Pie eyed Julie.

"A couple of times," Julie said. "More times than I need, really. Ranger?"

"My soul could always use some work," Ranger said.

Pie gestured to one of the younger men in her group. He stood and walked toward the vehicles. "You folks have any trouble along the road?" she said.

"Some." Ranger gave a summary of the recent excitement.

Pie poked the fire with her stick. "Get enough guns and knives together, every problem looks like something to shoot or stab."

The man came back to the fire with a wooden box. He lay it in front of Pie. "Thank you, Brother Skillet." She put both hands on the box and closed her eyes. Pie's lips moved in a short prayer, and she blinked her eyes back open again. "You ladies ever get high?"

"I've been known to," Ranger said, "and I expect my partner would be open to the experience. Runner?"

Julie's eyes moved from Ranger to Pie to Ranger again. "Sure," Julie said. "I guess it's been a while."

"Amen to that," Pie said. She opened the box. "Bowl, water pipe, joints, or edibles?"

"Edibles," Ranger said. "Definitely edibles."

"Praise Jesus," Pie said.

Julie woke up on her side with her face inches away from the interior wall of Ranger's van. Her head hurt a little, and mouth and eyes were dry. A stranger was snoring gently behind her. Julie rose on her elbow and craned her neck to see who it was.

Correction: Who *they* were. Two bedmates, draped in blankets, one a snorer, the other not. The inside of the van was rosy with body heat and musky with the smell of sex, clean sweat, and lemon-grass soap. *Had they...?* Yes, Julie distinctly remembered showering with at least two people, laughing and helping each other scrub those hard to reach places.

Julie lowered herself back down to her side. Now that she was more awake, the faces of her companions were clear in her memory, but their names were fuzzy. Dandy Lion and... someone else. Dandy Lion was a tiny thing with a bright smile and a puffball of hair dyed bright yellow. The other one was...

Contrary to Brickhouse's assumption, Julie was not totally inexperienced, but those fumbling, blink-and-it's-over encounters held nothing over the night before. Julie was tender and sore and relaxed in places she'd never been tender and sore and relaxed before.

Seal! That was other bed lump's name. Completely hairless, warm-handed, long-fingered with a quiet voice that Julie could still feel in her ear. *Do you like it when I do this?*

Yes!

Julie flushed. Once Pie opened her box of tricks, all bets were off. Maybe Ranger had started it by getting up to dance. But, no, Pie had already been there, swaying in the firelight. Someone had pulled Julie to her feet – Seal, probably – and then…

Night had flowed toward dawn in a warm muddle of laughter and skin.

Now Julie had to pee. She squirmed into the cab of the van and reached back for her clothes. The windows were fogged to opaqueness. Julie laced up her boots and, as quietly as she could, got out of the van.

Outside, the air was sharp but not as cold as she expected. The sun was high. It had to be noon or close to it. Ranger was by the fire drinking coffee. She looked at Julie and grinned.

Julie colored, her hands floating up in an I-can't-believe-it gesture. She couldn't help but grin back.

Ranger pointed with her coffee mug. "Pisser's over there."

Bladder emptied, Julie returned to the fire and sat beside her partner.

"Pie?" she said.

"Among others." Ranger reached down and picked up another mug. She filled it from the pot bubbling over the fire and handed it to Julie.

"Did you know that was going to happen?" Julie said.

"Know?" Ranger shook her head. "But once I heard what denomination they were I had an inkling." She smiled. "The Rollers are good people. I've run into them before."

"So they just…" Julie gestured helplessly.

"Drive around saving people with sex and good weed? Yep. Every night's a party."

"What about diseases?"

Ranger shot an eyebrow. "I don't know about you, sister, but I've had all my shots."

Julie nodded. "I guess I have, too."

"And, in spite of your busted emplant, you don't have to worry about getting pregnant because…" She pointed at the van.

"True."

"So, how does your soul feel this morning?"

Julie smiled. "Pretty damned good."

"Good. You deserve it. We deserve it." Ranger hauled herself to her feet. "Let's you and me make some breakfast for our hosts."

TWENTY-SEVEN

"I've got it!" Julie said. "Ranger Rick the raccoon."

Rick had enjoyed a moment of reboot stardom in Julie's youth as the mascot of the Domed-Forest Project, a program that had waxed in popularity and then waned as supporters realized it was too damned late.

"Nope. But the Domers didn't come up with him. He was a print magazine back in the 20th and early 21st."

"No way. I had Ranger Rick pajamas and everything."

"Challenge if you have the guts, rookie." Ranger grinned at her.

Julie didn't dare. She owed way too much in park chores as it was. Ranger's road games were wrecking what little free time she had. "You could just tell me why you're called Ranger," she said.

"Could, but won't. And if you cheat, I'll know."

Julie huffed. "I won't cheat." She pushed her shoulders into the seat padding and straightened her legs in a long stretch. "How much longer?"

"I murdered the last partner who kept asking me that." Ranger tapped the steering wheel, matching the beat of "Curb Your Heart," track three of the Subservient Puppies' greatest hits album, which was playing on the entertainment center. "I'll give you a hint: we came out of Daniel Boone National Forest about an hour ago."

"I didn't see a forest," Julie said.

"Which is why we didn't stop there. Whole thing burned down six years ago. So few people were still living in the area that no one bothered to come put it out. Feds ducked in, ran a bulldozer over everything, and called it good."

Julie looked out the window for signs of life. In spite of politics and the ocean's rise, the United States was still massive. Nature was trying to reclaim what mankind had abandoned, but except for the kudzu, wasn't finding it easy going.

"We'll park in about two hours if the road holds up," Ranger said. "I figure I'll drive on through since you have so much work to do when we land."

"Ha ha."

Julie leaned back to watch the world go by. Every once in a while they passed a boarded-up building, but most of it was acre after acre of green vine and leaf. Kudzu ruined the soil it grew in and choked out whatever it grew on. "It's too bad we can't eat it," Julie said.

"Kudzu? You can," Ranger said. "It's almost like spinach. Good for hangovers, too. The stuff that grows around here is probably not great for you because of all the shit they used in the coal mines. We'll grab some from a little further down the road and have salad for dinner."

The road twisted and turned but stayed relatively intact, so they made good time. "There you go," Ranger said. "Park, sweet park."

Above the parking lot, the remnants of a giant bird squatted on a round stone building. The nest itself appeared to have been built over a garage. "Is that a goose?" Julie said.

"Used to be a hotel, I heard." Ranger parked the van and shut down the engine. "It's been on the demolition list for years."

"Probably keeping it around because it's cute," Julie said. "No one can stomach tearing down a goose."

"Could be." Ranger reclined her seat and put her hands behind her head. She closed her eyes. "Let me know when everything's set up."

* * *

There wasn't much to setting up a park. Julie located the fire ring near one of the garage doors and rolled it to the center of the lot. There was a stack of dry scrapwood tarped in a copse of scrub nearby. Julie carried four armloads to the ring and used Ranger's hatchet to split off kindling. Coop had been a good teacher, and Julie soon had a strong fire going, its light and heat letting all comers know the park was occupied and welcome to good company.

She rapped on the van window. "Are we expecting anyone else tonight?"

Ranger held up her phone. "Just checking that." She scrolled through posts with her thumb. "Maybe. There's a group coming south. If the roads are OK, they might make it before dark."

"Should I put on some food?"

Ranger opened the door. "I better do it. Your cooking could gag a goat."

Julie frowned. "It's all prepackaged."

"Yeah, I don't know how you do it, either." Ranger pulled the big pot out of the back of the van and tossed in ingredients for a simple soup. She hung the pot over the fire and wiped off her hands. "Open for business."

"We're almost out of toilet paper."

Ranger nodded. "We'll be in Ohio tomorrow. We can probably pick up some supplies in Huntington. How's the firewood?"

"Enough for the night, but I'll need to refill the cache."

"Wait until morning and maybe someone from the other group will help you out." She looked down her nose. "Or I will."

"Bet your ass you will," Julie said. "I didn't lose that badly."

"Tell you what, rookie. You set the kitchen up tonight, prep the drones, and I'll promise to make pancakes for breakfast."

"Chocolate chip?"

"As you wish."

Julie opened the van's side door and hauled out the folding table and chairs. She set up the little electric stove on one end of the table and pulled the awning out to cover it all. She checked the weather and moved the rain collectors to a likely location. "Batteries are a little low," she called. "We could use some sun."

Ranger was resting near the fire. "Won't get it tomorrow," she said. "How low is low?"

"We're good for another day, day and a half maybe."

Ranger pulled her phone out of her pocket. "I'll put Juniper to sleep tonight to save some juice."

Julie peeked into the cab of the van and watched as a half-dozen telltale lights faded into darkness. A single blinking light, green, remained. She joined Ranger near the fire.

"You want to play a game?" Ranger said.

"Not on your life."

Julie stretched her legs after dinner, leaving Ranger by the fire with her reader. The older woman's literary tastes trended toward thrillers and romance, but Julie had found a small clutch of mystery and true crime in the device that she was quickly moving through. As a kid, Julie had been drawn to science fiction but the ideas and plots had either come too close to reality too quickly or been too outlandish. Special relativity and arranged marriages? Really?

She climbed a pile of rubble and approached the goose house. The thing was built on a single-story garage, each door of which was boarded over and plastered with "no trespassing" signs. Julie could see right through the goose in places, and it looked in jeopardy of falling off its perch in any kind of stiff breeze. *Who the hell would want to live in this?*

"Company's here." Ranger's voice crackled in Julie's ear.

"I'll be right there."

The windows of the house, a combination of broken panes and plywood, were egg-shaped. The walls, the nest of the goose, were tan stone and had survived much better than the goose's body. The bird's eyes caught the waning light. There was a brass medallion embedded in the wall, dated 2040, recognizing the goose's one-hundredth birthday and declaring it a historic landmark.

Julie shook her head. People had been so damned weird in the early twenty-first. The place was barely big enough for a family. She climbed up the other side of the debris pile, most of it made from the same stone as the house, and returned to the fire. Ranger was talking to a burly guy with red suspenders. He waved to Julie. "I'm Babe," he said. "Nice fire."

"Welcome to the park," Julie said. "Where are you coming in from?"

"Michigan," Babe said. "Soon as they get unpacked, I'll introduce you to the rest of my outfit."

"What are the roads like that way?" Julie said.

Small talk came easy because there was nothing small about it. Bad roads were to be avoided; good roads celebrated. Areas where the pigs were thick were problematic. What had Julie talked about back when she lived with her mother? She couldn't remember anything she had to say back then that would have been more important than the state of the road ahead.

They were joined at the fire by nine more people, including Babe's wife and two teenage sons. The boys went tearing up the rubble pile to inspect the house while their parents offered a box of crackers and a somewhat stale cake to go with the soup. Babe hiked over to the wood pile and brought a few armloads back to the ring.

"I'll set the boys to renewing the cache in the morning," Babe said. "They're pretty good at any chore that involves destruction."

The boys came back to the fire and declared the goose "cool." They finished off the soup and most of the cake before heading back to their vehicle to play games and sleep. Babe

offered around a case of beer, and they drank and talked until
the fire went to embers.

Julie set Ranger's surviving drones on a limited auto patrol
– once around the park every hour – and curled up in her
sleeping bag. She woke up in the morning to the smell of
pancakes and the thud of axes on dead trees.

"We got a problem," Ranger said. "Van won't boot up."

"Is it out of power?" Julie said.

"I shut it down to keep that from happening," Ranger said.
"Eat and then help me go over it. If we can't get the computer
back up, we're screwed."

TWENTY-EIGHT

Ranger had a program called Hot Girlfriend on her phone. It was designed to slip into bed with Juniper when she was sleeping too deeply and gently prod her awake. It had worked before, but this time there wasn't a moan, not a blink, not a happy gasp. The van was bricked.

"This is not good," Ranger said.

Babe's wife, Gremlin, her outfit's mechanic, agreed. "You've modded this thing beyond recognition, but we should have gotten something by now."

"Could it be the batteries?" Julie said.

"Your recharger is solar, and it's raining like a bastard." She scratched her head. "We have a little wind turbine. I can run that up and see if it makes a difference."

Julie helped Gremlin get the turbine mast in place and tightened the guidelines that kept it upright. Juniper's telltales fluttered red and orange when they ran a cable from the turbine to the van's power converter. Ranger flicked the battery indicator with her finger. "They're not taking a charge," she said.

"Give it a few hours," Gremlin said. "We can stick around for a little while."

Julie joined the teenagers in the work of renewing the firewood cache. She had a bad feeling she'd be using some of it that night. It wasn't overly cold, but the rain made it feel raw. Ranger watched the charge indicator like she could make it advance through willpower alone.

"It's not working," she told Gremlin after a couple of hours. "You guys need to get going if you want to get to your next park while it's still light out."

Babe and the boys unplugged the wind turbine and packed it into their trailer. "I hate leaving you like this," he said.

"We have about thirty hours before the pigs can start sniffing around," Ranger said. "We'll get moving before then."

Babe pulled Ranger then Julie into a bear hug. Gremlin asked if there was anything she could do before leaving.

Ranger said there was not and looked to Julie for confirmation.

Julie cleared her throat. "Got any toilet paper you can spare?"

"Did you put the type of batteries we need in your post?"

Ranger's face twisted. "Of course I put it in the fucking post! Try to remember which one of us is the senior partner here, rook!"

Julie threw up her hands. "I'm just trying to help. There's no sense biting my head off."

"I know. It's just–" Ranger growled. "Those batteries were supposed to last until…"

"Until what?"

"Just until." Ranger wiped her hands with a rag. "I'm calling neutral corners. You take this side of the park. I'll take the other."

Julie watched her stalk off. Over the weeks of travel "neutral corners" had become the code phrase for "I need some space," an important consideration for two people who lived in a van.

It was growing dark again. Julie built up the barrel fire. Babe's outfit had eaten all the soup but left an assortment of food bars and protein shakes in its place. Julie checked that the food was still dry in the supply box built into one of the benches. She took off her gloves and stretched her hands to the fire.

Without the "special" qualities of Ranger's rig, they were limited to a static version of the volksnet. Julie's plan to use the batteries from the drones to wake the computer had worked for about ten minutes before they ran dry, but it had been enough time for a version update and a single post. Without the benefit of a more recent update, they had no idea if anyone else was coming to the park, let alone if anyone had seen their post and could help. In the last hour, Ranger had been reduced to sporadic beatings of the battery casings.

Julie's shadow leapt across the bench beside her and raced to mirror the path of the vehicles pulling into the park next to the stalled van. She shielded her eyes and counted. Four vehicles, all of them fairly small. A man stepped out of the lead truck. "Hello, the fire," he said. "You traveling alone?"

Julie gestured in the direction Ranger had taken. "My partner's over there somewhere. Where are you coming in from?"

"Illinois, mostly," he said. "Heard there was some garage space here. We were hoping to get out of the rain."

"Garages are sealed up. But there's a fire and food," Julie said.

"That will do us." He patted the top of the cab, and a woman climbed out the other side.

Julie relaxed a little. "Welcome to the park."

Ranger came back as the new group was setting up camp. "Who are they?" she said.

"Said they're from Illinois. Eight or nine adults. One toddler. Little girl, I think."

"Got your stunner?"

"It's in the van. They caught me without it, and I haven't had a chance to grab it without being, you know, noticeable."

"They're probably fine. But grab it when you get a chance. Grab mine, too." She frowned. "Got pissy and left my pants down."

"We both did. I'm sorry."

The couple from the first car approached the fire. He jabbed his thumb at his chest and then at the woman. "I'm Hard Knocks, and this here is Shoelaces." The woman lifted her hand to waist level and offered a little wave.

Ranger cleared her throat. "I'm Ranger, and this is my partner Runner. We're headed north."

"We just came south," Shoelaces said. "Rain all the way down."

Ranger took a seat near the fire. "How are the roads that way?"

The heating unit in Julie's sleeping bag ran down around 3am, and she shivered until rising at dawn to stoke the fire. It had stopped raining, and Knocks was already there, warming his hands. He smiled at her. With a stunner on her belt, it looked less like a leer.

"Hope I didn't wake you," he said.

"I get up early."

He nodded. "Shoe and I talked about your problem. We can give you and your partner a ride to our next park. Maybe you can get some help there."

"I'll check in with Ranger about that," Julie said. "Thanks for the offer."

Ranger was back at the van wearing her leather coat. "You should probably take them up on it," she said. "Pigs'll do a flyby in about twelve hours. You'll be in jail three hours after that."

"You might be, too."

Ranger's laugh was choked. "I have so many illegal mods in the van, that's a definite."

"They might go easier on you if you aren't traveling with a runaway."

"Pigs pick me up, I lose the van. Doesn't matter what they charge me with after that. Juniper's gone, I'm done."

"I guess I'll stay, then." Julie checked the power level on her stunner. "I can get a flash charge for the drones off Shoe and Knocks."

Ranger adjusted her coat. "I'm not planning on going down in a blaze of glory or anything."

"Never hurts to be prepared."

Ranger checked the time with her phone. "That's it. We've officially overstayed. If the satellites are paying attention, we should hear pig props within the hour."

"If they're paying attention," Julie said. "I know how the system works, remember. That's a big if."

The sun was dropping toward the western horizon. The rumble of a giant engine shook the air near the park's entrance. "They're early," Ranger said. "Well, it's been fun, rookie. You've been a good partner."

Julie's eyes had started to burn, but she was more angry than sad. Months on the road, meeting new people, making a difference... *How is it ending like this?*

The vehicle came into view. It was a massive thing, with tires that came up to Julie's shoulders, armored doors, a long flat-bed trailer dragging behind it.

Ranger laughed. "Overkill much?"

A constellation of headlights and fog lights flashed on, pinning the two women's shadows in place. Julie's hand rose to the butt of her stunner. It wouldn't do any good against the tank, but if she waited until the people inside debarked...

Feedback whined. A woman's voice, distorted, emerged from the vehicle's outside speakers. "I saw your post. What flavor shit have you stepped in this time, Shannon?"

Julie glanced at Ranger. The older woman's mouth hung open for a second then closed into a wild grin. "I will be damned," she said. "It's Mom!"

TWENTY-NINE

"Put Juniper in neutral and make sure the parking brake is off. Then get your asses in here and get warm." The massive vehicle's passenger doors opened like wings. "There's hot water for tea, beer in the cooler, and homemade muffins."

Julie followed Ranger up the short ladder into the passenger compartment. The furnishings were mismatched but comfortable, the interior was deliciously warm, and there was, indeed, a half dozen blueberry muffins in the warmer. There was, however, no steering wheel, and no one appeared to be in the vehicle but Julie and Ranger.

"Who's driving this thing?" Julie said.

"I am," the woman's voice said. "Telepresence until we get on the highway then autos until we're a few miles from home."

Ranger pointed to the rear of the cabin. "Bet there's a bathroom right there. I'm going to go check."

Julie felt the vehicle lurch. "What's happening?"

"I have to swing this beast around and grab the van. Want to watch?"

The windows around Julie faded into transparency.

"You must be Julie," the woman said. "Shannon filled me in."

Julie looked at the overhead speaker. "Shannon is...?"

"Ranger. I'm Gretchen. I've known Shannon for years."

The big vehicle looped around the parking lot and backed the flatbed in front of the van. Hydraulic arms unfolded from the sides of the trailer and pulled the van up and locked it into place.

Ranger dropped into the seat across from Julie. "Plenty of toilet paper. Heaven on a roll. Shower, too, if you want one."

The monster truck lurched into motion again.

"We'll be in Jackson in about four and half hours," the woman said.

"Didn't think you trusted the main roads," Ranger said.

"Still don't. I'll be swapping out the IDs on this thing at least seven times on the way, and I've got drone-mounted decoys going in four other directions. This is a bad idea, but I believe I can get away with it."

"If anyone can, you can, Mama Bear." Ranger grinned at Julie. "I've been trying for years to get Gretchen to go by that, but she refuses."

Julie pulled a muffin out of the warmer. "So, Shannon."

"Yeah, you got me. But don't get any ideas. Mom's the only one I let call me that."

"I'm going to darken the windows in case the police buzz us," Gretchen said. The overhead light came up as the windows went opaque. "In about fifteen minutes I'm switching to auto and finding something more useful to do."

"Thanks for picking us up, Mom," Ranger said.

"Settle in. None of us got much sleep last night."

"You told me your parents died in a car accident," Julie said. Gretchen's truck ran more smoothly over the roads than Juniper ever did, and once they hit a highway there was little to keep them awake. They sacked out for at least two hours before the promise of muffins lured them awake again.

"Yeah," Ranger sipped her second beer and smacked her lips, "when I was a kid."

"So, Gretchen is your–"

"Guess."

"No." Julie squared her shoulders. "I'm too tired for guessing games. I was ready to take on the cops for you, the least you could do–"

"Adopted Mom. Informally adopted. Maybe more of a mother in-law." Ranger scratched her head. "Mother in-sin. Her daughter was my first partner, way back in the day."

"How far back?"

Ranger smiled. "We were just kids. I was seventeen, and she was a couple of years older. I inherited Grandma Trudi's car, but I needed a driver. So I asked Megan to come with me."

"Megan?"

"Yeah."

"Not Pencil Top or Lima Bean or something like that."

"Eventually we started calling her Doc. She'd been a medical student. Had enough credits to be a physician's assistant. Funny, when we started, she was the one with useful skills. Kept us fed. All I knew how to do was fold laundry and take care of kids."

"And she was your girlfriend."

"First one of those, too. And before you ask the next question, she died. Had a bad reaction to an airborne toxin in Philly. Something in the spray they were using on the tower walls."

Julie winced. "I'm sorry."

"Me, too. She really liked being on the road, helping people, making friends." Ranger pushed back in her seat and crossed her arms over her stomach. "She was a better person than me. Been trying to live up to her ever since."

"You do alright," Julie said. "At least you make the effort."

"It's not enough." Ranger turned to the darkened window; the only view it offered was a dim reflection of life inside the truck. "Never enough."

Julie rose to her feet and grabbed one of the overhead handholds. "I'm going back to check out the bathroom. Maybe take a shower."

* * *

Gretchen's truck was dwarfed by the steel-sided garage she parked it in. "Home sweet home," she announced via the van's speakers.

Ranger was slurring her words and nearly fell twice coming down the ladder. Julie grabbed her arm to keep her steady.

Ranger blinked owlishly at the battered van atop the high-tech trailer. "What a piesh of junk," she said.

"You're drunk, Shannon," said a sharp voice from behind them.

Gretchen was unbowed but worn in a way Julie had come to recognize. She didn't have time for artifice or smooth surfaces. Life had hardened her. The set of her mouth said she did not smile often.

Ranger smothered a cough. "A bit. You put the beer there."

"So, I did." Gretchen folded her arms. "I suppose you'll be looking for repairs."

"Runner, I'd like you to meet the most dangerous woman in America," Ranger gestured to Gretchen. "Hacker, mechanic, cook, and she can shoot the props off a drone at a hundred yards."

"Only with my good gun," Gretchen said. "I'd show you, but I think someone needs to sleep it off."

"Usual place?" Without waiting for an answer, Ranger headed for the back of the garage.

Julie felt her face flush. She'd seen Ranger drunk several times, but she'd never seen her rude. "I'm sorr–"

"Shannon and I don't always bring out the best in each other," Gretchen said. "I'm the one who should be apologizing to you."

"Thank you for coming for us," Julie said.

"She's family. Will you be needing a bed of your own or are you sharing?"

"My own, if it's not too much trouble," Julie said.

"No trouble." Gretchen gestured around the massive garage. "It's just me and my machines, and a lot of empty space."

THIRTY

Julie woke early to search out the bathroom.

Gretchen's living quarters spanned several stand-alone rooms built along the walls of her massive garage. Each bedroom was accessible by circular stairs, ladder, fire pole, and climbing wall. The living room required a nerve-racking, white-knuckled stroll across a narrow catwalk stretched at least forty feet above the garage floor.

The bathroom was at ground level, because that's where Gretchen spent most of her time. After descending the stairs, Julie wandered through banks of industrial-grade three-dimensional printers, a humming cluster of servers, enough heavy equipment to build a warship, a kiln, a laser cutter, a metal press, work benches covered in disassembled drones, a table laden with antique smartphones, and numerous vehicle carcasses. The bathroom was adjacent to Gretchen's primary workspace, and she was already awake.

"Good morning, Runner," she said.

"It's Julie." The screens Gretchen was working with were massive and crystal clear. Pictured on them was a strange mix of superheroes, fairies, animals, monsters, and clowns. Julie watched them for a moment. "Is that ThirdEye?"

"Are you familiar with it?"

"I should be," Julie said. "Spent most of my teens and early twenties in there."

Gretchen scratched the side of her head with a stylus.

"I'm sorry about that. It's not what I designed it for."

"You designed it?!" Julie's urgent need to pee faded.

"Well, not all of it, of course. But a lot of it. Most of the original code is mine or that of my team." She sighed. "It was supposed to be used in schools. Virtual field trips. Let the kids see places and things they'd never be able to visit otherwise. Now it's Bedlam." On one of the screens, a snake woman appeared to be having sex with a cyborg polar bear. "But it pays the bills. I have a maintenance contract for the source code. Not that it needs much attention."

"It's different when you're in it," Julie said. "On a screen like this it looks like a vid, but when you're in there, it's just like life."

"Do you miss it?"

Julie considered. Not long ago, she couldn't have imagined life without ThirdEye. "I've replaced it with something. Not everyone has that option. We can't all be out here roaming around."

"We were once, and look where that got us." Gretchen's lips flattened. "I suppose you're right. My little project has become a panacea for the troubles of the twenty-first century. Everyone locked away in Plato's cave watching the shadows of the fire on the wall."

"I was looking for the bathroom."

"That way." Gretchen pointed. "I'll make breakfast when Ranger wakes up, unless you're hungry now."

"I'm good."

"I already replaced the batteries in the van and rebooted the computer. She checked out fine." Gretchen turned back to her bench. "I don't need much sleep."

Headed back to bed, Julie considered trying the climbing wall but decided against it. She took the ladder up. Looking out the room's windows, now that she knew where to cast her gaze, she could just see Gretchen, still at her computer, toiling away on the virtual world that, for many, was replacing the real one. *Does that make her God? What would Happy Daze and his Bible-thumping pals think of that?* Julie yawned.

She crawled back into bed and slept for four more hours.

Ranger and Gretchen were in the kitchen drinking coffee when Julie joined them, limping.

"Fire pole?" Ranger said. "You need to use your legs to control the speed, not your hands. I made that mistake a bunch of times before I caught on."

"Had to try it." Julie filled a mug from the carafe of coffee waiting in the center of the table. It was hot and strong. "My ankle's just a little tender. It will be fine in a couple of hours."

In spite of Gretchen's tech savvy, she had the least modern kitchen Julie had ever seen. There wasn't an embedded screen in sight, and the coffee machine gasped and gurgled like the victim of a Dark Age plague.

Gretchen closed her laptop and wiped her hands on her jeans. "Well, that's done."

Ranger raised her coffee mug to Julie. "Congratulations, you are now legally an adult."

"Huh?"

"You're really not," Gretchen said, "but someone very like you – same fingerprints, same face, same name – is. It will pass a police scan unless they get really nosy."

"So, I can get a driver's license?"

"You have one. It's sitting on the printer at my work station with your birth certificate. You can apply for Basic, get a cube... Whatever you want to do."

"Thank y–"

Gretchen's lips twisted. "Show your appreciation by not getting in so much trouble that you draw attention to me."

Ranger sipped from her mug and murmured happiness.

"Mom's coffee is not to be missed. Megan and I once drove the entire New Coast in one swoop, drinking it all the way. Never had to sleep."

"You were both young and stupid," Gretchen said. Her voice was sharp.

"We got over the young part pretty quick. Verdict is still out on stupid." Ranger swallowed another mouthful of coffee and put the mug on the table. "Have you heard anything about the Panhandle that hasn't made the 'net? I'm thinking about making another run west."

"California in your condition?" Gretchen said. "I can fly you there if it means that much to you. I have the points."

Ranger reached across the table and put her hand on Gretchen's. "I know you would, Ma, but that's not what I want. I need get there under my own steam."

Gretchen was quiet as she looked at Ranger's hand. She closed her eyes and took a deep breath. Ranger grinned at Julie and counted to four on her fingers. She restarted the count at the top of Gretchen's exhale and made it to four again. She dropped her counting hand in her lap as Gretchen opened her eyes. Julie covered her smile with her coffee mug.

"I haven't heard much." Gretchen pulled her hand free and picked up her coffee. "A couple caravans have disappeared. Some singles have been picked off."

"Or they're just breaking down," Ranger said.

Gretchen shook her head. "I don't think so. Breakdowns usually resurface somewhere. They vow to try again or give up and move to the city."

Ranger poured Julie some more coffee from the pot in the center of the table. "Gretchen runs the volksnet. Created it. She usually knows what's going on better than most."

Gretchen snorted. "It was the only way I could keep tabs on the two of you. If I'd waited for you to message me, I'd still be sitting here on my thumb!"

"Speaking of thumbs and sitting on them," Ranger pointed

at Julie, "Runner needs a new pharma but all of her money is tied up in an account she can't get to."

"What happened to your old emplant?" Gretchen said.

"Carved out in a prison escape," Julie said.

"So she can't go to a real doctor. All she really needs is birth control," Ranger said. "She's taking care of her other shit with patches."

Gretchen rubbed her cheek with her knuckles. "I can help with the money, but I don't do pharma emplants."

"I've heard of a guy in Columbus who can handle that. That can be our next stop." Ranger leaned back in her chair. "I also think it's time Runner messaged her parents."

Oh, shit.

THIRTY-ONE

Julie and Ranger spent the day repairing Flutter and Nameless and calibrating the two replacement drones Gretchen assigned to them.

"I can replace all four," Gretchen said. "It's no more trouble than printing up two." She slid her hand over one of the new drones. "And I've made improvements. These guys are faster, smarter, and will run longer on a single charge. More range, too."

Julie looked at Ranger. Ranger shrugged as if to say it was Julie's decision.

"Sounds good to me, but I still claim naming rights," she said.

Later, Gretchen took Julie back to the kitchen for more coffee. She woke her laptop and connected it to a box made of wire mesh. She pointed. "Put your left hand in there."

Julie did as she was told. "What are you doing?"

Gretchen concentrated on her computer. "I'm waking up what's left of your emplant and pulling out anything stored in there. Then I'm bricking it. You have your phone?"

Julie fumbled the antique Ranger had provided out of her pocket and laid it on the table. The nanoink screen on Julie's left forearm woke up and started showing gibberish and error messages. Gretchen ran a thin cable from her laptop to the phone.

"First I'm moving any personal files from your emplant to the phone. Like so." The phone screen lit up. "Now, I'm

reformatting your emplant and permanently shutting it down."
The nanoink protested a few more times than faded.

"So everything I did on my emplant is now in there." Julie
pointed at the phone.

"Pretty much. Depends on how often you ran maintenance
on your emplant."

"Almost never."

"Then, yeah, every meme, message, or dick pic you ever
got is now on your phone. Lucky you." She told Julie to pull
her hand out of the mesh cage and disconnected it from the
laptop.

"Your old data body still exists," Gretchen said. "If I'd just
deleted it, it would have left a lot of loose ends. I don't like
loose ends, so I tweaked it so most searches will just overlook
it. It's there, but there's nothing to latch on to, if you get what
I'm saying."

Julie did not, but she signaled her agreement anyway.

"You had some money in the bank." Gretchen showed Julie
the balance. "If I move it out of there, it's going to throw up all
kinds of red flags. So, I created an account for your new ID and
deposited an equal amount of money into it."

"But that's your money."

"True. So when your old ID turns twenty-five, it's going to
empty its bank account and send the money to a secret account
of my choosing. Dig?"

"I'll be repaying you."

"Yes, you will. Deal?"

"Deal." They shook on it.

Ranger led Julie across the catwalk to the living room, which
contained little more than a lamp, a battered recliner, and a
free-standing set of shelves.

"Help me with this," Ranger said. She grabbed one side of
the shelving unit and started to pull.

Julie put her hands beside Ranger's and added muscle. The shelf unit was full of books. It took their combined strength to pull it away from the wall. The whole bookcase moved on a pivot, revealing a narrow opening.

"Gretchen has got to get rid of some of these things," Ranger panted. "Either they're getting heavier, or I'm getting older." She reached inside the hidden room, and LEDs flickered to life in the ceiling. "Come on in."

The entryway was so narrow Julie had to turn sideways to get through it. The little room looked like a robot had projectile vomited all over it. The walls were covered in circuitry embedded in some kind of tan resin. Julie had smashed a handheld in a fit of rage once, and the room looked like someone had done it to a hundred more and mounted the guts on the walls.

"What is this?" I said.

"The X. It lets you use the commercial network without being part of it."

Ranger handed Julie yet another antique phone.

"She loves these things," Julie said.

"Says they finally got them right in the late '60s. Indestructible, long battery life, plenty of processing power. Ten years after that everyone went quantum, but you really don't need it unless you're running an AI or something like ThirdEye." She tapped the phone she'd given Julie. "She pulled out all the ID programming, modded the whole thing. It's untraceable, but it only works in here."

Julie thumbed on the handheld and watched the display light up.

"Text only. Don't waste a lot of time," Ranger said. "The X only works if no one knows about it. From the outside it looks like a dead spot. The longer the spot is there, the more likely it is someone will notice it."

"What should I say?"

"Fuck'd if I know. My parents died when I was a kid. Keep it simple, I guess."

"Give me a minute."

Ranger patted Julie's arm and slipped out of the room.

It took a bit for Julie to puzzle out the handheld's user interface. It didn't use any operating system she'd ever seen. Once she found her bearings, she keyed in a message:

– Mom & Dad,

I'm safe, alive, and healthy. Sorry if I upset you by leaving. It was something I needed to do. I needed to start my life, and I think I have. I've seen amazing things and met a lot of great people. Don't worry about me. I will message again when I can.

Love, Julie –

Julie turned off the handheld and slid back through the door. Ranger was waiting outside. She reached through the door and turned the lights off, leaving the X to the shadows. "Help me with the door."

"How do you feel?" Ranger said.

"I don't know."

"That's probably about right."

THIRTY-TWO

The face of Anji's avatar was serene, but there were tears in her voice. "There's nothing for any of us there. Am I supposed to spend the rest of my life screwing around with you in ThirdEye? Look at this shit!" She pointed at a parachuting hedgehog, and it burst into screaming flames. "I'm glad I didn't run away with you and Ben. I'm glad I bailed on you! I'm just sorry I couldn't take you with me!"

"Fuck you!" Julie's avatar said. "You wouldn't know so—"

Julie pulled the ThirdEye visor off her face, cutting off the rest of the recording. Gretchen hadn't updated to the latest tech, so the recording hadn't been nearly as immersive as the real encounter. It still hurt, but less than expected. When Julie had recorded the exchange, her last contact with Anji months ago, she'd imagined she would play it over and over again.

At least arguments in ThirdEye were visually more interesting. *Won't be looking at that one again.* Julie deleted the recording from her phone. It was one of thousands of files she was slowly going through to clear space. She'd already lived through dozens of more recent messages from her mother and father, the police, even a few from Ben. They called her selfish, expressed concern, said they'd get her help, asked how she was doing, and advised her never to come crawling back, young lady. She'd deleted them all.

Figuring out what to do with the past was proving more difficult, but she didn't have to do it all at once. She slipped the phone in her pocket and rose from the chaise lounge Gretchen used as her ThirdEye immersion couch.

There was a squeaking sound behind her as Ranger slid down the fire pole from her room. "I think I got us a caravan."

"Paying?"

"Just a ride along. Leaving from Louisville, Kentucky, in five days and heading west."

"How far?"

"All the way. You interested?"

They'd been resting up at Gretchen's for a couple of weeks. Ranger had filled out some, but the more frequent showers and better lighting revealed a blue tint to her lips and fingernails.

"I'm in," Julie said.

Gretchen stood to rummage through a cupboard. She came back to the table with a battered metal thermos and filled it from the coffee pot. She handed it to Ranger.

"We'll stop in longer the next time we come through," Ranger said.

Gretchen handed her a paper bag without changing her expression. "For the road."

Ranger took the bag and hugged the older woman. "I miss her, too."

"I know you do." Gretchen rubbed Ranger's arm. "Get going before Runner leaves without you. Don't forget my errand."

"We won't."

Julie's goodbye included a stiff-armed hug. "Take care of her," Gretchen said. "She's not good at it. Take care of yourself, too. She's not always good at that, either."

"What's this errand?" Julie said as Ranger backed the van out of the garage.

"Little repair work on one of Mom's towers."

Gretchen had a fleet of twenty-five drones that she kept in the air constantly, plus a dozen or so crawlers on the ground. She was also a fan of redundancy and had two big transmission towers and a host of smaller, camouflaged backups. Julie was relieved to find out the repair only required them to climb one of the small towers and not one of the two-hundred foot monsters.

Ranger parked the van and handed Julie the component they had to replace. "I'll carry the tools."

Getting to the base of the tower required an uphill hike through scrub, and Julie was sweating by the time it was over. "What is this thing?" The replacement part she was carrying started out at around twenty pounds, but now it seemed to weigh at least four times that.

"No idea," Ranger wheezed. She pointed up. "I just know it needs to go up there."

The tower was eighty feet tall and disguised as a dead hickory tree. It blended in nicely with the rest of the dead trees on Gretchen's lot and the nearby Wayne National Forest. Julie slung the component over her shoulder by the built-in strap. "How the hell do we do this?"

Ranger kicked brush away from a metal box nearby and keyed in a security code. Inside were two climbing harnesses. "Buckle up for safety."

"You've done this before."

"Similar. Gretchen usually has a few chores for me when I visit."

The harnesses went around their waists, around each leg, and up over their shoulders like suspenders. Two stiff straps with clamps on the end extended from the front. Ranger demonstrated. "There are these staple-looking things all the way up. You clip into them with these," she opened and closed one of the clamps, "as you climb. Mostly foolproof. They won't open until the other one is clipped in."

"Mostly foolproof."

Ranger smiled. "The Well of Fools has no bottom." She showed Julie how to attach the replacement part to the back of her harness then attached the tool pouch to her own. "After you."

Metal pegs jutted out from the faux trunk at regular intervals, and Julie used them to climb the first six feet of the tower. "I'm at one of the staples."

"Clip in and keep going," Ranger said. "When you get to the next staple, clip into that then unclip the first one."

"Foolproof." Julie clipped in and continued the climb. The technique was pretty easy to learn. The trick was to remember not to climb so high between staples that reaching down to unclip was impossible. She made the mistake early and vowed not to make it again.

"Keep your body close to the trunk." Ranger was panting. "If you get tired, just stop and hang out for awhile."

For the first twenty feet, Julie avoided looking down. Then she glanced back to see how Ranger was doing. "I kind of like this," she said.

Ranger leaned away from the tree letting the harness take her weight. "It will get worse as we get higher. We're lucky there's not a lot of wind today."

About a dozen feet later Julie felt the tower swaying, but there was an easy rhythm to it. "Still not so bad," she said.

"Good," Ranger said, "next time it's all you."

Julie clipped into the anchors to the left of the hidden access hatch and waited for Ranger to catch up. She leaned back as far as she could. The hill they'd climbed on the way to the tower added to her total elevation, putting her above nearly everything in sight. "Which way is Columbus?"

"North," Ranger pointed. "You can sort of see it from here."

Julie shaded her eyes and looked in the direction Ranger had pointed. The city of Columbus was a dark smear on the horizon. That far inland, the federal reconstruction was less about height and more about density. The new Columbus was evolving into a tight circle of services, shops, and cubes. *The rich will still get the good seats.*

Ranger hauled herself the rest of the way up and clipped into the opposite side of the hatch. She lifted the fake, shaggy bark covering the keypad and entered Gretchen's access code. The hatch popped open. Ranger pointed. "You can clip the replacement there. We'll probably need all our hands for this."

It felt good to lose the extra weight. Julie's lower back was starting to feel the pressure of the harness. "Will we have to go back to Gretchen's to drop off the old one?"

Ranger's laugh turned into a hacking cough. "You tired of being alone with me already? That does not bode well, chum."

"She seems lonely."

Ranger took the pouch of tools off her waist and clipped it to the fake tree in easy reach. "No one is forcing her to be a hermit. She likes it that way. Always has." She used a power screwdriver to remove a water-resistant gasket from around the faulty part. "Even when we were kids. She put in all that playground shit – the poles and climbing wall – when Megan and I started to visit regular, but she always seemed a little relieved when we left. Hold this."

Julie took the gasket and its cover plate. Ranger pulled the faulty unit out of the snarl of electronics inside the fake tree. "And this," she said.

The part was warm to the touch and smelled burnt. Ranger pulled the new module out of its carrying bag and slid it into place. Its telltale lights flashed from yellow to green. "There we go." Ranger put the old part into the carrying bag and put the gasket and cover plate back on. She reached overhead to grasp the hidden hatch, and it clicked smoothly into place. "Grab the old one, and we'll head back down."

Ranger was wheezing badly by the time they made it back to the van.

"You drive," she said and dropped heavily into the passenger seat. As soon as Julie started the engine, Ranger flipped the car's air-purifier on and turned the fan up high.

"Are you going to make it?" Julie said.

Ranger was gray. "I just need to rest for a little while."

Julie pulled out carefully and headed down the road.

Ranger sat with her eyes closed and the air-purifier fan blasting into her face for nearly an hour before groping for the water bottle and taking a long pull.

"That's better," she said.

"How sick are you?" Julie said. She'd been tiptoeing around the question for weeks. Ranger was open about a lot of things but tended to get squirrely when people showed too much concern.

"Pretty sick."

"Have you been to a doctor?"

Ranger sighed. "Last year a doctor gave me about a year."

"A year to live or a year to get better?"

Ranger pulled out her phone. "It's about sixty more miles to Columbus. We'll park tonight so we can get into the city about noon tomorrow. Then we'll run parallel to I-71 to Louisville." She humphed. "Don't think I've ever stopped in Circleville."

"Where?"

"Says here it used to be home to the Great Pumpkin Festival or something. Mostly empty now. Bunch of tornadoes tore through it and people got sick of rebuilding. The park is in an old swamp right outside town."

"Sounds lovely."

Julie heard the rustle of paper.

"You hungry?" Ranger said.

"What is it?"

"Muffins. Homemade. Gretchen slipped them to me before we left."

"Whatever's in there, I get half."

"Deal."

Julie washed down two of the muffins with swallows of black coffee. "So, pretty sick, yeah?"

"Yeah."

After they bedded down that night, Julie pulled out her phone and looked again at the list of files from her own life. Vids, games, silly messages and pictures, angry bouts with her mother... She slid her finger up the screen and checked the box that would select them all.

Delete. No more past. This is where I need to be.

THIRTY-THREE

"The fire isn't burning." Julie leaned over the steering wheel to get a better look out the windshield. It was early evening, gloomy and cold, and a motley group of vehicles was parked in a circle at one end of the lot. Most outfits had a slew of lights, garish things: Christmas lights, strings of LEDs, plaits of long-burning glow sticks... Ranger had a string of antique hot-pepper lights that she hung up when the mood struck her.

But at the very least there was always a fire to welcome any fellow travelers.

Ranger yawned. "Maybe they can't get one going. It's raining like a son of a bitch, and not everyone had Coop as a teacher."

Julie flashed a smile that she didn't quite feel. She couldn't take her eyes off the circle of vehicles. "I don't see any lights at all. Not even interiors."

Ranger's features narrowed, and she sat straighter in the seat. "That's not good. Let's stop here and watch for a bit."

Julie brought the van to a halt about a hundred yards out. The windshield wipers flailed to keep up with the downpour that had been chasing them for the last thirty miles.

Ranger muted the entertainment center. "Beep the horn."

The van's horn, rarely used, sounded like a goosed duck. Julie stress giggled.

"I've been meaning to fix that," Ranger said. "Do you see anything?"

"No. But the rain might be covering it." Julie activated the horn again. This time the duck's throat was clear, and it blatted loud and long.

"Give it a minute," Ranger said.

The windshield wipers beat, and hot air from the defroster blew into their faces. "Nothing," Julie said. "Should we launch one of the drones?"

"If it's a trap, they already know we're here." Ranger's eyes narrowed.

"They might even be coming around behind us."

Ranger touched a slider on the screen linked to the back-up camera. The image went from visible-light black to night-vision green. She used a toggle to pan the camera right to left and back. "I don't see anything."

Julie's mouth firmed. "I'm getting out. Count to five and come out after me. Leave the doors open in case we need cover." She plucked the holdout stunner she'd started keeping in the cup holder beside her and flicked the safety off with her thumb. The little weapon wasn't as powerful as the one on her belt and carried less ammo, but she could conceal it in her hand. Julie pushed the button to open the van door and stepped out into the rain. "Start counting."

Julie's waterproofs were tucked away in the back of the van, and the thin jacket she was wearing soaked through in seconds. "Hello, the fire!" she said and walked slowly forward. She heard the passenger-side door open and held up her left fist to let Ranger know she should hang back. "Hello!"

If the horn didn't do it, my voice sure as hell won't. Julie's heart was hammering, and she forced herself to breathe slowly as she approached the circle. *Keep it out of the black.* She'd never met her armed-combat instructor in real life, but he'd been a fiend for breath control and using it as a tool to keep a clear head. Condition black meant out of control, jacked up to uselessness with adrenaline. A hard orange alert was OK. Red might become necessary, but black was no good to anyone.

Julie reached the closest vehicle, a mostly modern minivan, and slapped it with her free hand.

The flat sound shocked the air and died without further reaction. Julie put her back to the minivan's nearest tire and squinted back into the rain at Juniper. Ranger was peering around the passenger-side door, stunner in hand.

Julie pounded the fender above her with the side of her fist. She looked to Ranger who shook her head and held up her hand. The older woman slipped around the door and started to approach Julie's position.

She knelt down beside Julie. "It's hard to tell a lousy ambush from a good one until you're in it."

"I don't think it's a trap," Julie said. "Do you smell that?" It was a greasy odor, almost cheesy, gassy, with a sort of floral undertone. Julie's police-training package had included a set of smell strips, each laced with a blend of chemicals that might prove important to the job. The one she was remembering now had nearly made her throw up and lingered for days in her room.

Ranger swore.

"What do we do?" Julie said.

"Stand up and look, or walk away." Ranger pulled the flashlight off her belt. "Can you handle this part?"

"Can you?"

"No idea." Ranger took a deep breath and stood to point her light inside the minivan. "It's not too bad."

"Are they dead?"

Ranger rapped the window with the butt of her flashlight. "Yeah."

Julie peered into the van. The back had been converted into living space, and two human forms spooned under the blankets inside. They weren't moving.

"The windows aren't fogged," Ranger said. "Let's check the others."

The next vehicle had three bodies in it, the car after that only one. Vehicle five contained an entire family: two big, under-the-blanket lumps and three little ones. Twenty-seven corpses in all.

"Did they freeze to death?"

"I don't see how," Ranger said. "It's been cold but not that cold."

Julie scanned the circle again. "It doesn't look violent." She borrowed Ranger's flashlight and ran the circle of light on the ground around each vehicle. "No blood that I can see, but it's raining."

"How bad do you want to know?" Ranger's face was tight.

"We have to do something." Julie returned the flashlight. "Don't we?"

"No. But let's wait until morning. Maybe it will stop raining by then."

Waiting didn't mean sleeping. Ranger made a pot of coffee, and they sat up in near silence to watch the shapes of the caravan sharpen as the sun came up.

"Nothing we do is going to make anything better for them," Ranger said.

Julie slipped her mask over her face. It might be enough to cut down the smell. Might. "You can stay back here." *She's thinking about Euchre.* "That might be a good idea anyway."

Ranger snorted. "Who's going to save your ass when you throw up in that thing?" She wrapped a scarf around her mouth and nose. "This will do."

Neither precaution was enough. They jimmied the driver's door of the minivan and fell back, retching in the foul air that drifted out. "I really don't want to do this." Julie lifted the blanket. The little spoon – a woman, probably, though it was hard to tell – clutched something to its chest.

Julie's virtual Intro to Forensics trainer, Police Sgt Janey Lavois, had a voice like a piccolo and a macabre sense of humor. Julie tried to channel one of those things. "At least she died snuggling."

Ranger's eyes widened. "What the–"

"Coping strategy." Julie cleared her throat. "I don't see any wounds or blood."

"What's she holding?"

Julie lifted the woman's hand. "No rigor mortis. She's been dead more than thirty-six hours."

"Duh, Nancy Drew, she's been dead a hell of a lot longer than that."

Julie flushed. "I'm following procedure."

"Screw procedure." Ranger leaned past her and plucked the object out of the woman's grasp. "It's a book. A Bible." She held it out for Julie to inspect.

There was a bookmark inserted into the pages about three-quarters of the way through. "She was reading Revelations."

Ranger threw her hands in the air. "Fucking idiots!"

The bookmark was a plastic card with a raised design printed on it. "I think this is a pharma mod."

"Betcha anything that she used that, stuck it in that fucking book, and then lay down and died."

"You can't be sure."

Ranger gave Julie the hard eye. "I've seen some stupid shit out here, Jules. Ten to one this was a group of Rapturists who didn't want to see what came next."

The driver of the next vehicle was still behind the wheel. He also had a Bible and a little plastic card. The man's passengers, a man and a woman, had med patches up and down their exposed forearms.

"No pharma emplants," Ranger said. "Had to do it the hard way. We keep going we're going to find the same thing."

Or worse. "The kids."

Ranger slammed her hand on the hood of the car. Her face was ashen. "Oh, hell. God damn them. What kind of monster would do that to their own child!?"

Scared monsters. Desperate monsters. Monsters who had seen all their hope leave orbit. They'd planned this, thought about and prepped for it, worked up their courage and– *That's it, folks!*

"Why hasn't anyone seen this before now?" Julie said. "You said the police fly over the parks every couple of days."

Ranger smoothed her braids. "Maybe they missed it. This park isn't used much. Or maybe they saw it and left it as an object lesson."

"What do we do now?" Julie said.

"No pigs," Ranger said. "That's where I draw the line."

The fire they left behind them three hours later neither warmed nor welcomed.

THIRTY-FOUR

Ranger dropped lunch on the table. "The Jennifers gave us these. I've been saving them. The expiration date is only a little past."

Julie pawed through the small collection of readi-meals Ranger had spread out on the hood. "They don't really go bad."

Ranger's hand darted in. "Lasagna. Mine. I haven't had pasta, even bad pasta, in ages."

Julie picked a package that said "Apple Pie" and pulled the self-heating tab. The package inflated from the pressure.

"That's not likely to be real," Ranger said.

"What is?"

She humphed. "I see you're in a great mood today."

"And I see you're faking it."

"Usually am. Life makes it hard sometimes."

They sat at the table and ate with the plastic silverware that came in the packages. Julie licked her spork clean and burped. She rolled the packaging into a small ball. "How much of this is recyclable?"

"Probably none of it. Keep the spork. You can use it again. We'll put the rest into the trash bag until later."

Julie was quiet as she did her share of the packing up. The word "later" was fraught, but they'd already talked about it during the drive to the little park outside Columbus and again when they woke, still exhausted, late the next morning. What would happen if...? What should she do when...? The plan was simple enough. She and Ranger would drive into the city to meet someone who could set her up with a birth-control emplant, then rendezvous with a Louisville-bound caravan on the other side of the city.

"It's going to be fine." The van door made a satisfying thunk-click when Ranger closed it. She made a practice of unpacking and repacking the back every time they stopped. She said it was to keep the sleeping area clean, but Julie suspected it was more to keep the location of all the oddities stuffed inside fresh in her memory.

"You said you don't know even know this guy," Julie said.

"I don't. But I sort of know someone who does, and that's usually good enough."

Julie was still rocked by what she'd seen the night before and what she'd had to do. They'd posted a notice on the volksnet: a complete caravan, free for the taking, mind the smell and the pyre. It was an opportunity for someone, although Julie couldn't imagine anyone being eager to ride around in a corpse-scented minivan. "I just don't want to get caught," she said.

"You won't." Ranger opened the driver-side door. "Probably."

The holo map blinked out when Ranger started the engine, and she slapped some sense back into it.

"That's not going to work forever," Julie said. "There's a short in there somewhere."

"You want to poke around in there with a soldering iron feel free. Until then…" Ranger brandished her hand. "El Whacko speaks volumes."

The nav system beeped four times as it recalibrated and displayed their route. Ranger pointed. "See? It knows who's boss. Seventeen miles to go."

As crows once flew, the city was a lot closer than seventeen miles. It loomed on the horizon like a fairy land, all tall spires and shining solar panels. Here and there wind towers bloomed like alien flowers. Had Juniper been capable of highway speeds, they might have been there in five minutes. As it was, twisting around what was left of the local roads, the trip took nearly two hours over the broken pavement lacing together the abandoned suburbs.

"It's hard to believe people used to live here," Julie said.

Ranger drummed her fingers on the steering wheel. "Once enough people moved into the city, the government came in and knocked everything down. Keeps away squatters."

There was enough left of driveways and parking lots that Julie could get an idea of the geography. It had probably been a lot like the place where she grew up. She sighed. "It's all going to look like this one day. Brown grass, dead trees, and rubble."

"A lot of it already does," Ranger said. "Other places it's desert." She took a left and entered shadow. She flicked the headlights on. The GPS pinged. "Welcome to Columbus."

Julie craned her neck to look up and finally stuck her head out the window. On either side of the street, buildings rose like cliffs. Way, way up, she caught a glimpse of the yellow-blue sky and the daylight they'd left behind. "That's depressing." She pulled her head back in and raised the window. "There's not even anyplace to walk."

"There's a skywalk about midway up," Ranger said. "At the fifty-floor mark."

"You've been here before?"

"Couple of times."

A green autopod meeped at them as it scooted past. Julie got a glimpse of the occupant, engrossed in his emplant while the autopod's navigation system figured out the fastest route to his destination.

"Important enough for a private pod, but not so important that he can't avoid an appointment in the Dregs," Ranger said.

"Dregs?"

"Closest to the ground, closest to the bone. The more money you have, the higher up the towers you live. You go high enough you even get parks and windows. Down here...?" The GPS instructed Ranger to take a left at the next intersection and go up a ramp into a mostly empty parking garage. Juniper took up a space and a half and stuck out into the lane. "We won't be here long." Ranger pointed. "There's the elevator."

The elevator took them up nine floors and dumped them in a nondescript hallway filled with equally nondescript doors. Ranger consulted her phone. "This way."

Ranger led the way to a T-intersection and took them right.

"Every door is the same," Julie said.

Ranger tapped the phone. "The doors are coded. If you lived here, you could feel your own cube through your emplant." She stopped. "Here we are." Ranger stuffed the phone back into her long coat and rapped on the door with her knuckles.

A computer's voice responded. "Wait," it said. It said "wait" again, and repeated it every thirty seconds for the next eleven minutes.

"This is ridiculous," Julie said. She made a fist and readied it to knock again. The door slid open.

"Enter," the computer said. "Enter."

They crossed the threshold at the third "Ent –", and the computer fell silent.

The room beyond was dark and humid.

"Oh, God," Julie said. Her stomach rolled, and she raised her hands to her face. "The smell..." It was worse than a minivan full of corpses, like something rotten had crawled into a corner and died explosively. "I'm going to be sick."

"Shush!" Ranger frowned.

A panel in the far wall slid open, and the overhead light flickered on. The man who came out of the bathroom was beyond pale. His graying hair was long and lank. The green towel that circled his bony hips made his skin look sallow, and he was covered in sores. He shuffled toward them. "Which one of you is Ranger?" he said.

Ranger put her hand on Julie's back. "You're Oliver."

The man's eyes were pale and watery. He blinked. "Alex, turn the lights down by half. And give us a spray." He sniffed. "It's a little ripe in here. Pipes must have backed up again. Send another message to maintenance."

"Yes, boss," the computer said. The lights dimmed, and the ventilation system hissed. Something that smelled vaguely of apples and spice began to overlay the rot.

Oliver gestured to a small table and chair set. "Sit."

"I can stand," Julie said.

"Not if you want to talk to me. There's another chair folded up under the table. Get it down for me."

As Julie fumbled under the table, Oliver shuffled toward a locker on the far side of the room. "Message said you needed a birth-control implant." He turned and leered. "Which one of you has the cock?"

"I don't…" Julie frowned.

"Our money is good," Ranger said. "That's all you need to worry about."

Oliver finished his traverse of the floor and opened the locker. He plucked a box from a shelf inside. "I'll worry about whatever I want to worry about, tramp." He closed the locker and began to shuffle back. "Lots of people have money, but I only sell to the ones I like." He put the box on the table. "Untraceable. They don't even exist." He lowered himself into the other chair with a sigh. "What if I said you had to try it out with me before I agreed to sell it?"

Julie stood. "Ranger, let's go."

Oliver drew circles on the tabletop with his finger. "Your choice. Good luck finding an emplant this invisible. Worked in a clinic out in the burbs. Government razed it when it shut down. I logged them as destroyed." He tapped the box. "Tags on these aren't on file anywhere."

Julie pushed the box away from her. "I don't care how invisible they are. I'm not having sex with you."

Oliver's laugh turned into a coughing fit.

"He'd never survive the experience. Look at him." Ranger rested her hands on the table. "How long have you been in a cube?"

Oliver avoided her eyes. "What's it matter?"

"When's the last time you logged off?"

"Couple of days ago," he said.

"Couple of weeks ago, more like. You can barely walk. You're dying."

He pushed the box back at Julie. "You want one of these or not?"

Ranger put her hand in her coat pocket. "Maybe we should take all of them, Runner. You think Ollie here can stop us?"

Julie searched Ranger's face for some sign of how to respond. "He's not looking too good," she stammered. She looked inside the box. "There are seven in here. How much was he planning on charging us?"

Oliver heaved himself to his feet. "Hold on, hold on!" He raised his hands. "Alex, record everything."

"Recording," the computer said.

He shook a finger at Ranger. "If you touch me, the police are going to know who you are. They'll be on you like flies on shit."

"Maybe," Ranger said. "Or maybe you won't be worth their time. I bet they won't raise too much of a fuss about someone stealing something that doesn't exist from a ninth-floor slug."

"I wonder what else he has in that locker." Julie was warming up. She still wasn't completely sure Ranger was bluffing, but backing her play seemed like the only move. She rose to her feet.

Oliver slumped. "Look... alright." He raised his hands. "I don't want any trouble. Just take what you came for and leave. It's on the house."

"We'll pay what we agreed on." Ranger crossed her arms. "Julie, sit back down."

Julie took the empty seat at the table.

"Give her the emplant," Ranger said. "And no more screwing around."

Oliver reached into the box. "Take off your jacket and open your shirt."

THIRTY-FIVE

"I'm not proud of that." Ranger carefully backed Juniper out of the too-small space. "I shouldn't have let him get to me."

"Would you really have robbed him?"

"Of course not!" Ranger chewed on her bottom lip. "Probably. Maybe once upon a time... But no."

"He was an asshole," Julie said.

"He was. But he's just trying to live through this, same as us."

"Not the same." Julie shook her head. "We wouldn't dangle something somebody needed off the end of our dicks."

"He's not the worst I've met. There are all kinds of Olivers. Greedy fuckers who let what little power they had go to their heads."

"Like Kinks."

Ranger nodded. "I think they're all just scared of what they're becoming."

"Slugs?"

Ranger put the van in forward gear. "Irrelevant."

Back on the road, Julie took over the driving so Ranger could focus on their route. "Two hundred and forty miles to Louisville, Kentucky. No way in hell we're making it tonight."

"Cincinnati?"

"They practically fracked this part of the state to death in the '40s. Earthquakes. Nobody goes to Cincinnati." Ranger pursed her lips. "Maybe Xenia?"

"Never heard of it."

"Only town in the US that starts with an X, according to this. There's a park with a caretaker at some old fairgrounds."

"Sounds dreamy."

There was a fire burning at the park when they arrived, a big pot of soup over that fire, and a four-piece acoustic band trying to play a song called "Nine-Pound Hammer."

"Welcome to the park," said an older, short-haired woman. She took a break from nodding along to the too-slow music and waved. "My name's Ocean Lover, but mostly they just call me Ocean."

"Where are you coming from?" Julie dropped the leftover readi-meals onto the communal pile. She'd weeded out all the desserts and pasta before making the donation.

"Here and there." Ocean smiled encouragement at the musicians. "Last night we parked near Dayton. Mostly we go east to west then back again."

"All the way?" Ranger said.

Ocean pushed through the pile of readi-meals with one solid finger. "Sea to shining sea. We're on our way back to the New Coast. We'll spend some time near Newark, see the sights. Takes three or four months to make the crossing now, but," she finished her inspection, "what the hell else are we going to do?"

Julie took a bowl from the stack near the fire and filled it with soup. She knew there wouldn't be much flavor – tramp soup could generally be best described as "gently savory" – but it would warm her up. Her chest had felt empty and full of ice since Circleville.

"How's the Panhandle?" Ranger said.

Ocean squinted. "What did you say your name was?"

"Ranger." She jabbed her thumb at Julie. "This is my partner Runner."

"*The* Ranger?"

"One of them," Ranger said.

Ocean reached beside her for a flask and pulled the cork

out with her teeth. She took a long swallow and offered the bottle to Ranger. "I know a few. None of them match your description. You're the one who saved Brickhouse from–"

"Ancient history." Ranger took a pull from the flask and handed it to Julie. "You were about to tell us about the Panhandle."

Julie took a sip from the flask and then a mouthful. It burned her throat and warmed her gut better than the soup.

"It's getting worse every damn time we go through." Ocean's eyes were bright. "We lost three people."

"To what?"

"Name it. Bandits. A sinkhole near Guymon. One night the temperature dropped from 85 degrees to 29." Ocean's voice had gotten louder, and hearing it, the band stopped trying to play. She waved them on. "Keep going. You're getting a lot better." She smiled at Julie and dropped her voice. "I keep telling them that, it might come true. Let's take a little walk. You can show me the famous Juniper."

Ranger gave the older woman a hand up, and the three of them headed in the direction of the van.

"Pretty night," Ocean said. "Lots of stars."

Comparatively. They were far enough from the city to escape the light pollution, but the particulates in the upper atmosphere still cast a haze over everything.

"The others get worked up when we talk about it." Ocean cleared her throat. "That freak cold snap took our medic. Old guy, wasn't prepared. None of us was. I think I'm going to have a helluva time convincing everyone to go west again." Her mouth set. "Could be we stay to the one coast from now on. Could be we break up. I don't know." Her eyes brightened. "I don't suppose you'd–"

Join them? Nearly a thousand miles back the way they'd come.

"I'm sorry. I don't have time for that," Ranger said. "We're meeting up with an outfit in Louisville in a couple of days."

"Maybe I'm getting too old for tramping around anyway."
Ocean's lip trembled. "I hear the sea in ThirdEye feels almost
real. Does it?"

"I like her," Julie said.

"Ocean? Yeah, she reminds me of the old days. Just out
here to see as much as she can, live as much as possible. If she
knows Brickhouse she's been out here for a while."

Julie tried to make herself comfortable on the van's front
seat. "What did you save Brickhouse from?"

"A much-exaggerated bar fight in East Texas with some
Proud Boys. Couple of months before they seceded." She
laughed. "I was much younger and dumber then. Maybe even
as dumb as you."

"I seem to remember saving your ass a couple of times."

"What I mean by dumb. You need to learn to look around
before you jump into things."

"Sometimes not knowing where you're going to land is the
point," Julie said. "Things get predictable otherwise."

Ranger grunted. She was either losing interest in the
conversation or falling asleep. The subsequent snores proved
the latter.

Nearly four months since Julie had left home. What would
a year on the road do to her? Two years? Burn out and die like
Ranger. Age into oblivion like Ocean. Work until it was time to
be replaced like Coop?

Julie's head ached dully, either from the questions running
through it or the hormone manipulation of her new emplant.
She rolled over. *Maybe I just need to drink more water.*

Ocean's outfit was up and moving by the time Julie crawled and
stretched her way out of the van. She counted on her fingers.
Only two more nights in the front seat before she'd paid off her

debt accrued in Ranger's question-and-answer games. She did a few sun salutations to get her bones and muscles back into place and walked to the fire in search of breakfast. Ocean and Ranger were already there drinking coffee.

"Breakfast is whatever you can find." Ocean gestured to the pile of cartons. "A couple of my girls already refilled the wood cache."

Julie pulled herself a mug of coffee and sat to warm her fingers. "Chilly," she said.

"Probably going to get worse," Ranger said. "Ocean's hitting the road in about an hour. Figure we should do the same."

"Not much reason to stick around if it's just us," Julie said.

Ranger upended her coffee mug and shook it clean. "I'll get the van warmed up." She stood and nodded to Ocean. "You and your people ever been to Maine?"

The older woman shook her head. "Never had a good reason to."

"Funny how different the sea looks in Bangor compared to, say, Andalusia or Fayetteville. Almost like a whole other side of the world."

Ocean smiled. "I'll keep that in mind."

THIRTY-SIX

The sky was nearly crimson by the time they pulled into the small park outside Louisville.

Ranger took the van out of gear. "Red sky at night, sailors' delight. Red sky in the morning, sailors take warning."

Julie shook herself more awake. "What?" The miles since they bypassed Cincinnati had been slow and dull.

"Old saying." Ranger covered a cough. "Doesn't mean much with all the shit in the air these days. Once upon a time it meant we'd have a nice day tomorrow. Now, who the fuck knows?"

The westbound outfit they were meeting up with wasn't due for another day, but there were three small caravans already setting up for the night and sharing a meal by the fire.

"Lucifer," said the woman who rose to greet them. "My friends call me Lucy, but my husband will tell you Lucifer fits better. Welcome to the park."

Ranger had stopped in Scottsburg to scavenge cooking oil, and Julie had cranked out a new batch of soap. They ended the night lighter by several bars but with full stomachs and ten pounds of stock for the printer.

In the morning, they cleaned the van and made sure it was ready for the push to the Pacific Coast.

"Have you met this group before?" Julie said.

"Parts of it, maybe. It's fairly new. I don't know the guy they've hired as wagon master. His name is Sarge, apparently. Ex military."

"Be nice to be able to take it easy," Julie said. "Let someone else do the thinking." *And the staying up all hours and stressing out.*

"Mmmm." Ranger put her hands on the small of her back and stretched side to side. "Let's go over the drones, too. Might be they can mesh with whatever setup this Sarge guy has. Give him a couple of more birds in the sky." She smiled. "Team player. That's me."

It was nice to see Ranger smile. She'd been quieter since Circleville, more withdrawn. If she had any misgivings about heading west under someone else's flag, she didn't offer them.

The caravan rolled in around 1pm. Julie counted twenty-two vehicles, most of them modern, a mix of big and small. At the end of the line was an olive-drab truck about the size of a fire engine, raised up on over-sized tires, with an exhaust system that terminated in a snorkel.

Ranger shaded her eyes. "That must be Sarge." The caravan made a counter-clockwise loop around the parking lot before settling into precise spaces, front bumpers less than eighteen inches away from the one before it. "Tight ship."

The engine sound – a mix of biodiesel growls and electric whines – died away. The horn of the olive-drab truck blatted twice. The passenger-side door of every third or fourth vehicle opened and the occupants stepped out, weapons ready.

"Now, that's just showboating," Ranger said. "The park is already occupied by two caravans, family groups. If shit was going to go down, we'd already have eaten it." She pointed. "There were two of Lucy's kids standing over there waving them in. They're hiding in the scrub now, probably pissing themselves."

Julie squinted. "Are those lethals?"

"Some of them. Might be loaded with no-kill shells, though. Can't tell from here." She stepped away from the van and headed toward the circle. "Let's play dumb."

Julie followed, aping Ranger's decision to keep her coat closed and her hands loose at her sides. All of the guards, men and woman, were young, or youngish. Late twenties or early thirties. One of the men, strong-jawed with a long scar on the side of his face, barked at them to stop.

Ranger raised her hands. "I'm Ranger. This is my partner Runner. The Dame around? She's expecting us."

The man who'd yelled exchanged glances with another guard. "You hear anything about that?" he said.

The other guard – tall, startlingly pretty, with a bright red mohawk – grunted noncommittally. They leaned over and spoke to someone inside the car. The driver's side door popped open, and a woman with a blue mohawk jogged toward the other side of the circle. "Ice is on it." They looked down their nose at Ranger. "Sorry, you know how it is."

"Getting an idea." Ranger put on her best aw-shucks grin. "You folks have any trouble on the road?"

In the distance, the woman with the blue hair, Ice, had stopped at the olive-drab truck and was waiting by the side door.

"Little dust up near Roanoke," the tall guard said. "Nothing we couldn't handle."

"Looks like you all could handle a lot. Live ammo in those things?"

"You bet," the male guard said. "We–"

"Save it, King. Stick to the brief."

The side door of the truck opened. A man, giant even at a distance, stepped out. Ice pointed back toward Ranger and Julie, and the man followed her gaze. They started walking, the big man ahead, Ice a couple of paces behind.

"So, where's the Dame?" Ranger said. "Been going back and forth with her on the 'net for a couple of weeks now."

"We'll get her if we need to," the tall guard said. They moved the gun from one arm to the other and stuck out their hand. "Fire."

Ranger shook the hand and laughed. "I get it! Fire and Ice. You two been riding together long?"

Fire squinted. "About five months. We met in Newark."

"You part of the caravan or hired help?"

The big man came into earshot and cleared his throat. "I can take it from here, Wildfire." He turned a tight smile on Ranger. "Help you with something?"

He was close to seven feet tall and wide as a door. His face was baby smooth and topped by a crew cut. Muscles bulged underneath his T-shirt.

"We're here to join up," Ranger said. "I know the Dame through a friend of a friend, and when we heard you all were heading west, well, we just had to go, too."

"Ranger, right?" He looked them both over. "We've been expecting you. I'm Sarge."

His hand dwarfed Ranger's then Julie's when they shook hello.

"Glad to meet you," Ranger said. "I was getting a little worried. Your people didn't seem to know I was coming."

"He does that sometimes." Fire frowned. "Says it keeps us on our toes."

Sarge laughed. "It does. And you followed protocol, sure as shit. Good security follows protocol."

Sarge's voice didn't match his size. A light tenor instead of the big bass that should have come out of his chest. *Must piss him off.*

The big man pointed toward the fire with his chin. "See we got some neighbors over there. What do you know about them?"

"Couple of families," Ranger said. "Nice people."

Sarge grunted. "Fire, Ice... Go check them out. Then come back and help us get everyone square. We're leaving early in the morning."

"Anything we can do to help?" Julie said.

"Give your DBW code to Fire."

"Don't have one," Ranger said. "Van's not built for it." She did the aw-shucks smile again. "We'll keep up alright."

Something ugly flickered behind the big man's eyes. "You'd better. It's a long way to the Pacific." He turned on his heel. "Welcome to the park."

It took an abnormally long time for Sarge to recede into the distance and disappear back into his truck.

Ranger whistled. "Big fella, ain't he?"

"Ex-Marine." King smiled. His teeth, in spite of his otherwise rough appearance, were blindingly white. "Augmented. I seen him lift the front of one of our scout cars."

"Impressive," Ranger said. Her face was still open and friendly, putting Julie on guard. "Where can we go to pay our respects to the Dame?"

THIRTY-SEVEN

Julie nearly had to jog to keep up as they headed the way King directed them. "You're not happy."

"Oh, I'm fucking thrilled," Ranger said. She was nearly panting but refused to slow down.

"What's a DBW code?" Julie said.

"Drive by wire. Means all the vehicles in the caravan are on autodrive, controlled out of that truck of his via a satellite link."

"Why would he want that?"

"It was popular about ten years back. Kept groups together better. Allowed closer formations. Could be that's it. Could be he's a control freak."

"The van really doesn't have a DBW code?"

"Gretchen and I pulled all that shit out when I got her." She stopped beside a thoroughly modern forty-foot motor coach. "The Dame has money."

"Looks like a UFO had sex with a tank," Julie said.

"Wonder if she shelled out for the optional flight package." Ranger tapped the doorbell. "Let's ask her."

The Dame was a tall, slim woman who'd had paid a lot of money to look younger than she really was. In appearance at least, she reminded Julie of her mother. Carson S. Riley, however, would not have been caught dead in the gold-brocade jumpsuit the Dame answered the door in.

"Oh, hello," the woman said, "who are you?"

215

Ranger made introductions, and in short order they were in the sitting room of the land yacht with drinks provided by the Dame's butler, Stevedore. Ranger and Julie shared the couch. The Dame sat across from them in a gilded mechchair that whined quietly as it shifted to support her every move.

"I've heard so much about you!" she said, addressing Ranger. "You've been a tramp your entire life! Were you born on the road?"

Ranger took a sip of her gin and tonic. "Not quite. I was born in Norwood, Massachusetts. Hit the road when I was seventeen and never settled after that."

"The things you must have seen! Tell me everything!"

"We would be here a long time if I did," Ranger said. "If we add all of Runner's stories, we'd never leave this room. Why don't you tell us about yourself instead?"

"I'm not very interesting, I'm afraid. I'm from Charleston. My husbands died – one right after the other, poor dears – and I came out here to find my bliss." Her teeth literally sparkled when she smiled. "I'm sure I don't have to explain it to you. Every day of your life has been an adventure."

Ranger shot Julie a warning glance. "One after another. Where did you find Sarge?"

"Through an acquaintance. My personal lawyer, really. It was an extensive search. Then we spared no expense in outfitting him. Only the best!"

"I can see that. How big is his crew?"

"A half dozen. Plus his partner. They call him Fish Eye. He does look something like a flounder, I suppose."

"Have you been west before?" Julie said.

"Dozens of times." The Dame had a laugh like silver bells. "This will be the first time by road, of course."

"Of course." Ranger downed the rest of her drink and signaled Julie to do the same. "You must have plenty to do without us taking up your time."

The Dame floated to her feet. "Uneasy lies the head that

wears the crown, I'm afraid. Will I see you both at the fire tonight? Stevedore will be serving s'mores and hot cider!"

Ranger sent the folding chair clattering to the ground. "I'm going to kill her!"

"The Dame?" Julie uprighted the chair and sat on it. "She's crazy but probably not worth a life sentence."

"Not her." Ranger had enough growl in her voice that a few extra r's came out. "Keebler! I can't believe she recommended these freaks to us."

Awareness dawned. Keebler was the friend whose pal had pointed them to the Dame's outfit when Ranger cast a net looking for a west-bound party. "They're headed in the right direction. What more do we need?"

Ranger thrust her finger in the direction of the Dame's land yacht. "They're," her face curdled, "tourists! Fucking dilettantes on a disaster cruise!"

Slumming, in other words. Out to spend some time among the great unwashed as the clock runs out on civilization. I wonder if I'm any different. "We don't have to go with them," Julie said. "Get on the 'net. Find another group."

Ranger kicked the other chair, sending it careening away from the van. "I don't have time to find another!" She stalked away.

Julie hesitated and followed, leaving the toppled chair where it fell. She didn't have to go far. She caught up with Ranger near the ruins of a white, wooden building. She was leaning in an over-sized doorway, coughing her head off under a sign that said "Livestock."

Ranger rolled up her sleeve to show a line of med patches. "These are barely working anymore. The next step is an emergency inhaler and that's only..." She trailed off.

"Only what?"

"Only supposed to give me another few weeks." She pressed

the heels of her hands against her eyes. "I don't have time to find another outfit."

"Then we'll go alone," Julie said. "We can leave tonight. There's a town west of here called Santa Claus. Supposed to be a statue and everything."

Ranger wiped her eyes with her sleeve. "The statue's not there anymore. They moved it up to Indianapolis and put it in one of the towers." She straightened her back against the door frame. "We won't make it on our own, Jules. I won't make it."

A hug or a shoulder or a pat was the next logical move, but those things had never been part of their relationship. Julie settled for leaning against the opposite side of the door. "Then how bad could it be, traveling with them?"

"Bad," Ranger said. "Dangerous. I don't know about the rest of them, but I wouldn't trust the Dame to know when something's going wrong."

"Sarge looks competent."

"Looks. Augments aren't the most stable of personalities. Obsessiveness and anger issues are built in. He's probably on heavier meds than we are."

Julie flipped the hem of her coat to the side and stuck her thumb in her belt, leaving her fingers to rest on the butt of the stunner there. "Caravan might need us to save it from itself."

"Oh, yeah?" Ranger's face slowly spread into a smile.

"It's what we do, 'Burb." Julie pushed herself off the doorframe. "Let's go meet the neighbors."

"And grab some s'mores."

"Oh, hell yeah."

THIRTY-EIGHT

Fish Eye did look like a flounder. He had a pale, narrow face and watery, staring eyes. He didn't blink much.

"Bespoke." He poked one of Ranger's drones disdainfully. "Quaint. We can link them with our copters and fly them as part of the security screen. I'll send you the patch."

"We can do foot patrols, too," Ranger said, "and the crow's nest giv–"

Fish raised his hand to cut her off. "We have things under control."

Ranger's shoulders rose. "I've talked to your crew. The most veteran of them have been out here less than six months and none have run the Panhandle."

"I hear it's been a while since you've run it, too." The skin around his eyes tightened. "Ranger, the Terror of Terre Haute. I looked you up when the Dame told us you were coming." He smiled, but the tension didn't leave his eyes. "We got this. Put your seat back and enjoy the ride. Are there any problems with your vehicle I should know about? It's the oldest one in the caravan."

Ranger rotated her head a fraction of an inch to either side.

Fish flipped a mocking salute. "Thanks for the drones, ladies."

He walked toward the next vehicle. Fish Eye was Sarge's second in command and vehicle master. He'd spend the afternoon checking in with drivers to make sure their rides were ready for the road. "What happened in Terre Haute? Where even is Terre Haute?"

"It's in Indiana. Rampant stupidity happened." Ranger squinted ahead to where Fish Eye was talking to the next driver in line. "Still think this is a good idea?"

Julie picked at a pimple on her neck. "I'm taking my cues from you. If you say we go, we go."

Ranger grumbled some more and disappeared into the van for a nap. Julie put on her utility belt and went for a walk. She missed Lucifer and the kids, who had gotten back on the road earlier that afternoon. The boys' antics had been enough to knock a few bricks out of the funk that had been settling in since Circleville.

She waved to Fire and Ice, who were walking a patrol around the circled-up caravan. Sarge had six guards on staff, plus himself and Fish. Ranger had gotten a discount for contributing her drones to the security net, but there was no way – Julie counted on her fingers – that the full price multiplied by the ten other vehicles in the convoy would have been enough to pay for everything the caravan offered. The Dame had to be making up the surely huge difference. One big bus was a dedicated bathroom, complete with showers and a hot tub, and she'd hired a film crew to document the trip for the party she was planning for her return to the New Coast.

The documentarians, two slick thirty-somethings who went by Hitchcock and F.F. were ubiquitous. They'd poked around Juniper for a half hour, asking questions and shooting footage, until Ranger chased them off.

Julie jogged across the circle to catch up with Fire and Ice. The two guards were friendly and obviously smitten with each other. "You two ready to get back on the road?"

They glanced at each other. "Wouldn't mind sticking around for another day," Fire said. "We haven't had a real break since Roanoke."

"What was the deal there?" Julie said.

"Few losers tried to make off with some gear and the shower bus," Ice said. "We weren't on duty, but we heard it was no big deal."

"Anyone get hurt?"

Ice laughed. "They might have. None of our people did."

Julie tapped her stunner. "Are you carrying lethal?"

The lovers glanced at each other again. "Right now, no. But we have it." Fire lifted the barrel of their shotgun a few inches. "Rubber shot and bean bag mostly. Hurts like hell but probably won't kill you."

"Ever fired on anyone?"

They shook their heads. "Have you?" Ice said.

"Couple of times. I wanted to be a cop once, so I had a lot of training. You?"

"Not much." Fire looked at Ice and smiled. "We came out here to be together for real. Our first ride broke down near Charlotte, and we heard Sarge was hiring."

"Where is he anyway?" Julie made a show of looking around. "I expected him to be a bigger part of the prep."

"You won't see him much," Ice said. "Stays in the command center mostly and lets Fish do the legwork."

Fire snorted. "You won't see the Dame much, either. She has a ThirdEye suite in that bus of hers. Spends a lot of time back in the city with her friends." Their mouth twisted. "We don't ask questions. Fish tells us what to do, and we do it. Once the new van's paid for we'll part ways and see what's up the road. Portland is supposed to be a lot of fun, still."

They chatted for a bit longer and Julie excused herself to take on the real errand she'd set out to do. She crossed the circle again, smiling and waving to the few people she'd met so far. The medic's vehicle wasn't huge, maybe sixteen feet long, but barring some dirt and a few scratches it looked like it had just rolled off the line. Julie took the short flight of folding stairs into a comfortable waiting room with a simulated receptionist.

"Can I help you?" The voice and image were androgynous, a slight fuzzing at the edges of the hologram the only real indicator that it was made of light and controlled by an AI.

Julie pulled a strip of Ranger's med patches out of her pocket. "A friend of mine is on these." She slid the patches into the scanner. "She says they aren't working anymore."

"How many patches is she using per day?" the receptionist said.

"Probably too many."

"When you say 'friend' am I to assume you are romantic partners?"

If it helps. "Sure. Civil union or married. Whatever you like better."

"What is your partner's diagnosis?"

"It's called lung rot, I guess. Meso-something. Is there something you can do?"

"Possibly. Would you like to make an appointment for her?"

Julie imagined she heard worry in the simulation's voice, but surely it was a projection of her own concerns. "Yeah," she said. "Let me talk to her, and I'll get back to you."

THIRTY-NINE

Ranger's hands were tight on the steering wheel, but Julie pressed on. "It's just an appointment. You barely have to go anywhere. I'll even go with you."

"It will be like a spa day!" Ranger barked a harsh laugh. "You really think that will make things any easier?"

I have no idea. "You should see inside the place. You're not going to find anywhere that fancy outside a city."

"I'm sure it's the best rolling medical center the Dame's money can buy. Not interested." Ranger craned her neck to look at the film crew riding in the back. "And if you're recording any of this, I'll stab you both."

Hitchcock did something with his emplant, and the tiny drone that had been hovering in the driver's compartment returned to his side. "I'm just doing my job."

"Your job doesn't include me." Ranger glanced at Julie. "Yours, either. I've been to the doctor. I listened very closely to what she said. I'm dying. I'll probably be dead soon. Another appointment isn't going to change that."

F.F. cleared her throat. "I am very sorry to hear that. If you'd be interested in recording a messa–"

"Shut up!" Julie snapped. "If the two of you share a word of this conversation, I will stun you and drop you down a hole."

"Don't yell at them!" Ranger said. "You're the one who brought it up!"

"I…" *I brought it up super casually and very oblique. You're the one who started yelling about death.* "Fine. Forget I said anything."

The van traveled a slow, bumpy, and silent mile and a half. Ranger cleared her throat. "Look, I appreciate you looking out for me, but there's nothing a doctor can do. Terminal is terminal."

"A lot can change in a year," Julie said.

"Now you sound like Gretchen. She keeps sending me articles and vids about experimental treatments. None of it fits what I got, babe. It's a tramp disease. No one cares what happens to a tramp."

"We could try. That's all I'm saying."

"I'd try," Hitchcock said.

Ranger and Julie rounded on him together. "Shut up!"

Another half mile passed. The van rocked hard, sending Hitchcock's drone clattering to the van floor. Julie and Ranger shared a smile.

"It's just my time," Ranger said. "I've lived longer than a lot of people out here. The road catches up with everyone, eventually."

"That's just survivor's guilt talking," Julie said.

"None of us are survivors, baby girl. The survivors all left orbit." Ranger laughed. "Nah. I don't feel guilty about surviving. When I feel guilty it's because I couldn't save someone."

Or didn't try hard enough. One of Sarge's guards was a guy called Studman. Meeting him had gotten Julie thinking about Marty, the dude she'd gotten arrested. She'd scoured the volksnet for any sign of him but came up empty. She hoped he'd been able to keep his car. "How do you think I'm going to feel if I can't save you?"

"Bad, probably. But I'll be dead. That will be your data to format and wipe."

Julie folded her arms across her chest. "That's pretty selfish."

"I'm the one dying," Ranger sighed, "and I'm getting really sick of looking at that thing's ass." The back of Sarge's mobile command center filled the windshield. As the only vehicle not on drive by wire, Juniper had been designated "extreme sweeper" and sent to the back of the line. "I am perfectly capable of maintaining a proper distance between my bumper and the bumper of the car ahead. There's no need to stick us back here."

"I don't understand why we're here, either," Hitchcock said. "You made it perfectly clear you didn't want to be on camera. It doesn't make any sense to assign us to ride with you."

"It's probably a punishment," Ranger said. "For me. And Runner." She looked at Julie. "You don't want to be famous, either, right?"

"No thanks." Julie continued staring out the side window.

Ranger inspected the film crew via the rear-view mirror. "You twerps like musicals?" She reached for the entertainment center. "This is my favorite."

Music and the bag of THC candies Hitchcock produced from somewhere mitigated the mood inside the van. Within an hour they were singing along to "Greta's Braids." An hour after that they were at a dead stop, feeling their highs fade and irritation set in. King walked back along the line of vehicles and rapped on Ranger's door. "Fish Eye wants the vid guys to come up to the front."

"What's going on?" Julie said. "Why aren't we moving?"

King cracked his neck. "Building collapsed up ahead. Blocked most of the road. We should have it clear in a couple of hours."

Ranger pointed to the holomap hovering over the dash. "There's a bypass less than half a mile back. We don't even have to turn around. Just put everyone into reverse for a bit."

"Fish says he wants to clear the road."

F.F. climbed out of the van and slung her camera bag over her shoulder. "Duty calls, Hitch."

Ranger sucked her teeth and watched the film crew struggle to keep up with King. "Let's go," she said.

"Back to the bypass?"

"And ruin my good reputation by deserting the caravan on the road?" Ranger's laugh sounded wet. "No, we're not there, yet. We'll walk up to the front and see what's happening."

They each filled a bottle with water and left their coats in the van. The day was overcast but muggy, and sweat was trickling down Julie's back before they reached Sarge's truck, which was the next vehicle in line. "Think our fearless leader is up there directing traffic?"

"We really don't see much of him, do we?" Ranger flipped the top off her bottle and took a long pull of water. "Wonder why that is."

"Maybe he's shy."

As they walked they were joined by a few of the other drivers and passengers curious to see what the holdup was. About a half mile up, just beyond the bumper of King's little scout car, Fire and Ice had stripped down to tank tops to clear debris. Fire had muscles like a gymnast. Ice's arms were covered in tattoos.

"Get to work." Fish Eye said when he saw them approach. He was standing off to one side with the Dame. "This will look great on camera. The caravan coming together to clear an obstacle."

"That's going to take at least an hour." Ranger jabbed her thumb back the way they'd come. "There's a bypass back there. We could be moving forward again in twenty minutes."

"That's not the plan." Fish's face reddened, but it might have been the heat. "We're going through, not around."

Ranger walked forward a few yards and shifted debris with the toe of her boot. "Doesn't look like this came down on its own. See how it's all spread out and how far it goes?"

"An explosion?" Julie said.

Ranger nodded. "And the wood's not even weathered much. It came down pretty recently." She stuck her thumbs into her utility belt. "Sarge worried at all that this might be a trap?"

The color in Fisheye's face deepened. *Definitely not the heat.* "We know our jobs. We sent the drones out as soon as the scout reported in."

Hitchcock's tiny camera drones were in full force, too, buzzing around the work area as more members of the caravan joined in the efforts. The Dame's manservant, Stevedore, was setting up a table of snacks and drinks.

Ranger smiled. "Guess we'd better get to work then. Runner?"

"Right behind you. Help me with this beam thing."

When they bent to lift it, their heads were only a few inches apart. "Don't forget to smile pretty for the camera," Ranger whispered.

FORTY

"Twenty-five years ago, this trip would have taken forty hours," Ranger said. "Not counting sleep stops and pee breaks."

Julie yawned. Four days of following Sarge's mobile-command center at the mandated two vehicle lengths had neither challenged her driving skills nor her mind. "We could have been already if we'd flown."

"No fun in that." Ranger's feet were propped up on the dash, and she was changing the color of her toenails again, this time to something like safety orange. The color was covering a glow-in-the-dark green that had flickered like fireflies in the back of the van the night before. She had traded four bars of soap for a sampler pack of polish.

"Not a tremendous amount of fun in this." Julie forced her shoulders down and glanced at the speedometer. Twenty miles per hour on the button. *Suck it, cruise control!*

Ranger inspected her work, curling and spreading her long toes. "Imagine crossing the country two hundred years ago. No music. No A/C. Dysentery. Months staring at a horse's ass."

Julie gestured at the vehicle ahead. "Asses or assholes. How is this any different?"

"We get snacks delivered."

The Dame only emerged from her yacht for dinners and to "supervise" repair stops or road clearing, but she sent Stevedore out with trays of canapés every time the caravan came to a halt. The little gray man walked up and down the line presenting his tray at every window, his carry-all stalking on four spindly legs behind him. He offered little human interaction to go with his canapés, and he had no sense of humor that Julie could ferret out.

"Hey, I had a Sarge sighting this morning," Julie said. "I forgot to tell you. He was out on the porch of his HQ, just kind of staring at the sky. I waved. He turned and went back inside."

"That makes two appearances since we got joined up." Ranger tapped her forehead. "I don't think he's all there. I met one of the early augments, years ago. Doped to the gills all day, every day. Sarge looks the right age to have been in the last batch. The big success story."

The augmented Marine program had failed spectacularly a decade before – a super-soldier program that resulted in enhanced muscles, reflexes, mental focus, and off-the-charts rage issues. Julie dimly remembered learning something about it in high school. There'd been a propaganda video for the Mark V program, a squad of buzzcuts crushing Olympic records, throwing motorcycles around, and lifting pianos. The Mark V augments made a single deployment to the Panama Canal. The lucky ones had ended up dead. The others were flown home as war criminals, declared criminally insane, and locked up for their own safety.

Ranger frowned when Julie recounted the memory. "The Dame must have called in a few chips to get a superman sprung for her personal-security detail."

"Where are we stopping tonight?" Julie said.

"Officially, I have no idea. I am quote outside the security loop unquote. Unofficially, Gretchen hacked into Fish's itinerary and sent it to me this morning. Willow Springs. There's a park in Mark Twain National Forest."

"I wonder how you get a forest named after you."

"Maybe he planted it. Either way, we're going to be stopping there in about four hours." She coughed into the crook of her arm.

"How are you holding up?"

"Fair." Ranger probably had less to do in the Dame's outfit than any other caravan she'd ridden with. The rest should have been doing her good, but all it seemed to be doing was making her tense. "Little bored. Starting to wish something would happen, even though I know that's a really bad idea out here."

The population had always been spread thin between the Mississippi River and California. The Green Laws and other legislation to move people out of areas continually ravaged by drought, storm, earthquake, and fire had virtually emptied it. Trading a mighty piece of it to China in return for trillions in debt relief and cash had been a no-brainer. Now, past a certain point, caravans were completely on their own. Emergency services were scarce and responded at a crawl.

"Entertain yourself by coming up with more bullshit to share with the kids tonight," Julie said.

Once the younger members of the outfit had figured out how long Ranger had been on the road, she'd become a folk hero. At night, around the fire, they begged her to share war stories. Ranger usually complied. Most of her stories started with, "It wasn't that big a deal, but one time..."

"All my stories are one-hundred percent true," Ranger said.

Julie lifted an eyebrow. "You snuck into the Chinese States to rescue a political dissident?"

"Absolutely."

"Held off a squad of Texas Free-State Rangers until a caravan of refugees made it over the border?"

"It was more of a distraction than a stand-off, but sure."

"Drove Juniper into a tornado to rescue a family that had taken shelter under an overpass?"

"Might have exaggerated that one. Call it fifty-one percent true." She considered. "Maybe forty-nine. Forty on the outside." She pushed back her seat. "I'm taking a nap. Wake me up when you want to trade seats."

* * *

Ranger wrapped her jacket more tightly around herself and stretched her feet toward the fire. "I don't have any stories tonight," she said. "It's your turn."

Fire and Ice glanced at each other. A scruffy guy named Stoner shuffled his feet and poked at the fire. Julie used a mug of tea to cover her smile.

"Nothing?" Ranger said.

Stoner's partner, a model-pretty, long-limbed girl named Grass, looked flustered. "What do you want us to say? None of us have been at this very long."

"Just be interesting," Ranger said. "You can do that, can't you?"

It's like poking kittens with a stick. "How'd you two get hooked up?" Julie said.

Grass smiled. "We bought into the same weed-share. I was cubed up in Boston. He was paying his way with deliveries."

"Love at first toke?" Julie laughed.

Stoner colored. "Something like that."

"So, you were already tramping when you met her." Julie reached to refill her mug from the pot steaming by the fire.

"Not really. It was a company car. A full auto. I just rode along for security." Stoner pushed a shock of tangled hair out of his eyes. "I was squatting mostly. Abandoned buildings. Storage units. I, uh, liberated some of the stock, and got fired."

"He showed up at my door with his backpack over his shoulder," Grass said. "I let him in. My cube felt too small for two, so this seemed like a good thing to do for awhile."

Ranger whistled. "Serious commitment to give up your place like that."

The girl's eyes widened. "Oh, I didn't give it up. It's still there waiting for me."

Ranger's eyes narrowed. "How much pot did you guys 'liberate'? That little camper of yours didn't come cheap."

"It's the Dame's," Stoner said. "We can use it as long as we are part of her caravan."

Julie looked at Fire and Ice. "You guys said you were paying her off by working security for this trip."

"Everyone has their own thing going on with her, I guess," Fire said. "The Dame put most of this outfit on the road herself."

"I don't remember seeing anything about this on the volksnet," Ranger said.

Stoner snorted. "That antique? We were recruited directly. Well, Grass was. She got a message in ThirdEye."

"Just like that?" Ranger said. "Come join a tramp caravan to the Pacific?"

"Her people said I fit the profile," Grass said. "My agent took care of the rest."

"Your agent?" Ranger said.

Grass flushed. "It's only a bot. I don't get enough work to afford a real person."

Ranger stabbed a finger at her. "You're an actress." Her finger moved to Ice. "What about you two?"

"Not me. Fire's done some modeling."

"I did a commercial, too. Melo-Tonic." Fire glanced at Ice. "Before we met."

"Anyone else here a secret vid star?" Ranger said.

"Not me," Stoner said, "but King's done some motion-capture work and one of the other guys has a game stream." He looked at Grass for help.

"I think most of us worked in the biz at some point or other. King and I are represented by the same agency."

Conversation changed to work and the entertainment business.

Julie leaned close to Ranger. "You got your wish. You are not the center of attention."

"Yeah, but what the hell kind of party documentary hires actors?" Ranger said.

Alright, fine. "I have an idea how we can find out," Julie said.

FORTY-ONE

"Are you eating?" Carson S Riley said. "Your avatar is so pixelated you might as well be a tossed salad."

"I'm fine, Mom. Healthy. Well-fed," Julie said. "Doing yoga. I even learned to drive. Real driving, not just poke and proceed."

"Where are you staying? I don't want specifics. I gave you my word that I wouldn't look for you, but I am not immune to temptation."

"We're on the road a lot. All the time really. Right now, we're part of a caravan heading west."

"Living in a van by the river," Carson snorted, "and talking to me with smoke signals and lantern flashes. Truly the American Dream. What's next? A drum circle?"

Contacting her mother using her new ID and Ranger's arcane system had required a number of patches, bypasses, emulators, and reach-arounds. There was no telling how the final product looked on ThirdEye's quantum servers. Her mother's image, created by top-of-line gear in her new tower digs, had been reduced to a fuzzy, doll-sized holo-projection on the van's dashboard, recognizable mostly by her posture. "How's Mark?" Julie said.

Holo-Carson pushed back her hair. "I'm getting a cat. Dr Bevins wrote me a prescription. They say I need something to exercise my maternal instincts on now that my child has become a criminal."

233

Julie whistled. "That's expen–"

"My health insurance is covering most of it. I put an order into the clone bank a month ago. Male, short-haired Tabby, loving disposition, congenitally testicle-free. Probably what I should have done years ago, but your father convinced me that children would be fun."

"I was fun," Julie said.

"Maybe until you turned eleven or so, and a little bit between seventeen to twenty. All that hope and promise. The rest of the time you were a pain in the ass."

Julie took a long pull on the THC rig she'd loaded up in preparation for the call.

"What's that?" Carson said sharply. "What's that you just did? It looks like your head caught fire."

More smoke slipped from Julie's mouth and rolled around the van's ceiling. "I am consuming marijuana so that we might have a more enjoyable conversation."

Carson tsked. "You're gone for four months, and you're already doing illegal drugs."

"Pot's been legal since before you were born, Mother." *And I know damn well you have a healthy supply of trans-dermal THC in your medicine cabinet.* Distance or time had made the banter easier. Less personal. Below the nagging, Julie could hear fondness, even love. "It's good to hear your voice."

"This connection is so bad, you sound like a recycle unit breaking down a piano. I'm not even sure it's you."

"It's me, Mother."

"Are you coming back?"

"You said, and I quote, 'Don't you dare come crawling back.'"

"So don't crawl. Come back with your head held high. Are you seeing anyone these days?"

"Like a shrink or–"

"L.O.V.E.," Holo-Carson spelled carefully. "Or at least fucking. One of us should be."

"Not really." Julie had enjoyed a brief flirtation with King the week before, and while he was pretty it wasn't enough to make up for his narcissism. He was also dumb as a dead battery and not nearly sweet enough to make excuses for it. "Did you find the information I asked for?"

"Who says I even looked?"

"You can't help yourself. There's always the possibility you'll find a story in it. I'm just surprised it took you so long to dig something up."

"Two weeks." Carson sniffed. "I put Dallas on it. You remember Dallas?"

Dallas was Carson S Riley's 32-year-old intern. He'd been working for her for seven years, holding out a vain hope that a permanent position would open up at the network. "Yes. How is he?"

"Redundant. The network replaced him and all the other interns with an AI last week. A real one, not a toy. My instance is named Taylor. It's an idiot, but the network expects it'll take over my job in five or six years. Can you imagine?"

"How did Dallas handle being fired?"

"He overrode the safeties on his balcony and jumped off."

"Damn, Mom, I'm really sorry." Julie took a longer pull on the rig.

Holo-Carson broke into static and reformed. "He was technosexual. Did you know that? He was living with a sexbot, not that there's anything wrong with that, but who am I supposed to send flowers to? Or a card, even? He hated his parents. The sexbot had been customized to look like me, so I suppose I should be flattered but–"

"Where is it now?"

"The bot? It's in my spare bedroom. It didn't seem right to let them recycle it with the rest of his stuff. It's a surprisingly good conversationalist. I think I'll keep it around to pet the cat when I'm away."

"How do you feel about being replaced by an AI?"

Holo-Carson picked something up and held it to her mouth. A cocktail? A cup of tea? "I'll be retired by then. The fuck do I care?"

Definitely a cocktail. "Are you, like, training it?"

"Training sounds like I had a choice. Motion capture. It's been linked to my emplant. Probably listening to every word we say. Part of my latest contract renewal. I'm being paid to make myself – my entire profession – obsolete."

"Start working on your last show now. Set the whole network on fire on the way out the door."

"Maybe." The cocktail moved to the blur's mouth again. "I like you better now that you're gone. You sound good. I mean, you sound like a robot, but there's strength there. Like you got your shit together."

"I might have. A little. It's still a work in progress."

"Join the club." Holo-Carson lifted the cocktail again, tilting back her head to drain the glass. "The sexbot makes a good Old-Fashioned, too. Anyway, after Dallas got canned I put that cunt of an AI on it. Fucking thing put everything together in about five minutes. You want the scoop?"

The camp chair went careening across the ground again, and Ranger stalked after it. "It's not the damned chair's fault," she said, putting it back into place and sinking into it. "Keep going."

"The Dame's real name is Martha Kavanaugh," Julie said. "Stupid amounts of old money. Mostly media and power. Her grandfather was a judge or something. Nine months ago, she registered the word Glamping as a trademark and incorporated as Glamorous Tramp Productions, LLC."

"And she's making this whole trip into a vid series."

"And a ThirdEye game. But that's just the start. Eventually, it's all going to be about adventure excursions. In a couple of months, after the series goes live, she'll sell tickets to be part of the next season. She gets money and footage for the show, sells advertising, and her customers will get a safe, catered safari through Old America."

Ranger looked as if she wanted to kick the chair again.

"Fish Eye is the director. His real name is Christos Binder. He was part of the crew on *Just Plain Volks*."

"And based on that fucking puff piece he thinks he knows how the world works." Ranger rubbed her face with both hands. "Plus, our security team is a bunch of porn stars and motion-capture actors and their boss is a headcase."

"Mom didn't know anything about Sarge."

"She doesn't have to. No one has seen him in days. He's probably on a drug holiday in that truck of his. Plugged into a nice, calm VR scenario. He's useless."

"I wouldn't want to fight him."

"We'd have to wake him up and unplug him first. This is not good. We'll be in Guymon in a couple of days."

Guymon, Oklahoma, was the last stop before the caravan threaded the hundred-mile needle eye between New China and Independent Texas.

"What will happen there?" Julie said.

"Probably nothing. It was all robofarms and natural-gas wells the last time I was there. The park is at an old animal refuge nearby. There's a semi-permanent market there. We can stock up. It's the travel days after that I'm worried about." Ranger scratched her arm absently. The limb was covered with a patchwork of dirty, discolored days-old med patches and bright, fresh ones right off the roll. "I don't need this right now."

The volksnet was heavy with posts about the dangers of running the Panhandle. With routes south and north blocked by border security, the only way out was through. Solo travelers and small groups were advised to avoid it until they could join or form a big enough caravan to make the passage safely.

"From a distance, we probably look pretty secure," Julie said. Fish Eye was a stickler for security, keeping up a full flight of drones every night and sending his crew out on foot patrols. If it weren't for his weird obsession with clearing every obstacle they encountered instead of going around, they might have made it to the Pacific already.

"I don't like it," Ranger said. "If we get hit, it's all going to come apart. People are going to get hurt."

"I'm surprised no one's done this before," Julie said. "*Just Plain Volks* has been out for years. I know it's mostly bullshit, but maybe a regular show and some tourism is a good idea. At least people will finally see how bad things are out here."

Ranger's face tightened. "Bad out here? It's a thousand times worse in there!"

"In some ways, yeah," Julie said. "But–"

Ranger pointed east at some unknowable metropolis. "Tramps are not society's victims! I thought you'd figured that out by now. We chose this. We don't need to be saved!" The camp chair tumbled on the ground again. This time one of the sides snapped free. "And we're not entertainment. This is our lives, not some kind of a freak show!" Her face twisted. "Not some debutante's disaster porn!"

"That's not what I meant." Julie's chair rocked as she stood, but it did not fall. "But there are problems out here. We've seen them. Sometimes people need help. Think about Circleville. They didn't have to die that way."

"If you'd rather die in a cube, I'll drop you off at the next city. I'll stay out here where I'm free!"

"Free?" Julie laughed. "Free to eat bad food and wear dirty clothes and not shower for days at a time, maybe. Free to make your kids take poison and live off piss water." She jabbed her finger at Ranger. "You are sure in hell free to cough your lungs into bloody scraps."

Ranger's smile was cold. "Is it too tough out here for you, 'Burb? Maybe your mother will buy you one of the Dame's safari packages for your birthday. You can travel west in style." Her breath caught, and she fumbled for her inhaler.

"Maybe if we were on a safari you'd go see the doctor." It was Julie's turn to point. "It's right over there. Big white trailer with the snake thing on it."

"I'm not doing this with you again." Ranger took a shuddery pull on the inhaler. "My ride, my rules, rook. You don't like it, feel free to stick out your thumb."

Julie felt dizzy. "Maybe I will." *Call Neutral Corners!*

Ranger straightened her back like someone had dropped an ice cube down it. "Maybe you should. Better do it now before it really gets tough."

FORTY-TWO

The rugged little sportswagon rocked through a washout. The driver turned to look at her rear passenger. "You should talk to her."

"I don't want to talk to her," Julie said. *She threw me out. And left all my shit outside on the table and changed the access codes to the van.*

Fire looked at Ice, who shrugged helplessly.

"It's not that we don't like you," Fire said, "but the wagon's too small for three for the long haul. And we're going to want to have sex soon. Maybe even tonight."

"Definitely tonight," Ice said.

Julie's craned her neck to look out the side window. The backseat of the little car had been folded down into a bed, and she was riding prone among the duo's worldly possessions. "Once we stop, I'm out of your hair, and you can fuck all you want."

"What are you going to do?" Fire said.

No idea. Riding in the middle of the caravan with Fire and Ice, Julie hadn't laid eyes on Ranger for nearly a day and half. She'd seen the van, of course. It was hard to miss the old eyesore among the sleek and modern vehicles of the Dame's rolling reality show.

"It's easy to get on each other's nerves in such close quarters." Ice looked at Fire as if seeking permission to continue. "Our first fight was really bad. This was maybe four months ago, in the old car, which was even smaller than—"

240

"Ranger and I are not a couple, and this wasn't our first fight." Julie lowered her head back to the pile of mostly clean laundry she was using as a pillow. "I appreciate what you're trying to do, but it's complicated. I'd explain it, but it's not all my baggage to share. Get it?"

"Yeah," Ice said.

"Just get me to the park, and I'll figure things out from there."

She was free. A legal adult, at least on paper, with money in the bank and more, thanks to her enrollment in Basic, on the way. She finally had a few options. Find another ride to the Pacific. Maybe head back east and see if Coop's offer was still good. Get a cube somewhere. Go back to Boston. *Don't crawl*, her mother had said, *come back with your head held high.*

"Is there a plot twist scheduled for today?" Ice said.

Fire's mohawk shook. "Not that I know of."

Julie tuned back in. "What are you talking about?"

Fire glanced at her in the rearview. "You aren't on the security team. It's need to know."

"Whatever. It's not a big deal." Ice turned to face Julie. "Every couple of days King gets a few miles ahead of us and causes an accident. Drops a tree on the road or knocks over a fence. Something like that. Fisheye calls it a plot twist."

"So all those times we stopped to clear the road..."

"Plot twists. Most of them." Ice grinned. "They'll look great in the Dame's party doc."

Julie frowned. "Here's a plot twist for you. She's not making a party doc. It's a reality series." She told them what she'd learned from her mother.

It was Fire's turn to frown. "I better ping my agent. I should be getting paid more if it's not for private use."

"You better get a copy of that contract," Julie said. "I'll bet money there's more they haven't told you."

* * *

According to the volksnet, the park in Guymon, Oklahoma, was the only tramp gathering that could be seen from orbit with the naked eye, and that was only because everything around it was so damned dark. The first thing Julie saw was the Ferris wheel, LED lit and turning slowly against a soft glow on the horizon.

Ice pointed at it. "We've got to try it! Do you think it's safe?"

"Good luck finding someone to sue if it's not," Fire said. They squinted at the car's navigation screen. "We are officially off the map."

The land the park had grown up on was federal, but control over it was a snarl of international treaties and backroom handshakes. Hemmed in from the north by Chinese security fences and drones and from the south by Independent Texas border patrols, the park – a mishmash of tents, trailers, and tiny houses – perched on the shifting rim of the New Dust Bowl, semi-independent and ever ready to take flight.

Extremely awkward and slow flight. There wasn't a permanent structure in sight. Everything had come in on wheels and on wheels it remained, ready to be packed up and towed away at a moment's notice. However, some of it had been parked so long and rebuilt so high that it would take a miracle of engineering and physics to set it in motion and keep it upright.

Julie made her goodbyes and thank-yous and slung her bag over her shoulder. An old man sat in a lawn chair to one side of the gate leading from the visitors' lot to the heart of the park. "Hello, the fire," she said.

The man lifted a hand in greeting. "Welcome to the park, young traveler! What can I do for you?"

"Food, shower, and a place to stay for a couple of days. Not necessarily in that order."

He squinted at the circle of vehicles Julie had just left. "That's a mighty pretty outfit to walk away from. Lover's spat?"

Julie shook her head. "This is just my stop. How are the roads looking?"

"Slow. Folks are coming in and only heading out in bigger groups, so they're staying longer. Good for the local economy as long as their money holds out. Strains the infrastructure, though." The man reached into the cooler beside him and pulled a beer from the swamp of ice inside. He popped the tab and took a swig. "You'd best walk down the Midway, where all the lights are. Toward the end there's a pole with paper tacked all over it. Dig around, you can find a place to stay cheap. Showers, too. It's hard to avoid food." He patted his stomach. "Trip over your shoelace, and your hands will land on five or six food trucks. Best one, in my opinion, is Jebena. It's Ethiopian. Owner is a real asshole and the hours are screwy, but the food is fantastic."

Julie followed the directions onto the Midway. She scented it long before she saw it, a mix of cooking smells and hot printer stock. She stopped short when she got to the top of the row, which stretched ahead and out of sight. Everything she'd ever and never wanted was on display in the market stalls lining each side. The space between was filled with customers, drifting with the current mostly but occasionally moving with purpose. The purposeful ones were the locals. They knew which stall they wanted and where to go. The rest were travelers and tramps like her.

She smiled. *I feel like I'm skipping school.* Back at the caravan, Ice, Fire, and the rest were unpacking and setting up camp. Someone would be building a fire. Ranger would be... *Fuck Ranger!* Meantime, Julie was standing in front of a modified tiny house that smelled amazing and sold – she puzzled out the hand-lettered sign – "Real Texas BBQ." Considering the ban on meat from Texas, at least two of the words on the sign had to be an outright lie. She walked over to check.

"What'll be, hon?" The woman inside wiped sweat from her forehead with a terry-cloth band wrapped around her wrist.

"What's safe?" Julie said.

"Safe?" The woman blinked at her. "It's all safe. Anyone gets sick off my food I'll lose my spot." She pointed at a printout on the wall. "I've been here for nearly five years."

"Is it real meat? From an animal?" Julie had eaten chicken a few times, steak once, and fish twice. Her mother could have afforded to eat it more often but avoided it on principle.

The woman stuck her head out the order-here window and looked both ways before answering. "Sometimes. I got a couple of boys keeping an eye out for livestock that wanders across the border. Happens more often than you think. Patrol drones are calibrated for people not cows."

"I just need some dinner," Julie said. "Nothing too expensive."

The woman's price netted Julie three pieces of some kind of barbecued protein, a side of beans, spicy greens, and a piece of cornbread as big as the palm of her hand. She found a table off to the side and sat down to people watch and do some math. If all her meals were going to be as expensive as the first, her savings weren't going to last long, and she still had to put a roof over her head. The temperature was fair, and it wasn't likely to rain, but dust storms were common. Waking up buried in powdered dirt didn't sound the least bit fun. Julie yawned. She spotted a couple of people she recognized from the caravan, but no one she knew well. They'd either ducked out on their camp chores or rushed through them to get to the Midway. Just from her table Julie could see a body-mod shop, a metal printer, three food stalls, a tarot-card reader, and a shop that specialized in goods smuggled down from New China. How a buyer could tell the "genuine" silk scarves from something a printer had produced, she had no idea. *Maybe the real thing smells different?*

Julie pulled out her phone. The park had an independent network and an electronic bulletin board where residents and tramps could post goods and services to trade. She looked up lodgings and winced at the results. Staying in Guymon with nothing but Basic supporting her would be a fool's quest. She needed a job. She searched for postings on the board. There were plenty, but most were offering money or housing in exchange for sex work, and she wasn't nearly that desperate, yet.

She tossed her trash into a nearby recycler and shouldered her bag again. The old guy had said something about a pole with paper tacked onto it, somewhere at the end of the Midway.

The Ferris wheel wasn't the only entertainment on offer. Julie passed by a corral of rusty-but-running bumper cars, some kind of death trap that shot its riders into the air then dropped them, and a strip club on wheels. Clean-limbed examples of human beauty stood on the little porch out front and whistled to passersby. Julie recognized the name of the place from her job search. She kept walking.

At the end of the row a thick wooden pole had been pounded into the dry earth and riddled with staples and tacks. A dozen or so paper fliers fluttered there. Julie perused them carefully.

Cheaper housing to be sure and jobs that fit her skill set better. Julie pulled one off the pole and folded it into her pocket. "Bartender/bouncer wanted. Small room included," it said. She turned to retrace her steps.

FORTY-THREE

Julie paid for the basket of tempura and took it back to her tiny room above the bar. There was barely enough space inside for her and the roll-out mattress, but it had a lock, a light, and access to the bathroom downstairs. Home for now, and her next shift started in four hours. She rolled out the bed to take a nap. The first night's work hadn't been overly difficult – she'd been mostly running drinks and pulling beers – but Yurts So Good stayed open from 8pm to 4am seven days a week, and Julie was the only employee.

When she woke, the owner Ray – just Ray, he said, none of those stupid nicknames – was getting ready to open. He grunted when he saw her coming down the tight spiral staircase from the loft.

"Any questions?" he said.

"As long as it's pretty much the same as last night, I think I'm good."

He grunted again. Ray looked older than the dirt he'd pounded his yurt stakes into fifteen years before. He held the record for longest operating stall on the Midway and lived in a rotting tiny house two rows behind it. He said he'd posted the job opening because he wasn't up to working seven days a week anymore.

"Why don't you just shut down a couple of nights?" Julie had asked him.

He'd stared at her like she'd just shat on the floor. "Don't want to lose my spot, 'course."

There were plenty of shops among the residential rows, too, but the big money was on the Midway, where business was all about foot traffic and getting as much money out of visiting outfits as possible. Space on the Midway was rent-free and first come, first served, but the Chamber of Commerce had a long list of eviction-worthy infractions and a squad of roughnecks to enforce it.

Julie got to work unlocking the cabinets and coolers that served as the bar's infrastructure. Ray used the same code for all of his locks, 2074. It was even the password to the jukebox and cocktail maker. Julie punched it into the latter and watched for a few seconds as it ran through a self-diagnostic.

"You wouldn't believe how much that cost me," Ray told her for the third or fourth time.

"Says it's low on vermouth," Julie said. "What's vermouth?"

Ray showed her where he kept it and taught her how to refill the machine. "Should be a quiet night," he said. "The only outfit parked here right now is that rich bitch, and her people can't be bothered with us."

That suited Julie just fine. The Dame and her convoy of reality stars were scheduled for a "Four R" stop: several days of rest, recreation, repair, and refueling. Plenty of time to create and record lots of drama and pathos for the film. Julie had spotted more people from the outfit shopping on the Midway but had thus far avoided conversation.

"Pour me a beer, willya?" Ray took a seat at the end barstool. "A dark one."

Julie slid the glass in front of him.

"Let's see…" Ray scratched his chest. "It's Thursday. We'll say Monday is your first solo, OK?"

"As long as I get a couple of nights off in there."

Ray sipped the beer and made a face. "I swear this shit used to be better."

"Do you want something different?" Julie said.

"Nah. Just get me a bowl of peanuts and turn on the vids. There's a game on."

That night Julie worked the bar while Ray and most of the customers ignored her in favor of the action on the vid screen. It was the North American Wizard War championship: USA versus the Chinese Protectorate. Julie tried to care, but watching the teams' avatars running around the play map casting spells at each other just wasn't doing it for her.

Ray, however, was ecstatic. He cheered every point the American team made and urged his customers to drink more and cheer along. His response to one play was so enthusiastic he knocked over his beer – his sixth, if Julie had the count right. His semi-toothed smile was one of the ugliest things Julie had ever seen, but there was no malice in it. "I used to be an e-thlete, believe it or not. I played 'Belt Pirates' back in the '30s. Made a bunch of money."

"What happened?"

Ray swore. "Life. Kids. Bad decisions about all of it. Now I'm here." He smiled again. "But here's not so bad, right?"

Julie reached for a towel to clean up Ray's spilled beer. *Yeah, not so bad.*

FORTY-FOUR

Julie stowed the roll-out and did yoga stretches in the tiny space it left behind. The bar downstairs was quiet. Ray was probably sleeping the night off in his moldering house. She'd practically had to carry him there after closing and was surprised the floor of the thing still supported his weight. The house still had wheels but there was no way it would survive a move.

She climbed down to the bar's tiny kitchen, made a sandwich and pulled a beer for herself. She ate at the bar, perched atop one of the much-repaired stools. Yurts So Good looked a lot different empty and by daylight. The age and grime showed more clearly. The dishwasher's work on the plate and glass she used was fair at best.

Julie propped her elbows on the bar and rested her head on her hands. Ray was a skuzzier version of Coop. A few beers into her first solo shift he'd introduced her to the crowd and said she'd be his successor, taking the bar over after he'd gone "tits up."

The customers, most of them around Ray's age, cheered and ordered more drinks to celebrate. *What is it about old people that makes them think we want their shit when they die?* Julie washed her breakfast dishes by hand and checked the locks before heading into the residential section. She had a tip she wanted to check out.

Fifteen minutes and four hours' pay later she was soaking in deep tub of hot water. Her clothes were being laundered in the next room, and there was a thick robe and towel on the chair next to her. She let the water dissolve the knots in her back and shoulders. A middle-aged woman wearing an eyepatch had told her about the place the night before, swearing up and down that it was the best bathhouse in the park. Julie wasn't sure what quantified as best, but the place was clean, the water was hot, and there didn't appear to be any cameras spying on her. It would certainly do and was definitely a big step up from nothing or the tepid stall shower she'd paid to use the day before. She needed it. Sleep hadn't been coming easy the last few days, and what little she'd found had been visited by Circleville dreams. *Resentment of the doomed.* The kids especially haunted her nights with empty eyes and wet mouths.

The Dame's outfit would resume its trek west soon. *Not a call. Not a message. Not a post on volksnet.* It was entirely possible she'd already been replaced in Juniper's copilot seat. She was tempted to use her phone to get a peek through one of the drones but didn't know how she'd react if her credentials had already been erased. Julie sank deeper into the tub and tried not to think about any of it. The bath bombs she'd purchased sizzled as they dissolved and released a cocktail of euphorics and muscle relaxants into the water. *Bliss.*

It was over too quickly. Cleaner in body, if not in mind, Julie retrieved her things, dressed, checked the charges on her weapons, and headed back out to explore.

Ray drew her aside at the start of the shift. "Could get a little rough tonight," he said. "Some boys parked today been kicked out of every other decent place. Watchtower tipped me off."

Watchtower was the old man Julie had met at the gate. When he wasn't on duty he was a Yurts So Good customer and got half-price drinks for keeping Ray in the know about the comings and goings in the visitor's lot.

"Why do you let them in?" Julie said.

Ray's eyebrows shot up. "They been kicked out of everywhere else! Where do you expect them to go?"

Part of Julie's job description included crowd control. Her police-training and utility belt full of weapons had tipped the balance during her brief interview with Ray. "How will I recognize them?"

"They look real rough. Two or three of them, I guess. Men. Bigger than me."

There were peanuts among the bowls of mixed nuts lining the bar that could wrestle Ray to the ground.

"Anything else? Hairstyle? Scars or tattoos? Gang colors?"

"Some of 'em have got hair." Ray tapped his nose. "Some don't."

Julie kept her belt around her waist instead of hanging it behind the bar like she usually did and stared hard at everyone who came in the door. They all looked rough. A lot of them were men. Most of them, even the women, were bigger than Ray. The majority were bald or balding, just like the night before and the night before that. When midnight rolled around she started to relax.

"Give me a beer."

Without looking at the speaker, Julie pointed at the holo menu glowing and turning above the bar. "Four kinds. Which one?"

"A lager."

The man grabbed her wrist when she set the glass in front of him. "Did you used to work for Kinks?"

Julie twisted her wrist free. "Touch me again, I break your thumb."

The man narrowed his eyes. "Naw, you didn't work for us. You were with that bitch got our girls all riled up."

Julie smiled at a regular who was settling his tab before responding. "You see her around here?"

The man – Julie recognized him now as the one who'd told her about the showers – drank some beer. He made a face. "Nope. But you were with her, sure as shit."

"Well, I'm not anymore. Now I work here. You need anything else?"

"Good for now." He sipped at his beer and moved toward a cluster of men standing near the jukebox. Julie kept an eye on them while she filled orders. From the way Shower Man was gesturing and nodding, she'd become the topic of their conversation.

"You know them?"

Julie glanced over to the speaker, barely taking her eyes off the men. "They the ones you told Ray about?"

Watchtower sneaked a look at them. "Yep. They've come into the park five or six times over the past month or so. Selling salvage, or so they say."

"I'm surprised you keep letting them in." Julie put a fresh beer in front of the old man unbidden.

He reached for it. "People want what they got. Besides, it takes a ruling by the Chamber of Commerce to keep someone out, and they ain't done anything too bad, yet."

"If they make trouble, do you have my back?"

"What? No! I'm way too old for that shit."

"I thought you were a security guard."

"Hell, no. I'm just a greeter." He looked into his beer, which was already half empty. "But if it gets rough I can call a couple of folks I know."

Julie ran drinks and pulled beers for another hour, watching the clock. If they were going to do something, they might wait until it was closer to closing, when the bar had fewer people in it. *Fewer witnesses.* On the other hand, they might want an audience that could testify to how bad ass they were.

Ray waved her over. "You keep moving so slow, customers are going to complain."

Julie pointed to Kinks' old pal with her head. "Those are the guys Watch told you about. I think they're going to try something."

"Try what? There are two dozen people in here." Ray squinted blearily at them. "They look alright to me. They paying?"

Julie nodded.

"Well, leave them alone. Let them have their fun long as they don't go busting the place up. You know how much I paid for that drink machine."

Shower Man stopped her on the way back to the bar. "Kinks was a friend of mine. You know what happened to him?"

"Don't know. Don't care." Julie tucked her thumbs into her utility belt, her fingers close to the stunner on the right side and the collapsible baton on the left.

"You and that bitch partner of yours took everything he had. Stunned him, kicked him, took his money, trashed his ride." Outrage and anger looked natural on his face; it had been there a lot. "What are you going to do about that?"

"Nothing," Julie said, "and I'm going to need you to go back to your pals there and calm down. If you can't–"

"Fuck you!" Shower Man swung his glass at Julie's face. She blocked it with her left arm, and he slumped to the ground with a whimper like a kicked dog. He lay on the ground and quietly pissed himself.

Ranger was standing behind him, her stunner already cycling up for another shot. She squinted at him. "Do we know him from somewhere?"

"What're you doing here?" Julie said.

"I came to apologize. I said some stupid things I didn't really mean and overreacted to some stuff you said."

"You're not wrong," Julie said. "I think I said some stupid shit, too."

"We're leaving tomorrow morning, and I really want you riding beside me."

"That it?"

"And I miss you." She rubbed her forearms. "And the patches aren't working at all anymore. I might need someone I trust to roll me across the finish line."

"And?"

She rolled her eyes. "And I'll see the damned doctor."

Shower Man groaned and rose to his elbows. Julie pulled her stunner and shot him in the back. He went down again. "Ray," she called, "I'm sorry, but I quit."

FORTY-FIVE

Two days down the road, at a park outside Questa, New Mexico, Ranger woke Julie from a lovely dream by shoving her feet out of the driver's seat and screaming at the navigation system. "Fucking start!" She upped the ante by slamming the dashboard with both fists.

"What's happening?" Julie pulled her feet out of Ranger's way.

"Very bad shit!" Ranger said.

While Ranger battered the dashboard, Julie blinked her eyes clear. Far to the right, directly across the defensive circle from the van, King's fast little scout car was awash with flames. It wasn't alone. "What happened?"

"Fire bombs. I saw them hit." The biodiesel engine woke up angry. It didn't sound right, and it made the van rattle. Ranger laid on the horn, and put Juniper in reverse, ramming the car behind them hard. "That should help wake 'em up." She shifted gears. The van surged forward, tagging the trailer in front of them, and made for the closest exit. Ranger leaned on the horn again. "Make sure we're not followed!"

"Fire bombs?" Julie stared at the backup screen dumbly; it was blank. "Wait, is this even real?" She'd filled Ranger in on Fish Eye's little plot twists.

The van bottomed out as Ranger took a speed bump without slowing. "We'll get clear and circle around to take a look."

Ranger kept the headlights off. After two hundred yards or so, she took a right turn into an unused lot overlooking the park and pulled up to the guardrail. "Hold here until I signal." She disabled the overhead light and crept her door open. Ranger bent low and jogged to the guardrail. In a minute she waved Julie out, gesturing for her to stay down. Julie crawled into place beside her, wishing she'd grabbed some gloves. The air was fiercely cold, and the wind was picking up.

The attackers were moving their vehicles into a loose formation around the trapped outfit. At least half of the caravan was in flames.

"Looks real to me." Ranger gripped the guardrail.

"Why is no one running?" Julie said. "Where's security?!"

"See if you can get a link to the drones we lent Sarge. Maybe we can see what's happening."

Julie pulled her phone out of her jacket pocket. "My phone's down," she said. "What the fuck is going on?"

"A hack. Or a virus, maybe," Ranger said. "We would gotten an early warning otherwise. The van's not running right, either."

The driver's side door of one of the burning vehicles swung open and a figure toppled out. It could have been Fire. It could have been anyone. It rolled to its feet and aimed something at the attackers. Before it could fire, the figure was brought down by a swift whisper of flechettes.

Julie gasped. "Are we going to do anything?"

Ranger shook her head. "There's too many of them. Nothing we can do but lie low and try to help the survivors."

Julie clutched Ranger's arm. "There won't be any survivors!"

Ranger shook Julie's hand off and focused on the devastation below like she was recording it. "There are vehicles missing from the line."

Julie glanced back at the van; the driver's side door was still open. She ran for it. Ranger grabbed for her and ended up sprawled on the pavement.

She flung herself behind the wheel and pulled the headlight switch. With the other hand she searched for the horn. Juniper's high beams showed like twin cones through the smoke. Julie pumped the horn like she was giving CPR.

Ranger yanked the passenger door open and climbed into the seat. "You got your wish, asshole," she said, panting. "Two scouts coming this way. Drive!"

Julie wheeled the van around so the hood was pointing back toward the exit. She dropped it in drive and jammed her foot on the accelerator pedal. Juniper's tires squealed as Julie turned right out of the exit. "Where?"

"Map's not working. Get on the Interstate!" Ranger said.

"You said Juniper didn't like the Interstate!"

"Just do it! Right there!" She pointed.

The on-ramp came up fast. The van's worn tires protested at another hard right, and it heeled way over as they took the curve. Juniper seldom moved faster than thirty miles per hour, and as the speedometer crept toward sixty, the engine shuddered and screamed. The van fought hard, tugging against Julie's hands like it was trying to crash them into the guardrail.

Ranger swore. "I never thought I'd be traveling with anyone stupid enough to purposely piss off a raider gang."

"We couldn't just leave them!"

"You didn't save them, Jules. You just made sure everyone was in trouble."

Julie closed her mouth and focused on the road. A reflection from the side mirror dazzled her, and she glanced to see it being filled by the grille of a triple-decker passenger bus. The bus flashed its lights at them, and Juniper's rear-collision alarm sounded.

"The bus wants you to speed up," Ranger said.

"I can't go any faster!"

"Hopefully, they'll figure it out and go around instead of coming right through."

Modern vehicles were rigged to keep track of the road and each other via satellite uplink and constant check-ins. Juniper couldn't do any of that. The bus likely didn't even recognize her as a vehicle; she was just a slow-moving obstacle. It slid into the passing lane and accelerated past. Juniper rocked violently in the wake and tried, more intently than ever, to drive herself off the road. Julie fought the wheel and kept her in the lane. Barely. "We need to get off this."

Ranger craned her neck to study both side mirrors. "Not yet. I can't tell if they're following or not."

A robotruck hauling a half-dozen trailers rocketed by, nearly sending them into a spin and tumble. Julie's hands were white-knuckled on the steering wheel. A harsh buzz from the dashboard made her heart jump. Every warning light there was flashing orange or red. The engine hitched. Ranger swore. "Looks like I'm outvoted. Let's hope we can make it to the next exit."

Juniper stalled out as they made the exit, and the steering wheel seemed to gain forty pounds.

"Don't touch the brakes," Ranger said. "Coast as long as you can. We need to get off the road."

Momentum took them into the parking lot of an abandoned gas station. Ranger got out almost before they came to a stop and started pushing from the rear. She didn't make much progress until Julie hopped out and added her weight and muscle to the job. They switched places, and Julie pushed from the back as Ranger steered and pushed from the driver's door. They managed to get the van up the sloping parking lot and behind the building.

"Now what?" Julie said once she could catch her breath.

"We keep moving. Grab your sleeping bag, a light, and some food."

"We're leaving the van?"

"They could be right behind us. We can move. She can't."

Julie stuffed the sleeping bag, a couple of water bottles,

and some food packets into her backpack. "What about your oxygen?"

Ranger's appointment with the caravan medic had resulted in a tank of pressurized air and a breathing mask to wear when she slept.

"Too heavy. Leave all the doors unlocked," Ranger said. "I'd rather come back to an empty van than one that's been smashed open."

Ranger led away from the roadway, down a slope that ended back at the Interstate. Moving as fast as they could, they picked their way down the hill and helped each other over the animal fence. Traffic whipped by only feet away.

"Are we looking for a ride?" Julie said.

"No one will stop. We're crossing. When I say run, run."

Seconds ticked by as she stared at the Interstate traffic.

"Run!" she said.

The backpack thumped against Julie's back as she sprinted across eight lanes. Ranger's feet pounded behind her. She slammed into Julie, knocking her into the divider. Julie sat up in time to get a face full of dust as a freight truck hurtled by less than a meter from her feet.

Then they did it again. Pell-mell across another eight lanes and another gasping sprawl.

"Get up!" Ranger's voice gurgled in her throat, and she spit something onto the ground. "Up the hill! Now!"

There was chain-link fence at the top of hill. They helped each other over it, and Ranger sagged, leaning her back against the fence for support. She collapsed into a coughing fit.

"We need to get you inside," Julie said. "This cold air isn't helping anything. And it's starting to snow." A rusty billboard loomed about a hundred feet ahead and thirty feet above, lit with a single floodlight. The sign welcomed them to "Store-Eaze."

"I'm going to look around," Julie said.

Ranger grabbed her leg. "Watch out," she said between wheezes, "cameras."

Store-Eaze was five or six rows of single-story buildings with wide metal roll-up doors, bordered by chain-link fence and freaky shadows. The few cameras she saw had been smashed.

There was an oasis of civilization near the front gate, and Julie snuck up as close as she dared. An older man with his feet up on a desk faced a bank of vid screens inside. Only a few of the screens were on and those were tuned to entertainment programming.

Bent double, Julie slid along the buildings back to where she'd left Ranger. She ran her hands along the bottom of each door she passed and stopped when she found one without a padlock. She pulled up on the door's handle. It moved. Julie let go of it and started to jog, counting the doors as she went.

Ranger had crawled into the shadows, and it took Julie a couple of minutes to find her. She was wheezing again and didn't respond when Julie touched her shoulder. Julie whispered her name a few times and tried shaking her. Nothing. She grabbed her under her arms and started pulling.

Ranger woke and tried to help. Her efforts set off another round of coughing, and she passed out again. The next time Julie pulled her though a lighted area she saw blood around her mouth.

When they got back to the unlocked door, Julie opened it just enough to roll Ranger under it. She squeezed under it, too, snagging the edge of the door with her backpack. The flimsy material tore, dropping everything inside onto the storage unit's floor.

Julie unrolled her sleeping bag by touch and squeezed the tab that activated the heating circuits. She took off Ranger's outer clothes and wrestled her inside. As the bag warmed up, Julie inventoried the rest of the stuff in the backpacks: several packets of food, a couple of bottles of water, a tin cup, and a bar of soap. Ranger had been smarter about packing her rucksack. Along with her sleeping bag and some food, she'd packed the small camp stove, a squeeze-lamp, her poncho, and a collapsible fuel jug.

Julie pumped the squeeze-lamp and got a cold, blue glow that barely reached the walls. She grunted. "Better than nothing." The storage unit wasn't empty. One corner was piled high with trash, another looked to have been used as a sleeping nook.

Ranger's sleeping bag had reached the cozy point, but she hadn't woken up. Each of her breaths ended in a gasping whine. Julie shook her. "Can you hear me?"

Ranger stirred. Julie held up the light and looked around the storage unit for a good place to set up the stove. "I'll boil some water." All the tea was back in the van or, worse, ground into the dirt under some gang-member's boot.

There was a bench to one side that was perfect for the stove. Julie set the little burner up and started heating some water. Next to the bench was a cardboard box full of water bottles, some full, others empty.

The stove and the heat escaping Ranger's sleeping bag were taking the edge off the temperature. Julie explored the sleeping nook she'd found. A thin mattress with a sleep sack folded neatly in the center. Next to it was a backpack, containing a dozen food packs and clothing.

"We'll just hope they don't come home tonight," Ranger said.

Julie turned her head to see her. Ranger's skin looked like wax and her eyes were so shadowed they looked bruised.

"Do you think they will?"

Ranger shrugged inside the sleeping bag. The movement made her look like a convulsing caterpillar. "Either way, we can't stay here long. Is the door secure?"

"You can only do that from the outside."

"Give me some of that water."

Julie took the tin cup off the stove and passed it to Ranger. She stuck an arm out of the sleeping bag to take it.

"I should've listened to you," Julie said.

Ranger closed her eyes, her face contorted like she was having a sharp pain. "Maybe I should have listened to you. There couldn't have been that many of them."

"Can we go back?"

"Not tonight. We'll make the hard decisions in the morning."

FORTY-SIX

There was just enough light outside the storage unit to let Julie see the silhouette of two legs and an arm as the door slid up.

"Ranger?" she said. "Is that you?"

The person outside froze in place. Ranger coughed weakly from her corner.

The stunner was in Julie's utility belt, but she was no longer sure where that was. She'd gotten up to pee, and the sleeping bag had snagged on her foot for a step or two. When she'd finished she had crawled into the bag where it lay and went back to sleep.

"Who's there?" It was a man's voice.

"Don't come in here," Julie said. She slid her hands and sleeping-bag-trapped feet across the floor in search of her weapons.

"Who are you?" he said.

Julie found her backpack and shoved it aside. "We needed a place to–"

"My rent's all paid up. You got no business being in here."

Shit. "Look, I'm sorry. My friend's sick–"

The man squatted down beside the door and shone a bright light into Julie's face.

Julie froze. The man had less than five feet to cross once he rolled under the door. The back of her head hit the floor as the weight of him landed on her chest. The door slammed to the ground in his wake.

The man dropped the flashlight and scrabbled for Julie's arms.

Julie tried to push him away, but the side of her face blew up. He had hit her with his fist, a rock, maybe a planet. His flashlight rolled and lit up an empty corner. Julie kicked, but her legs were trapped in the sleeping bag.

He hit her in the mouth. She gagged. She was drowning in blood. His knees were on her chest. She couldn't breathe, but her heart was leaping like she was running a marathon. She gritted her teeth and tried to force energy into arms and legs. It didn't help. She was moving through water, and all she could do was gasp. Something cracked. Cracked again.

Julie stumbled into darkness.

The side of face throbbed with her heartbeat.

"Lie still," Ranger said.

There was something pooling in the back of Julie's throat. It made her cough. "I can't see."

"Give me a second." Ranger pumped the squeeze-lamp, and the little blue light came on.

One of Julie's eyes wouldn't open right. "What happened?" She couldn't get her tongue around the "d" sound.

"You got beat up pretty good."

Julie tried to answer, and her stomach leapt out of her mouth. Ranger rolled her to her side, and darkness smacked Julie in the face again. When Julie woke again she was warm and could smell puke. She groaned.

Ranger's face wavered back into view. "Don't move." She held the light close to Julie's face. "Your pupils are dilating equally. That's good." She moved away. Julie resisted the urge to turn her head to see what she was doing. "Try to drink this. We'll go slow."

Julie drank the whole cup of water one little sip at a time. Ranger smoothed a patch on the back of her hand. "It will take the edge off the pain."

The squeeze-lamp dimmed – it was only good for a few minutes at a time – and Ranger pumped it up again. "You hit the back of your head pretty good on the floor, but I think the sleeping bag caught some of it." She stroked Julie's hair.

Julie fought to stay awake.

"Rest for a while," Ranger said. Her voice was breathy. "I'll make you some soup."

Morning light was creeping through the thin gap running across the top of the door frame. *Morning. After such a long night of...*

Julie tried to sit up.

"Don't," Ranger said. "Not yet." She put her hand on Julie's chest. "How are you feeling?"

Julie moved her arms and legs and carefully rotated her head. "Better," she said. The right side of her jaw popped, and she put her hand up to touch that side of her face. "My neck hurts, but my face is the worst."

"Does it feel like you have any teeth loose?"

Julie probed at them with her tongue. "No." There was a lump on the back of her head. It hurt when she touched it. "What happened?"

"A guy came in and attacked you."

"After that."

"I took care of it." Ranger turned to fuss with the stove. "We can stay here until it gets dark again, but then we gotta get out of here."

"Took care of it how?"

"I... He's dead."

It took a few seconds for the words to kick in, then Julie felt the man's knee on her chest again. The edges started to get dark. She dragged in a long, shuddery breath and willed herself to stay conscious. "You killed him?"

"My stunner isn't working. Yours, either, by the way. And

he was too far away for the baton. I have a holdout pistol.
I shot him. Twice." She twitched her head toward the door.
"He's over there."

Julie struggled up to her elbows, fear clamping down on the
pain and nausea. An emergency blanket covered his face and
body, but she could see socks peeking out of the other end.
The left one had a hole in it, and she could see his big toe. A
kid's rhyme, the one about the piggy who went to market, ran
through her head. She made a sound that was part giggle, part
sob. "He wasn't wearing shoes?"

"I took his boots. We might be able to trade them. They're
almost new."

It was the saddest thing Julie had ever heard. "We were in
his house."

"That's no reason to attack you."

"What are we going to do?"

Ranger pointed at the body. "He stays. We go tonight with
everything we can carry."

"What about the police?"

"None worth talking about out here. Think about it. He
lived in this shit hole, and his boots were almost new. Odds are
he was not a nice guy."

"He stole the boots."

"Probably." She sighed. "Maybe he didn't. Maybe he's really
a wonderful person who lives in a storage unit full of stolen
property and was coming home with his new boots and a
backpack full of small, valuable, easily-traded items." Ranger
helped Julie into a sitting position and handed her the soup.
"Either way, he shouldn't have attacked you."

"Am I going to be all right?"

"I'm not a doctor, but I think so. I hope so. I have no idea
where the closest hospital is." Ranger slid into her sleeping bag
and wiggled closer to the stove. "Get some sleep. We'll leave
after it's dark."

Julie tried to nap, but there was a dead body near the door, and she was a murderer now. Well, really, Ranger was the killer, but Julie wouldn't let her stand up to that alone. Julie drifted in a half sleep until she felt his knees on her chest again and saw his fist reach back for another blow.

She yelped and sat up, breathing hard. The fading glow of the squeeze-lamp gave her just enough light to see him lying near the door. "Are you sure he's dead?"

Ranger grunted.

"Maybe he's just waiting for us to sleep."

"He's dead." Ranger rolled over to face the wall.

Julie lay back down. She dreamed she heard someone crying.

Ranger woke her up by pumping the squeeze-lamp next to her ear. The pulsing wheeze pulled Julie up from a dream and the four-course meal she was enjoying there.

"Get your hustle on," Ranger said, setting the lamp on the floor. "We need to get back over the highway to check on the van."

Julie fought her way to her knees and rolled up her sleeping bag. The bag was cool. The heating elements needed charging.

"Stuff it into his backpack," Ranger tossed it into Julie's lap. "It's better than yours."

Ranger went through the dead guy's pockets, turning out scraps of trash and a roll of patches. She held it up to the light. "I have no idea what these are, but someone will want them."

She pulled a switchblade out of his pants and handed it to Julie. "Put it in your pocket."

She fumbled at the catch and flicked it open. The blade was dark gray, some kind of ceramic, and wickedly sharp. Ranger had to show her how to close it. Julie slid it into the pocket of her jeans.

They searched the storage unit again. If the renter had some kind of organizational system, it wasn't apparent, but he'd tucked away a tramp fortune in easily movable goods: food, medicine, booze, and camping gear. Julie found a yellow knit hat wedged on one of the metal wall studs and tried it on.

Ranger laughed. "It's got ears. Cat ears."

"Warm, though." Julie pulled the hat on her head. It was a little small. "Maybe I can cut them off."

"Later." Ranger lifted her rucksack into place. "Come over here and let me see your face."

Julie held the lamp high as Ranger prodded her injuries. "It'll be a few weeks before you're pretty again, but you'll heal." She touched a spot over Julie's eye where tape was holding a wound closed. "That one's going to scar, though. How's your vision out of that eye?"

It was still mostly closed. "Just warn me if I'm about to get hit by a truck." Julie moved her jaw from side to side. It popped like a firecracker. "What did he hit me with?"

"Sap gloves. Weighted. I would have taken them, too, but they got – you know – gross." Ranger peeked out of a hole in the door before bending down to grab the handle. She held the door open while Julie crawled under.

"We're going to leave tracks," Julie said.

Ranger pointed to a set of footprints leading from somewhere behind them to the door of the unit. "If someone finds them, hopefully they'll think they're his."

"There are two of us."

"Walk in my prints and maybe it will look like one person. Let's go. I want to find a way across that doesn't involve sprinting. I don't think either of us could handle that."

FORTY-SEVEN

Juniper was right where they'd left her, covered in a thin blanket of snow. She hadn't been touched, but she still wasn't running.

Ranger closed her toolbox. "I don't know what they hit us with, but I can't fix it."

"Phones are still dead, too."

"It's all fucking dead." Ranger dropped a battered and much-altered spiral-bound road atlas on the hood and stabbed her finger at it. "We can't be too far from the park at Questa. We went west for maybe ten minutes on I-64."

Julie traced a line on the paper map with her finger. "Is this accurate at all?"

"The distances and directions should be." Ranger pointed over her shoulder with her thumb. "Seventeen miles back that way should be the park."

"Is that the only option?"

"Can't stay here too much longer. We've got food and water, but all the electronics are bricked. As overcast as it is, we wouldn't get much out of the solar panels anyway, and it's going to get colder. There might be someone at Carson, but this late in the season…" She threw up her hands. "Plus, it's a lot farther to walk."

"Alright."

"We'll try to get some sleep and leave in the morning."

The shared the bed in the back of the van, piling it high with blankets and spare clothing to ward off the chill. In the morning, they packed lightly and used the last of the juice in the stove to make coffee and fill the thermos. The sky was gray despite the sunrise, and the air was frigid.

"I thought this part of the country was turning into a desert," Julie said. "What's with the fucking snow?"

Ranger laughed. "When I was a kid-blah-blah, the weather used to make sense." She pointed west. "We might be in for more, too. I don't like the look of those clouds."

They took it slow, but it wasn't long before Ranger was having trouble breathing. She'd covered her mouth and nose with a somewhat clean T-shirt they'd found in the dead guy's bag, but it wasn't doing much. Julie's mask wasn't, either. She lifted it to spit. It was too dark to see where the spittle landed, but it was a tossup whether it was lighter or darker than the ash-colored snow.

They'd walked for about two hours before Ranger pointed to a playground in front of an abandoned fast-food restaurant. "Let's take a break."

The playground's outer gate was hanging from one hinge, and they squeezed underneath it. The fast-food chain had bought into the drone-delivery market before Julie was born, but the playground had held up well. A plastic clown kept guard on a bench right inside the gate. Dirty snow filled his lap and crowned his faded-orange head. His grin looked insane.

"In here." Ranger pulled Julie out of the clown's eyeshot and through the door of a plastic playhouse. She handed Julie a sleeping bag. "Unroll this and get it going."

Julie eyed the charge indicator. "There's not much power left."

"It's better than nothing. I'll unpack lunch."

Just getting out of the wind was a relief, although the yellowing plastic walls didn't offer much insulation. They sipped lukewarm coffee and thawed out. Ranger propped their packs inside the doorway to block the wind. It was almost cozy compared to the gray chill outside.

"How much to go?" Julie said.

"We're about halfway, unless I'm really wrong about how long we were on the highway. We'll warm up for twenty minutes or so and then get going."

"Is it worth trying to get into the restaurant? Maybe there's something in there we could use."

Ranger shook her braids out. "Anything in there is dried up, cleaned out, or frozen solid. Besides, until we get the van started it's just more to carry." The dark circles were still under Ranger's eyes. Even a full night's sleep couldn't bring her back up to even.

"Nap for a bit," Julie said. "I'll keep watch and wake you when it's time to go."

"Don't let me sleep any longer than fifteen minutes."

Julie woke her in thirty, earning a half-hearted scowl. Julie handed her a food bar and a water bottle. Ranger was a little peppier when they left the playhouse five minutes later, but her breathing still rasped.

She called a second halt in the doorway of an abandoned building a while later and consulted her battered road atlas. "Three more miles maybe. Last break before the final push."

"What are we going to do once we get back on the road?"

Ranger leaned against the boarded-up door. "We find another caravan and keep going. What else is there? Ready?"

"No, but we should get moving."

"We'll make a tramp out of you, yet, 'Burban girl."

Ranger was stumbling by the end of the next mile, and there were scarlet holes in the snow around her, burned there every time she cleared her mouth. Her face was gray above the dirty white of the dead man's T-shirt.

Julie took her arm. "Let me help." Ranger tried to shrug her off. "Let me help you," Julie repeated. "At least give me your pack."

Ranger's wheezing counted out the beats in a long moment of stillness. She shucked off the pack and handed it over. Julie put the pack on backward, over her chest.

"Thanks," Ranger said.

It was getting dark again by the time they made it back to the park's upper lot. Ranger scanned the scene below with binoculars from the van, panning left to right. The scan ended in a coughing fit. She handed Julie the glasses. "You try."

"Why would they still be there?"

"Why wouldn't they be? Lot to haul away with one trip."

Julie adjusted the field glasses to fit her face and did her own slow survey. The vehicles were still there, drawn into a circle and blackened by fire.

"Look for any movement," Ranger rasped. She cleared her throat. "Keep it slow. Don't attract attention."

Julie made another pass. Odds were good the attackers hadn't stuck around any longer than they'd had to, but luck hadn't been doing them any favors lately. She lowered the field glasses. "I don't see anything."

"Neither did I. Wait fifteen minutes, and we'll try again."

Julie had never been so tired in her life, and she had no idea how Ranger was keeping going. The asphalt sucked the warmth out of their bodies. They had knelt on it long enough that Julie began to wish they were still walking. Ranger held the binoculars back up to her face and scanned back and forth, again and again.

"Let's go," she said. She slipped the glasses into their case and slid it into her jacket pocket. "Stay low and go around. Head away from the stairs."

It was the longer, colder way to go, but Julie didn't complain. The stairs would have made a pretty sweet spot for an ambush. They crawled beside the guardrail as it followed the roadway and curved into the lower parking lot. Ranger got out the binoculars again at the bottom of the ramp. She looked through them for several minutes before putting them away.

"They might be really good hiders. If I say 'run', you run. Don't wait for me. I won't be able to keep up."

"What if they catch you?"

Ranger patted her jacket pocket. "I have one bullet left."

"That won't do you any good if there's a bunch of them."

"It won't be for them." She stood. "Let's go. No sudden movements."

Julie's knees popped like bubble wrap.

"You see anything moving, make sure I see it, too," Ranger said.

Julie pulled the baton off her belt and flicked it open.

The thin crust of snow over the asphalt crunched as they got closer to the convoy. Ranger grabbed Julie's hand when she reached out to brush snow off the windshield of King's red car. "You don't want to do that."

Julie let her hand drop. "You think he's still in there?"

"If he is, we can't help him."

Julie looked at the little car for a couple of long seconds. She'd known him in a fumbling, halting sort of way, and hadn't liked him much. He'd been less than a lover, far less than a friend, and, really, kind of a self-centered asshole. But he'd been alive and now...

When the dry heaves subsided, she ran to catch up with Ranger.

"I don't see anything," she reported.

They held still long enough for Julie to get shivery again. Ranger took her hand out of the pocket where she kept the gun. "There's no one here. Let's go."

The bathroom truck was closest. Ranger made Julie stay outside while she went in. Julie heard her moving around inside, and the camper rocked a little on its springs. After a minute or two she reappeared at the door. "It's empty. It looks like they got everything worth getting."

About six paces down the side of the RV a green hose peeked out of the fuel tank. Julie pointed it out.

"They got the fuel." Ranger swore. "Another reason to keep it all from blowing up."

"Why aren't there any bodies?" Julie said. "Did they get away?"

"I don't know." Ranger kicked a can that had come to rest beside one of the vans. The attackers would have taken everything they could – tires, spare parts, batteries, and belts – there wouldn't be a single vehicle in the convoy that was roadworthy anymore.

"Where would they go if they did?" Julie said.

"Maybe they started walking. Maybe they hid and another convoy showed up before we got here." She frowned. "I don't see the Dame's land yacht or the command center."

"Were they here when we left?"

"Remember I said there were vehicles missing…" She licked her lips. "I don't know. Maybe."

"Everything was happening so fast." Julie turned in place. "We should set up camp in the shower truck. Beats sleeping on the ground."

They set up camp in the center of the truck, in the largest shower stall, and rolled their sleeping bags out on the bare floor.

"These aren't going to do us much good without a recharge," Julie said. "Can we make a fire? With all the windows smashed out, ventilation won't be a problem.

"If you find something that won't off-gas us to death in our sleep. Don't go too far."

Ranger got food ready while Julie went in search of burnables. Some of the plastics would catch, but the smoke would make them sick. She found a dirty rag that smelled like someone had been using it as a gas cap and stuck it in her pocket.

The wind was picking up. She was maybe fifty meters from the entrance of the former Hotel La Fonda. There was a metal trash barrel there, like those the caravans made their campfires in. Julie jogged toward it

Her footsteps echoed on the frozen pavement. It took her

only a minute to cross the distance, but with every step she expected someone to run at her from an abandoned vehicle or empty shadow. Her heart was hammering by the time she stopped beside the barrel and looked inside. It was empty. A blast of frigid air slapped her from behind, sliding up her back inside her unzipped jacket. She shivered, nearly gasping. It was going to be a cold night.

There was another entrance and another trash barrel around the corner. The shower truck was still in sight. The wind blew cold and strong enough to make her breath hitch and flood her eyes with tears. She snugged her hat down and walked along the face of the building, heading to the corner.

With her left side protected by the building, she only had to watch ahead and to the right. Julie walked faster, almost jogging again, until she got to the corner. Jackpot.

Julie looked around once, twice, then sprinted to her prize: a large metal dumpster. Fear gave her wings, and she came to a halt by slamming into the side of the thing. The dumpster rang like a gong while Julie cowered and crouched like a rat beside it. No one came.

The dumpster was too high to see inside, but there was a metal ladder welded to it. The rungs felt like ice. Julie climbed as quickly as she could until she could get her elbows on the top.

A riot of staring faces and naked limbs waited inside. One pale hand with crooked fingers reached higher than the others, almost to the dumpster rim, as if the owner was hoping Julie would grab it and pull him somewhere calmer and less embarrassing. A burnt, twisted thing wearing Fire's face spooned with Ice. She stared at Julie through the frost that had formed in her eyes. Neither one of them blinked.

Julie trapped the scream building inside her with the palm of her hand. If she woke them, they might pull her inside with their broken fingers and warm their chilly flesh against her own.

She withdrew by inches until her head was below the dumpster's rim. She dropped to the pavement and ran back to Ranger.

FORTY-EIGHT

"We should leave," Julie said.

Ranger rubbed her eyes. "I can't do another hike right now."

"What about –" She swallowed against the bile rising in her throat. "What about them?"

"They were our friends. Mostly. They wouldn't have hurt you when they were alive. They're not going to hurt you now. Do you think they're all in there?"

Julie put her hand over her mouth. "I don't know." She clamped her lips shut and took several deep breaths. "I didn't stop to count."

"I can look later. Someone should know." Ranger punched the metal floor beneath her. "Goddamn it. They didn't deserve that."

Julie crossed her arms over her chest like she was giving herself a hug. "I'll help you look in the morning."

"It will be full dark soon." There was a new hitch in the rasp of Ranger's breath.

"I'm sorry I couldn't find anything for a fire."

"I'm just glad you got back in one piece." She pointed at Julie's sleeping bag with her chin. "That's totally out of juice?"

"Yeah."

"We can zip the bags together. Do you mind? Don't want you to be weirded out by snuggling with the big, bad lesbian."

"You're not that big."

It took most of Ranger's energy just to get out of her sleeping bag. Julie got them zipped together after a couple of false starts and helped her back in. Ranger was shivering hard when Julie crawled in beside her. "I can't get warm," she said.

The truck rocked as a gust of wind caught its side.

"Roll over." Julie squirmed closer and put her arms around Ranger. "Better?"

They lay there listening as the wind howled through the window holes and feeling the truck sway on its springs. Ranger's shivering slowly subsided.

Julie sniffed. "You need a bath."

"You smell like puke."

"That's because I threw up. What's your excuse?"

"Busy couple of days."

They dozed, missing the last of the sun as it dropped past the horizon. Ranger woke them with renewed shivering.

"How you doing?" Julie pumped up the squeeze-lamp.

Ranger tried to curl up to conserve her heat, but the position sent her into a coughing fit. "Not good." She sat up. "Maybe I should walk around some. Warm up."

"Not a great idea." Julie peered around the inside of the van with the squeeze-lamp. "Gimme a minute."

Julie slid out of the sleeping bag, trying to keep as much of the warmth inside it as she could. She grabbed an empty jar from the pile of supplies they had rummaged and poured it about half full of biodiesel.

"What are you doing?" Ranger said through chattering teeth.

"I won't use it all."

She pulled the greasy rag out of her jacket and cut a long narrow strip off it with the switchblade. She handed the knife to Ranger. "I still can't close the damned thing. You do it."

Without waiting for her response, Julie turned back to the project. The strip of fabric went into the jar. She pushed all of it under the surface of the liquid fuel.

"I get it," Ranger said.

Julie looked over her shoulder at her.

"You're making a lamp."

"My friend's dad showed us how to make one. Years ago." Julie's fingers felt thick as she fumbled one end of the wick out of the jar and suspended it with a wire across the top. "Cold." She blew on her fingers. "Where's the lighter?"

Ranger fumbled inside the sleeping bag and handed over the lighter and the switchblade. Julie put the knife in her pocket "You'll have to show me the trick of it again," she said.

"Just light the lamp."

The lighter's heating element glowed, and Julie touched it to the fuel-soaked cloth. It caught and burned with a bright, smelly light. Ranger held her hands over it. "Nice work."

"About time I brought something to this relationship." Julie squatted down next to the lamp to warm her hands beside Ranger. The lamp smoked and stank but gave off a good amount of heat.

"You sorry you left home, yet?" Ranger said.

"This was supposed to be all about philosophers and artists sitting around campfires." Julie shifted her weight to spare her knees. "It's harder than I thought."

Ranger drew herself up in the sleeping bag and sat with her back against the shower wall. "When I first came out here it was more like that." She smiled. "A lot more kumbaya and a lot less every man for himself."

"Why did it change?"

"The world got worse. More people lost their jobs." She shook her head. "The colony missions were supposed to give everybody hope, but that doesn't last long if you know you're not one of the people who gets to leave."

"There's not a lot of hope for the people who got to go, either. Who knows what they'll find after all that time?"

"At least they'll get a fresh start." Ranger pointed at the lamp. "How long are you keeping that going?"

"As long as I need to. The fuel won't do us much good if we freeze to death."

Ranger closed her eyes. "I want you to have Juniper when I'm gone."

"You're not going anywhere."

She smiled, but she looked more tired than anyone Julie had ever seen. "I'm not going to make it much longer."

"You're not dying on me."

Her grip was weak. Julie could have pulled away easily, but the tone in Ranger's voice stopped her. "Julie, don't. Please. At best I'll get another couple of years in a cube. They'll keep me alive until I'm nothing but tubes and wires."

To someone like Ranger that would be hell. "You're not doing it tonight." The cold seeped through the metal panel behind her and into her back. "We have a place to sleep." She gestured at the lamp. "We have fire." She pulled the metal cup out of her pack and held it in the air. "We will have tea."

In a little more than thirty minutes they were sipping warm water, and Julie was nursing a burned hand. Julie pumped up the squeeze-lamp again and set it on the floor between them. "Feeling better?"

"A bit." Ranger's smile was wan.

"We could play I Spy, but there's not much to see. Why did we come out here, again?"

Ranger's grin was skull-like. "Freedom and adventure."

Julie lifted the cup. "Here's to it."

The temperature was still dropping. Julie had stuffed anything she could find into the empty windows, but it was doing little to keep the heat in. Next time she ran away she'd remember to bring some extra blankets and maybe a self-heating tent.

"Talk to me," Ranger said.

Julie shook her head. "You know all my crap. You talk to me." She poured more water in the cup and held it over the little lamp flame. This time she remembered to put on a glove. "Tell me how you got out here."

"That's a story not a conversation." Ranger propped herself up against the wall of the van and pulled the sleeping bag up to her chin. She left the bag unzipped just enough to stick her hand out for the next cup of hot water. "I went into federal care after my parents died. I was about eight."

"How did they die?"

"The Russians. This was back when they were hacking everything they could get into. They got into the traffic grid and caused a seventy-three car pileup. My parents were in car thirty-one."

Julie rubbed her arms. "I can't imagine how that felt."

"I didn't find out until my grandmother picked me up at school that day in her new Volvo. 'Best car in the world,' she said."

"The first Juniper."

"She lasted longer than Grandma." Ranger chuckled.

"She just showed up and told you your parents were dead?"

"It took her a couple of days to tell me. I didn't really understand it until the funeral. It was a Catholic thing. Open casket."

"Sounds horrible."

"I don't remember much of it. What people said." She shook her head. "I remember Grandma slapping my hand because I tried to touch my mother. I thought I could wake her up."

"Sounds like a bitch."

"She really was. She put me in the foster home because my psyche tests said I had 'homosexual tendencies.'" She smiled. "Guess I showed them."

"She dumped you for that!"

"She was religious." She coughed. Julie handed her a rag. She spit something into it and cleared her throat. "Maybe it was more than that. I don't think she liked my mother much."

"Still."

"It was a long time ago." She handed Julie the cup for a refill. "Anyway, I got a message at the foster home telling me she'd died, and I'd inherited all her stuff. The house, the car, the furniture. I was seventeen, so I had another year before I could leave. The lawyer said they were going to sell everything and set up an account for me."

"What if you'd wanted the stuff instead of the money?"

"If I'd been eighteen I would've had the choice." She sipped the hot water. "There was this girl who worked at the home. Part-time. She was twenty, doing pre-med. She was there mostly to get experience with working with kids. She lost her college funding a couple of days after I got the message about Grandma. She told me she was turning tramp."

"You asked her to take you with her."

Ranger grinned. "I told her I'd take her with me. In the car I'd just inherited from my dead grandmother."

Julie laughed. "Could you even drive at that point?"

"Megan could. That was part of the deal."

"Gretchen's daughter."

"I got a weekend travel pass to go to my grandmother's house. I said I needed closure." She smiled. "Megan came along as my chaperone."

"And she liked girls, too."

"Lucky me. We had some good times together."

"Back when it was kumbaya," Julie looked down at her cup where maybe an inch of water was cooling.

"I'm going to try to sleep," Ranger said. "Join me?"

"Should we let the lamp burn?"

"We can wake up in a couple of hours and relight it, if we need to."

Julie made sure the lamp wasn't going to tip over and burn them to death. "Move over." She squirmed into the sleeping bag beside Ranger, and they curled up like quotation marks. Ranger drifted off to sleep first.

Julie didn't know when she followed, but her dreams ended when a short sasquatch stuck his head through their makeshift curtain. "Y'all still alive in there?" it said.

FORTY-NINE

"You're gonna die if you stay here."

Julie forced herself up to her elbows. She was too tired and cold to be startled. After the events of the past few days it almost made sense that a skinny teenager dressed in furs would stick his head inside the shower stall they were curled up in. "Who are you?"

"Devin Jones." He nodded at the human-shaped lump beside her. "That one still breathing? Be easier if she ain't, just sayin', not that I'd be happy about it."

"She's alive," Julie said.

"Well, let's go." Devin rubbed his sparsely-whiskered face. "Reckon you can walk on your own?"

The kid leaned over and gathered Ranger in his arms, doubled sleeping bags and all. "Got a sled outside. Grab anything you want to take wit' you."

Julie put on her coat and slipped a backpack over each arm. The storm had come in early that morning, dropping a half foot of snow atop the inch or two already on the ground, and now it was snowing sideways.

Outside, Devin was securing Ranger to a sled that looked to be made from tree branches and boot laces. "She's alive, but she ain't doing good."

"Where are we going?" Julie said.

"Not far. You can put those packs on the sled, too. It's no trouble." He waited while she did just that and put the sled's

284

tow rope over his shoulder. "Follow best you can. Holler if you fall in a hole or something." He set off across the parking lot, away from the entrance and roadway.

Julie folded her arms around herself and trudged in the sled's wake.

"I'd be more worried about tracks if it weren't snowing so hard." Devin moved easily through the snow and barely seemed affected by the cold. "Reckon we'll get another foot by sundown."

"T–t–tracks?" Julie said. Movement was warming her up, but it also seemed to be making her shiver.

"Pa don't like folks knowin' where we've holed up." He looked up at the sky. "Won't be a problem today."

The boy hauled the sled over a divider and into the parking lot of a boarded-up motel.

"You live here?" Julie said.

He laughed. "Hell, no. Building like that's full of toxins. Mold, dust. Hard to heat, too. Wouldn't have it if you paid me."

The boy's path took them behind the hotel and up the hill into the dense patch of woods beyond.

"You girls were lucky I spotted you," he said. "Got a couple of traps set on the other side of the park down there or I wouldn't have. Up here." He powered up the steepest part of the hill, and Julie fought to keep up. There was less snow among the dry trees and undergrowth, but he seemed to have little trouble with the sled. The forest ended at a chain-link fence with a large hole hacked into the middle. Julie smelled wood smoke. "Almost there," the kid said.

A hundred yards further on, Devin stopped in front of a low rise and dropped the tow cable. He pointed. "Right in through there. I'll bring your friend in."

Julie walked where the boy had pointed. The snow had been shoveled out from a crude wooden door that appeared to be set right into the side of the hill. She pushed it open.

"Is this a cave?" she said.

"A soddy," the boy said, coming up behind her with Ranger in his arms. "Sod house. Pa's built a bunch of 'em. This is the best one." Beyond the door was a short corridor lit with an oil lamp. "Hang your coat on the wall there. Then take your boots off and go on through."

A rough blanket hung over the doorway at the end of the corridor. Julie pushed through into firelight, heat, and the smell of food.

"Got 'em, Ma," Devin called. "Only one of 'em's walkin', though. She got lung rot."

"Put the other in your sister's bed." The woman who spoke was tall and strong-looking, her hair tied back in a messy bun. She put her hands to the small of her back and looked at Julie. "My name is Linda, and you've already met my son, Devin. His little sister is over there by the fire."

Julie squinted. Sure enough, a little girl in worn clothes was perched on a stool near the open maw of the fireplace. "Is Ranger going to be alright?"

Linda looked over at the bed then smiled tightly at Julie. "Was she sick before?"

"She got lung rot, Mama," Devin said. "I told you."

"And I told you to hush," Linda said. "Go over there and play with your sister before I find some work for you to do."

"Aw, Ma!" the kid huffed.

Linda's face didn't change, and Devin stalked over to the fire. The little girl squealed then laughed.

"Jerry, my husband, is checking his trap lines. Probably won't be home until tomorrow," Linda said.

"Is he going to be OK out there?" Julie said.

Linda laughed. "He lives for this shit. He's probably hunkered down somewhere in an emergency shelter he made using only tree branches and old yoga pants. Warm as a tick, happy as hell." She pressed her hand to Ranger's forehead. "It's just about over anyway. We get a bad one once or twice a month during the season. This was the worst I've seen in a while. Can I get you anything?"

"Water?" Julie tried to get a look at Ranger. "Is she asleep or unconscious?"

Linda pointed to a plastic bucket on the crude kitchen counter. "Either way, she's resting. So it doesn't much matter, does it?"

The water was lukewarm and heavy with minerals, but it cooled some of the fire Julie felt every time she swallowed. "Our phones got bricked. If you let me borrow yours we can be out–"

"No phones. No power. We gave all that up when we moved out here. Totally off the grid." She glanced at the two playing a game by the fire. "Jerry and I agreed this would be a better life for them."

"You're Apes!" Julie flushed. "I mean–"

"I know what you call us." Her mouth twisted. "I don't suppose we say much better about you."

Apes. Anarcho-primitivists. They believed the human race had been going downhill ever since it gave up hunting and gathering and that all the problems of the day could be traced back to the evils of society and technology. *Not that they are totally wrong, but…*

"How long have you lived like this?" Julie said.

"Devin was two when we left the city," Linda said. "So thirteen years or close enough."

"And all that time, no doctors, no computers…"

"You don't need all that if you live right." She cleared her throat. "I got a fire going in one of the other houses for the two of you. I know Jerry wouldn't want the kids talking to you much, so I'll get Devin to take you over there once you have something to eat. He got a turkey yesterday, and I made a nice stew. You can rest and figure out your next step. You're survivors of that ambush over there at the mall?"

Julie nodded.

"I'm sorry that happened to you, but that's what you get when too many people are together. We weren't made to live like that."

The little girl laughed again. She was playing some kind of counting game with her big brother. Both kids were a little grubby, maybe, but they looked healthy and happy enough. "I see your point," Julie said.

Ranger roused long enough to eat some stew. It was thick and good and had a lot of things in it that Julie didn't recognize. She ate two bowls and tried not to think about heavy metals and other contaminants. After breakfast, she and Devin put Ranger back on the sled and dragged it a hundred yards west to another soddy.

"How many of these do you have?" she said.

"Lost count. Anytime Pa gets bored he goes out and builds a house. All different kinds. I got a little Pict house in the woods back there that I use in the spring and summer." He helped Julie get Ranger inside the crude little space and into a bed near the fire. "It's not as nice as ours, but it's warm and dry. Pa's been using it as his library."

The back wall of the little place was loaded with books and binders of magazines. "You can read 'em, but don't mess them up."

Julie helped him fill the wood box, and he showed her how the compost toilet in the corner worked.

"Probably come over later with some more stew," he said. "You can keep the fire going?"

Julie told him she'd had a good teacher. He grinned. "Betcha mine was better. I can start one three different ways without a match. You?"

Julie admitted she needed matches or a lighter. Devin shot her a grin. "You stick around long enough, I can show you."

"Do you like living like this?"

He scratched his ear. "What's not to like? Work when you need to, read, make things, go hunting when you're hungry."

"What about friends?"

"Couple of other families live over there a few miles." He pointed toward the bookshelves. "Don't see 'em much in the winter but spring and summer we do."

"What do you do for fun?"

"Trap. Hunt. Fish. Sometimes we creep up close and spy on the caravans." He grinned. "Probably know a lot more about you people then you know about us."

"Probably. Thank you for coming to get us."

Shrugging seemed to be his favorite expression. "Couldn't leave you out there to die."

Julie waited until the door closed behind him then went to check on Ranger. "How are you?"

"Feel like shit," she wheezed. "Wish'd I'd grabbed the oxygen."

"Sleep for a while and then we'll figure out how to get out of this."

"I got an idea about that," Ranger said. She slipped her hand under the pillow and pulled out a phone. "Someone left us a present."

FIFTY

Julie reread the note attached to the phone. "Says here she doesn't want us to let Devin or her husband know she has this."

Ranger coughed. "Can't blame her. Sort of flies in the face of everything they're doing."

The phone flickered on. It was three-quarters charged. According to the note, Linda kept it in case someone in the family had a medical emergency. "How do you think she keeps it charged?"

"If she doesn't turn it on, it might last six months or so. She probably trades for a recharge every once in awhile." Ranger smiled. "Or maybe she has a solar panel hidden somewhere, too. She strikes me as a smart lady."

"Should I message the cops?"

Ranger frowned. "Last resort. For all we know, I'm wanted now." Julie added a log to the fire while Ranger considered their options and struggled to breathe. "I'm not sure how long I can hold out."

"Do you know anyone around here?"

"Probably some of the people in the outfits running around, but no one with the resources to come and save our asses." Ranger shifted in the bed. The mattress was homemade, and the stuffing had a tendency to poke.

"I could call my parents. They could get us back east, but we'd probably have to leave the van."

"I'm not leaving the van," Ranger said, "but it could be a way out for you."

"What about Gretchen?"

Ranger sighed. "It's not her side of the country, but if anyone can make something happen she can."

Julie sent the message, making sure it was properly tagged with their GPS coordinates. A response beeped in a few moments later. "Idiots," it said. "Give me a few hours."

She surveyed the bookcases. There was little fiction. The titles trended toward DIY and crafts. An entire shelf promised to teach her how to build her own underground house. The magazines were antiques. Bound issues of *Popular Mechanics* and *Mother Earth News*.

"What are we going to do about Devin and Linda?" Julie said. "You've seen how they live. That stew of theirs had to be full of toxins. They're going to get sick."

"You still don't get it." Ranger struggled to sit up in the bed. "She's not a victim. Linda's not being held prisoner. She knows what she signed up for." She pointed at the phone. "She's got it handled. She doesn't need to be rescued until she says she does."

"But the kids–"

"For now, they're healthy and happy. Eventually, they may get sick, and Linda and her husband will have to make some decisions. Living here is no worse than living in the van or in a cube. It's just different. You need to get your head around that. Apes and tramps are not sob stories, Jules."

The phone beeped again. "How long would it take you to get back to the mall tomorrow morning?" Gretchen asked.

"I'm not riding in the sled again," Ranger said. "I can walk."

"You can, but you don't have to," Julie said. "Devin's going to come along to show us the way anyway. You might as–"

"Not going to happen," Ranger said. She nodded to Linda. "Much obliged for you taking us in."

"A little food and a night's sleep," the woman said. "It's not so much."

"Considering the last people we saw tried to kill us, I'd say it's quite a bit." She smiled. "You have a lovely family." She stuck an elbow in Julie's side.

Pa Jones had finally made an appearance after a night in a wikiup. He'd been all smiles for his kids and wife but glared suspiciously when they introduced him to their guests. He was splitting wood off to the side of the house, but still keeping an eye on what was going on. Devin's little sister was digging out a snowcave, and all Julie could see of her was her rear-end and mukluk-clad feet. "Lovely," she said. "Your home is amazing."

Linda smiled. Ranger had put the phone back under the pillow, and it disappeared when Linda came in with a breakfast of bread and hard cheese.

Falling snow had filled in the sled tracks from the day before, but Julie began to recognize landmarks as she and Ranger trailed along in Devin's wake. The woods. The boarded up hotel. Finally, the snow-covered lumps that used to be The Dame's caravan.

"You're lucky you got your phone workin'. You want me to stick around until your ride comes?" Devin said. He dropped the bundle of wood he'd carried from the soddy and began to set up a fire.

"It shouldn't be too long," Julie said. "I think we'll be OK."

Ranger dragged a crate over to the fire and sat on it with her sleeping bag around her shoulders. Even the short walk had left her gasping for air.

"If you're sure." Devin stood and dusted his hands off on his pants.

"What are you going to do when you grow up?" Julie said. "Do you want to go to college or something?"

Devin looked at her like she was crazy. "Why'd I want to do that? Pa says school is just guided reading. I got plenty of books."

"Do you want a family of your own? A girlfriend? A boyfriend?"

He defaulted to shrugging again and looked embarrassed. "I was kinda hopin' you'd come back for that fire-building lesson. Show you how to dig out your own house, too."

Julie forced a laugh. "I'm an old lady. You need someone who can keep up with you."

"Maybe so. Well, if you don't need me," he waved, "catch you all later." He turned and began to retrace his steps.

Julie sat on an overturned bucket and warmed her hands.

"Looks like. You have. A. Boyfriend," Ranger wheezed.

"Shut up you. Save your breath."

They'd burned through half the firewood before the truck came, a four-door monster with an extended bed. A woman with short gray hair was behind the wheel. She unrolled the driver's side window. "You Gretchen's friends?"

Julie stood. "I'm Julie, this is–"

Ranger rose to her feet but collapsed into a coughing fit. Her breath whooped in and out of her damaged lungs.

"Shit!" Julie said. "Help me here!"

FIFTY-ONE

Bright, blurry lights. Words that made no sense. Warm water held her. The hand behind her head kept her face out of the water. Clean blankets tucked around her body. The bed was soft. It was the best dream she'd had in weeks, and she fought to stay in it.

She lost the battle. Her eyes opened and focused on a woman's face. "Mom?"

"No, dear. But you're fine. Don't get upset."

The rest of Julie's vision kicked in. The room was windowless and dim. She really was in a bed. "Where am I?"

The woman put her hand on Julie's arm. "Don't worry about that right now." She smiled, wrinkles forming around her mouth. "You're safe."

"Where's Ranger?"

The woman's forehead creased. "The doctor will be here in an hour or so. You can ask her."

"Doctor?" Julie looked around as best she could. "Is this a hospital?"

"Close enough. And I'm close enough to being a nurse to know that you need to stay quiet and rest. You've had a rough time." She smoothed the hair off Julie's forehead. "How long were you out there?"

"In the parking lot?"

"On the road."

Julie tried to think, and counted back as best she could. "Nearly five months, I think."

"Well, I'm sure there's no permanent damage." She patted Julie's hand. "Can I get you something? Some juice? Something to eat."

"Water would be fine."

"I'll be right back."

Julie's thoughts were a broken kaleidoscope. The road. The caravan. The storage unit. The snow. The bodies in the dumpster. The van. Ranger and the gun. The family of Apes. The truck. She shook her head to settle the shards. It made her dizzy. Her head sank into the pillow, careful not to disturb the broken glass inside. She focused on her breathing. The air came in, the air went out. One. She sucked in another lungful and let it go, slowly. Two. She inhaled again – Clean. It smelled clean, like filtration and air-conditioning. Like her room at home.

She remembered getting into the truck. *Did they drug me?*

The nurse lady came back in with a plastic pitcher and a glass. She set the glass on a table near the bed and filled it with water from the pitcher. Ice cubes clunked against the plastic sides. "Let me unstrap your hands so you can drink this."

Julie tried to lift her arms. They moved about an inch, kept in place by soft cuffs. She pulled again, harder, feeling the muscles bunch in her arms. "Why am I tied down?"

The woman had been reaching for the cuff on Julie's left arm. She adjusted her aim and patted Julie's arm again. "For your own safety, dear. We didn't want you to hurt yourself."

"Why would I hurt myself? What is this place?"

The woman picked up the glass of water. "If you calm down I can give you this. If you don't, I'll have to hold it for you."

"Where's Ranger?"

"The doctor will be here soon." She waggled the glass. Julie could see the clear water sloshing around inside. She could almost taste its coolness on her aching tongue. "Make a decision."

Julie took a deep breath. "I'm OK."

"Good." She put the glass aside again and unfastened the straps on Julie's hands. They made a ripping sound as she pulled them loose. She handed Julie the water. "Drink now."

The water was good. There was none of the rusty, stale taste Julie had so much trouble getting used to on the road. She drank greedily.

"Give it a few minutes to settle then you can have more." She took the cup from Julie's hand and put it on the table. She flipped the bottom corners of the blanket, one at a time, and freed her feet. "Don't try to get up. We had to give you a catheter. Do you know what that is? I'll check back in a few minutes. Try to rest."

"Did you drug me?" Julie said.

"Yes. We also scanned every inch of you and drew blood. We had to make sure you weren't contagious or dangerous in some way."

"I've had all my shots."

"As you say, but your emplant wasn't working to tell us that. We had to figure it out the hard way."

"Who are you?" Julie said.

She smiled, making wrinkles again. "I'll give you mine if you give me yours."

"Julie." She stopped herself before saying her last name. The less they knew the better. "Just Julie for now."

"That's not one of the names you kept mumbling when you were asleep. Looks like I won the pool." She held out her hand. "I'm Beth."

Julie arm felt heavy as she lifted her hand for Beth to shake. "I guess I should thank you."

"We'll talk about it more when the doctor comes. Get some rest."

Julie was asleep before Beth was out of the room.

* * *

In spite of the water, Julie woke with a dry mouth. She rubbed her eyes, dislodging a buildup of sleep. Her arms and legs felt like they'd been bolted onto her body as an afterthought, but they weren't strapped down. She reached for the pitcher of water on the little table and slopped the glass full.

Julie drank carefully, not wanting to fumble water all over herself. Beth or someone like her would likely rush to her side to keep her from drowning. She put the glass back on the table all by herself.

The walls were a sunny yellow, a good complement to the green bedding, and an obvious attempt to make up for the lack of windows. The floor was dark gray tile, probably for easy clean up. There were no cameras that she could see, but they had to be keeping tabs on her somehow.

The only real hospital she'd seen was the one Ben's dad spent his last few weeks in. Julie's family had gone visit him, small and weak among the beeping machines and servo-nurse arms. He'd tried to talk, but Julie didn't much understand what he said. One of the servo-nurses injected him with something. He had smiled at her before he fell asleep. It was the last time she'd seen him.

This place looked nothing like that hospital, nor like any of those she'd seen on the vid. She might as well have been in someone's spare bedroom.

She slid her hand beneath the covers and slipped it under the waistband of the purple pajamas someone had put her in. Beth had said there was a catheter, but she couldn't find anything unusual down there. To be on the safe side, she moved slowly as she slid her legs over the side of the bed and stood.

No alarms went off, and there was no sudden gush of pee or blood from a hidden tube. She put her hand on the table and waited for her head to stop swimming. There were two doors in the room. The one she'd seen Beth come through probably led to a hallway. The other door either led to a bathroom, which she didn't need at the moment, or to a closet, which might have her stuff in it.

Julie shuffled to the door she hoped led to a closet. She started out with one hand on the bed but was moving just fine, albeit slowly, by the time she got around to the other side.

It was a closet, but there was nothing of Julie's inside. It was full of shelves and plastic totes of craft supplies: spools of thread, glue, scraps of cloth, foam heads, jars of pins, and googly eyes. She grabbed a pair of scissors and slid them under the waistband of her pajamas. The tail of the striped-pajama shirt covered the handles.

Getting to the other door took only a few seconds. Her legs were feeling almost normal. She pressed her ear against the door and held her breath, hoping to hear if anyone was passing by outside.

She tried the knob. It turned smoothly under her hand and three moves later she was outside the room with the door closed behind her. The scissors fell out of her pajamas and onto the floor with a clunk. Beth looked up at the sound. "I was wondering when you'd try that." She patted the couch beside her. "Come sit down."

Julie used her foot to push the scissors under a chair. "You live here? I've been in your house all this time?"

"Apartment." Beth gestured to the door Julie had just come out of. "Spare bedroom slash craft room."

"Who are you?"

"Someone who had a spare bedroom. The doctor will be here to talk about that in a few minutes." She put something down on the couch. She'd been knitting. Julie wondered if she knew how to make a hat.

"How are you feeling?" Beth said. "Any tenderness from the catheter?"

"I'm fine. How long was I out?"

"Nearly three days. Are you hungry? I made some soup."

Beth left the room and came back in with a tray. She placed it on the low table in front of the couch and returned to her knitting.

Julie's thoughts were as hazy as the steam rising from the bowl. "The last thing I remember is the truck pulling up. Was that you?"

"It was. Do you remember that I offered you some water? There was a sedative in it. Then you were in quarantine. So was I for that matter." The door chime sounded. Beth put her knitting down again. "That should be the doctor now." She patted Julie's knee. "Stay right there."

Beth opened the door for another woman, maybe fifteen years younger. They whispered to each other for a few seconds before Beth waved the woman in. "Julie, this is Dr Shah. If you owe anyone for your rescue, it's her."

"Nonsense. If we had not done it together, it would not have been done at all." Dr Shah stuck out her hand. "You are Julie."

Her hand was small and cool, and she had an accent like Anji's grandmother crossed with Sherlock Holmes.

"Thanks for the assist. What the hell is going on?" Julie said.

The doctor flashed a smile. "May I sit?"

"Beth is the queen bee around here. Ask her."

"I'll make some tea while you talk." Beth smiled. "Or would you prefer something else?"

"Tea's fine. Maybe hold the knockout drugs this time."

Dr Shah and Julie sat on opposite ends of Beth's small sofa. "You are well, I trust," the tiny doctor said.

"I feel kind of shitty, thanks."

"Let me see your hands." The doctor pinched Julie's fingertips. "No numbness? No dizziness?"

"Not since I started moving around."

"You are eating?"

"I had a couple of sips of soup."

Dr Shah released Julie's hand. "I do not expect you to experience any permanent trouble."

"What was wrong with me?"

She ticked the medical issues off on her fingers. "Minor frostbite on hands, feet, and face. Bruises and contusions to the face and back of your head. A mild concussion. A vitamin deficiency."

"But I'm fine."

"That depends entirely on you. If you go back on the road, you will almost certainly get worse."

Beth interrupted with the tea and sat in the armchair closest to Julie's side of the couch.

It was peppermint tea. "When can I see Ranger?" Julie said.

Dr. Shah put her cup on the table, next to the cooling soup. "Whenever you please."

FIFTY-TWO

Ranger looked tiny in the big diagnostic bed; the only sign of her personality were the telltale lights pushing into the red zone. *She always has to live on the edge.*

"Why is she still unconscious?" Julie said.

"Heavy drugs. She's in a medical-induced coma to help her heal." Beth brought up Ranger's chart on the screen embedded in the foot of the bed. "Looks like she went into hypothermia at least twice. Frostbite, same as you. Pneumoconiosis." She looked at Julie's face. "Lung rot, but you knew about that."

"Did you cure her?"

Beth wiped the chart. "It would take more than a few days to do that, if it could be done at all. She has a very advanced case. Come on, we'll let her sleep."

Julie followed Beth out of the room. "Where's all of her stuff?"

"In storage."

"I want to see it."

Beth led the way to a small room bathed in ultraviolet light. "Let's not linger or we'll get a hell of a sunburn," she said.

Ranger's clothes had been laundered and neatly folded. Her heavy jacket was hanging from a hook. The contents of her pockets were carefully arranged on the table.

"We went through it to make sure there was nothing dangerous," Beth said.

Some of the items were familiar, others Julie had never seen before. She picked up a heavy metal pin, a six-pointed star with the word "sheriff" engraved on it. The picture of Ranger and Euchre was folded under the clasp.

"Do you want to take that with you?" Beth said.

"I just wanted to make sure everything was here." Julie put the pin back with the other items. "What is this place?"

"The future, maybe." Beth smiled. "The past, too. It's hard to say. It's too new."

"Are we in the city?" Julie said.

Beth shook her head. "We're not in the suburbs, either. It's a new place, a new idea. Dr Shah will tell you about it after we eat."

They went back to Beth's apartment. Beth went into her room and came out with a stack of clothes. "I washed them for you," she said, handing her the neatly folded bundle. "Mended a few of the holes."

Julie took the stack into Beth's craft room and changed. After so much time in pajamas, her old clothes felt like armor against her skin, thick and stiff. She stomped into her boots and studied herself in the mirror. The face above the collar of her coat looked like it was better suited to the pajamas. *Who is this woman, and why does she look so young when I feel so old?*

"You won't need a coat where we're going," Beth said, coming into the room. "It will be plenty warm." She led the way up two flights of beige walls and concrete stairs. The stairs ended at another metal door. Beth pushed it open and stepped through.

The space on the other side of the door was like something out of ThirdEye. It was huge, bigger than anyplace Julie had ever been before, bigger than anyplace needed to be. Sunlight poured through a glass ceiling at least a hundred feet above her head. The floor was tiled, the wide path bordered on both sides by long, low boxes of plants. On either side of the garden space walls rose, five floors high with balconies, to meet the ceiling.

Beth twisted a ripe tomato from the box to her right and handed it to Julie. "This is where we grow our food," she said. "We can have that for lunch."

The air was thick with moisture and oxygen. It tasted cleaner and more natural than anything Julie had ever sucked into her lungs. She was dizzy.

"Let's sit down for a minute." Beth claimed a bench off to one side of the path. "It takes a little getting used to." She handed Julie a bottle of water. "I told you you wouldn't need a coat."

Julie drank the cool water and closed her eyes until her head was less swimmy. Beth took the empty bottle back and tucked it into her bag. "Do you know where you are now?" she said.

Doors and huge glass windows led into empty storefronts all around them. "We're in one of the ghost malls."

Beth patted her leg. "Let's go see Neha. Dr Shah."

Dr Shah's office was on the second level. It was small and plain, but, with its glass front wall overlooking the mall's courtyard garden, the doctor had a hell of a view. Beth tapped on the glass, and the little woman beckoned them in.

"Tea?" she said.

Julie nodded dumbly.

Dr Shah slid cups in front of them and sat back behind the desk. She laced her fingers and rested her hands on the clean surface in front of her. "Welcome to Ark Four."

"Like Noah's Ark?"

"Minus the water and the religion, perhaps. We are a secret. One that you are most lucky to know."

"Because of Gretchen."

"Dr Frost is one of our founders, although she's chosen not to work on site."

"You called this Ark Four."

"Of seven. There are more planned. The mission to PC may save humanity but will do nothing for the people remaining. The tower projects are little more than warehouses. Our founders see us as the last hope." Dr Shah rubbed the bridge of her nose. "It will not be enough, of course. Many will die in the years to come."

"So what's the point?"

"To buy time."

Julie laughed. "Time for what? Do you know what it's like out there?"

"Time for you to have children, maybe," Beth said. "And those children to have children." She picked up her tea. "Maybe time enough to allow the world to heal, or for some of us to adapt to the new one."

"That's not much of a plan."

"Not all of us can fly out of the solar system and not all of us want to." Dr Shah stood. "It makes a good deal more sense than riding around in cars until you get cancer or freeze to death."

"We didn't know this was an option." Julie's eyes narrowed. "And it's not an option for most of us, is it? Gretchen would have told Ranger about it."

"Julie…" Beth looked down at her hands as if they contained the words she was looking for. "What we're doing here is very important and very fragile."

"And we will do our best with it," Dr Shah said. "Come. Let me show you our ark."

Outside her office, Dr Shah stayed a couple of steps ahead while Beth walked right beside Julie. The doctor led the way to a balcony overlooking a courtyard. Below, a dozen men and women were tending the fruits and vegetables. "We have forty-three people living here. In time, we expect to be able to support up to two hundred families."

The Ark residents had set up their homes in the abandoned storefronts, each apartment looking out over the garden courtyard.

"With all this up here, why do you live in the basement?" Julie asked Beth.

"To be close to my work. We're using the subbasement for biofuel production, using bacteria to convert waste oil and sewer grease." She wrinkled her nose. "We expect to be able to use it to trade with members of the volksgeist soon."

"So, you'll trade with them, but you won't let them in."

"Not everyone will want to come in, Julie. And not everyone should." Beth looked away. "Some may be too damaged to live among us constructively."

"You can't just let them die out there!"

Dr Shah started walking again. "We will do our best to make their lives comfortable. If they fall sick, we can make certain…" She hesitated. "We have drugs to ease the transition."

Suicide at best, passive-aggressive euthanasia at worst. If not for Gretchen, Beth and Dr Shah might have offered Ranger death on a med patch.

They descended a flight of stairs to the mall's ground level. Steel-shuttered storefronts slept on all sides of them. Dr Shah had a smile on her face when she stopped and turned. "The skylights let in a lovely amount of sunshine." She pointed up to the ceiling dozens of feet above. "No matter what happens down here, the sun will continue to do its job."

The garden was huge, running through the wide corridors shoppers once used.

"The tile underfoot is original to the structure," Dr Shah said. "The gardens are planted in raised beds, with a built-in irrigation system."

Julie didn't understand much of what she was hearing. The little doctor led them on a brisk hike through the mall, pointing out things of interest: a fountain, bee hives, a small grove of trees. She patted the trunk of a sapling. "An experiment. We will see how well they do without driving their roots into the basement."

"Will people live down here, too?" Julie said.

"Most of this will be our public space. The stores around us will become art galleries, restaurants. Concert halls."

"Who's paying for all this?"

"Private investors. They purchased the mall properties and set things into motion."

"And your job is to get everything up and running so your

investors will have a place to go when things start getting bad."

Dr Shah blinked slowly. "Things are already bad. You of all people should know that." She made a scan of the garden before resuming her measured pace. "Things will get worse."

"And your rich friends will come here."

"They're not all rich. Many are just concerned for the future. Beth, for example." She smiled at the gray-haired woman. "She is a doctor twice over. Biochemistry and medicine. Her investment, like mine, is expertise." Dr Shah looked at the clock built into the fountain. "I must leave the rest of the tour to her, I am afraid. I am late for a meeting."

Beth took Julie's hand. "Let's go back to my apartment, and I'll answer all your questions."

Dinner was soy curry and rice, all the ingredients of which had been grown in the ark. Beth was a great cook. She made her own wine, too.

"Not all the arks will be like this," Beth said, leaning back in her chair and letting her stomach expand. "The later ones will be pretty basic. A roof, sanitation facilities, and food tanks. They won't be comfortable or pretty, but they'll keep people alive." She put down her wine glass and dabbed at her mouth with a napkin. "We're the test kitchen, developing the means of survival."

"For who?" The idea of Carson S Riley and her high-level friends sitting down to a meal of Tasty Paste and recycled water was laughable.

"We have a recruitment program in the works through ThirdEye. We'll find likely candidates and offer them a place with us."

"Those aren't the people you want," Julie said. "I mean, some of them might be, but most of them don't have the imagination. You should recruit from among the tramps," Devin's grin swam into her head, "and the Apes."

Beth frowned. "We'll need people who can live together

and build a new society, not ones who can't live within one."

"Then you definitely don't want people from the city," Julie said. "At least not at first. Tramps aren't perfect, but they know how to work together. A lot of the cube dwellers barely interact with real people. They've forgotten how."

"You sound like Gretchen. We've studied this carefully. Our research teams followed the caravans for months."

"Followed not lived with?"

"Yes."

"I bet the only people they talked to were the outliers."

The conversation continued long into the night. Beth pulled a couple of old board games out of the closet, and they played Scrabble and talked about Julie's adventures on the road until neither could keep their eyes open. The next morning Julie met the rest of the ark's staff. There wasn't a single one who wasn't a master of something or a doctor of something else, and they doubled up with fancy hobbies. The dentist was also some kind of martial-arts black belt. The chief botanist played in the station's string quartet with Beth. None of them were under thirty.

Julie checked in on Ranger and spent the day resting, eating well, and walking around the gardens. That night, she attended a concert in a café set up in what used to be a clothing store. Beth played violin, and Dr Shah took to the piano bench for a jazz set. Julie could make an oil lamp and soap. She could shoot straight, block a punch, and drive. But compared to the people in Ark Four she felt useless.

The next morning, Dr Shah called Julie to her office. She invited her to sit and stared at her over steepled fingers. "You will be happy to know that your friend will be waking up today or tomorrow. She'll be ready to travel in a week or so after that. What will you do now, Julie Riley, age twenty-three, and formerly of Massachusetts?"

I never gave them my name, and that's not right age for cover ID Gretchen set up for me. "Did Gretchen rat me out?"

"She is not the only hacker on the team." Dr Shah put her

hands flat on the desk. "We have as much interest in not being found as you do. You are a minor child and a runaway. We are not in the business of sheltering such. You have many fine qualities, I am sure. Dr Bernhardt... Beth... has grown quite fond of you during your time here. But you are not what we are looking for at the moment."

"What will stop me from telling everyone about this place?"

"Your honor, I hope. If necessary we can tell the authorities who you really are, but I trust it won't come to that."

"What if I come back? You said you might be opening the doors in a few years."

"We will of course review your résumé for any changes that might have made you more useful to Ark Four." Her polite smile flashed into a grin then faded. "No promises."

Julie knew the start of a negotiation when she saw it. She'd learned from the best. "I want something from you in return for me staying out of your hair until then."

"Continue."

"Number one, I need some repairs for our van."

FIFTY-THREE

Julie sat up in bed, her heart fighting with everything it had against the weight on her chest.

But there was no weight. She was in Beth's spare room, not the storage unit. The bins in the closet were full of craft supplies not corpses.

I'm alive, I'm alive, I'm OK, I got this.

StudMan Marty had developed night terrors from his time in the service and years on the road. *Was this how they started?*

Julie got up to go to the bathroom and pulled on her boots. No one had said anything about being a prisoner, and no one stopped her as she left Beth's apartment and sussed out the route to the hospital.

A woman was on the desk there, reading a book.

"Can I see her?" Julie said.

"She's sleeping."

"I won't wake her up." Julie flushed. "Please. I had a bad dream."

The woman put a piece of paper in the book and closed the pages around it. "Just for a few minutes, OK?"

Ranger was indeed asleep in the dimness. A dark lump in the bed, breathing and snoring almost normally.

"Can I sit with her for a bit?" Julie said. "I promise to be quiet."

The woman's face moved in interesting ways as she considered the request and finished in a terse smile. Julie moved into the chair beside the bed.

I had a bad dream. She mocked herself. How many years had it been since she'd used that line to get her mother and father to open up their bed to her? The nightmares had been less specific then. A combination of global terrors and existential dread as only a nine year-old could feel them. Will it be OK? she'd asked her parents. Yes, they'd said.

Liars.

Listening to Ranger – Shannon? No, Ranger. Always Ranger – breathe made her feel better. The older woman, even stuffed with tubes and covered in sensors, beat back the bogeyman.

I am really fucked up.

In an hour or so, Julie returned to the apartment to try to sleep again. She roused herself early to make eggs and coffee and greeted Beth when she came blinking out of her room.

"Have a good night?" Beth said.

"No." Julie told Beth about the dream and her trouble sleeping. "Is there anyone here I can, you know, talk to?"

Beth smiled. "I think I can scare someone up."

FIFTY-FOUR

Dr Shah had pronounced Ranger's health "poor but stable", and Juniper was in similar shape. Ranger laughed herself into a coughing fit the first time the holo display flickered out, and Julie brought it back with a practiced whack.

They hooked up with a west-bound outfit outside Jicarilla Apache Territory a couple of days after leaving the ark and traveled with it all the way to the Grand Canyon. There, they rested up, saw the sights, and joined an ad-hoc caravan for the rest of the trip to Oceanside, California. Ranger drove the last leg of the trip, and didn't object when Julie offered to shoulder her portable oxygen tank for the short hike. Julie wore her new filtermask for the walk but took it off when they hit the beach. Life was precious but there was more than one way to show it.

They took their shoes off and dug their toes into the sand. Ranger stripped naked and flung herself into the water. Julie hesitated until Ranger called her a chicken, and then she waded in too. The water was warm and clear.

"Worth it?" Julie said.

"Fuck yeah." Ranger grinned, some of her old energy at play in her eyes. "You?"

"I liked the Grand Canyon better."

She hiked back to the van before the sun set to get their gear, and they camped right on the beach. Julie built a little fire. Similar campsites dotted the beach on either side, none too close. There was plenty of room. They spread their sleeping bags on the sand.

In the morning, Julie woke to find that Ranger had already gotten up. She had a few moments of anxiety before spotting her at the water's edge, barefoot and looking west.

"Looking for China?" Julie said, joining her.

"We passed a big chunk of it getting here," Ranger said. She pointed across the sea. "Japan is closer if we're heading that way."

"You wanna drive or should I?"

Ranger's smile was wan. "I met someone who made the crossing. Sailboat. I always thought I'd try it out some day."

"Find us a boat, and we'll head out."

"Not today." She fished in her pocket and pulled out her keyring. "I'd throw you these, but you'd miss, and we'd spend the next three days dredging for them."

Julie took the keys. "Back east already?"

"Your pal Beth offered me a job." She smiled. "She wants me to set up a recruitment program for tramps. Find some likely candidates to move into the arks."

I was more convincing than I thought. "Is that what you want to do?"

Ranger looked back across the water. "For a while. They have some pretty good doctors. Beth thinks they might be able to do something about–" She patted her chest.

"Really?"

"Maybe. Only one way to find out. I've seen a lot of death recently, Jules. Even caused some. Thought I was ready for my exit, but now I think maybe I'm not."

"I can't stay there with you. Dr Shah said I'm not useful enough."

"She's wrong about that, but I don't think you're ready to settle down."

Julie tossed the keys up and caught them. "Probably true."

"So, once you drop me off, the van's yours. Oh," she fumbled in her coat pocket, "and this."

Julie looked at the brass star Ranger handed her. "Looks vintage."

"Full-blown antique. Euchre gave it to me. She said as long as I kept playing the part, I should look it, too. I stopped wearing it after she died. Couldn't save her. Didn't deserve it."

"Are you sure about this?"

"Just make sure you find a good partner."

FIFTY-FIVE

The fuel jugs in Julie's hands sloshed as she carried them up the driveway and behind the abandoned house where she had hidden Juniper. Portland, Oregon, was as interesting as advertised, but it lacked parking for anything bigger than a scooter. It had taken more than a few stern words to get the autocab to make the trip from the city center out to the decaying suburbs where she'd stashed the van.

For the last few months she'd been running up and down the Pacific coast, trying to get a feel for life as a solo act. She talked with Ranger nearly every night on her new-and-improved phone. New phone, new meds, new virtual therapist…

Julie rounded the corner of the house.

"The fuck do you want?" The girl was dressed in cheap print, her words muffled by a midrange filtermask. "I don't have anything for you." Her voice was pitched high from nervousness, her teeth chattering with cold. The low-power light on the portable heater at her feet was flashing.

"That's my ride, 'Burb." Julie patted her coat pocket. "Got the keys right here." *Not to mention the codes for the new security system*. Anyone trying to break in would end up mighty surprised.

"It's no one's," the girl said. "I've been here two days, and no one has come near it."

Julie reached into her back pocket and pulled out the switchblade. "I've got a knife, too. Sharp. It opens just fine but doesn't like to close." She put her finger on the button that released the blade. Ranger's heavy coat felt like armor. Like a hug. "Get me?"

The girl stood by and shivered as Julie poured twenty gallons of biofuel into the van's fuel tank. Juniper started right up when Julie turned the key.

"What about me?" the girl said. "What do I get?"

The girl was younger than Julie. Her clothes were dirty. A runaway. Not out on the road long. "Help me clean the snow off, and I'll give you a ride."

"What are you doing out here?" Julie said.

The girl hadn't been able to open the passenger-side door until Julie showed her the trick. Now she was staring out the window like there was something interesting on the other side. "What's it to you?"

"I'm guessing you want to steer clear of the police."

The girl pulled her eyes off the roadside. The angry expression she'd been cultivating slipped. "Yes."

"You kill anyone?" Julie said. "Steal anything important?"

The roadway recaptured her attention. "No."

"Where are you heading?"

The girl didn't answer.

Julie took her right hand off the steering wheel and held it out. "I'm Runner."

The girl ignored the hand. "Phoenix."

"That's a terrible name," Julie said. "You picked that yourself didn't you?"

"Screw you," the girl said.

Julie let a mile pass before trying again. "I don't suppose you know how to drive."

"No."

"Can you knit? Do anything useful?" Julie cleared her throat.

"Fuck you." Phoenix tugged her collar tighter around her neck and crossed her arms.

Julie put on the brakes harder than necessary. Phoenix's – *we have to get her a better name* – hands slapped the dashboard as she lurched forward. "What the hell?" she said.

"Look, kid," Julie took the van out of gear, "I'm not in the best of moods. I'm not your mom, and I'm not interested in having sex with you or stealing your shit." She reached across the girl's lap and opened the passenger door. "You can get out or you can stay, but I'm not playing this game with you."

Phoenix's hands found the seatbelt release then went back to her lap. "I'll stay," she said. "I'm sorry."

"Close the door." Julie pulled the shifter back into Drive. "Where are you going?"

"I don't know."

"Dude, I just –!"

She raised her hands. "Really, I don't know. I came out here to be with someone, and it didn't work out. There's this new vid series he wanted us to try out for."

"What happened?"

"I don't want to talk about it."

"I'm headed south to look in on someone. After that I'm going east," Julie said.

"How far?" Phoenix said.

"All the way to the ocean." The brass star pinned to Julie's coat caught the light. "Want to tag along?"

ACKNOWLEDGMENTS

Julie Riley has lived in my head since 2010, when I wrote draft one of the short story that was to become my first published fiction (*It Pays to Read the Safety Cards*, "Something Wicked," March 2012). In that early draft, 12-year old Hayley O'Brien sailed for Proxima Centauri aboard the good ship *Sam Walton*, exchanging letters with Julie, her best friend left behind on the ailing Earth. Revisions erased the letters and, eventually, Julie. Ben survived in name only.

Ranger/Shannon showed soon after in a short that was eventually published as *Grandma's Redemption* in the autumn of 2012. Shannon and Julie found each other – as I suspect they were destined to – and shared roughly equal space with Ben and Anji in a YA novel called *Leaving Home*, which I completed as my MFA thesis in June 2012.

It is hard to recall who had their fingers and toes in the text at what times, and subsequently difficult to know who to thank for their labors. Twenty-Five to Life is a third of and three-times the book Leaving Home was, and I am indebted to everyone who poked, prodded and massaged it along the way. Certainly I owe thanks to Merle Drown, Katie Towler, and Craig Childs, who served as my thesis advisors, and to Gary Devore who read and remarked on Leaving Home when I pulled it out of the drawer a few years ago.

It can take a long time for a story to take flight, and this book and I were truly granted wings by super agent Sara

Megibow of KT Literary Agency and the well-oiled machine called Angry Robot Books. Without Eleanor Teasdale (my editor), Gemma Creffield (my guru), Sam McQueen (my robot pal), Andy Hook (my face saver), map maven Kieryn Tyler, and cover designer Glen Wilkins, this book would be naught but a dream and a Word doc.

Recent years have proved weighty and fraught, and I would be remiss in not paying homage to those who helped me shoulder the load and keep my head up. First, in the #TranspatialTavern – a sort of online Algonquin Roundtable – featuring Dan Hanks, Ginger Smith, Reese Hogan, Chris Panatier, Halla Williams, Zig Zag Claybourne, Charlene Newcomb, Gabriella Houston, Sara Jean Horwitz, David Lawrie, and Patricia Jackson, as well as in the Bigfoot Appreciation Society starring Elaine Isaak, John Murphy, Robin Small, Iain Young, and Kevin Barrett. Good people, great writers all. I would happily let them join my outfit, so long as they brought their own vans.

My thanks go out to all the reviewers and book bloggers – most of them unpaid – working to help others find their Next Great Read, and to the independent bookstores that ensure books and readers enjoy meets-cute every day.

Finally, thanks to my parents who read me to sleep until I could read myself woke and to Brenda Noiseux, my First Reader, who makes everything possible and a good deal more fun. Brenda, you are loved by me.

Fancy some more apocalyptic fiction?
Check out the first chapter of
The Offset by Calder Szewczak

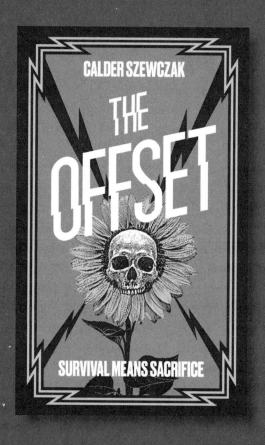

Out from Angry Robot Books
14th September 2021

A hand over hers, the chafe of skin on skin. The first touch in months. Miri lashes out, thrusting an elbow hard into the stomach of the person who has come to stand too close; a tall figure who neatly side-steps the blow and, undeterred, presses forward. A dazzle-patterned scarf is bound over their mouth and nose, and above it are two black eyes that gleam like oil on water. Miri tries to draw away but is not quick enough to escape the strong fingers that circle her wrist and restrain her. A rough slip of paper is pressed into her open palm. Then the fingers loosen their grip, releasing her, and the masked figure disappears into the crowd.

Alone again at the edge of the square, Miri takes several steps back to shore up the distance between herself and the mass of people gathered there. Then she examines the paper. A flyer, bearing the usual line – *Say no to life* – above a short quotation. She balls it up in her palm and shoves it into her pocket.

She is only here to see the Offset. She wants – needs – to see the execution, but the longer she waits the harder it is to stay. The unexpected physical encounter has set her on edge. Without noticing, she starts pressing finger to thumb in a repetitive gesture she half-recalls learning in childhood. There is, she thinks, a rhyme that should accompany the motion but she cannot remember what it is. Something about an inch-worm. No. A spider. A spider and a flood borne of a cleansing rain that hammered the earth for forty days and forty nights. Or is that something else? Her brow creases into a frown as she tries to remember, but it's no good. All she has left is the mime. Finger, thumb, finger, thumb. There's something about it that makes her feel still. Calm. As though that one repetitive movement is enough to slow her racing heart: her nerves transformed into kinetic energy and heat. For as long as she can keep it up, she is safe. Or should be. Right now, it isn't working too well.

The square is packed. Miri struggles with crowds at the best of times and it's been a long time since she's seen so many people in one place. It's too much to contemplate, all those lives compacted together into one vast, sprawling beast. Even standing apart from the worst of it, the stench is inescapable; a pervasive musk of stale sweat beneath the occasional tang of urine and sulphur that wafts through in the heat.

For one fleeting moment, Miri imagines herself standing atop the empty capital of the blackened pillar at the square's centre. From that giant height, the crowd becomes no more than squirming ants. In her mind's eye, she lifts a heavy bucket aloft and tips it until water comes pouring out, crashing down onto the masses below, flooding the square until it becomes a sea, a watery grave thick with the bodies of the drowned ants. Then, just as suddenly as it came, the image is gone. Now, when she glances at the crowd swarming around the base of the column, the vacant plinths, she sees herself as part of it; another cell of the fetid mass that grows like a blight in the earth. Her heart spasms with revulsion and she stares down at her hands, focusing on the movement until the sense of stillness returns. Finger, thumb, finger, thumb.

Slowly, she turns her attention to the feel of the November heat on her hands and face, the scratch of her threadbare shirt against her arms and back, willing her consciousness out into her skin to acknowledge the barrier that holds her together and keeps her separate from the world. It helps. When she next looks up, she observes the crowd with newly impassive eyes. Even so, she is neither quite brave nor foolish enough to relinquish the protection of the childish ritual. Finger, thumb, finger, thumb. Like a talisman to ward off evil.

Now she's regained her composure, a wary voice in her head tells her to go, to leave now rather than risk suffering again the sensation of being subsumed into the heaving crowd. Or worse still, *touched*. But she can no more bring herself to turn away than she can learn to breathe underwater. Her place is in the square. She must stay and watch. She must give witness to the execution.

She's not sure how long it's been since the last Offset – she doesn't venture often into this part of the city. But, from the excited activity of the ageing crowd, she figures that it must have been quite some time. The mass of bodies swirls with eddies and currents as people make their way through to meet old friends, to get a better spot, to get closer to the action. But there's no mistaking where the focus lies: the steps that ascend from the square to the Gallery, an ancient building with a monolithic edifice of cracked white stone.

For now, the Gallery steps are empty save for a glass-fronted booth that stands between two of the crumbling pillars. It's a broad, squat structure, purely functional in design and comprised of little more than painted timber frame and glass. What lies within the booth changes from Offset to Offset. Sometimes it contains gallows and sometimes a guillotine. Today it holds a wooden chair, tall and narrow, with a number of broad leather straps hanging from it, rusted buckles trailing to the floor. A metal rod runs up the back of the chair like the frame of a medical drip and a round, metal bowl hangs from it at approximately head-height. A thick wire leads from the metal rod to a generator at the back of the booth.

Miri doesn't know anything about the person who is due

to die in that chair, but she knows everything she needs to about the crime they have committed. It is the only crime still punishable by death the world over: the mortal sin of procreation.

Historically, the transgression was voiced by one of suitable authority – a mayor, a judge, a religious leader – who stood before the crowd and explained that the Offset was perfect retribution, exacting and brutal. How every birth, every act of creation, every new life threatened the fragile equilibrium of all things. That the imbalance had to be righted, and that the wages of sin was death. "For every birth, a death," they would say, in recitation of the law.

There is no such pronouncement anymore, though. There is no need.

The part of the crowd nearest the steps is thick with activists, including anti-natalists baying for breeder blood. They are all dressed like the one who gave her the flyer, dazzle-patterned scarves bound about their faces. The banners they wave are daubed in red and depict graphic scenes of environmental destruction. Several bear the image of a bloodied ouroboros. Miri can't hear the slogans they chant but she can guess their meaning: save the planet, the earth is suffocating, no mercy for breeders. In their midst, Miri spots one or two people who don't look like anti-natalists. They are white-haired and bear green spirals painted on their faces, and they are trying to tear down the banners. Miri thinks she could almost admire their courage if she didn't find their views so abhorrent. One of them has a crudely-made megaphone and attempts to drown out the anti-natalists' shouts, but only serves to silence the voices of their own group. Others in the crowd – those marked by neither ouroboros nor green spiral – roll their eyes or laugh. Every Offset is the same; the Activists come in their droves to shout and mock, some in favour of the ritual and others against it. No one else pays them much heed. May as well protest the heat of the sun, for all the difference it will make.

Miri turns her eyes skywards. The sun is distant and remote, obscured behind the thick haze that permeates the city. Far off, a solitary tree rises up amongst the buildings, listing at a precarious angle, its charred branches stripped bare. Miri's eyes snag on its grim silhouette. For as long as the dead tree stands, it serves as a monument to the wildfires that coursed through the heart of London the summer before. Soon, though, it will fall and the fires will recede in public memory until they are as hazy as the smog that even now chokes the streets.

Even though Miri knows how easy it is to not see, and how much easier it is to forget, it still seems unbelievable to her that anyone could be quite as blind to their surroundings as those wearing the green spirals. They protest against the Offset even as they stand within sight of the most recent natural devastation. It's as impossible to understand as the selfishness of those who, like the person due to be executed, wilfully continue to add to the world's burden by creating more parasitic mouths to feed on the lifeblood of the earth.

Parasites like you, says the voice in her head.

She quickly pushes the thought away. Finger, thumb, finger, thumb.

Silence falls on the square like an axe. At once, her attention snaps back from the sky and down to the booth, where two pigsuits have appeared. Their terrible forms cast dark silhouettes against the glass. They are vacant shells, dreadful chimeras of dented aluminium and transparent acrylic, each one encasing a fleshy hollow moulded into the shape of a body. The pigsuits have been empty for years; have long since outgrown the human officers who once wore them. Now they are driven by the frenetic command of their programming, of the sensors and circuitry that laces their articulated exoskeletons.

There's a sharp intake of breath somewhere nearby as fear pulses through the crowd. Heads jerk upwards. It reminds Miri of old footage of herds on the African savannah, before severe droughts turned the grassland to desert. An antelope catches the scent of a prowling lion and, one by one, the rest of the herd raises their heads in search of the coming danger. Unlike the herd, the crowd in the square doesn't turn tail and flee but merely cowers, trying to reassure themselves they have nothing to fear.

For now, at least, they do not. The pigsuits' interest is confined to the thin woman who stands between them, small and fragile. She is there of her own volition, honouring the choice that was made by her child, offering herself up in sacrifice. A mother.

Miri feels herself incline forward, rocking onto her toes, eager to drink in every detail of the woman. Next to the degenerating pigsuits – their fasciae blossoming with rust, their clear central casings so grease-smeared as to obscure the chasm within – her appearance is neat. Fastidious, even. She wears a plain brown skirt with a white shirt tucked into the waistband and her wiry ash-blonde hair, freshly dyed for the occasion, is drawn back into an elegant twist. She does not look up at the crowd but keeps her eyes downcast as she moves into the glass-fronted booth and drops herself heavily down into the wooden chair. Once she is seated, she waves a hand to indicate that she is ready. The closest pigsuit bends and reaches out a handless glove to fasten the straps, looping several around the woman's arms and legs and then another across her torso.

Miri wonders where the woman's partner and child are. Perhaps they are somewhere in the crowd, watching, revelling in this moment of glory, of righteous revenge and absolute power. If she were bolder, she would push through the crowd to get as close as possible, to be right up against the glass when the electric hits. But the very thought of stepping further into the mass makes her lungs tighten and constrict.

Finger, thumb, finger, thumb.

The woman is shaking with fear now, violently enough that Miri can see every quiver, even from her poor vantage point. The smaller of the two pigsuits is busy adjusting switches on the generator whilst the other straps a wet sponge to the woman's forehead. As it crushes the hanging metal bowl on top of the sponge, lines of water run down the woman's face, pooling in her eye sockets and making her blink hard. Miri can see her thin arms uselessly straining at the straps in an attempt to wipe the water away. The pigsuit, ignorant of her discomfort, sweeps a greasy brown blindfold over her face and pins it there. A small pool of damp spreads across the woman's skirt as she loses control of her bladder. The anti-natalists jeer.

Miri scans back past them, looking to see how the rest of the crowd are responding. They are quieter than the Activists, transfixed and silent. Insignificant details spring out at her; a man kneading a dry earlobe between his knuckles, a couple clasped together with circling arms, an old woman absently clutching a lumpen teddy, threadbare and grey, to her chest.

Miri turns back to the booth. It seems that the pigsuits are finally ready. The smaller of the two, the one that has been tending to the woman, straightens up and retreats into the shadows. As soon as it has, the other pigsuit raises an arm to the lever on the generator.

This is the woman's moment.

The crowd watches her intently. She wets her lips, tongue darting, and then nods. The pigsuit pulls the lever down.

Two-thousand volts shoot down through the metal bowl and into the woman's body. She braces hard and then falls out of consciousness before beginning to thrash and jerk violently against the restraints. Blue lines of electricity crackle along her limbs and torso. The generator whirs loudly. Somebody in the crowd screams.

Without warning, the pigsuit throws up the lever. A sudden stillness. Ten seconds pass. Twenty. The woman's chest rises and falls with a weak, rattling breath.

Her respite is short-lived.

With another crank of the lever, the pigsuit sends out a second wave of voltage. This one ensures death. The frantic thrashing and jerking start up again but this time steam begins to emanate from the woman's body. Vast waves of it churn out from the glass front of the booth, making towards the crowd in the square.

The pigsuit raises the lever, allowing the woman's body to slump forward in the chair. The other steps forward and tugs at the bowl on her head. Once it comes free, Miri sees that the woman's hair is aflame, blazing so furiously that soon her entire head is consumed. It is no ordinary fire, but threaded through with electricity and unnaturally ferocious. The front rows of the crowd begin to retreat, even the Activists. Miri can see people turning away from the Gallery, gagging, hands pressed over their mouths and noses. The stench hits, dreadful in its familiarity. She thinks of the summer's wildfires; the blackened bodies laid out on the heath. Bile rises in her throat. Behind the glass, the pigsuits battle with the flames while the woman slowly burns.

Beyond the edge of the square there is a strip of wild grassland that once served as a road. Miri stumbles through it, beating aside the ragweed, thistles and yellow toadflax to scatter the air with clouds of dry, shrivelled seeds. Standing half-submerged in a dense thicket of blood-red filterweed is an old bus stop; a rusted metal frame is all that remains of the modest shelter. Miri lowers herself onto the rickety bench and takes a few deep breaths, stuffing her fists into her pockets. In one pocket is the crumpled flyer and in the other a folded postcard, a willing reply to Miri's request to meet at seven the following day, in the cool of the evening. It's from someone they call the Celt, a woman who she got to know in the volunteer-run ReproViolence Clinic out by the Soho tenements. Although she hasn't had cause to return there in the last few months – not since she recovered from that last bout of pneumonia – she finds her thoughts turn to the Celt with increasing regularity.

Just thinking about her now, she can feel the blood begin to pound in her ears. Miri's not sure how she ever worked up the courage to ask the Celt to meet. She's glad she did, though. The chance of seeing the woman so soon is enlivening and fills her with anticipation.

Just then, a flash of movement catches her attention and snaps her out of her reverie. Leaning forward, she warily eyes the patch of filterweed. For a moment, everything is perfectly still. Then the weeds shiver in the windless air. There's another loud rustle and now she's sure that something is headed her way through the undergrowth. Tensing, she recalls the swarms that have plagued the city in years gone by – species of all kinds either fleeing fire, flood and famine, or simply surging unchecked with every new imbalance wrought in the food chain.

A rat darts out from the undergrowth and then sits back on its haunches, nose twitching. Miri notices at once the fleshy protuberance that stands proud of the creature's matted white fur, running like a ridge along its back: a human ear spliced into its spine. In all other regards, it is a perfectly ordinary white rat, with pink feet and a long scaly tail. Miri laughs, partly in relief. She's been half-braced for the harbingers of a carrion-beetle swarm, but after all that it's only a rat, no doubt escaped from some nearby laboratory.

"Hello," she says, stooping to lower her hand towards the creature. Tentatively, it noses at her fingers, its whiskers tickling her skin. Then it clambers up onto her palm, the ear on its back rigid like a sail. She lifts the thing up onto her lap and makes a maze of her hands for it to run through. It seems to know better than she does what her next move will be.

Although she guesses a laboratory rat would probably be used to humans, she is astonished by how much it appears to trust her. It makes no bid for freedom and seems quite content in her company.

Perhaps it thinks you're an escaped lab rat too, says the voice in her head, which she ignores. Probably the creature is from a long line of animals bred for the trait of docility. Yes, that vaguely chimes with what little she recalls of her half-forgotten genetics lessons. Assuming she's right, she doesn't see how a creature so tame could possibly have escaped of its own accord. The only other explanation is that the thing was set free. This is, she thinks, a cruel trick to play on such a beast. It won't survive the London wilds for long.

While she supposes that a docile lab rat would be more useful for experimental purposes than an aggressive one, she can come up with no good explanation for the human ear growing on its back. Try as she might, she cannot see the utility of it and suspects that it has been done for the oldest of reasons: simply because it is possible.

It's hardly the first time a genetic experiment has got out of hand. The crimson filterweed that surrounds the bus stop is a case in point. Although the intention was to create a super-strain of knotweed capable of filtering small amounts of carbon – and so improve the local air quality – the plant spread more aggressively than anticipated and spawned several new mutations, overwhelming other flora in the process. Worst of all, its effect on local air quality proved negligible. Several of its later variants seemed not to sequester carbon at all.

Idly stroking the rat, Miri stares out at the square. Now that the pigsuits have dealt with the fire the crowd is beginning to disperse, surging down the arterial lanes that feed the square in clots of twos and threes.

Someone peels away from the crowd and heads towards her. It's a boy, a few years older than her, with a strong brown face and a crop of curly hair, an anti-natalist dazzle-pattern scarf pulled down beneath his chin. She recognises him at once as the figure who approached her before. Seeing him again, Miri notices that there's something in his bearing, in his artfully crumpled stretch suit, that reminds her of the kind of people she grew up with. As he draws near, her fingers twitch. It's all she can do to stop herself from slipping back into that repetitive gesture of finger over thumb. She knows instinctively that she must not, that it invites attention, that it makes her appear vulnerable; an easy target. To steady herself, she closes her hands tighter on the rat, taking comfort from the warmth of its fur and the strange feel of the ear's helix against the skin of her palm. Then the rat squirms and she becomes suddenly aware of how small and fragile its skeleton feels beneath her fingers. She loosens her grip.

"Alright?" says the boy, now a few feet away.

Miri tenses herself, ready to run. Seeing this, he stops, and raises his hands in the universal sign of peace. On his face is a blank expression that she can't read.

Miri switches to the defensive. "Your parents know you're an anti-natalist, do they?" she asks pointedly.

"*Parent*," he corrects her in a languid tone. "One of my dads died when I was a kid."

Miri chews on this, thinking, *no Offset – good for you*. All the while, the boy's eyes search her face. After a moment, his lips carve upwards with a triumphant smirk. "It *is* you!" he exclaims.

Miri's stomach drops. She isn't used to being recognised these days. There isn't much left of the girl who used to feature so frequently alongside the famous Professor Jac Boltanski in the news clips and promotional materials that document nearly every aspect of her mother's work.

Though Miri hasn't had much cause to look in a mirror since she left home, that doesn't mean she hasn't noticed how her body has changed. Two years of being constantly on the move and never knowing for sure where the next meal would come from makes a mark on a person. She is skinnier than she ought to be, ribs and collarbone pronounced and visible beneath her skin, which is so pale as to be almost translucent. Despite her gaunt frame, her stomach is constantly bloated, hanging low and distended, and her feet and ankles often swell dramatically, filling with fluid that puffs them to twice their usual size. She is always cold, even in the midday heat. A few months back, she found a heavy cable-knit jumper in an abandoned tip and she has barely taken it off since, even though it is threadbare and smells faintly of urine. There are sores on her face, chest and back. Her hands, once soft and delicate as befitting her cloistered upbringing, are rough with callouses and her fingernails are torn to the quick. Her hair, which she wears short and streaked through with bright reds and oranges, hangs in greasy ropes about her face and is beginning to thin. She wonders what it would take to completely erase her genetic inheritance and every trace of her mothers: Jac's hard features and Alix's freckles.

"What are you doing here on your own?" asks the boy when she doesn't respond.

"None of your business."

"Your life is everyone's business."

Miri closes her eyes. He's right, in a way.

She gets up to leave but he grabs her thinning arm with enough force to bruise. She catches the smell of lemongrass, an expensively synthesised scent of the kind that often graced a home just like hers. The home that used to be hers.

"Hey – tell me who you're going to choose–"

Before he can continue, his words give way to a sudden howl of pain. He snatches his hand away as though it has been scalded and clutches it to his chest, peering down to examine where there are now two deep punctures in his skin, the red-wet marks of an animal bite.

Angry now, his dark eyes search out the cause of his pain and he finally sees the white rat, clambering down the leg of the bench. The boy lunges for it, set – Miri is certain – on grabbing the rat by the tail in order to smash its skull against the side of the shelter. Miri tries to block his path but the effort is needless, for no sooner has she scudded forward than the boy falls back, his face twisted in alarm and disgust. Miri follows his gaze and realises that he is seeing the ear half-sunk into the rat's back for the very first time. Judging from his expression, it's a sight he finds deeply abhorrent. It transfixes him for a moment and then he tears his eyes away, staggering back and shooting Miri a last, horrified look. Steadily, Miri releases a breath she didn't realise she'd been holding and then, for good measure, makes the sign again. Finger, thumb, finger, thumb. The rat on the ground at her feet now sits back on its haunches and begins to clean its long pink tail.

The boy is already out of sight, but his words ring in Miri's ears for a long time after.

Tell me who you're going to choose.

It's the question the whole world is waiting to be answered. They won't have long to wait. Miri's Offset is in two days' time.

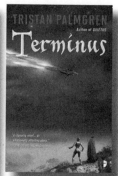

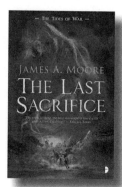
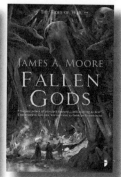
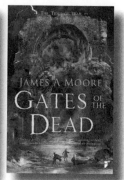

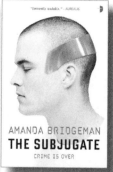

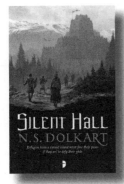
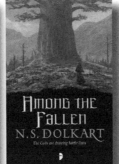

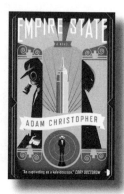